# NAUGHTY PARIS

# Jina Bacarr

# NAUGHTY PARIS

Spice

Spice

NAUGHTY PARIS

ISBN-13: 978-0-373-60517-0
ISBN-10:     0-373-60517-X

www.Spice-Books.com

**Printed in U.S.A.**

To my husband, Len LaBrae, an artist in his own right.

## Acknowledgments

My love affair with Paris began years ago when I visited the City of Light as a struggling art student and fell in love with everything Parisian, including the world of the Impressionists. I visited the Louvre, the art studios, the cafés where the Impressionists had hung out and an idea began to form in my mind: what if I could travel back in time and become part of their world? Now that idea has become a novel, but not without the hard work and perseverance of three special and dedicated women.

I wish to thank my editor, Susan Pezzack, whose artistic sensibilities helped me fine-tune my manuscript; Leslie Wainger, the editor who opened the door for me, and my friend and agent, Roberta Brown, who loved this story from the first time she read it and never gave up on me. *Merci.*

I loved the film *Moulin Rouge* about Paris and La Belle Époque and wondered what it would be like to be slim and gorgeous like Nicole Kidman, fall in love with a handsome hunk, and sing on key when I'm having an orgasm. I thought about it at lunch when I dieted on herb quiche with low-fat cheese and gulped down latte without whipped cream. I thought about it when I showed commercial properties to boring old men with lust in their eyes and soft putty in their pants. I thought about it when I got jilted at the altar and went to Paris for my honeymoon *sans* the groom.

Then I didn't have to think about it anymore because it happened. To me. Autumn Maguire.

It all started with:

*Désir (Desire)*

I am not a woman—I am a world.
My garments only have to fall
and on my body you will find
a whole series of secrets.
—Gustave Flaubert
(1821-1880)

# CHAPTER ONE

*Paris Today—An Art Studio in the Marais District*
*The Model*

"You want me to take off my T-shirt?"

"Yes, mademoiselle."

"*And* my yoga pants?

He nods. "Yes, mademoiselle."

"Hold on a Paris minute," I protest, glancing over at the old artist with a Gauloise cigarette hanging out of his mouth like a limp penis. He takes a drag without taking his eyes off my wet T-shirt sticking to me like a Post-it. "I ducked in here to get out of the rain, *not* sign up for strip aerobics."

Husky voice, low in the back of my throat. *Jeez, is that me?* Got to be nerves.

I had the same catch in my throat when I swallowed the mint in my mouth after David, my ex-fiancé, insisted I give lousy BJs and he couldn't go through with our wedding because he had issues with us.

*The jerk.*

As if flunking a postgraduate course in blow jobs is a top-ten reason to send me into therapy and sic my mother on me for the prepaid, nonrefundable honeymoon to Paris. But here I am, wandering around the Right Bank in the rain like Jean Valjean in squishy Nikes. Jilted and miserable.

*And* wondering how I let silver-tongued David—a guy who knows how to use that tongue to trigger my starter button—talk me into charging everything on *my* credit card. I've worked my ass off climbing the corporate ladder since college, putting my dream of opening my own art gallery on hold. Now I'm not only groomless but I had to dip into my 401-k account to pay for twelve bridesmaids' dresses with matching dyed Jimmy-what's-his-name stilettos, not to mention more than two hundred pounds of prime rib. Rare.

After I cut up my maxed-out credit card, I guzzled down the last bottle of champagne then tossed my white satin Vera Wang knock-off into the closest trashcan. The next morning I took off for the birthplace of Godiva chocolates to sweeten the bad taste in my mouth. And I don't mean spending time on my knees sucking on a guy wearing a raspberry-flava condom. I mean something dramatic and wonderful, heart-stopping and sizzling with pent-up energy. I want to feel *alive,* desired.

Who am I kidding? I want to be a drop-dead-gorgeous sex goddess.

*Youth and a fab bod aren't everything, you know.*

Ha! David thinks so. That's why I'm not all snuggly and warm with him between the sheets in my Paris hotel instead of sneaking through the city like a rat in an underground sewer.

*You're not young anymore, kiddo, and you are, oh, so not thin. That's why you lost David to that Aphrodite, an insipid skinny-as-a-toothpick, not-old-enough-to-drink-yet blonde. Your assistant, yet. How could you be so dumb?*

Dumb? I was stupid, insane, a complete idiot for letting that bitch take David away from me. I got punked.

*Zap!* As if agreeing with me, lightning rips through the long multipaned window, hitting me in the eye like a redlight camera, illuminating the faint light in the studio and diluting the smoky atmos.

I blink, then blink again. A B horror film mentality creeps me out, making me shiver. It can't get any worse. Storm clouds hide the afternoon sun. A rush of rain falls outside, banging against the windowpanes shimmering with a wet sheen. Thunder cracks like a boombox bursting with outta control volume. The old building shakes. I cringe. Do I *really* want to go back outside into that stormy mess? That's why I don't protest when the old artist hustles me toward the platform in the back of the art studio.

"*Hurry,* mademoiselle, we're losing the light."

A pungent whiff of burnt tobacco shoots up my nose. *Who is this putz?* For sure, he's no panting Adonis who can seduce a woman to take off her clothes with a smile. He's short, balding, sporting a little paunch and he smokes too much.

"Watch those hands, monsieur. *I* know karate." I'm bluffing, but it works with the geek corporate types I deal with every day who think a physical workout is something you do by yourself with one hand.

By the way, did you notice the old artist was impressed

when I said kah-rah-tay with the accent on the tay? I may give lousy blow jobs, but I'm not Gallic challenged. I got an A in French in college. I can rattle off enough swear words to impress the surliest taxi driver, from calling him a *salaud,* bastard, to a *quel casse-couilles,* pain in the ass.

"You made a mistake, monsieur," I continue, now that I've got his attention. "I wouldn't look as soggy as over-cooked lasagna if I owned an umbrella, which I don't. Nobody from the O.C. does. It ruins our image, not to mention Nielsen ratings."

He makes a face. Silly me. As if he understands my pop-culture rhetoric to explain why he doesn't want to see me naked, why I slap on phony tanning stuff rather than sport a citrus-yellow bikini on a SoCal beach. I don't tell him cellulite and I are as tight as sorority sisters. Not to mention my stomach is upset and I feel like I'm going to pass gas from the greasy *pommes frites* I gulped down at the flea market.

"Then you're *not* a model, mademoiselle?" The old artist gestures with his two hands like he's feeling up melons in the *supermarché.*

I shake my head emphatically. "No."

"Pity." He coughs, tosses his cigarette into an empty saucer, then does a mental strip search of my bod from the top of my red Angels baseball cap to my DKNY white cotton T-shirt, mauve yoga pants with a white stripe running up the side, and comfy walking shoes. "I'd still like to draw you."

I tilt my head to one side, thinking. What's holding me back? Posing in my bra and panties isn't any different from sporting a bikini at a pool party, right? So why not go for the win?

I nod. "Okay. It'll be a fun souvenir to take home."

He smiles, then drops the bombshell. Right into my lap. "*Bon*. Good. You must pose in the nude."

"Are you sure Madonna started like this?" I ask, holding on to my panties, pulling on the elastic waistband until it snaps against my bare skin. *Ouch*. I've already taken off my wet clothes and left them hanging on the tall black screen standing in the corner, along with my waist pack with my money and passport.

"Mademoiselle?"

"You know, the pop star? 'Like a Virgin'?" I sway my hips like the superstar diva. Somehow it doesn't have the same effect. The old artist shrugs.

"I don't care if you're a virgin—"

I'm not, but I smile anyway.

"—I wish to sketch you, mademoiselle, not make love to you."

That did it. Can my ego get any flatter? Ever seen a used condom?

Well, here goes.

I wiggle my peppermint pink panties down over my thighs and let them drop onto the small platform. There. I've done it. I'm nude. No turning back, even if I haven't shaved below my bikini line.

*Vive la nue* me.

I glance over at the old artist wiping down his posterboard with a damp cloth. The look on my face says, What do I do next?

He coughs, wipes beads of perspiration off his forehead, then points to my feet. I look down. I'm up to my ankles in pink nylon. I shift my weight from one foot to the other. The wooden platform creaks. Loudly. Urging me to hurry. Okay, okay. I scoot my panties off the platform with my bare toes. Wearing nothing but my sweat, I grin.

The old artist nods, picks up a Conté *carré dessin,* drawing charcoal, and waits for me to get into position. I hold my hand over my crotch. What a silly thing to do. I must relax. Relax. Keep up my courage. A chill slithers up the back of my neck, making my nipples harden and point straight out. I know now how guys feel when they get a hard-on in the middle of a heated business meeting. They can hide it behind this week's market stats report. Me? I'm as naked as a low-carb burger going solo.

I know you're sitting there all comfy in your sweats, shaking your head, pinching your thighs, wondering how a thirty-something woman could even *think* about taking her clothes off in front of anybody but her gyno. Brace yourself. It ain't pretty. Here's the skinny, which I'm not, so it's even more outrageous.

I'm desperate for excitement, a cheap thrill, and if it cost me a new pair of La Perla panties, then let them fall. Nothing exciting ever happens in corporate real estate sales, though I keep hoping I'll run into Donald Trump between bankruptcies and wives.

Unfortunately, time is running out for this apprentice wannabe. I'm thirty-four with more than a little tummy since David took off with my heart *and* my willpower stuffed into his back pocket. The idea of posing nude evokes a sexual charge in me, an irresistible allure of the forbidden without putting myself in danger or jeopardizing my corporate reputation, a unique twist to my personality I never dared explore.

Until now. This moment. My world is so frustratingly normal, so *conservative* in every way, that although I'm shocked at the artist's request, I'm also terribly intrigued. It's my nature.

Besides, I want to show my ex-fiancé I'm still hot stuff.

I grind my teeth. Just thinking about David makes me cringe. When I discovered he used me to get info on a major land development deal in Wyoming, I should have broken up with him then. But he was so convincing in his "I'm doing this for us" speech, I put aside my fears and didn't protest when he proceeded to slide my panties down between my thighs and do more with his sexy mouth than give me spin.

Even my mother warned me about David, said he was looking for a hot body with a trust account, but I didn't listen. She oughta know. My mother and her talking mirror just divorced their third husband.

I'm not in the mood for advice so I clicked off my cell phone. Mother drives me insane with her text messages that resemble the bottom-of-the-screen news headlines on CNN. Don't get me wrong. I love my mother, even if she collects marriage licenses like some women clip grocery coupons.

For your information, I left her blissfully engaged in bringing down the French national debt single-handedly on the fashionable rue Saint-Honoré while I wandered around the Marais district. I was looking for a poster or painting to take home to add to my collection of lowbrow work by un-discovered artists, or to put it bluntly, cheap, when a summer storm hit. A refreshingly cool rain blew in from the west, twirling over the blue-tiled rooftops and pelting down the narrow alleyways. The raindrops fell in bunches and splatted on the stone streets like water balloons. I got drenched. Not a pretty sight. I took refuge in an art studio with faded lettering over the arched entryway: House of Morand.

House of Wax is more like it.

Looking around the studio, the place looks like something out of a scary movie. Dirtballs fill every corner, mustard-yellow newspapers sit piled up on chairs, and a bookcase filled with art books stands alongside a tall, ebony pearl-inlaid screen. A hotplate with dirty red pots sits atop a Chinese coffee table alongside paint brushes sitting in trays in a liquid that smells like turpentine.

I hear the old artist clear his throat.

"Are you ready, mademoiselle?"

I nod.

Wetness drips down the insides of my thighs, a wetness which makes me twitch when I see him smoking and humming to himself, waiting for me. I can't back out now. I exhale deeply. This is it. My destiny on canvas. I'm hot, sweaty and perspiring.

I strike a pose.

Who knew standing still for twenty minutes would be so difficult, especially since I was trying hard not to concentrate my energy on my throbbing pubic area? Okay, my pussy. Yes, I'm embarrassed to admit it, but I got turned on posing nude. No, the old artist didn't come on to me. He's very professional.

It's *me*.

I'm sexually frustrated, and not even a stiff neck—oh, for

the delights of a stiff dick instead!—and achy back can stop me from daydreaming about moving my body in a brisk rhythm, my lover licking my clitoris, then the lips of my pussy, digging his tongue into me, and then back on my clit. Back and forth until I'm buzzing down there with an undulating energy that never stops...never stops...

*Mmm...keep dreaming.*

I take a break behind the screen to soothe my sore muscles and wipe off the sweat between my legs. That's what it is, isn't it? I smile, then sniff. Maybe not. Letting go of a sigh and a little gas—I couldn't help it—I grab a faded smock off a coat hook. Gray-tinged and splattered with dried paint, it looks like it's been hanging there since Paris was liberated but it's dry. My clothes are still wet. *Drip, drip.* I tiptoe through puddles of water on the wooden floor. Or is there a leak in the roof?

I look up. Unlike the rest of the studio, the ceiling is a square skylight. High over my head rain beats down against square glass panes framed with lead, blocking out what little gray daylight can slide through the pelting drops. I shiver. It's creepy back here. I wonder what the old artist is hiding under the black velvet drape covering the wall? Dorian Gray in his jockeys?

Before I can pull back the curtain to find out, I see an object that intrigues me. It's about a foot high, battered bronze, and grimy looking: a statue wearing a feathered crown, carrying a flail, and with his erection protruding straight out in front of him.

Did I say erection? As in penis? A dick? Oh, yes, I did.

This is *way* better than any hotel souvenir. Oozing with

curiosity, I reach down and wrap my fingers around the statue's penis and continue to hold on to it. I have no idea why, I just can't let it go. I smile. It's been a while since I've held such a hard penis in my hand.

I peek over the screen and ask the old artist about the statue.

"You're holding *la gaule*, the erection, of the Egyptian god Min," he says, tapping his cigarette pack. It's empty.

"He should be the poster boy for Viagra," I say, trying to make light of my awkwardness. The statue's kinda cute, if you dig a walking Egyptian with spiked hair.

"Min is the god of fertility, mademoiselle. His symbol is the thunderbolt."

Thunder cracks. How apropos.

The old artist never misses a beat, as if he's told this story a hundred times. "He has the power to grant youth and sexuality—" he pauses, then lowers his voice "—if you're willing to pay the price."

"Price, monsieur?"

"You must sell your soul, mademoiselle."

I cock an eyebrow at him. "Sell my soul?"

"Yes. You'll be young and beautiful—"

"Get out!" He's kidding, isn't he?

"—but you can never fall in love."

No chance of that happening. Not after David.

I ask, "What happens if I do fall in love?"

"You change back to the way you were."

In other words, middle-aged and overweight. Thinking, I run my fingers over the statue's, um, dick. The statue is for sale, according to the old artist. It's tempting. No more vanity sizing? A flat stomach? Perky breasts? What a fascinating idea, a tantalizing, sexual black magic. FX to the max. But is it worth braving an airport security search? I shake my head. I still have not-so-fond memories of smirks and pat-downs when my ex-assistant—yes, she and David are now a twosome—sneaked a lipstick vibrator into my carry-on bag when I flew up to San Francisco last month. I don't want to go through *that* again.

Smiling, I tell the old artist I'll think about it. He shrugs, then disappears to get another pack of cigarettes. I look around to see what other goodies I can find. Nothing here. Cracked vases, old books, a Tiffany lamp and a charcoal-tinged red pot emitting a weird odor. Not unpleasant, just weird. I take a sniff. Coriander, wine…and is that ginger I smell?

Within seconds dizziness muddles my mind as if the wine gremlins have invaded my head and are using my brain for a grape mosh pit. Is it the bottle of Pinot Noir I washed down those fries with? Or the smelly stuff in the pot? The bile in my stomach crosses paths with frying grease and adds fruity alcohol to the mix, flipping out my equilibrium. Whatever, my knees go weak, as if I'm moving in slo-mo. I try to focus, but everything looks blurry. What if I pass out? Go into a coma? Without a prince to wake me up with a French kiss? No frickin' way! I sink to my knees, but I refuse to succumb to the sleepytime trolls dancing in my head. I grab on to the black velvet drape to steady myself when—

*Swwooosh!*

My hands fly up as a heavy thump of velvet comes down on top of my head, suffocating me. Gasping, I struggle to wipe the soft darkness from my eyes, free myself from the giant bat cape covering me from head to toe. Loud breaths, husky, panicky, invade my ears, making the hairs on the back of my neck stand up. I hold my breath and listen. Who is it?

I let out my breath. Damn, it's me. Panting like a porn star having a fake orgasm in cyberspace.

Okay, so now I can relax. I'm not trapped in here with some spine-tingling apparition chatting me up with nocturnal moans, but I can't get this velvet drape off my head. Every time I pull one way, the drape goes the other, making me queasy. I gotta shake this nausea. Breathe *in* then *out*. Two, three times. I'll never dip greasy French fries into red wine again. What was I thinking? Then…

…over my rapid breathing comes another sound. Laughter. *Laughter?* Is the old artist back? I have the odd feeling he's choking on his ciggie *sans filtre,* enjoying this. I'll give him something to laugh about when I unravel this velvet mess and—

—ooohhh, *wait.* That's not him. The laughter is low and sexy and so close to my ear a chill slithers up and down my vertebrae knocking together like Lego pieces that don't fit. Something creepy is going on here. Drops of perspiration form between my breasts, wiggle down my ribcage, then drip down my thighs as I pull and tug on the black velvet drape. I can't thrash loose. My breath becomes sharper. The back of my neck is damp. Finally, I rip the heavy fabric off my face and—

—I see *him.* Staring at me with his eyes. Dark blue eyes that intrigue me.

A life-size painting of a man over six feet tall.

I grin, relaxing the tenseness in my face. So *that's* what

the drape was hiding. A superstud. Arms crossed, feet spread apart, and wearing tighter-than-tight pants that outline his impressive cock and he's—

*Laughing?*

Creepy bumps pop up on my bare arms. The more I think about what I heard, the more I believe I must have imagined it. Hearing the man's sexy laughter stirred carnal desire so dormant in my female psyche that I can't tell what's real or in my head. Well, look at him, will ya. He's a painting, dammit! Touch him, no, not *there*. There. On his hand. Cold. See? He's not human, so get off this goth kick and get the hell outta here. Oh, I forgot. I can't. I'm naked.

*So, girlfriend? He can't see you.*

I smile. *Yeah.*

So why not have a little fun and flirt with him?

With my eyes still on the man in the painting, I trace the fullness of my breasts with my fingers, cupping them in my hands. Playfully, I rub my nipples, hard and brown and pointy, licking my lips again, then as I become more comfortable with my teasing game, I move my fingers down to my belly, then between my legs. I sway my body gracefully, in a classy manner. This is art.

Art? C'mon, a lifetime of *Cosmo* signals to me loud and clear this is sex, pure and simple. My juices flow and the fullness in my groin swells as I hear the old artist scuffling out front.

He's back.

I hear him strike a wooden match. He's lighting another stubby Gauloise cigarette. A wavy swirl of smoke snakes over the screen. Smoke has no effect on the man in the painting. He's still smiling. Me? I cough.

Not taking my eyes off this macho pin-up, I call out from behind the screen in what I hope is an I'm-just-curious voice, "I found a painting I like."

"Mademoiselle?"

"The good-looking guy in tight pants under the black velvet drape." I wet my lips. Ooh la-la.

"Ah, you found Paul Borquet."

"Who is he?"

"He was considered a genius in his time, mademoiselle. The painting is a self-portrait he did in his studio in Montmartre."

"I never heard of him."

"After his strange disappearance in 1889, the art world forgot about him. I covered him up years ago."

"Covered him up? Why?" I lean my hip against this lost artist. So close our thighs touch. I tingle. He has an electric charisma that transcends three-dimensional space. Or am I just horny?

"The models spend too much time looking at him—" the old artist laughs "—and arousing themselves."

Even in the murky light, I can see why. The man is dark, dangerous looking, with a raw aura of lust about him that makes my skin crawl with ideas of back alley cafés, strong liqueur and sweat-drenched nights of passion. An erotic hero.

My eyes travel down to the big bulge between his legs, confirming my suspicions. No doubt he has an ego to match. He's handsome with chiseled, though slightly misaligned features, giving him a cocky air. He stands with his legs apart, his longish dark hair swirling around his open collar and contrasting with the musculature of his chest, visible under his white ruffled shirt.

Looking at him starts a slow burn down in the unexplored area below my phony tan line. He makes me squirm. I remind myself he's just a painting. Then a sneaky thought hits me. How would it feel to make love to him? *Why not?* After David gave me the heave-ho, a girl's got to rev up her mojo even if he *is* a two-dimensional hunk in tight pants.

I drape the black velvet curtain around my shoulders in a provocative swirl, letting it slide down my bare back, and wiggle my butt. I wonder what it would feel like to run my fingers over his chest, touch his hot flesh, then grab on to the mauve-colored scarf wound around his neck in a graceful swirl and pull him close to me. So close I can inhale his musky scent, then lean my cheek against the deep satin blackness of his cape slung over one shoulder.

I feel my inhibitions rise up and escape from me like someone sucked the breath out of me with a long, deep kiss. French kissing. I can't get the desire of wishing for a deep kiss from him out of my mind.

I shudder. Sweat trickles down my neck. *What am I doing?* Making love to an artist who died over a hundred years ago? I *am* losing it. I should run out into the rain and let a good soaking clear my head.

*Flash!* Lightning dances over the varnished ebony screen, making the surface shimmer. I flinch, turn my back to the painting. I won't look at him. *I won't.* Thunder echoes in my ears, as if Paul Borquet is daring me to look.

I ask, "Was he an Impressionist?"

"Paul Borquet was among the best, mademoiselle," says

the old artist. "Monet, Renoir, Toulouse-Lautrec, they all admired the young artist's work. *And* his bravery."

I cock my head and sneak a peek at Paul Borquet. I know I shouldn't, but I can't help myself.

"Bravery?" I ask. Okay, so he was a real alpha male. Interesting. *Very* interesting and just what I *don't* need. Another stud who pops steroids like they're purple M&Ms.

"He died in a fire, mademoiselle, trying to save the woman he loved."

That's cool, but I've had my fill of macho overkill. So why can't I stop looking at Paul Borquet? I'll tell you why. No cosmetic effect of darkness at play here. I know art. His work has energy. Vibration. He really understands color. His use of paint becomes a vehicle for the perception of light. He seems suspended, shimmering and vivacious within the frame of the portrait. There's a snapshot quality to the work, a sense of immediacy and spontaneity as if he were here now in front of me, alive.

"Paul Borquet," I mumble, putting my thumb to my lips and sucking on it, wondering if he was as good in bed as he was with a paintbrush. A sexual hunger awakens inside me and makes me reach down into myself, *way* down.

Wetting my lips, I imagine him naked. I slide the heated palms of my hands over my thighs, imagining the sticky, dewy liquid dripping from his penis, glistening. I savor this moment. The artist's use of bold brushstrokes and harsh lines suggests a mad aggressiveness about his personality that excites me. Gives me chills, then makes me hot. *Very* hot.

I keep my eyes riveted on the painting as I wiggle my hips, dreaming about how it would feel to have the paintbrush of this lost Impressionist sliding down over my belly, down between my thighs, then tickling me with its soft bristles. Running his fingers up and down my torso, lingering here and there, taking his time. Then licking me with his tongue, drawing his finger in and out of my pussy. In and out. In and out.

I sway, shake, moan, barely keeping my urges under control. The strong smell of oil paint mixes with the sweet smell of my own desire as I move in time to music in my head. I swear Paul Borquet winks at me. I take one step backward, then a second. His eyes seem to follow me. A tremulous hunger swells up in me, aching to be satisfied.

I bend forward, touching my breasts, squeezing my nipples, swaying my shoulders back and forth. Then I rub my pussy slowly, daring the man in the portrait to kiss me. I pretend I'm kneeling astride the lost artist, locking my legs slowly around his neck, his longish dark hair tickling the insides of my thighs as I press my soft mound on his mouth, brushing my body back and forth across his lips. A tingling vibrates between my legs. Melty, sweaty heat wiggles deliciously down to my pussy and a subtle, yet burning sensation flows through me as he tickles the sensitive button of my clitoris with his tongue.

I squeeze my pubic muscles together. My pussy is tight and hot, though I haven't come. I want him to fuck me. I want to clamp down on his cock as if it were deep inside me. I want to keep it there forever. My mouth is dry. I lick my pink glossed lips, then give out a low moan.

*Can I push the limits? Can I climax in my fantasy?*

I smile. No one can see me behind the screen. No one but

Paul Borquet with his broad shoulders, bulging biceps, narrow waist and hard lean thighs. And, oh yes, his squeezable butt.

My heart is pounding, *pounding* in my ears. I abandon all my sensibilities, grabbing the statue of the Egyptian god Min and holding it between my nude breasts, its firm erection nesting in my cleavage as I climax wildly, warm sweetness oozing in my cunt as melodic waves of pleasure hum through me, a seamless tapestry of buzzing and purring and sighs and moans weaving through the air, some breathy in tone, others louder, still others painfully ecstatic.

All of these sounds only make my climax more intense, more lasting than anything I've known in a long time. I don't close my eyes, but continue staring at Paul Borquet, wishing I could feel his arms around me, his lips kissing me, his body pressed against mine.

"You wouldn't stand a chance, monsieur, if I were young and beautiful," I whisper in French, shifting my weight from side to side. The wooden platform bends, squeaking under my wet bare feet. Lightning flashes overhead through the skylight, stinging my eyes like a thousand-watt lightbulb slashing through the air. "I'd make you fall in love with me—"

I cry out when electricity jolts the bronze sculpture I'm holding between my breasts, sending a hot current through me and vibrating through my brain, raising the hair on my arms, and making my eyeballs bulge out.

Somewhere in the back of my mind I hear the old artist calling out that he's going for help, but I can't answer, can't focus. All the muscles in my body tighten and I feel myself lifted up off my feet and zooming through space, as if something is flinging me skyward. An unexplained chill settles in me as if I'm in a swirling vortex as electricity flashes over my skin, racing in and out of my bod faster than I can blink.

What's happening to me?

This isn't my normal world. I want things dry and safe. Not wild and crazy. The electricity dances a choreography of darkness and light all over me, tracing the path of my sweat. I'm breathless and more than a little bewildered. Mix in bewitched and my trip to Paris is turning into the *Rocky Horror Picture Show* with French subtitles. *This can't be happening!*

Thunder claps in my ears with a loud boom then—the lights go out.

Darkness. The humid air suddenly reeks of a strong musky scent. Male.

Coming closer...closer...yes...I hear that sexy laughter again as someone blows hot air into my ear, making me shiver. I twist my fingers on the statue until they burn, then my nipples harden into pointy peaks as if someone pinched them. Becoming aroused again, I let out a sigh when someone squeezes my breast and sucks on it, then moans. *Who? Where is he?* I can't open my eyes, swallow or talk, or move my legs or hands, touch him, *anything*.

I can't do more than make a desperate breathing sound as I lie—

*Where?*

Where am I?

# CHAPTER TWO

*Paris 1889*
*The Artist*

*I can't paint, I can't move. Alors, I can't believe what I saw. A moment ago I swear the night was slashed open by a strange light and I saw a redhead stripped naked, teasing me, flirting with me, her bare shoulders swaying and dipping provocatively.*

*I continue to stare into the gauzy-thin darkness veiling a corner of the room, a rapturous chill shooting up the side of my face, then wiggling down my spine and meeting head-on with the slow burn pulsating in my groin. Ready to explode. No. I must be going mad. Delirious. What occurred stunned me, like lightning flashing through my body.*

Exhaling slowly, blinking, trying to ease the strange headache that came upon him—brought on by too much absinthe, or so he wanted to believe—he regained control of himself. Barely. He tapped the tip of his cane against his leg, keeping time to a strange rhythm in his soul only he could feel. He gripped his cane tighter, trying to hold on to the moment. How was such a thing possible? No candle or lamp illuminated the corner where he'd seen the redhead, no moonlight drizzled through the open window. He'd heard no one enter through the thick wooden door. The only sound in his ears was a soft whisper.

"I'd make you fall in love with me," she said, taunting him. A sensual giggle escaped her tinted lips, no pretense of innocence shading the moaning sounds coming from her throat. Then she slumped to the floor, the life gone from her, like the morning sunlight dissipating over the stacks of hay in the wheat fields, leaving behind only deep shadows. Cold. Lonely.

He moaned.

Tonight, working in his studio, he had the unnerving feeling someone had been watching him. Lusting after him. Undressing him. He grinned. It was the redhead. A familiar tingling inside him made him squirm with frenzied energy as if thousands of carmine-red lips, wet lips, *her* lips, kissed and sucked the long shaft of his penis. Up and down, circling around it with her tongue.

A spasm of anticipation within him caused his hard cock to press against his tight pants. He was excited, stimulated by this redhead. He felt his penis bulging and swollen with a great need he couldn't conceal.

But first he must find out if she was real.

Paul Borquet approached the dark corner with fear in his heart. Fear of discovering she *was* but an illusion. What else could she be? The whisper he'd heard in his ear came from a long way off, fading so slowly, like the long sigh of a young girl as she peaked during her first sexual climax.

He drew in a long, deep breath.

The beautiful girl lay on the floor, not moving. She *was* flesh and blood.

And she was nude. The pale sheen of her skin enchanted him, her face bewitched him, her breasts thrust forward with one hand lying lightly between her thighs, as if daring him to peek and savor her pussy. Her slim hips, long legs, all delighted his artist eye with a sensual harmony so perfect he could do nothing but stare at her.

Strangely, as if in the grip of an unseen hand, he couldn't concentrate on anything but the redhead. Not the model waiting for him in the small studio upstairs, not his unfinished drawing, not his need for more absinthe. He'd raced down to the study to indulge his thirst for the green liqueur when a sudden lightning shower drew him to this room. Then he'd seen her.

And nothing else mattered.

He breathed in deeply, and the shadow of her erotic perfume descended over him, holding him in a sensual moment so real his hand shook when he felt for a pulse on the side of her neck. His dark blue eyes widened. Yes, blood beat in her veins, but her skin was hot, as if a fiery flame danced over her body without burning it. He couldn't stop himself from reaching out to touch her face, her lips. Her breasts. The desire to twist the pointed nubs of her breasts with his eager fingers heated his groin. He yearned to lick them with his red-hot tongue, then nibble on them. He moaned, wishing he could bury his face in her creamy white flesh and smell the aroma of her female sex. Sweet and pungent. Erotic.

He must paint her. *He must.*

He closed his eyes in ecstatic torture. Touching the beautiful redhead raised him out of his deep depressive mood. He had been melancholy earlier, sitting silent and withdrawn in his studio, his head sunken to his chest, his hair hanging in his face as he drank absinthe. Night after night he sat, condemning the art world for not recognizing his genius.

In the late afternoon he had roused himself out of his drunken stupor and gone to the Louvre to study the works of Delacroix, Poussin and the Dutch masters of the seventeenth century. It provided him with the perfect release when the headaches and dreams crowded his brain with such pain he could no longer hold his brush steady.

Then he had come to his small studio in the Marais district in the town home of *la comtesse,* his one-time mistress, and prepared his paints, but nothing happened. Nothing. His creative urges were stalled. He could no longer reach into the most remote parts of his mind and explore the vast universe of his imagination, that *mystique* of sensation he knew he could achieve, allowing him to put his feelings into art. Yet he wouldn't give up. Couldn't.

He drew in his breath, a sudden longing for the smell of paint under his nose and the sound of short, quick brushstrokes whispering in his ears. With a haunting clarity, he conjured up in his mind a dazzling painting of this redhead, already seeing his bold colors on canvas. Red. Blue. Yellow. Shocking colors, passionate colors. Colors that *lived,* that captured the moment.

His heart raced faster, a thin veil descending over his sense of reasoning, the veil of madness that was often a companion to his art. Always striving to sell just enough of his work to buy more paints, while at the same time he struggled to express a feeling, a thought, a human need in his painting.

Could not hope be expressed by a star in the heavens? The hunger of a soul looking for love by the brilliance of a sunset? The beauty of all women by the luminous eyes of one woman?

He was certain the redhead _was_ that woman.

How had she come to him? She was here in the room with him, this seductive creature of the night. And if so, she must be skilled in black magic and a follower of the occult. He exulted in the idea she would be a fitting partner to join him in his ongoing journey of mystic and sexual exploration into the Paris underworld of hedonism and excess, where women danced naked, titillating the madly decadent men.

He called it his _cirque érotique,_ where beautiful, young _mesdemoiselles_ rode from room to room in sumptuous private mansions on bicycles _sans_ pantaloons, naked below the waist, giving the gentlemen an exquisite view of their nude buttocks; or where women offered themselves as love slaves, willingly partaking of strong intoxicants to increase their pleasure as they did their masters' bidding; or where they engaged in salacious threesomes, making certain the gentleman always had twice the fun.

He embraced this world, watching women performing and arousing, seducing and being seduced. A world where there was magic in every kiss and every kiss was magic, a world he found strangely evocative and compelling.

The world of the Black Arts.

The girl moaned. She was stirring.

"Oooh…" She crossed her arm over her chest, her hand pushing together the luscious swell of her breasts. He gasped. The sight of her white flesh delighted his eye, but his mind told him to cover her, lest she catch a chill. He was acquainted with the wardrobe of the mistress of the house in an intimate manner, so it didn't take him long to retrieve a long, hooded red velvet cloak from the *garderobe*. He placed the cloak over the girl's nude body, then picked her up in his arms, reveling in the lightness of her slim body when—

—her other hand opened and the object she'd been holding dropped onto the carpeted floor.

His throat tightened. *No, it couldn't be.* But it was. His small statue of the Egyptian god Min. Had the girl sneaked into the town house to steal it? What other treasures did she seek? Jewels? Gold louis? Silks? Was she but a thief of the night and not a goddess as he believed?

He should toss her out into the street, be done with her. Such women, he knew, were sensual creatures who plied their trade with kisses and promises of forbidden sex. Naked young women in the throes of passion, kissing, sucking, restraining the man with silken bonds, blindfolds and cock rings to keep his erection until he satisfied each girl and she cried out in orgasmic bliss.

Was she such a girl? He looked down at her lovely face, the fullness and beauty of her breasts, the elegant curve of her heaving rib cage so white and pure against the lushness of the red velvet cape. He'd go mad if he couldn't paint her, and so he would keep her. But he would be very careful with his feelings. *Very.*

He placed her upon a rose-colored *meridienne*, putting a red silk pillow under her head, then stroked her cheek, her straight nose, her full lips, her breasts. Then his fingers traveled down her sleek midriff to her flat belly and the insides of her thighs before tugging on the curly reddish hairs covering her mound. His dream was in his arms, an enchanting mademoiselle, but one thing still puzzled him. Why had she stolen his statue of Min? *Why?* Did she know its power?

*Did she?*

He did.

He became interested in the occult when the owner of the red velvet cloak, a beautiful and wealthy *comtesse*, presented him with the small statue as payment not only for his portrait of her, but for his performance in her boudoir. *La comtesse* claimed the statue was discovered in the pyramid of a powerful pharaoh known for his sexual prowess. The statue had magical, sensual powers she was only too happy to teach him as she lay upon the bed, waiting for him. He held her face between his hands, then lowered his mouth to kiss her deeply until she wrapped her legs around him and gripped him tightly around the waist, her ankles crossed above his back. Then he ground his hips, pushing his cock into her in slow rhythmic thrusts, then faster and faster until she climaxed with so many orgasms she lost consciousness.

Bedding the countess wasn't the only game he indulged in. From time to time, sexual orgies occurred in the grand houses here in the Marais district and he eagerly took part, wearing only a long red cape over his nude muscular body. He hid his identity behind a fox mask, though many young women claimed to recognize him by what he *couldn't* hide. His cock. Long, hard and perfectly shaped.

His favorite trick was making his cane disappear, then inviting the eager young women to duck under the wings of his cape and search for the missing cane in between his legs. They ran their fingers, their lips, even their *melons,* large breasts, all over his body until his penis found them, filling their *connasses,* cunts, between their legs with his magic.

*"Hélas, tu es bien monté,"* the women whispered, telling him he was well hung. Then he would sweep through the bevy of naked girls, pushing up against them, pumping, thrusting forward his cock, huge and fully aroused. He kept his handsome face hidden, his piercing, dark blue eyes watching the eager women through the holes in his mask, women all vying to be pleasured by him.

Not tonight. Passion for his art triggered a reflex action in his fingers, making him open, then close his fist. Slowly. A stimulating flash of inner heat, as though he'd reached through the arc of what was real now and what could be real beyond this moment, surged up in him.

Tonight he must paint.

*Her.* The redhead.

But first…he must get rid of the blonde.


"Do I not *please* you, monsieur?" a feminine voice asked, emphasizing the world *please* with a pretty lip pout. It had no effect on him.

"I've changed my mind, Lillie." He buttoned the deep blue, paint-splashed jacket he wore and tightened his flowing neck scarf, the color of a velvety plum. It was his trademark, his style, and he guarded it carefully. Then he forced his eyes to look at the model, a pretty girl from Madame Chapet's *maison tolerée*, brothel. Lillie de Pontier was the prettiest of all the girls at the House on rue des Moulins. He picked her out of three girls simulating sexual encounters with each other, writhing all over a large four-poster with abandon, touching, caressing, kissing and sucking on each other's breasts.

She seemed pleased when he chose her, snuggling up to him, blowing in his ear, rubbing her firm *derrière* back and forth across his crotch, making gestures about the firmness of his buttocks. But he no longer needed her services. He was nervous. Edgy. The redhead would be conscious soon. He must sneak Lillie out the back way without the two girls seeing each other. He was frantic. He didn't have much time.

"I will show you for free, monsieur, what all Paris would pay to see." Lillie pulled off her tight black garter and her rose-colored silk stocking slithered down her creamy thigh in a slow, serpentine crawl.

"Put your stocking back on, Lillie."

The girl ignored him and leaned toward him. He noticed beads of sweat between her nude breasts. For a moment he couldn't take his eyes off her. She wore only a corset in peacock-blue satin, tightly laced around her tiny waist and pushing up her exposed breasts. Her ample bosom swelled out in all directions in delicious curves, pleasing him. Full, bulbous cups of white flesh seduced his eye with the promise of delights to come. A crinkly pink ribbon tied in a neat bow around her neck completed the effect.

He reached out to untie the bow when—

He stopped, his hand raised in midair. A sound from

downstairs caught his ear. Was that a moan he heard? The redhead?

"Your private show is about to begin, monsieur," Lillie said in a husky voice, curling her lower lip and hissing the phrase with a deliberate purr. Her long white fingers pinched the end of her pink stocking as she pulled it off, then she wiggled her naked toes playfully before slowly spreading her legs to expose a gentleman's peek at the yellow-gold triangle of pubic hair between her perfect thighs. *Sa chatte.* Her pussy. Well-groomed and beckoning him. He had not expected this. She tilted her head toward him, her eyes asking, What do you think?

"You tempt me, Lillie, but I—"

Did he hear someone moving about downstairs? Opening drawers? Banging them shut?

"I'm the best at Madame Chapet's at *chevaucher.*" Lillie chewed on the end of her fingernail then touched the inside of her thigh, running her fingers up and down, ever so lightly, coming closer and closer to her soft pussy. "I can ride the stallion for as long as the gentleman desires."

She slapped the air with an imaginary riding crop, and for a moment he was tempted. *Very* tempted. He was in need of release from the pent-up passion throbbing within him. He could imagine himself sitting on a chair with Lillie spread out over his lap, his cane sliding up and down her toned calves, her thighs. Then, slapping her firm, naked buttocks ever so lightly before turning her over, he would take her, her mouth wide open, his tongue licking her lips, his hands grabbing her all over, her breasts, her waist, her thighs, *everywhere.*

He ignored the bold desire in her eyes, eyes telling him

what she wanted. *Baiser*. Make love. To her. Tonight. He shook his head. No, he couldn't, though she *was* beautiful. Her angel-pale skin gleamed white with rice powder from China with skillfully applied brown pencil arching her brows. Deep blue shadows flowed across her eyelids and over her temples, enhancing the size and luminosity of her eyes. He could see where she had dabbed the color of a pink dawn over her cheeks with a hare's foot, the lobes of her ears and her chin. The touch of artificial gold rinsed her hair. Garish but effective.

*La belle fille* possessed all the skills of a woman schooled in the art of illusion. And that was why *she* could never be his perfect model, why he could never paint her with the vigor of reality, because everything about her was an illusion.

*Mais non,* it was someone else who held him in rapture, someone more provocative, more alluring, more sexually exciting.

"I have no need of you tonight, Lillie," he said, dismissing her. He should have known a woman with Lillie's skills would not give up so easily.

"Watch me, monsieur," she whispered, twisting her pubic hairs then inserting her fingers inside her pussy, "as I wind up my music box to play a tune that will please you."

He wasn't surprised when she began moaning, quite convincingly. He had no doubt she'd had much practice, but he had no time for love. It was a foolish emotion he refused to give in to; it drained his energy, his passion to paint. *Art* was his mistress. He could never love a woman as much as his art.

*Never.*

He ran his fingers over the ebony handle of his cane carved into the shape of a couple making love. His own penis was also hard, unbending, like the unique design of the male figurine hovering over the woman, lowering his erect *outil,* tool, into her. Lillie, moaning louder, also noticed his hard cock. She kept repeating what a strong, muscular body he had, and how she would find such delicious pleasure burying her face between his hard thighs, sucking on him. He tried to ignore her obvious overtures. He must get rid of her. *He must.* But how? Sweat slicked his grip as he slid his hand up and down the cane. Why was he so tormented, so affected by his passion to paint the redhead?

He knew why. She was the seductress chosen by the gods to be the perfect model for his masterpiece upon which he could stamp his art with an impulse of his true feelings, the inner emotion of his soul. He never would have believed it possible such a woman existed in his world.

A different urge settled in his groin. Primitive. Lusting. He couldn't wait any longer.

"Put on your clothes, Lillie," he ordered. "I can paint no more tonight."

Her chemise lay on the floor, crumpled into a thousand fine little wrinkles, with one rose-colored stocking strewn carelessly on top, along with her violet two-piece taffeta dress and petticoats, violet button shoes and tiny matching hat with its long, curling veil.

"*Pardon,* monsieur?" she asked.

"You're leaving."

"But we haven't played the game—"

"I have no time for games. I have another engagement."

"At five o'clock in the morning?"

"Do as I order or Madame Chapet will hear about your insolence."

"That old *garce?* Bitch. She cares only about making money, and I make plenty for her." Lillie threw on her petticoats, then her shoes, though she didn't button them.

A door slammed. Downstairs.

She laughed. "I believe your other engagement couldn't wait, monsieur."

He panicked. "*No!* She can't leave. She can't!"

Paul grabbed his cane, then his voluminous black cape and swirled it about himself like a creature of darkness about to take flight on the cloud of a dream. He raced downstairs, flung open the door, then ran outside, blending into the landscape of mendicants scouring the boulevards of Marais, their baskets on their backs but no names on their souls. The clean, dry air was still.

Where had the girl gone?

He stopped a poor *chiffonnier*, ragpicker, and asked her if she'd seen a young girl in a red velvet cape running from the townhouse. The old woman held out her hand and, after he folded a bank note into her palm, she pointed toward rue Saint-Merri. Joy raced through him, sharpening his eye to see the truth. Then she *wasn't* an illusion. She was out there somewhere. But where?

Gripping his cane, twirling his cape, he raced out into the night with a quickening sense that he had no choice but to find her.

No matter what he had to do.

# CHAPTER THREE

Jesus Christ, what the hell happened?

*Zzz-zap. Zzz-zing. Bang.*

Energy pulsated through me like a thunderbolt, giving me the wildest orgasm I've ever had. It started at the center of my vagina, way up inside me. Sizzling like a hot fireball, pulsating, increasing in size until it filled my pussy. Then my clitoris burst into flames, and dazzling fireworks exploded before my eyes. Silver, red, blue.

Hot, hot, *hot*.

I experienced the most exquisite, soul-melting ride: my whole bod jerking with each jolt, my legs thrashing in midair as I flew through space, an electrical shower falling around me, singeing my skin and making me yell out. I moaned so much, I sounded like I was crying. Long rhythmic shudders traveling up and down my body thrilled me, telling me the peak of my passion, my climax, was near. Then my pussy began a series of spasms, clamping so tightly on—

*Hold it.* How could all this happen with no penis filling me up? Plunging deep, totally possessing me? My pussy muscles *tried* to draw him in deeper and deeper.

No go. It was all in my mind.

Or was it?

Paul Borquet.

I *swear* I saw him through the slits of my eyes, leaning over me. His manly scent ignited my desire for sex all over again, and his arrogance at taking what he wanted set off my emotions in a frustrating state of upheaval. I felt his hands squeezing my breasts, then rubbing his thumb over my rigid nipples, sliding his palm down across my waist and digging his fingers through my pubic hairs. Oh, it was delicious.

*Him.* Moaning, gasping. His body tense, hot, slick with sweat.

*Me.* Tingling. Glowy. Trembling, aching for him to touch the soft mound between my legs, push aside my pussy lips, insert a finger—

Then he was gone.

Where?

And where the hell am I?

Isn't it time we answered that question?

I walk with my arms swinging, bare thighs rubbing together *sans* panties, feet burning, striding up rue Saint-Merri, looking everywhere at once. I see a few electric lights glowing in the nest of small streets crowded together, mostly gaslights from the grand houses throwing a yellow tone upon the cobblestones and tossing eerie shadows everywhere. An exquisite haze, barely a mist, covers everything like a delicate veil. I see a man standing on the corner, tending to a big copper cauldron. He pulls down his black felt hat, then flips up his coat collar as he rattles the steaming-hot chestnuts roasting in the pan. The nutty fragrance floats across the square and tempts me to stop, ask the questions lingering on my lips. I don't. I want to see more.

I'm not disappointed. I see horse-drawn carts, wagons, a horse cab, even a lone bicycle at this early hour, the traffic flow following no specific order. The *clop-clopping* sounds of horses' hooves fill my ears. You'd think I'd get it, wouldn't you? But I don't. Can't. It's still too weird.

I keep walking, pulling the red velvet cape closer around me, shutting out the early-morning chill. I love this cape. Lined with a slippery red satin as soft as nude skin, I snuggle within its folds, lapping up its luxuriousness with a greedy hug. *Sooo* sinfully elegant. Where did it come from?

When I came to after the best orgasm I've had in years, the cloak covered me from head to toe, but my clothes, my waist pack with my money and passport, *everything* had disappeared. A girl needs more than red velvet to find her way back home.

Or back to the hotel. That's where I'm headed. I intend to go to the police and find out what that old artist did with my stuff.

I'm still groggy and drained from climaxing like I was the star attraction in a *ménage à trois,* but here's what happened when I woke up. Darkness invaded the studio except for an electric light with an opaque, fluted shade. *One* electric light? I questioned, noting someone hung a pink chiffon scarf over it, giving the room a soft glow. That should have been a dead giveaway, but I didn't let it sink in. I was more fascinated with the wardrobe of costumes I found. Petticoats, stockings, garters, button-up shoes. No underwear. But in my present state of undress, I couldn't be choosy.

I wiggled into a soft white petticoat with layers and layers of frilly lacy ruffles and pert pink bows, then slipped on a silky apricot-hue dressing gown so thin it was transparent. I let out a girlish giggle when I saw my breasts standing up and not sagging and my hard nipples popping through the silk like I was nineteen again.

Isn't that what expensive lingerie does for you? Makes you feel sensual and thin?

Or was it something else? Something black magical?

After tying a silver cord around my waist—which seemed smaller—I laced up a pair of tight-fitting pearl-gray leather button shoes with stubby two-inch heels and threw on the gorgeous red velvet cloak. No mirrors, so I couldn't see how I looked, but everything fit perfectly, as if I'd lost a few pounds. *Very* strange. I wanted to believe the statue had worked its magic on me, but I couldn't. Not yet.

My calf muscles pull, legs tighten in the morning chill, and I walk stiffly across the boulevard toward what I hope is the rue Saint-Honoré. Up in the sky the fading moon ignores me, along with the dark clouds trying to blot out its glow. No storm clouds. No thunder, and God help me, no lightning. No rain puddles, either. But it's cold, much too cold for an early summer dawn breaking over the elegant edifices of the pink-brick and white-stone mansions. A cool breeze plays with the heavy velvet whipping around my ankles, as if it knows I'm pantyless and wants a peek. I pay it no attention. I have to get some answers, and fast.

Why did the Marais studio look so different when I came to? Where was the old artist? How long was I unconscious?

And what about Paul Borquet?

He couldn't have been real. I only imagined him.

I exhale deep lungfuls of air that puff in front of me like smoke. Yet I'm sweating despite the chill. I hear only my own panting, the swoosh of my long cape hitting the pavement as I plod along the cobblestone streets in two-inch-high button shoes with squared-off toes that wouldn't know a Blahnik from a Choo. I don't want to accept the crazy notion skirting through my orgasmic-maxed-out brain. *Nothing* I've seen is real, I tell myself. Can't be. The reality is I'm lying in a Paris hospital, tubes coming out of my nose, my mouth, *everywhere,* my mother hovering over me while she flirts with the handsome French doctor who assures her I'll wake up soon.

*Only a bump on the head when she slipped on the floor during an electrical storm,* he tells her.

My mother reacts. *You said she was nude? And holding on to the erection of an Egyptian statue? My daughter?*

Yes, Mother. *Your* daughter, who's having the sexiest wet dream of a lifetime and I have no intention of waking up just yet. So, let's get on with it! I want to see what happens next...

I look to the pavements. A soft sigh escapes from my lips, frustration following, as if my breath catches on a feather and hangs there a moment. I see construction, houses the color of milky limestone going up, streets being widened, as if the city of Paris is getting a facelift.

I can't put into words my fascination, but I feel it down to the core of female sexuality. As if *I'm* the city of Paris and my body, my spirit, my fucking sex life, is reawakening and filling me up with so much energy, so much furiosity I feel my body regaining its suppleness, its curves. I'm lethal, baby. A sex pistol.

This sensual feeling takes possession of me and won't let go. I breathe it in. Suck it in, dammit. Power is a thrill ride. *Sexual* power is a thrill ride in overdrive. So, power up, because here I go.

I cross the street, the intoxicating floral scent of nature in an aroused state—ask any bee—seducing me. Moisture glistens on the canvas awning of a flower stand. Underneath I see an old woman wearing a tattered black shawl and a long, heavy dark skirt lovingly arrange her roses, lilies and violets. The woman pulls the shawl back from her face and smiles at me. I'm so absorbed in watching her I don't see the man come up behind me—

"*Pardon*, mademoiselle," drawls the young dandy, bumping up against me. Wearing a polished black hat and evening tails, he weaves past me in complete bewilderment of either me or his surroundings. I wrinkle my nose. The strong smell of alcohol lingers in the air. I assume the slender shape of a wine bottle holds more appeal for him than the curves of a woman. The young man dawdles down the boulevard, muttering to himself, when from out of nowhere a ragged creature with a wicker basket strapped to its back shuffles closely behind him.

I turn my head, sniffing. Did the air just get heavier with a foul scent? Unpleasant, as if they haven't washed in weeks.

Carrying a lantern in one hand and a sharply pointed

hook in the other, I watch in amazement as the creature picks several items out of the young man's coat pocket with its hook then tosses them into the basket.

"*Watch out, monsieur!*" I yell out, trying to warn the young man, but he's too tipsy to realize what's going on and dawdles on his way without looking back.

"Mind your own business, mademoiselle."

Is it a *woman?* The voice is gruff, gritty but definitely female.

"I will not," I shoot back, insulted. "You're a thief, madame, or worse."

*None of this is real,* I keep telling myself, so I edge closer, fascinated by this creature.

"Sassy, ain't ya, mademoiselle?" Surprised by my boldness, she stands down, shifting her weight under the heavy pack. I judge her to be around forty, but her hunched-over posture makes her appear much older. Swathed in gray-stained rags with an occasional patch of fancy silk plaid showing through her torn muslin petticoats, she has the look of a woman worn out by poverty, but crafty nonetheless. What surprises me are the fine black leather boots on her feet. She notices my stare. She grins with glee. "You like?"

"Where did you steal them?" I ask her, smirking.

"Yesterday these fine boots belonged to a fancy lady on the rue Saint-Honoré." She raises her skirts with her hook and shows off her boots. "Now they adorn Old Mathilde's callused feet, *ma fille.*"

Did she just call me a ho?

"*You* may be a thief," I insist, "but I am *not* a whore!"

"*Eh, bien?* Really? What else could you be with that red

Titian hair, mademoiselle?" I flinch when she reaches out and touches my hair, but I don't pull away. Something about this woman intrigues me, as if she's a key player in this melodrama. "I've never seen hair this color except on a beautiful *demi-mondaine,* gentleman's mistress, decked out in fancy feathers and soft silks and smelling like faded carnations and Rachel Rose powder."

I make a face. "Don't ask me what *you* smell like—"

Before I can stop her, the creature bumps into me, then rips open my long flowing cape, nearly tearing it off me. My bare breasts peek through the silky material of the dressing gown, my nipples brown and pointy, the apricot-hue giving my skin a natural peachy tone.

The woman's eyes widen. "By all the angels in heaven I've never seen *anyone,* not even a *dégrafée,* unhooked one, running through the streets of Paris in her underwear."

I pull my cloak closer around me. "Someone stole my clothes." I have no intention of explaining further.

Old Mathilde fiddles with her smooth, wooden rosary beads. "I know, mademoiselle. I've been watching you."

"Me? Why?"

When did she hop on for the ride in my orgasmic wet dream?

Stooped over, her wicker basket heavy with the night's pickings strapped to her back, she sniffs me. "I followed you through the streets from rue Saint-Merri, past the boulevard de Sébastopol to rue Berger." She chuckles softly. "You have the smell of sex on you, mademoiselle."

I roll my eyes and wet my lips. "You have no idea."

She smirks. "Is that artist as good with his cock as they say he is?"

In the early-morning mist, I can see she enjoys toying with my emotions. "Artist? *Who?*"

"Paul Borquet."

I grab her by the shoulders, though the smell overpowers me. Think vinegar with dead rats floating in it. "What do *you* know about Paul Borquet?" My pulse races. *"Tell me!"*

"You must have a hot cunt, mademoiselle. All wet and juicy and tight. Ripe for a man to slam his hard cock into and shoot his heavy load." Licking her lips with her wet tongue, she points it at me. The effect is more comical than sexual, but her comment unnerves me.

"I've had enough of your tricks," I yell. *"Tell me what you know about Paul Borquet."*

"He's looking for you, mademoiselle," she hisses. "And when he finds you, *beware!* He has an appetite for sex that derives its power from the occult." She crosses herself. "He's a master of the Black Arts."

Creepy chills come over me. I pull my cloak tighter. Black magic? Then the old artist was right about the power of the Egyptian statue. Oh, shit, then that means...

...this isn't a fantasy?

The old ragpicker says, "He can make any woman his slave."

"Any woman?"

Even a woman from another time?

"Yes, mademoiselle. Even a woman as young and beautiful as you."

*Young and beautiful? Red Titian hair? Small waist?*

Before I have time to contemplate whether or not I really have sold my soul to be young and sexy, I lose my balance when the creature jerks my arm back and grabs at my breasts and squeezes them. Hard.

Something snaps in me. Regaining my balance, I throw a punch at her. She bounces backward but recovers quickly. With a disgusted grunt, she shoves me to the ground. I go down hard, hitting with such force my teeth rattle in my head. Before I can react, she shifts the basket on her back, then takes off, wobbling down the street faster than I would have believed possible. *She's* wearing leather boots that fit. I'm not so lucky. The chick who owns the shoes I'm wearing must have only four toes.

I shout at her to stop, but she looks back at me and laughs.

"You won't get away with this!" I yell, taking off after her. I see the elusive creature weaving down the boulevard, paying no attention to whether or not I'm following her. She knows the streets better than I do, but I can't lose her. She's my only link to Paul Borquet.

I kick my stride into high gear, pushing myself to the max. I ignore the *Exercise Overload* red light flashing in my brain. Anger, like good sex, has a way of making you endure. I'm not even gasping for breath. I see the street thief about twenty feet in front of me. My long legs pumping, arms swinging, red velvet cloak blowing up around my bare legs like a battle flag. I'm no marathon runner, but when I'm desperate I can move out. Fast.

I catch sight of her turning onto a crooked little street so narrow only pedestrians and baby carriages can fit through its open-air portal. Pumped with adrenaline, I rush down the street. Where did she go? Inside a house? No, everything's shuttered up tight. Where then? The scene in the street looks like something out of an old black-and-white *film noir*. Plain, multistoried row houses, broken stoops, uneven cobblestones.

I shiver as a misty breeze tickles my bare neck. Sweat oozes down my cheek and settles on my lower lip. Salt mixes with what's left of my pink lip gloss. I lick off the sweat and wrinkle my nose. The pickpocket has disappeared, but her dirty smell lingers in the air. I race down the street, looking everywhere at once. I'm not sufficiently paranoid to think I'm being led into a trap.

I dart into one doorway, then another, trying to follow her tracks. I bet she's watching me from her hiding place, laughing at me, waiting for me to give up. I won't.

Won't. *Get it, you old ragpicker?*

Because the street is bending and winding, with crumbling Gothic stonework caving in on either side of me, and because the alley is the only escape route visible to my eye, I surrender to my female impulse. I proceed without caution into what I believe is a small alleyway. Deserted. Quiet. I walk up and down the alley, going a little deeper into the darkness. *Any* excuse not to go to back to the hotel and face my mother and the French police and end this thrill ride. I don't want to lose the feel-good vibes surging through me from my fantasy fuck.

I'm having too much fun.

I cock my head to one side, looking for any sign of the old ragpicker. I slow down, painfully aware I've lost her. Just when I was getting started. I'm pumped with energy, like I could run all day. I don't turn back, not even when a cold wind penetrates my red velvet cloak, slicing through me like the steel blade of a knife. My teeth chatter. Dampness inches under my clothes, pricking my skin with tiny bumps. The alley leads me into the back entrance of a large, run-down building.

A curious urge guides my footsteps into the cool vastness of the gigantic wrought-iron framed hall. I crane my neck and look upward. An awesome panoramic view. Dizzying. Breathtaking. It's as big as an airplane hangar, stretching off to a misty vanishing point. The gigantic umbrellalike building with wrought-iron-and-glass roofing looks old, *very* old, and goes on for what appears to be miles. I count as many as ten pavilions with iron girders and skylight roofs, as well as large cellars for storage. Then I hear voices. I turn around and see merchants unloading their crates of wares and piling them ten, maybe twelve feet high, between rusty-looking scales and anywhere else they can find room.

At the same time, a steady congestion of traffic of hand carts and vendors passes by me, delivering their produce or selling their trade outside the market to the early morning shoppers. What time is it…5:00, 6:00 a.m.? Knife sharpeners, dog washers, even a fuzzy burro pulling a cart of rush-bottomed chairs with the rush badly broken, passes by me. Retail meat sellers, coffee, soup and milk stall keepers, fruit merchants and oyster sellers hustle and jostle each other for the best position to sell their wares.

I sniff the air. The scents of mint, thyme and tomatoes all

mix together under my nose. It's overpowering. Rough, raw, lusty sights and smells and sounds. Rats running in and out of the vegetable sweepings strewn about on the ground. Prostitutes soliciting from shadowy corridors. Accordion players piping out a melancholy tune. Mountains of pea-green cabbages. Orange pumpkins. Crates of ripe red tomatoes.

Funny-looking goose bumps pop up on my bare arms. Pointy, like needle marks.

Where the hell am I?

The *crack* of a whip catches my attention. I spin around, alert. I see a man weighing at least 250 pounds with long, dark, curly hair and a big, black beard hurrying up what I assume is his poor wife. The pitiful woman is attached to the cart by a harness and pulling a heavy load of vegetables, her labored breaths making each step painful.

"Hurry up, bitch!" the man screams at the woman, then turning around he snarls at me. "Out of my way, stupid!" The man pushes by me, cursing.

"Watch who you're calling stupid, you *patapouf!*"

"You whore!" he yells.

*Crack!* comes the sound of a whip striking a wooden post near me. Startled, my heart pounding, I can't move. The impact is so hard the splinters break free and breeze by my cheek, grazing it slightly. Blood trickles down my face and into my mouth, but I don't taste it. I spin around and see this same ferocious bear of a man coming straight at me, wielding a whip in his hand.

"*Arrête!* Stop, thief!" he yells, "or I'll shred the flesh from your bones with my whip."

"I'm *not* a thief!" I cry out. The nerve of him. Just because I called him a tub of lard, he calls me a thief. Blood curdles in my veins when I see the man raise his arm and crack his whip in the air like a dragon's tail. I swallow hard. This time he won't miss.

I fling myself on the ground and cover my head with my arms, rocking back and forth, ignoring the sting of wooden scraps and sawdust cutting through my cloak. I'm shaking, my teeth chattering. I clasp both hands to my head, striving to understand what's happening to me. It's harder to hit a moving target, so I roll into a dark corner away from the man with the whip, then get to my feet.

I bolt through the market, bumping into carts and knocking over crates of vegetables and fruit. I keep going. I have to get out of here. *How to escape?* The market entrance is blocked by piles of crates stacked up high over my head. I look the other way. Blocked as well. I run faster, experiencing a rush to my brain I don't understand.

With the wind ruffling the stray wisps of hair escaping from my hood, I keep running until—

"Not so fast, my young thief."

"Stop calling me a thief!" I spin around as a strong hand grabs me by my red velvet cloak and grips me so tightly I can't breathe. I hear the crackling of his long cape hitting the ground before the heavy woolen material slaps against the backs of my calves, stinging me. The man's other arm goes firmly around my waist and he lifts me off the ground as if I were as light as a *poupée*, a doll.

He carries me into the shadowy doorway near a restaurant with the picturesque name *au Chien qui Fume*, The

Smoking Dog. I sniff the air. The bitter smell of alcohol lingers on the man's breath. And licorice. I squirm, twisting my body this way and that, pressing my hip into his groin, but I can't see the man's face.

"*Let me go!*" I cry out, irritated.

"*Never.* Now that I've found you, mademoiselle, you won't escape me again." My captor begins laughing, a rich, hearty baritone edged with a sensuality that sends a tingling to my brain that shoots down to my pussy and makes it throb.

*I know that voice.*

My heart beats so fast I can't catch my breath. The strength of his hands holding me does strange, wonderful things to my libido I don't want to admit. Can't. This fantasy has gone too far. I've been jostled by a ragpicker, labeled a thief, chased, grabbed and manhandled. And now I'm turned on by a voice I only imagined I'd heard.

Fear tightens my throat as he turns me around and I get a good look at him. I gasp. Loudly. I can't believe what I'm seeing, even if the man is in my face, the darkness of his eyes glaring at me. Eyes *alive*. Lips pressed together in an amused manner. Pulse beating rapidly at the side of his neck where his longish dark hair curls around his cape collar.

God help me. It's him.

Paul Borquet.

No wonder I'm turned on.

"I want another look at you, you little hellion." He reaches inside my cloak, then pushes aside my dressing gown and cups my breast in his hand. I struggle, but he holds me with a firmness that lets me know resisting him is futile. "Yes, perfect." He slides his hand under my petticoat and runs his fingers up and down my thigh. His breathing is heavy, guttural, like an animal assessing its prey. "Slim, firm. You'll do."

"Do" for what? What am I? A prize pony? Doesn't he know I'm running this fantasy gig?

"If you touch me again, monsieur, I'll grab your balls and—" I slur what I think is the slang word for twisting off his testicles. He gets the idea.

"Damn you, mademoiselle. You should be grateful to me for saving you from Monsieur Renard."

"Who?"

"The beast of Les Halles."

"*You're* the beast, monsieur, for treating me like this." I squirm in his grasp, turning my head first to one side, then the other. "I'm *not* for sale. I demand you release me."

I kick him in the shin. He yells an obscenity.

"I'll teach you a lesson, *ma belle.*"

He turns me over his knee, his hand wandering under my cloak until he finds my bare buttocks, then he begins to stroke my skin. I moan, my breath ragged, my senses reeling. I cry out when he slaps my butt. Once, *twice*. It stings, but it's a delicious sting, igniting the nerve endings around my perineum. With two fingers he massages the sensitive area between my pussy and my anal hole. I hear him draw in his breath as his fingers push, probe and knead my quivering flesh.

I close my eyes and enjoy the feelings of tingling warmth as he traces his fingertips around the area, gently but with a purpose, knowing exactly how to arouse me. I feel my face flush and my ears turning red. It feels so good, I want more, *more*. But I'd rather die than admit it.

"*Zut alors,* if Monsieur Renard finds you, mademoiselle, your pretty young arse will end up on the wheel."

"Wheel?" I ask, refusing to give up the pleasurable sensation shooting through my groin. *Very* pleasant. "What are you talking about?"

Paul Borquet smacks my bare butt again. I moan. "If you do as I tell you, mademoiselle, I'll save you from such unpleasantness."

"Oh? And what is that?"

"*Alors,* mademoiselle, I want you to—"

He closes his hand over my cunt and pushes his finger in between my pussy lips. *Oooh*...his thumb finds my clitoris and rubs it, not too hard, just enough to awaken sensual, warm feelings in me. I sigh with pleasure.

Then he whispers into my ear the naughtiest, most sensuous, succulent act of lust I've ever heard.

Goody. Goody.

# CHAPTER FOUR

**A**s slippery with his sweat as with her hot juices, Paul sniffed his fingers, reveling in the aroma of her youth filling up his nostrils. Such delights energized him with renewed passion, vigor and sustenance to indulge in his art.

*I must be alone with her. Taste her cunt, wet with her* jus de miel, *her honey juice, a few inches above my mouth.*

First he must seduce the redhead to go with him to his studio in Montmartre. He would tell no one about her, not even the other artists he often painted with at L'Atelier Gromain. Who knew how they'd react when seduced by her opulent beauty?

His gaze traveled up and down her body in a long, continuous curve, the delightful journey beginning at the top of her silken red hair and ending at the tip of her button shoes. She could never compare to a mere mortal. Tall and regal looking, she held her head up with pride, like a goddess carved in white Carrara marble. She was perfection in a world of imperfect flesh, driving men mad.

She was safe only in his hands, he thought, inserting

his fingers into her again and massaging her clit with an expert touch.

The girl squirmed in his arms, the smell of her female scent assuring him she *was* real and not an hallucination induced by his indulgence in absinthe. Breasts, round and firm, responded to his probing fingers, her nipples puckered and dark. He was surprised she wasn't laced up in a whalebone corset, yet she was slender with a natural waist so small he could almost span both his hands around her.

He wanted desperately to seduce her, grab her everywhere, kiss her everywhere. Never had he dared to imagine he'd find her in Les Halles, the rumbling central market of Paris. He had meandered around the market, smelling the unpleasant odor of sea snails on the fish counters while looking for her, before wandering into a small restaurant to partake of a bowl of *gratinée* to cure his hangover. He had almost given up hope of finding her when the flash of her red velvet cape caught his eye. Racing after her, he'd sobered up quickly.

Now he couldn't let her go. He suspected she hadn't savored what he could teach her. He imagined her nipples, hard and pointy, pierced by silver rings. Her pussy framed with a delicate blush of raspberry curls and glistening with the moisture of her juices, waiting for his tongue to lick her essence, savoring the taste of her. She moaned and sighed with so much joy, as if she were discovering sex in its purest form with his fingers probing her. Inexplicably, each thrust of her lower torso into his hand heightened his anxiety.

What if she wouldn't pose for him?

"Does mademoiselle agree to my proposition to save her

from the humiliation of the wheel?" He looked up toward the high, high ceiling at the big, horizontal wheel attached to the flat roof of the hangman's stone tower. How many times had he seen thieves and unscrupulous merchants imprisoned in the rim of the medieval torture device with only their heads and hands showing, the hangman turning the wheel tighter every quarter hour?

The girl followed his gaze, then shivered. "You're not kidding, are you?"

"Word spreads around Les Halles faster than a careless indiscretion of *l'amour*, mademoiselle. Come with me."

"And if I *don't* play your lascivious game, monsieur?"

"Les Halles is swarming with gendarmes, mademoiselle, eager to wield their sticks. Apprehending a thief is great sport for them."

She grinned. Or was that a smirk on her pretty pink lips? "But I have *you* to protect me, monsieur. Lucky girl that I am."

"You won't smile so easily, mademoiselle, if they stretch your beautiful naked body out on the wheel, your legs spread so far apart to reveal the delicate inner pleats of your pink pussy lips, your breasts pointing outward, your nipples sucked on at the whim of the hangman, his ugly tongue licking you wherever he wishes."

A bad taste lingered in his mouth. The wheel was too cruel a punishment when the girl's only crime was foolishness. He remembered how many years *he* had suffered pain, stiffening in fear, never knowing how long the blows from his stepfather would last.

In his mind now, his thoughts went back to Giverny, to

his childhood home with heavily fringed lace curtains keeping out the light and sending him scurrying out into the fields to paint. He could see the soft fields of poppies, azaleas, peonies, begging for him to take up his brush, hours he spent painting, knowing when he returned home, his stepfather would try to beat this "painting nonsense" out of him. Sometimes he couldn't paint at all. The years of beatings by his stepfather took away his sight and set off a painful emotion that pressed upon his artist's soul, dragging out the mental effect of the beatings long after the physical pain had ceased.

The girl knew nothing of his pain. Innocent of life's harshness, she blinked, running her long fingers up and down her cheek. Such soft skin, untouched. "You *are* a pervert, monsieur, though a handsome one—"

He dug his fingers into the soft flesh on her buttocks, squeezing her until she squealed. "I promise you, mademoiselle, I won't hurt you. I wish only to pleasure you."

A saucy laugh escaped the redhead, but unlike the girls he met up with in the brothels of Paris, she didn't lower her eyelashes or coyly turn her cheek to allow the morning sun streaming through the glass roof to highlight her bone structure. This girl was the exception, and that intrigued him even more.

She said, "If you only knew what pleasure you bring me."

"*Zut alors,* mademoiselle, you surprise me with your boldness."

She laughed, throwing her head back. Her voice was low and husky. His cock hardened with desire, straining against his pants. "But if you try to fuck me, monsieur, you'll be limping home. I know karate."

Kay-rah-*tay?* What the hell was that? A devil's curse?

"*Pardon,* mademoiselle?" Paul blinked, frustration slowing down his exploration of her cunt. He removed his fingers from inside her, but that didn't stop her from pressing her slim hip up against his thigh. He suppressed a groan. He was never a man to let his physical needs override his reason. He'd been nurtured in a society where manners were more important than emotion. *This* little firebrand, he noted with wry amusement, *had* no manners.

"No man ever dared proposition me as you have, monsieur, asking me to…to…it's so unbelievably erotic, so *sensual,* it takes my breath away." She pulled away from him, but he held on to her. "Are you real? Or are you a dream?" She squeezed his forearm. "Mmm, you are real *and* ripped."

"Ripped, mademoiselle?"

"Buff. A hunk. Pumped-up."

Her words sounded strange to his ears. A country dialect? She spoke with a peculiar accent, lapsing into English, using words he didn't understand, although he knew a little of that barbaric language.

"I'll rip 'off' your clothes, mademoiselle, and make love to you not once but twice before the cock crows at dawn."

She laughed. "I love the B horror movie dialogue."

Ignoring her, he continued, "I'll make you beg for *mon mandrin,* mademoiselle."

"*Mandrin?*" she asked, not understanding. "Dick, penis?"

He pulled her closer to him. "You fascinate me, mademoiselle, with your choice of words. Parisian females need very little language to get their meaning across, using the elegance of their bodies to let a man know what they want."

"I *know* what I want, Monsieur Borquet."

He drew in his breath. "You know my name, mademoiselle?"

She smiled. "I've seen your work, monsieur. *Very* impressive." Her eyes moved downward. She squeezed his crotch. "Like the rest of you."

Gritting his teeth, he ignored her squeeze *and* her sarcasm, his hands moving up and down the slender form of his captive with an experienced touch. "Obviously, mademoiselle can't wait to experience the pleasure of my cock in her."

"I warned you, monsieur," she said, bringing her knee up to his groin, but his hands were faster. Not only was he a master with a paintbrush, but he had the hands of a boxer. Big. Strong. He grabbed her arm and swung her around, his face so close to hers he felt her breath on his cheek.

"I can't wait any longer, mademoiselle. I want to taste you."

He bent down and kissed her on the mouth. Kissed her hard. He parted her lips easily, thrusting his tongue into her mouth. She moaned, and he felt her body shudder. A more delicious sensation reveled through him as the half-dressed young woman struggled like a wildcat. He sensed in her a fiery passion that could make the night sparkle. Like a sweet, pink champagne.

Finally she let her body relax, her anger fading. "None of this is real, so why am I fighting you?"

"*C'est si bon,* mademoiselle. Good, because I'm not letting you go."

"Don't get so cocky, monsieur. I haven't agreed to your insane proposition." She squeezed his crotch again. Harder this time. "Not yet."

"Who is that dirty-looking harlot in your arms, monsieur?" Lillie asked, her eyes blazing.

Paul spun around, twirling his cape, but he didn't let go of the redhead. "How did you find me, Lillie?"

"Everybody in Les Halles is talking about the girl in the red velvet cloak and how you stole her away from Monsieur Renard."

He could see the blond prostitute fighting to keep the muscle at the side of her mouth from twitching. The look on her face told him she'd been following him from one tiny bistro to the next, looking for the redhead.

"I dismissed you earlier, Lillie. Be on your way."

"Not until I have a look at the slut."

Before he could stop her, Lillie yanked the hood off the redhead and, seeing the girl's beautiful face, slapped her.

"*Bitch!*"

"Keep your hands to yourself, sister!" yelled the redhead, slapping Lillie's face. Hard. The blond girl's hand flew up to her cheek, already burning red.

"*Quel cockatrice,*" Lillie said, spitting at the girl.

"What did she call me?" the redhead asked him in English.

Trying not to show his amusement, Paul said, "An old, worn-out whore."

"I'll tear her hair out by its dark roots," the redhead threatened, making Paul wonder if he should let her do it. It would be quite a show, these two beautiful women tearing the clothes off each other, grabbing hair, their nude breasts heaving up and down, pulling on each other's nipples, the smell of their fury mixing into an erotic musky perfume. But *les chipettes,* women such as Lillie, could attack their victim with a knife as easily as they plucked their eyebrows. Not a pretty sight.

"Not so fast, *ma belle,*" Paul said, trying to keep the two females apart. "Mademoiselle de Pontier isn't a woman to be tampered with. She is a *calège,* a high-class woman of pleasure, from one of the best brothels in Paris."

That didn't impress the redhead. She started laughing, then wet her lips before she said, "Where I come from, women who sell their bodies are known by the same four-letter word, whatever their price."

She glared at the blonde, making Paul uneasy. Trouble of a female sort was brewing. Silently he shot Lillie a glance that told her to keep quiet. She paid his warning no heed.

"*Alors,* mademoiselle," Lillie shot back, hands on her hips. "A girl of your sort would *never* be accepted at the House on rue des Moulins."

"Oh?" the redhead challenged. "And what sort is that?"

"I've heard gentlemen at Madame Chapet's say women like you are like a cheap sauce—once you find out what they're made of, you don't want to taste their pussies."

The redhead bolted toward Lillie, muttering, "Is that so? Well, I'll take the puff out of your French pastry—"

"*Cochon,* you little tramp!" Lillie yelled, ready for a

fight. "You're nothing but a *marcheuse,* a streetwalker haunting the boulevards, stopping in front of a shop and playing with your cunt to entice a man to follow you."

"*Me?* From what I can see, mademoiselle, *you* do a good job soliciting with *your* hips," the redhead said with a flippant attitude. Paul noticed she had lost none of her courage.

"*Zut alors,* you know *nothing* about pleasing a man, mademoiselle," Lillie said, wiggling her body and emphasizing her catlike litheness that hinted at the claws hidden under her cloak. "I'm the most popular of all the girls at the House on rue des Moulins."

"I don't care where you live or who pays you to moan when you're lying flat on your back with a dick in you," the redhead said, her frustration spilling over. "I don't want any trouble."

She looked very confused, and in that moment, Paul wanted only to take her in his arms and hold her. To do so, he knew, would anger the beautiful blonde, and *that* would make matters worse.

"Enough of your silly jealousy, Lillie. Be on your way!"

It was Paul who spoke, his voice cutting through the heat of the moment. The look in her eyes told him she knew he meant it. Although the cool morning mist mixed with the lingering night chill, Paul began to perspire. He turned to the redhead. She smiled at him, and was that surprise, then gratitude he saw in her eyes when he smiled back?

He didn't have time to find out. Lillie claimed her rights, insisting Paul pay her extra francs for her services, which he did, then fretted about how he'd be sorry he didn't let her ride the stallion tonight.

Lillie also had parting words for the redhead. "It's not over between us, mademoiselle," she said. "I never forget a face."

"I, on the other hand, find your face utterly forgettable," the redhead returned.

Paul could see Lillie barely holding herself in check, but she knew when to retreat, especially with the extra francs he stuffed in her bosom. Parting her pouty carmine lips, she hissed at the girl, though the redhead refused to flinch. Then Lillie was gone, her scent tagging along on a breeze, subtle but strong enough so Paul couldn't forget it.

"*Merci,* monsieur, thank you," the redhead said, her face flushed. "I let my anger get the better of me when that girl insulted me, but I couldn't stop myself. I feel like I'm starring in the French version of a bad slasher movie."

"'Movie,' mademoiselle?"

"Yes, a film, a flick." She shrugged her shoulders. "I guess movies haven't been invented yet."

She offered no further explanation, and he didn't ask for one. A strong wind heavy with anger ruffled the cape between his legs. More trouble, he knew instinctively before he turned.

*"There's the thief!"*

Paul saw the big, ugly Monsieur Renard push his way through a small group of stall keepers huddled around him, his stubby finger pointing to the redhead.

"*I* will capture the beautiful thief, monsieur," another man said, "then strip her naked and put her gorgeous body on display for all to see!"

Paul looked to see who had spoken, the threat made in very bad French with an English accent. It was a curious young gentleman, dressed in fine broadcloth, obviously very drunk, and arm in arm with a luscious young woman, her bare shoulders rubbing up against his white shirtfront.

The young Englishman wiped his mouth then rubbed his crotch, but he couldn't take his eyes off the redhead. Paul gripped his cane tighter. Stupid fools. Couldn't they see the girl was with him?

He held her hand tighter, shielding the girl from their eyes with his heavy cloak. Her hand was warm, the pulse in her wrist beating rapidly. She was his to protect, to keep safe on a distant plane in a faraway place where only he could travel.

"Let me go, monsieur, before my dream turns into a nightmare," the redhead demanded, begging him to listen to her with her beautiful green eyes.

Paul studied her face, fascinated by the way her perfect lips formed the sounds of her strange accent.

"As long as you're with me, mademoiselle, no one will harm you. *I promise.* Quickly, follow me."

Paul ignored the ranting of Renard, along with the Englishman's wailing, threats and bad French as he walked purposefully through the tarpaulin-covered stretch of stands in the market, his cape fanned out around the girl like a cloak of invisibility as she moved in tandem with his step. Out of the corner of his eye, he watched her. Their eyes met and her look set his heart racing. She drew him inside her like the green enchantress, the name given to the heady absinthe that gushed through his veins, arousing him out of his black depression.

He exhaled slowly as his eyes swept over the girl's blossoming curves, experiencing a rising surge of creativity bubbling to the surface and spilling over into a bluish pool of desire. Desire to possess the girl's soul on canvas. The whiteness of her skin bedazzling him, the erotic pout of her lips tempting him to kiss her again. The lingering desire in her eyes,, arousing him. Her face an alluring shade of pale. His fingers skipped playfully over her slender neck, then toyed with the curling red hair sticking to her forehead, her face an alluring shade of pale.

"*Arrête,* monsieur, stop!" shouted the Englishman, close behind them. Where did he come from?

"Ignore him, mademoiselle."

"You don't have to ask twice, monsieur," she said. "I'm outta here,"

"*Stop, I say!*" the Englishman called again. "You're shielding a criminal, monsieur. In England, you'd be hanged for that!"

Paul turned and noted with dismay that despite his tipsiness, the Englishman was quick on his feet and nearly upon them, all the while thoroughly enjoying the entire incident.

More disturbing to him, where had Renard gone? Paul didn't trust the man. Though he was rumored to have a cock as limp as the rotting asparagus in his vegetable cart, he had a reputation around Les Halles for seducing young girls, then raping them. Tearing apart their pussies with the black leather shaft of his long whip. He was probably waiting in the shadows somewhere in the vast market to grab the girl the moment he let her out of his sight. This Englishman, however, with his wild accusations, was an immediate threat. *Alors,* he'd have to change his plans.

Paul spun around, folding the massive swirl of his black cape around the girl. He couldn't hide her completely from view as the foreigner cut them off between the meat stalls, his goblin face lit up with a grinning smile of white teeth, a lustful snarl rolling over his lips as he reached out to grab the girl's bare breast peeking through her cloak.

Paul was tempted to use the sharp knife concealed in the end of his cane to convince the man to go about his business. A dryness caught in his throat at the thought of her pure, lovely skin being touched and tainted by the overly eager Englishman. Pampered and smooth-skinned, the gentleman probably hadn't had his balls stroked by a woman since he was an infant at the breast of his wet nurse.

"Run into the Black Beau, mademoiselle," Paul whispered to the redhead, indicating with a nod a tiny bistro nearby.

"Monsieur?" she questioned.

"Do as I say or the Englishman will cause enough commotion to have your beautiful ass hanging upside down on the wheel." He opened his cape and cleared a path for her between the stalls. "Run, *now!*"

The redhead rushed past him, so close to him his fingertips brushed up against the exposed skin on her neck and a hot flush warmed his groin. She *must* be his.

*"Stop that thief, monsieur!"* shouted the Englishman.

"Thief, *what thief?*" Paul mumbled, twirling his cane

and gracefully pirouetting around in a circle, his wide cape swirling around him. "I see no thief."

"That one, monsieur." He pointed to the redhead pushing through the crowd and heading toward the tiny bistro. "She won't get far." He elbowed past Paul, shoving his shoulder into the artist.

"*Quel bâtard,*" Paul muttered under his breath. "Mongrel." Such poor manners. The Englishman deserved to be taught a lesson.

Quicker than the flick of a brush, the artist thrust his long, ebony cane out in front of the Englishman's feet and tripped him.

The Englishman cried out, tumbling onto the ground, his arms and legs flailing in the air in all directions before he landed with a loud thud.

Paul smiled, wiping his cane on the ends of his black cape with the tips of his fingers. The dirty hands of the Englishman would *never* touch the girl, he swore, sweeping the cane under his cloak with little effort. It disappeared like grains of sand caught on the wind.

"You *tripped* me, monsieur," the Englishman accused, struggling in his drunken state to stand up. "I should call you out for that, except I've already sent my bodyguards home for the night. And I refuse to dirty my hands on the likes of you."

"*Me,* monsieur?" Paul couldn't help but snicker. The man resembled a pot of jellied consommé, dumped onto a saucer. "I am but a poor artist."

"I don't believe you, monsieur," demanded the Englishman. "You're a magician. What have you got in your hand?"

"Nothing, monsieur—" The artist feigned a look that clearly said he was insulted. Adding to the effect, a muscle in his neck twitched and his eyes loomed large in his handsome face, casting a surrealistic, dangerous twist to his features. Smiling, he threw open his cape, his muscular chest straining against the thinness of his white shirt, "—but *this!*"

With a grandiose gesture he pulled out a faded handkerchief and waved it under the man's nose. The Englishman reeled backward, caught off balance by the heady smell of patchouli, a minty perfume from India that spoke of long nights of exhaustive pleasure.

Paul bowed slightly. "Your servant, monsieur."

The Englishman shook his head in disgust. "You and your magic don't fool me. You helped that girl to escape."

"You are mistaken, monsieur."

"You have insulted the Duke of Malmont, monsieur. Next time we meet, it won't be under such unsavory circumstances in front of peons. And when we do, *I swear I will kill you,*" the Englishman threatened, squaring his shoulders and wiping the dust off his coatsleeves. He stalked off in another direction, his battered British pride flattened in front of the market jammed with porters, commissionaires and wholesale and retail buyers stocking food on their hand carts.

Paul tapped his cane on the sawdust-strewn floor in an uneven rhythm, a mental fear engulfing him. He was rid of the Englishman, his threat meaningless to him, but the redhead wasn't safe with Monsieur Renard looking for her. He *must* get her out of here, this goddess who couldn't be more than nineteen, not yet a woman.

Where did she come from?

He often frequented the back doors of the cabarets and theaters where the women he met were victims of lascivious upper-class diversion long before he stroked their feminine egos with compliments and money. These women had succumbed to a living death on the silken sheets of sexual perversion and greed. One fed off the other. He merely provided a way out for them, indulging in their fantasies, giving them the joy of his cock for one night.

Unless he helped her, he had no reason to believe the future for this redhead would be any different. He tried to imagine her life on the streets. Begging for a sou might buy bread, but the day would come when her pitiful plea would buy nothing but an offer to take from her the one thing she could sell but once: her virginity.

He wondered what hope she would have then when she lay on her back with languid eyes turned away from the stranger thrusting inside her so deep, the walls of her cunt grabbing for him hungrily, betraying her. Hope that died with each thrust, each sweaty moan, each careless fondle. Paul knew the darkness of perversity came next. It always did.

He rubbed the handle of his cane between his fingers. Sticky sweat imprinted his fingerprints on the smooth ebony. He must save her from that darkness.

# CHAPTER FIVE

Running from the beast they call Monsieur Renard, I've never been so scared as when I saw him spring toward me like a wild animal. I *swear* I saw him pull out his dick, dark and meaty, and wave it at me. The pungent smell of his sweat overwhelmed me. Repulsive. Because of him, I've lost Paul Borquet.

*You fool.*

Okay, so the artist is sexy, gorgeous, and has a cock that lives up to his reputation, *if* it's as big as it felt pressing against my hip. And when he spanked me, I squealed with both surprise and pleasure, arcing my back up toward him. I'll never snicker at those SM personal ads again. There's something about a little whack on the butt that sets off a girl's libido like a vibrator on autospeed.

But if you think I'm going to tell you what he whispered in my ear when he was playing with my cunt, *dream on*. I can't think about it now. I gotta haul my butt outta here before that creepy Monsieur Renard finds me and turns me into his own private peepshow. Why do I get all the corpulent creeps? Why don't I get the Disney dream with the dorky dwarves and cute little elephants?

*You got the handsome prince, kiddo. What more do you want?*

Yeah. I can't keep a smirk from crossing my lips. What hands that artist has. Stroking, rubbing my clit in perfect rhythm. I imagine him licking the insides of my thighs until I can no longer stand up; then I collapse into his arms and he catches me; before I can think of the right French idiom for *fuck me hard,* he kneels and puts his mouth on me and makes me climax *un, deux, trois.*

Yes, I'm willing to believe I've traveled back in time, if that will keep this scenario going and help me find Paul Borquet.

First, *escape.*

Inside the Black Beau bistro I'm surprised to find it so small it has no table. *And* no customers. Only a bar and a couple of chairs stacked in the corner. Heavy steam pours out of the big pots cooking on the stove. I pull back to escape the hot vapors before they scald my exposed skin. I hear the angry stomping of leather boots outside. Close, *too* close. I take one step backward, then a second, and find myself flattened against the back wall of the tiny bistro.

Crazy. I'm hiding out in a deserted restaurant in a market demolished long ago, the dark, worn wooden chairs and dented pots casting distorted images of a past where I don't exist.

Until now.

My heart races; my body is flushed.

"Where's the girl with the red hair?" I hear a man's voice

yell, the crack of his whip cutting through the still morning air. I peek through the tiny hole in the door. It's Monsieur Renard.

"She went into the Black Beau," someone says.

I look around. Where can I hide? There's no back door, and no one attending to the steaming pots of hot liquid boiling on the stove. Talk about lousy customer service. I wish I knew what to do next, but I don't. I've used up my smart chick trick quota for today. A wave of fear washes over me as I grab a big, heavy broom to defend myself. I'm not going down without a fight. I will *never* allow that thug to snatch me, grab my breasts, his yellow teeth closing around my nipples, biting hard.

I begin whacking a big pot of boiling soup across its belly, sweating and grunting, until the kettle starts wobbling back and forth on the stove and the steaming hot liquid splashes out onto the floor. One more *push*. I strain with a loud grunt and over goes the pot, crashing and splashing over the worn, wooden floor.

"*Attention!* Watch out!" someone yells outside as the flood of scalding liquid spills out of the tiny bistro.

I protect my face from the hot steam with my hands, peeking through my fingers to see what's happening. Outside I see the angry crowd, including the black-bearded man and another man, jumping and bumping into each other, shrieking and cursing. A melody of yells, then accusations.

"It's *your* fault, monsieur!"

"Not so, monsieur—*you* started it."

I've got to make a run for it. I take a deep breath, lower

my head, gather up the soft folds of my red cloak, when I hear—

"Over here, mademoiselle," whispers a man's voice. *"Hurry!"*

*Who? What?* I can't believe it when I see a trap door in the floor rise slowly like a musty clam opening its shell and a hand beckons me.

What have I got to lose?

Without hesitation, I run toward the trap door and peer down into the hole. A rich, velvety darkness awaits me below. Okay, so it's not a good idea to jump into a black hole that could lead me to nowheresville. I should have thought about that when I imagined this madcap adventure. I didn't, so I don't have much choice. It's that or be ripped apart by an angry mob, my body bucking against the intrusion of more than one vile cock.

"Jump, mademoiselle," urges the same voice from deep inside the cellar. *"Jump."*

I hear a crackling sound as a bullet shatters a hanging oil lamp, splattering the thin glass everywhere. Someone's shooting at me! I take a deep breath and jump...

...and land unhurt on top of what I think is a large wine barrel. I can't see much. Carefully feeling my way in the dark, I let my legs dangle over the side. Only a faint sliver of light beckons me into the darkness. Before my eyes can adjust to the dim light, a breeze skirts past me, making me hold my breath. I smell strong liqueur.

"Shut the trap door, mademoiselle, before they find us and we go together to claim our place in hell," orders a man's voice. Impatience slurs his words, but I get his drift.

I pull the cellar door shut, fasten the handle in place, then turn my attention to the caped figure holding a candle in one hand, a cane in the other.

Paul Borquet.

I smile. I've never been so happy to see anyone.

"I owe you my life again, monsieur." Our eyes meet and I begin to understand the flurry of emotions engulfing me. From the first moment I saw him, I was wildly attracted to his gallantry as well as his cock.

"*Mais non,* mademoiselle, it is *I* who owe you. Your beauty inspires me, fills me with passion to paint."

We face each other, and in that breathless moment, I recognize he's more than a dark and mysterious superhero clone in a black cape and crotch-hugging tights. We are artist and model, a creative work of art yet to be defined that defies time and rationale. I lean into him and he strokes my neck, his fingers working at the fastening to my cloak, then stops. I sense his pleasure and something else. *Fear.* We're not out of danger yet.

Nibbling on my lip, I ask, "How did you find me?"

"No time for questions, mademoiselle," the artist says, the light making a halo around him as he extends his hand out to me. "Take my hand. We must move quickly. It won't take that beast Renard long to start tearing up the floor, looking for you."

His strong, muscular hand grips mine as quivering candlelight guides me down to the dirt floor below. Then, wrapping his cape around him, the artist leads me through a twisting, underground tunnel barely big enough for him to crawl through on his knees. Pulling my cloak around me,

I follow him, crumbling dirt hitting the top of my head, the tip of my nose. I keep his tight butt in sight. I've spent a lot of time on my knees with David, but the view was never *this* good.

Then, without warning, the candle flickers and goes out. I panic, but instead of being thrown into blackness, I'm surprised to see a spotlight of sunshine greeting me like a warm smile. I look straight up. The way out of the tunnel is an old, dry well laced with rusty, iron rings and small stone steps spaced about a foot apart on the cracked stonework.

"I've used this escape route many times when my taste for liqueur overrides my taste for a woman's pussy," the artist says with amusement. "Every sharp cut of stone is an old friend." He clasps his hands together and bends over to give me a boost. "After you," he urges.

I lift my eyebrows. "So you can stick your fingers up my rear end?"

"You have a sharp wit, mademoiselle."

"Not as sharp as the end of your cane." I cast my eyes downward. He's sliding his cane up and down my butt. Sensuous. Provocative. No mistaking his visual cue. I wet my lips.

He laughs. "*Allez,* go!" he calls out, insisting I start climbing up the wall whether I want to or not. To my delight, I find it easier than I thought as I grab onto the rings embedded in the scaly stone wall and climb up the side of the well. My heavy breathing mixes with that of the man following me, the sound of our feet scraping over the broken stones filling the echo of the empty water hole.

"I love the smell of freedom," Paul says, taking in a deep

breath of air when we reach the top and vault easily over the side of the well. He turns and looks at me with a sensuality I find not at all disturbing. "But not nearly as much as I love the smell of a woman."

"Don't look at me. I don't smell so good after crawling through that old tunnel," I say, dusting off my cloak.

"Let me be the judge of that, mademoiselle."

He leans down, his clean-shaven face so close to mine I breathe in the lingering odor of the strong liqueur. It makes me dizzy. His lips brush my cheek as he pushes aside my cloak and kisses my shoulders, then delicately up the sides of my neck. Little shivers of pleasure flow through me. I have to steady my nerves, slow my racing mind, get some answers.

God help me if he comes any closer.

"Where are you taking me?" I ask, not knowing what else to say. He shifts his attention lower. He caresses my breasts, taking the time to rub my nipples in such delicious circles, I can't catch my breath.

"Where you will be safe, mademoiselle."

*Safe?* With his hands doing this to me?

"To your studio in Montmartre?" I ask.

"How do you know I have a studio on the hill, mademoiselle?" He gives me a look that is neither friendly nor hostile, but probing.

*Don't stop circling my nipples!* I want to cry out. Coward that I am, I don't. Instead I say in a shaky voice, "Someone told me."

"Who?"

He slides his hand down to my waist. He fumbles with the metal clasp on my petticoats. Damn this ridiculous outfit.

I say, "An old artist. He showed me your self-portrait."
I don't tell him about the statue of Min and its prophecy.
Why spoil *his* fantasy?

"Where did you meet this artist, mademoiselle?"

Still fumbling. Has he lost interest in my clit? Or is he
more interested in his own self-portrait?

"In an art gallery in Marais," I say, not giving away *when*
I saw the painting. "The House of Morand."

Paul shakes his head. He's not even touching me. Oh, the
*frustration*. "I know of no such gallery in Marais."

I frown. My breasts feel cold without his touch. Is the
whole thing a dream after all? Okay, let's try again, appeal
to his male ego. Better known as his dick.

"I *did* see such a painting," I insist. "Life-size, in *every*
way." I can't resist letting my gaze drift downward to the
bulge between his legs. A movement that doesn't go unno-
ticed by the handsome artist.

He moves closer to me, then whispers in my ear, "Ah, you
mean the self-portrait I gave to La Comtesse du Chalons.
*Hélas*, you must be mistaken, mademoiselle. *La comtesse*
took the portrait with her to London."

"No mistake, Monsieur Borquet," I say, playing the game
and enjoying it. Evidently the portrait I saw in the modern
art studio traveled from one owner to another through the
years. "I like the real thing better."

"*Pardon?*" he says, not quite understanding me.

"American humor."

"Ah, so you're *une Americaine*, mademoiselle."

I nod. "Autumn Maguire from—"

No, don't tell him any more. Not now.

Paul raises his eyebrows, then laughs. "It doesn't matter to me where you're from, mademoiselle. You're not like the English girls who raise their skirts in the dance halls. Cheap and bawdy with a smirk on their lips and fat arms and legs." He leans closer, looking at me curiously. "You have the body of a goddess, made *pour faire l'amusette,* love play."

He lifts my petticoat with his cane and rubs the inside of my thigh with his walking stick. What took him so long? I tingle all over, warm and happy and *very* aroused. I don't pull back. I try taking slow, deep breaths. Instead, my breathing becomes wildly ragged.

*Don't get turned on, kiddo. You don't even know where you are.*

My eyes dart around the ancient courtyard. I can't deal with this insane situation until I find the courage to accept the fact I've traveled back in time. I have to do it quickly before my angst swells into a panic I can't control.

Face it.

This is Old Paris.

Grime-crusted towers and turrets, broken cobbles. A medieval atmosphere hangs in the air like an old tapestry fraying at the edges, its faded glory begging for a second look. I see several ramshackle town houses huddled together around a small square of broken stones with piles of rags neatly lined up in a row around the perimeter.

Suddenly the rags move, and tiny, taut faces peep out from underneath their dirty shells of clothing. The smell of unwashed, diseased bodies overcomes me. The scene is like a curtain opening on the final act, where the near-dead play at living.

*This is Old Paris.*

In a instant where I am, who I am, why I'm here, are all erased in one breathless sweeping moment when Paul draws me into his arms and does what I've been wanting him to do again. Kiss me. Hard. Deeply. Like a man who doesn't like his pleasure to be hurried. A man who knows what he wants. It isn't like any kiss I've ever experienced. His mouth moves slightly over mine, his tongue touching the insides of my lips, exploring. *Damn him.* I can't move. Arms pinned behind my back. Breasts pressed up against his chest. My whole body is tense. I feel breathless but for all the wrong reasons.

I try to wiggle free but he pulls me closer.

"Don't be afraid, *ma belle.*" The handsome artist laughs, spreading his arms wide, opening his black cape like angel wings reaching up to the heavens. "No harm will come to you with Paul Borquet as your protector."

"Who's going to protect me from *you?*" I look hard into his dark blue eyes. They hold secrets I must know, but they're impossible to read.

"When the time comes for you to fulfill *your* part of our bargain...

That lascivious act I mentioned earlier.

"...I will arouse you to such heights you will feel no pain."

"Why would I feel pain?" I have to ask. A whack on the butt, okay, but let's not get carried away.

"Your cunt is hot and tight, even for a girl so young."

*Young?* Can't he see I'm a woman, not a virgin school-girl? Though I admit, I'm a woman falling ridiculously in love with a man younger than myself. *Much* younger. He can't be more than his midtwenties. I haven't given it much thought until now, due to the lingering effects of this entire fantasy on my brain.

Yet I have to admit I feel different. I put my hands on my waist—it *is* smaller—place my palm on my stomach—flatter. Damn, I wish I could find a mirror, find out if the Egyptian god Min worked his magic on me.

Paul has no idea what's going through my mind and thinks I'm teasing him.

"Mademoiselle feels sexual excitement, *n'est-ce pas?*" he says, placing his hands on mine, squeezing my waist, moving his hand over my stomach, down…down…lower. Is he counting the rows of ruffles on my petticoat hiding my pussy from him? If he's not, I am. Okay, I'm stalling. I can't let myself get carried away. Who knows who's watching us? All I have to do is part my legs and he'll move his head between my thighs to my cunt. And you *know* what happens next. Tickle and tingle. Big-time.

I shake my head. "Not with everyone watching, monsieur," I say firmly, looking around. "Where are we?"

"These are the homes of the *truands,* the beggars, the lame and the blind. They're my friends."

As if on cue a tiny rag-covered child—or is it an adult?—hurries up to Paul and whispers in his ear. I watch silently as he draws a coin out of his pocket and gives it to the beggar. Then he grabs me by the arm and pushes me into a tiny alleyway.

"*Vite,* quickly," he says, "we must leave here."

"Why?" I ask. "What's wrong?"

"Word is out on the streets Monsieur Renard is looking

for a girl with red hair wearing only a red velvet cloak. They will look for you here among the beggars. *Vien*, come—"

"Where are we going?" I ask. I won't listen to the little voice in my head, telling me if I *am* young and beautiful, then I've sold my soul. Telling me what I don't want to believe. All I feel is the sting of the artist's kiss lingering on my lips.

I have no choice but to follow him, hugging the doorways and staying close behind the artist as he heads down the twisting rue des Halles toward the Seine. Everywhere I look citizens attend to their daily lives—going to the market, the cafés, the shops, their offices, cleaning the streets. I slip in and out of reality, a worrisome fear bobbing up and down in my stomach. A fear that grows with each moment.

After a few blocks, Paul slows our pace, though I stay close behind him as we walk along the edge of the Seine near the Pont Neuf. Standing on the quay under the trees shading the banks of the river, I look out over the Seine, puzzled. In my time, the river is filled with foam plastic cups, ducks, even used condoms. Now it ripples along its mile course through the city filled with boats carrying cargoes of grain going upstream, wine going down. Heavy traffic of brightly painted barges, *bateaux-lavoirs* for the city's washerwomen, as well as commuter boats, congest the canal. People scurrying about, everyone is caught up in their daily lives.

I grow cold all the way through my cloak to my petticoat to my bones. I hug myself, shivering all over. "Tell me, monsieur, what year is it?"

"*Alors*, mademoiselle, it's 1889."

*1889.*

I start to laugh, choke on the laugh, then seek refuge in incessant babbling. *I'm alive in 1889 Paris and the artist in the portrait is also alive and here with me.*

Silly words, meaningless words to Paul Borquet. Puzzled, he takes a flask out of his jacket and the violent whiff of alcohol pushes through the stale air, its scent making me dizzy. The artist holds the flask of strong liqueur out to me, its heady bouquet making my eyes water. He passes his hand over it, as if to make it disappear, then sniffs it with approval.

"You need a drink, mademoiselle."

"Why not?" I say. Something, *anything* that will help the throbbing in my head go away so I can think out this whole crazy situation.

I inhale deeply, then take the flask Paul offers me, drinking the liqueur down quickly, noting its bitter though licoricelike taste, hoping it will take away the chill in my bones and put some sense back into my head. I must play my part in this Parisian soap opera, though I wonder when I'll wake up.

I blink several times, swallow. My head feels woozy, funny…

I want Paul to hold me again…in his arms…play with my clit.

Oh, I'm dizzy. My legs rubbery. A tingling sensation scrambles down my arms, running like trickles of rushing water to the ends of my fingers. I start breathing faster, yet I feel an overwhelming sense of fatigue grip me and not let go, as if my body is shutting down, exhausted by everything I've been through since that electric current zapped me. I can hear Paul's voice talking to me, but I can't see his face clearly. Fuzzy shapes—he looks blurry...so blurry. But, oh, so handsome.

"What is this stuff?" I ask curiously, licking my lips. Peppermint. Licorice. And something else I can't identify.

"Absinthe."

*Absinthe.* A strong anise-flavored liqueur illegal in my time because of its druglike properties. Powerful stuff. Addictive and known for causing madness. Toulouse-Lautrec, Baudelaire, Degas. They were *all* absinthe drinkers, as was Oscar Wilde. Didn't the Englishman say something about absinthe making you see things as you wish they were, then as they really are?

I blink. Once, then again. It doesn't do any good. Everything around me starts to move. Dizziness overcomes me, then a pounding in my head. I feel consciousness slipping away from me and I'm powerless to stop it. Powerless to stop Paul Borquet from suddenly pushing his fingers in between my labes, thrusting up into me. He's caught me by surprise again, and the throbbing sensation blocks off my thoughts, my ability to enjoy the pleasure of his thumb rubbing my clitoris. What's happening to me? Am I waking up? Is the dream over?

No, I don't want to wake up, not when it's getting this good. Oh, damn—

—*damn!*

# CHAPTER SIX

P aul Borquet pushed open the window and hung out over the second-story sill. He looked down into the courtyard below where moss grew between the flagstones and the plants in the garden were covered with straw. Breathing in deeply, he cursed the grayness of the day. *Merde*, he needed more light. Only a faint glow stole through the open, airless window of his studio and hung over his shoulder, trying to enter his domain.

Containing his annoyance, though only barely, Paul pushed the low and broad divan with the unconscious girl closer to the window. She lay upon the couch, not moving. Pale, her eyes closed. He couldn't tear himself away from looking at her, her glorious cloud of red hair floating around her head, her full pink lips, firm breasts. Her skin was so smooth, so flawless. Skin like perfect white clouds on a fresh spring morning. He couldn't believe she was here with him.

He'd acted quickly after the redhead passed out from the effects of the strong liqueur, carrying her in his arms, then taking her by hansom cab back to his studio. Once inside the closed conveyance, Paul pressed himself against her, caressing her sleeping body, pushing aside her red velvet cloak while his other hand snaked around her shoulders until one of her breasts rested in his palm. Squeezing firmly, his thumb and forefinger found her nipple which, though she was unconscious, hardened under his touch.

Now, watching her with a mixture of pleasure and excitement, he drew renewed energy from her. He held her captive with the green enchantress as her manacles, but he couldn't take the chance of her escaping him. He was still gripped by the fear she would disappear, vanish into some unknown dark shadow, an abyss of black magic that haunted the deepest recesses of his mind.

He picked up his cane and came toward her, wielding the handle about, as if he were painting the heavy air between them. Then he pulled the handle off the cane to reveal the silver blade of a knife, its sharp point catching the glint of the lighted candle overhead. He took the precaution of securing her by cutting the silken fringed cords from the pillow and wrapping them around her wrists, then tying her to the curved, closed opening on the gilded caning framework of the divan.

Next, with the sharp tip of his cane, he lifted off the piece of midnight blue silk he'd laid over her naked breasts, her chest heaving up and down so slowly that if he laid a feather between her breasts it wouldn't move. He could see the trembling pulse in her neck and the bubbles of perspiration between her thighs. He *must* capture that purity, define the graceful, continuing line that swirled in elegant curves from her white shoulders down to her hips, then down to her ankles.

"I can deny my passion no longer, mademoiselle," he whispered, admiration enriching the deep, hypnotic tones of his voice, though he knew she couldn't hear him. The effects of the absinthe put her into a state similar to that of *s'évanouir,* losing consciousness during sex.

He dampened a clean, white, preprimed linen canvas and made a quick, deft pencil sketch of the redhead reclining nude on the couch. He could see in his mind her red hair scorching the canvas like brilliant fire, the pink of her nude flesh layered in rich, wayward strokes, her skin as luminous as a winter moon.

He wet his lips, then with the saliva on his tongue, licked the bristles of his sable brush until he formed a perfect point. He dipped the reed into the green- and red-orange mixture of oil paint and applied a flat plane of flesh tones to the cardboard canvas on the easel, filling in the empty spaces in his drawing and blinking several times to clear his blurring vision. He was near exhaustion, having not slept for two days. Or was it three? He didn't know.

He marveled as the color from his brush was partially absorbed into the linen, giving the painting a curious fluidity and an effect of movement that came alive on the canvas. He could almost feel her breath on his face as he painted her. He *must* have more absinthe to continue his work. He swallowed liqueur from his flask, its wormwood flavor lingering on his tongue and dulling his appetite. He was feeding off his creative frenzy, a frenzy that forced him to put aside everything else but his need to paint this beautiful girl.

He dipped his brush into the pale ivory, blues and greens on his palette, oblivious to the strong scent of oil and turpentine that prevailed in his studio. His nostrils stung with a different scent. The smell of the girl. It was a sharp sexual odor, blending with the mixture of her perfume and sweet body smells. He sniffed the air, the headiness of her aroma overwhelming him.

He painted for what seemed like hours, never giving a thought to anything but the joyous parade of color taking shape on his canvas. Pink dawn, crushed yellow butter-cups, the flyaway feathers of a bluebird. Listening to the dictates of his mind, his fingers had a will of their own. His brush fluttered impulsively but unerringly, finding a harmony of color that vibrated with energy.

He watched the girl, still in a deep sleep, stretch her arms upward, easing the tightly knotted tension in her shoulders. Her playfulness gave way to a moody restlessness as she struggled against the silken bonds restraining her, though not hurting her. He smiled, undaunted by the redhead's show of defiance.

He gazed at the girl who called herself Autumn Maguire, her eyes closed, her long lashes resting against her cheeks like sooty smudges. Unaware of his personal torment, she twisted her body like a lazy caterpillar reveling in a floral paradise, pulling on her restraints, parting her legs to reveal the curly red hairs around her pussy, and arousing him. A light sweat sparkled on her nude body like the glitter of a perfect diamond emanating its own light, her mouth open, her wet tongue licking her lips.

He breathed in deeply. *That's* what was missing in his work. He must capture that erotic expression on her face. He put aside his sketch, deciding to use her body as his living canvas. He took a dry brush with very soft bristles and painted her breasts with dribbles of her sweat, then down to her rib cage, over her flat belly and lingering in the soft thatch of her *jouet,* her toy. She took a deep breath as she spread her legs and a sweet, satisfied smile lighted up her face. Her mood was light, carefree as Paul continued painting bubbly beads of perspiration all over her smooth, nude breasts.

When she was fully aroused, he put his fingers into her pussy and wiggled them inside her until he felt her *languette,* clitoris, become hard and pulsating. His fingers pressed deep inside her, exploring the moistening contours with tender strokes. Although her voice was barely above a whimper, in the heat of the moment it was raw and husky.

"Oh...ooohhh..." she moaned, a look of ecstatic torment on her face. She squeezed her closed eyes tighter as a slow, warm pleasure filled her. Did she ejaculate? No, she couldn't have, not yet. He wasn't ready. He put his hand between her legs. Wetness stained the silk. Droplets. Not nearly enough.

Exhausted, he rested his head in his hands, but his body didn't relax. His pupils were dilated, his breathing heavy. A cordon of muscle bulged out at the side of his neck and his passion steeped upward in a heightening spiral of anticipation. His painting was not done, though he felt godlike, all powerful, fueled by a terrifying but irresistible need to create. To do so, he must capture her fluids. *But how?*

The redhead was stirring. *Bon.* He ran his hand over her breasts, and was rewarded by a faint ripple spreading out from under his fingertips. Yes, that was it. He would pleasure her, every nerve ending in her body in tune to his touch.

He bent down and pressed a kiss to her peach-soft lips, his tongue pushing inside, then lingering on the hard bud of her clit. She responded with a guttural moan low in the back of her throat and grind of her hips. Yes. He would make her juices flow and flow until her whole body pulsated for want of his cock—

—and then he would take her again. And again. Every hour. Until his masterpiece was finished.

I awake into a reality that pushes the absurdity of my situation back into my mind, back into my body. In other words, I have a hangover. Dry mouth, achy eyes and the *worst* headache. Slowly I become aware of the hardness of the couch pressing uncomfortably against my back, the staleness of the air, an unpleasant taste in my mouth. An overpowering hunger makes my stomach hurt, as if I haven't eaten in days. If this is 1889, it's been a long time since I scarfed down those *pommes frites* at the flea market.

Not so fast.

It's drafty in here.

I dare to peek down at—

—my belly button? I'm an inny, but whose flat stomach is that along with the tuft of red hair between my legs staring back at me?

Ohmigod, I'm naked.

*Naked?*

I'm simultaneously shocked and turned on. This is the *second* time I meet an artist and I end up nude. What gives? The last thing I remember was standing on the Pont Neuf looking out over the Seine and taking a drink of a pungent liqueur from a flask. Absinthe.

I vaguely remember taking the drink, then falling into a deep sleep, though I was conscious of Paul Borquet carrying me into what I suppose was a carriage and holding me close to him as we bumped over the cobblestone streets. I remember curling into that special space against his shoulder, his arm around me, my cheek leaning against his broad chest and listening to his heartbeat. I also remember him copping a feel…and my nipples hardening. *Mmm.*

Talk about a welcome mirage in my romance desert.

Between glances around his small studio in Montmartre—I assume that's where I am—I take a deep breath and lay my head back, content to stare at the ceiling until my hunky dream guy shows up.

Mirrors. Everywhere above me. In my reclining position on the divan, I can see a girl's nude body reflected full-length in the mirrored ceiling over my head like a digital pic on a giant computer screen.

Run that picture by me again. Yeah, *that* chick. The *Playboy* centerfold staring back at me from the mirrored ceiling. Gorgeous body. Tiny, nipped-in waist, full breasts, slim hips, sexy shoulders. Who is the bunny with the bod to die for?

Can it be me?

I close my eyes, believing when I open them again the girl will disappear; if she doesn't and the beautiful girl *is* me, well, this *is* my fantasy, isn't it?

Avoiding making any silly wager with myself, opening one eye at a time, I stick out my tongue. So does the girl in the mirrored ceiling. I draw in my breath. It *is* me. Interesting.

Still not believing, I blink several times, turning my head from right to left, each time catching tantalizing glimpses of my nude body in the mirror that makes me utter tiny sighs of disbelief followed by admiration, then again disbelief. I stare fixedly at the glass ceiling, amazed by my own vivid imagination and so very pleased with this free and independent spirit that has come to inhabit my mind *and* my body.

Thank you, Min, you naughty boy.

I watch the girl in the mirror on the ceiling draw her legs up, cross her ankles, press her thighs into the divan so her knees point in the opposite direction. I've never seen myself from this position and it's quite interesting. I have no idea what to make of it. I can't see my pussy up close and personal, but what I *can* see makes me appreciate the guy's point of view when he heads south for a nibble.

A little tremor goes through me. I hope Paul Borquet also enjoys the view.

I lift my body up slowly, trying to feel if there's any sensation in my arms, my legs. A tingling makes me aware of my limbs, although a supreme heaviness keeps pulling me down, as if wet sand traverses through my veins. What's wrong? I can't sit up, something is pulling on my wrists, making them numb. I pull again. What's holding me down?

I lean my head back and, with a hopeless sigh escaping loudly from my lips, I collapse back on the divan. My God, I'm tied to the couch, my wrists bound by silken cords. This fantasy has taken a wrong turn. I'm in a danger zone.

Helpless. Paul Borquet can do anything he wants to me and I can't stop him. *Anything*. Lock a collar around my neck, secure my wrists in handcuffs, cover my head in a leather hood that cuts out every ray of light and nearly every sound. The only thing I'll have left is physical sensation.

What's to restrain him from shackling me to his bedposts or rings in the ceiling? Next, I'll hear the hiss of the whip cutting through the air and draping across my shoulders or my bare butt. Or the kiss of his cane. Pain coursing through my body as thin red welts lift on my flesh. No, thank you. I'm outta here—

—but maybe I'm not.

What if he just wants to turn me on? Bondage, as in *erotic* and only if the right man is pulling my strings, *may* be kinky but I've always wanted to try it. If Paul Borquet wants a willing pupil for his night games, I might be interested. Fear is not something I'm unfamiliar with, not after what I've been through, but I'm just as sure something mystical lurks here, flooding my mind with thoughts of dark passages, ghostly bones and black magic à la Hollywood hunk. Why not? Silk restrains my wrists. Silk cradles my buttocks. Warm air blows over me from an open window. I don't feel threatened. Bondage may appeal to my Darth side, but only if we're talking about chick comforts. No cold cell or dungeon for this slave wannabe. I want to feed my hunger in style.

Bring it on.

A web of pleasure begins to weave itself in my belly and between my legs as I think about his tongue flicking back and forth across my clitoris, while his pinching fingers send exquisite sensations though my nipples and breasts. And I have to lie here and enjoy it.

*Poor baby.*

Waiting for you-know-who to make his entrance, I'm content to lie perfectly still on the divan, staring up at the high ceiling, a suspended candle in a glass jar swaying back and forth on a rope above my head. Lower and lower it seems, its blue-yellow flame taunting me. I wiggle my butt, now glowing white hot in anticipation, the seeds of arousal I've planted in my mind sprouting into blossoms of pleasure and screaming for release.

But wait, I'm not the first woman the artist has brought here. I see a pile of feminine clothing, including scraps of red and yellow silk, a black stocking, a lace-ruffled petticoat, crisp and white, and a brown-checked taffeta dress sitting in a heap near the divan. A persistent jealousy settles in me then. Lies heavy in my stomach. A new thought disturbs my fantasy. What if this Paul Borquet intends to make me compliant, make me wet, not with *his* lips but with the kiss of a woman? How will I react if he brings in a female like that blonde in the market and she straddles my shoulders, lowering her pussy over me? What will I do? What if her tongue opens my pussy and slides effortlessly over the swollen bud of my clitoris? Will my body betray me and my hips move in rhythm to her sucking?

I don't know the answers to these questions, never thought about it before. I never experienced the touch of another woman in my world. But this isn't my world, this is Paris in 1889.

*Get ready for some action, kiddo.*

Sniffing the air like an alleycat poking her nose in somebody else's kitty litter, I smell strong liquor and the residue of—do I dare say it?—sex.

Pungent. Like pollen. *Fresh* pollen. Monsieur Borquet is a *very* busy man.

"Ah, *ma belle* has awakened, ready to torment my soul with her beautiful eyes. Dazzling green eyes, *n'est-ce pas?*"

I jerk my head forward, but the lighting is poor. I can't see who spoke, but I can hear him. A low, raucous laugh oozing sexuality, the words slurred by alcohol. I twist my neck, squinting my eyes, knowing before my gaze settles on the man, who it is.

Paul Borquet.

Brimming with the exuberance of drink, tottering with unsteadiness from the lack of sleep, he is nonetheless a handsome sight with his long, black hair swirling around his face and over his shoulders, his shirt open to the waist and soiled with paint splashes. I see him pulling the string around the waist of his pants and tying it tightly. He must have come back from relieving himself. I wish for a daring moment he didn't draw the sting of his trousers so tightly.

The hungry look in his eyes shakes my sanity and makes me tremble. Reluctantly, I close my legs as a strange curiosity pricks my skin. I watch his face and see his expression deepen, his eyes half closing with desire, his cock swelling up under his pants. Does he intend to fuck me? Why else would he tie me to the divan? Back in my old corporate life, I'd say the man was into stocks and bondage.

"Why did you bring me here?" I ask, trying to keep my

voice steady. *Don't show him you may be willing to play his game.*

"To paint you, *ma chérie,*" he says, laughing, then drinking from a flask. A long, satisfying drink, spilling onto his shirt.

Paint me? What kind of BS is that? I want to yell out. I'm primed, pumped up, and ready for a good time and all he wants to do is paint?

The *audacity* of the man.

He turns his back to me, takes another drink, then goes behind his easel and begins pushing paint from a tube and mixing it on crackly brown paper.

I push out my breasts in a defiance that surprises him, though he says nothing. I'm steaming, fit to be *un*tied so I can kick him in his tight pants. I'm so aroused by my own daydreams, all I have to do rub my butt against the silk to experience acute spirals of delight forming in my belly. Though the silken cords aren't bound tightly, only a magician could get out of the intricate knots. I pull on them as if to prove my point. The artist looks up quickly, a flashing in his eyes with a warning that says if I disturb him again I'll pay for it.

Goody. Goody.

With that lascivious act I teased you about earlier?

Has to be.

He wants to paint me *and*—

—here's the kinky part—

—take the fluids from my pussy and mix it with his paints. I grin. Is that possible?

I smile, feeling not only amused but aroused. He looks so, so...*what is it?* So nineteenth-century-hero sexy standing there with his shirt open to the waist among the haphazard placement of junk, canvas and beaten-up brushes and paint-smeared wooden palettes, old and crusty, scattered everywhere. But it's the smell of turpentine and sex in the air co-mingling with the rich, oily smell of paint that makes me queasy. At least that's what I tell myself. It can't be because he's obviously hard, the bulge in his pants pushing out against his tight velvet trousers.

"Why did you tie me up?" I ask, pulling on my silken bonds for effect.

"I was afraid you'd run away, mademoiselle, before I finish my masterpiece."

His *masterpiece?*

I feel my heart racing, pounding in my ears. Does he mean a painting of *me?* Surely if such a painting exists, I would have seen it.

Or would Paul Borquet disappear before he completed it?

This new idea doesn't make my situation any easier. I'm more intrigued than horrified at my present predicament. This is something I never expected. The old artist said Paul Borquet disappeared in 1889. Sometime *this* year. I take a deep breath. Can I solve the mystery of this lost Impressionist?

Get him to keep talking, find out what's on his mind.

"Why paint *me* for your masterpiece, monsieur?"

I can't call him Paul. Not yet.

"Your hair, mademoiselle. It's the color of poppy fields. Up here—" he points to my head "—and down there." He indicates the exposed hair on my pubic area with the tip of his paint brush. Why did I get a shiver just then? Because I *want* him to make love to me?

Damn, I can't think clearly. Don't want to. A wave of dizziness hits me. My stomach turns triple cartwheels, tripping over itself. My legs feel rubbery and a light-headedness begins to overtake me as he puts down his paint brush and slowly unties the silken bonds around my wrists.

"Why are you untying me?" I ask, hoping the game is not at an end.

"You won't run away, mademoiselle." It's a statement, not a question.

"How can I? I don't have any clothes."

"If I had my way, you'd *never* wear clothes."

I wet my lips, then say naughtily, "Aren't *you* over-dressed?"

Paul cocks an eyebrow. "*Zut alors,* mademoiselle, you make a man so hot with desire he can't think about painting."

I say, "Then why paint?"

"What did you have in mind, mademoiselle?"

"Come closer and I'll show you."

Slowly, the feeling comes back into my upper body as Paul pulls me into his arms and holds me so tightly that for a moment neither of us can breathe. Then he kisses me. His lips are hot and probing, his cock hard and throbbing beneath his trousers, pressing into the softness between my legs.

He unloosens the string on his pants.

Long live the king—

—and long may his semen rain.

Panting like a pussy in heat, aren't I? Nicole Kidman, eat your heart out. You got all the guys in Moulin Rouge, but I've got Paul Borquet. In the ultimate act of coolness, I get caught up in my fantasy.

Paris in a wild and bawdy era.

My body morphing into a gorgeous chick.

Danger propelling me into Paul's arms, his strong body, the feel of his rigid cock when it nudges against me, the urgency of his breathing, the faint smell of our sweat mixing…

You know where I'm going with this, don't you?

Wanna come along for the ride? Fasten your seat belt, it's gonna be a bumpy, I mean, humpy night.

Because after desire comes:

*Passion*

She did not know whether she regretted
having let him love her,
or whether she wanted
to love him even more.
—Gustave Flaubert
(1821-1880)

# CHAPTER SEVEN

God, I want him.

I keep my eyes on Paul as he finishes untying the string on his tight velvet pants, then letting them drop to the floor, the ache in the pit of my belly heating up with a white, blinding fire at the sight of him. The sinewy muscles in his arms bulge hard and taut as he reaches out to me and pulls me into his arms, close to him. He smells musky, sexy, and his hair is soft, making it easy for me to draw my fingers through the dark silky strands.

"Kiss me again, Paul."

After a kiss like that, it's time we're on a first-name basis, don't you think?

"And lose my soul?" he whispers, a low growl in his voice. "You've already taken my heart."

I chew on my lower lip in a teasing manner. Sex kitten all the way. "Aren't my kisses worth the price of your soul?"

"*Alors,* your kiss inspires me to continue with my work, with my painting," Paul utters, nuzzling my ear.

"Then let me inspire you a little more." I lower my eyes, tantalizing him by kneeling on the divan with my legs spread, one hand on my hip, my other hand casually playing with myself.

"Ah, mademoiselle, you're too much temptation for this poor artist," he says, blowing out his breath, shaking his head, wiping sweat from his brow. "I can't hold myself back, even if I lose the one thing I can't live without."

"What do you mean?"

"*You,* mademoiselle."

"Me?"

"*Mais oui,* yes, I've always believed my art was like sex, something so transforming, so refreshing that someday I'd be able to capture that emotion on canvas. When I saw you, I knew you were the inspiration I've searched for everywhere in Paris, from the dance halls to the brothels to the *salons.* I *must* finish my painting of you. Now. Before you disappear, and I'm left without you in my world."

I frown. "You speak strangely, Paul, as if you expect me to disappear."

"It's a feeling I have…one that troubles me."

Paul sighs and holds me closer to him, as if willing me to stay. Moving forward with a fearlessness that seems to come out of nowhere, I reach out with my hand, daring him to escape from me as my fingers make contact with the hardness of his shoulder. The smoothness of his white Cossack shirt awakens a pleasurable sensation on the ends of my fingertips as I slide my hands slowly up and down his powerful arm. My eyes widen with approval when he pulls his shirt up over his head, revealing his upper body. He's wonderfully built: muscular chest, narrow waist. My pulse racing, I draw in my breath. The broadness of his chest, the width of his shoulders, the ripples of his abdominal muscles play upon my senses, daring me to continue my downward exploration, the flowering heat emuanating from within me dangerously close to making me forget Min's rules.

Fucking, yes. Falling in love, no.

I hear nothing but our breathing in unison, nearly as one. He wants me as much as I want him, but he's holding back. Why? As if he's reading my mind, he whispers in my ear what he wants, one of his hands caressing my hair, the other squeezing my left breast. I giggle. He wants to capture my live essence in his work. Oh, it's such a naughty idea, but then again, this *is* Paris.

*Go for it.*

I force a sound from my throat. "And how do you propose to gather up my honey juice?"

He inserts two fingers into my pussy, then draws them in and out of me, taking his time. "Simple. You're very wet, *ma belle.*" He reaches over to where his palette lies and picks up a small round clay pot. It's empty. Not for long, if he keeps touching me like this. "I'm not surprised your juices flow so quickly," he continues, "*tu es une hirondelle,* you're a—how do you say in English, rosebud?"

*Rosebud?* The word makes me smile, but it doesn't deter me. Not one bit. I *know* what I want.

"I'm a woman, Paul," I whisper, perturbed he's only interested in my youthful juices. "A *woman* who wants you to make love to her."

"You're a goddess, and I worship you," he says, his voice husky and deep.

"Then make love to me, Paul." No way am I going to let

this strong and virile young man out of my life. Although it's obvious he's very much in command of the situation, I feel compelled to seduce *him*. Is it because I want to prove to myself I'm still desirable? Show him a thing or two? Like how to find my G-spot? Not that I know where it is. David could never find it, but I read a book about it. How a woman can ejaculate several teaspoons of fluids with digital stimulation to her G-spot.

Just keep stroking me, Paul, and you'll get enough honey juice for the whole damn painting.

He touches my cheek with his lips, then kisses the throbbing pulse at the side of my neck before sliding his arm around my waist and crushing my breasts against his chest. I don't stop him. My body is obeying the need I felt since that first moment at Les Halles when I ran into his arms. I succumb to the ache to grab on to him, to whisper my desire, then let my instincts take over and shower me in a whirlpool of erotic sighs and spent passion. I surrender to him, exhausted by the intensity of my inner struggle to resist him. I close my eyes and my sense of touch reveals to me what I denied to myself all along. I needed only to alter my point of view, let my heart tell me what my mind doesn't want to accept.

I'm falling in love with Paul Borquet, a man who doesn't exist in my world, but I do in his.

*Watch out, kiddo. If you fall in love with him, that fabulous bod of yours will turn to fat. And don't forget those little lines around your eyes you noticed on your last birthday.*

Yeah, I know the rules. I'll be careful.

I hear him breathing, feel his warm breath upon my skin.

I lean my face up to his, the sign he's been waiting for. His lips come down on mine in a kiss that burns through to my soul. His tongue inflames me with a searing fire that arouses me, melting my resistance.

I kiss him back with a fierceness that reveals my need for him, then I lean back when he caresses my hair, running his hands down over my bare back, sending delicious waves of excitement shivering through me.

He tilts my chin up to meet his face and brushes his lips against my ear, nibbling gently, then darts his tongue in and out in a flurry of tiny probes. I draw in my breath. I'm on fire, my breath coming in deep, sensual gasps.

I moan when he says, "I want you, Autumn."

"Oh, yes, Paul, *yes*."

I writhe in delicious agony as he strokes my soft skin and continues teasing my hard nipples with his tongue. I pay no attention to where we are or what this will mean tomorrow or the next day or the next week. This moment is all that matters.

The late afternoon light is fading, tempting a faint glimmer of orange sun into the small studio and reflecting off our nude bodies. Heart pounding, wanting to believe everything I see, touch, feel is real, but afraid to believe it, I surrender to him. I lie back on the divan as he bends down and bites softly on my nipples. *Des fraises,* he calls them. I giggle. "Doesn't that mean strawberries?" Ah, what an insanely wonderful language French is. In the mirrored ceiling above me, I watch my dark-haired artist lover moving slowly over my breasts as he kisses them, bites on my nipples—excuse me, my strawberries—so many times I lose count.

"*Te plaît?* It pleases you?" he whispers, never stopping, never taking a breath as he continues his quest down over my rib cage until I feel his lips kiss the silky patch of red hair that adorns what he calls my *minon*. Got to mean pussy.

"Oh, Paul, I've never known such delights, such sensation…" I hold back, stop short of telling him he's the best lover I've ever had. What would he say if he knew I'm *not* the gorgeous nineteen-year-old staring back at me from the ceiling mirror, but a woman with experience? Would he understand that?

Instead I say nothing, choosing to keep this moment in the secret part of my mind, reveling in his sighs of joy as he continues his discovery of me while I watch us in the mirror on the ceiling, observing our naked bodies aligned together, moving in tandem to our tremors of passion. I cry out when his fingers find the tiny swollen bud within me, hard and bursting with want of release. I respond to his touch, my belly and hips rolling in a series of sensual rhythms, pressing against his fingers. As I do so, I look at Paul, handsome, naked, yet mindful of *my* needs as his other hand massages the firmness of my hips, over my taut belly and down to stroke my clit, his touch making me shiver and wiggle. I spread my legs wider, revealing more to him so he can see the glistening moisture of my juices gathering in the sensitive folds of my pussy, beckoning him.

I smile when he puts pillows behind my back to support me, amused at his gallantry but loving it, then he moves his body so close to mine we seem to melt into each other. I tingle; actually it's his long hard cock that makes me tingle.

Before I can take in its beauty and marvel at its size, he parts the soft lips beneath my red pubic hair and slides his cock inside me. I look down. No, it's only the *head* of his penis in me, but so exquisite is the feeling, it's more than I can bear.

"I've never felt like this, Paul," I whisper, clinging to him, looking into his dark blue eyes. He's clearly flattered by my response to him.

"I want you to feel the same ecstasy I feel when I look at you, *ma chérie*," he promises, and for a few brief seconds, it can't be more than that, I look at my reflection in the ceiling mirror and see the ecstatic look of a girl yielding to unbelievable pleasure. I have to admit I'm stimulated by the sight of my own nude body with the head of his stiff cock lodged in it. I sigh deeply when his grasp becomes firmer and he pushes himself deeper into me, a little at first, then a little more, deeper now, until I'm filled with all of him. His thrusts became more probing, up and down, up and down, and all I can do is moan, my face flushed with hot-pink desire.

He keeps thrusting, his breathing ragged, his body wet with sweat. The intensity of emotion we both share is over-whelming, our need for each other rising with each thrust of his penis. I'm seconds away from feeling long rhythmic shudders and I wonder, what will happen at the moment of my climax?

Will I wake up afterward back in my own time on the cold floor of the art studio in Marais, hot and sweaty, my body wet with the passion of my own dream?

Or will I wake up next to Paul Borquet?

Whatever happens, I'm determined not to close my eyes and be swept away by delicious sensation. No, I'm going to watch in the ceiling mirror, see my own body in its gentle throes of passion, see Paul, this wonderfully sexy young artist, pumping his desire into me and giving of himself to satisfy my needs as well as his own.

His pace quickens, becomes urgent, and before I can catch my breath, the supreme moment comes, sending incredible sensations pulsating through my body. I try to keep my eyes open, but I can't. I blink as wave after wave of pleasure surges through me, trying unsuccessfully to force my eyes open to view the tremors of my body as he pumps his throbbing cock deep within me, sending me into a graceful climax of ecstasy, then he—

—pulls out? *What?* I clench my pubic muscles as hard as I can, but he's gone and I can't stop. *Oh!* I gasp and groan, moving my hips up and down, crying out in pleasure with each contraction of my pussy walls, my mouth open wide in a piercing scream of delight as I toss my head back in wild abandon. *Ooohhh...* then it's over.

I can't move. Deep inside me I feel numb with relaxation and satisfaction. Before I can catch my breath, fluid erupts from my body. A fresh and light smell intoxicates me. Paul captures what he can in the small clay pot, then without missing a heartbeat, he puts my hand around his cock. Instinctively, I fondle him until he's rock hard again—a few secs, believe me—then open my legs and guide him between them.

"Push into me!" I call out. He thrusts forward with his hips, and his cock sinks into me. The thrill of my release from this torment of desire brings Paul to his own climax, his cock pulsing and thrusting within my shaking body as he empties his seed into me. It seems like an eternity as he pours his passion into me, his brisk up and down motions producing wave after wave of delicious pleasure. I want these sublime sensations to go on forever. The feel of him inside me, sending me into a torrent of ecstasy, taking me away from the worry and images of another century. Far, far away from anything I've ever known.

A moment later I'm writhing underneath him as I reach the height of my passion, my fingers digging into his back. Paul bucks hard, sending me into such an explosive orgasm I can't stop moaning and panting hoarsely. *Who am I kidding?* For the first time in my life, I'm experiencing *multiple* orgasms during sex. Something I never believed I was capable of feeling. It hits me then. I've never met a man like Paul Borquet, a man so responsive to me, to my needs, a man who plunges so completely into lovemaking that all else is forgotten. A man whose desire matches my own—

—*but wait!* Where's Trojan Man when you need him? We didn't use protection. I'm on the Pill, but who knows if it works with time travel? And what about STDs? Does a safe-sex guarantee come with this fantasy package? I hope so. I don't want to leave. Paris in 1889 is one rocking town, complete with the hunk, the sex and more excitement than a girl could ever need.

My mojo is *definitely* working.

Sunlight reflects off the mirrored ceiling, rippling down onto our nude bodies and forming dazzling gold sparkles on our arms, our legs. I look at Paul's tight butt, his broad shoulders. His penis flaccid. Still big. Bursts of a new morning sun shimmers over every curve of his nude body, and I'm drenched in the joy of my spent passion just looking at him. I breathe out, relaxed. I can't believe it. Paul Borquet is lying next to me, his arm wrapped protectively around my waist.

*I'm still here.*

I stretch, yawn, then wiggle my hips as I look up again into the ceiling mirror to make sure that nearly perfect female body *is* mine. Yep. I see flickers of light and shadow bouncing off the walls, swaying gracefully off the ceiling and making our nude reflections in the mirror blur like ripples on a lake. The welcome sunshine feels like a warm shower on my bare breasts, my belly, my legs.

I'm ready for another orgasm.

Seems I'll have to put off my quest. Paul is fast asleep, his long, dark hair wet with perspiration, sticking to his face. And is that a smile turning up the corners of his mouth? Indeed it is, and it warms my heart and makes *me* smile.

It's not lust I feel for this young man, but something I'm afraid of admitting because I couldn't bear it if I lost him, so I won't say it, won't think it, won't feel it.

That crazy thought, like a fragment of a forgotten dream, spins through my mind, making me feel warm and fuzzy all over, and when I try to hold on to it, squeezing my pubic muscles tightly together, my practical side butts in and I can't grasp on to it.

While I continue to push down this elusive romantic emotion, my rational why-the-hell-are-you-here mentality removes Paul's arm from around my waist lest I awaken my sleeping tiger. I pull myself up off the divan, steady myself when dizziness hits me, then I look around for something to throw on over my new, slim body.

*Not yet,* my romantic self urges. *Enjoy it.*

Feeling giddy, somewhat silly, yet *all* female, I prance around the studio in the nude, giggling and thoroughly enjoying myself. I haven't felt so uninhibited in years, so...so bohemian. Yes, that's it, *bohemian.* Ever since real estate deals and corporate planning meetings took over my life, my dream of living the bohemian life crash-landed like my virginity during homecoming week.

Now I have that dream back. Paul infused me with his exuberant artistic vision and his sensual desire for me. We're like two sexually charged animals embracing the discovery of each other.

And I can't *wait* to see his painting of me.

Tiptoeing over to his easel—I have no idea why, for nothing short of a cold north wind could awaken him—I gaze upon the Impressionist's work. Confused, I can't believe what I see. Oh, it *looks* like me, red hair flowing around my bare shoulders, soft like petals of poppies sunning themselves in the fields, but the face in the painting is pure. Innocent. The eyes, the mouth. The tilt of my head, my hands, the sway of my body.

Yet I'm amazed by the lightness of his brushstrokes, his ability to catch my image in a very spontaneous way. It's then I realize I'd forgotten what Impressionism means, about looking at the beauty of the world in a minimal way: nature, the colors, the people, and simple emotions, something so deep and beautiful. I'm so brainwashed by the overhype of

Impressionism in my own time I've lost the depth of its meaning. I've never seen such beauty of line, such richness of tone and color, but it's not *me*. It's the spiritual recreation of a beautiful vision of a girl on the threshold of woman-hood, as if he, the artist, will be the one to take her there.

I pick up the empty clay pot sitting next to his palette. *Empty*. While I slept, he mixed my fluids with his paints. Weird to think my love juice flows across his canvas in wild brushstrokes instead of flowing from my pussy.

I pace back and forth, thinking. Though I'm willing to accept the fact that any moment I could be hurled back to my own time, a part of me, romantic beyond my under-standing, longs to make him see me as the woman I *am*. I have to become part of this world if I'm going to survive and make Paul Borquet fall in love with *me,* the *woman*. Not the body. Damn right I will. I can't bear to think what would happen if he saw me as I really am. Thirty-four, okay, almost thirty-five, with a tummy and a few wrinkles.

As white heat surges in my loins, I push my sexual urges aside and go through the discarded women's clothing piled up in a heap. The dark moment passes and I regain my senses—such as they are in this erotic fantasyland—pushing aside empty green bottles that smell like…

"Absinthe," I whisper, getting a whiff of the now-familiar strong licorice odor. Obviously artists drink more than they eat since I find no food. And slim body or not, I'm hungry. *Very* hungry. Surely I can find my way to a *boulangerie* or *patisserie* once I find suitable clothes. From the top of the pile, I rescue my white petticoat with pert pink bows embroi-dered on it, along with a pair of yellowed pantaloons, a brown-checked taffeta dress cut *very* low in front and with a small waist, black stockings, two garters, soft beige slippers that look like a dancer's shoes—I'm ditching those button shoes with the pointy toes—a small white hat with a long, curling black ribbon and a red silk corset with black lacings.

Where's my red velvet cloak?

A quick search around the small studio provides no clues. I do find painting after painting of women in various stages of undress, along with charcoal sketches of nudes, as well as dried-up brown paper with paint smeared all over it. I sniff the paint, wondering if it's mixed with my you-know-what, then write a fast note to Paul with fresh red paint. "Paul, gone out to get some food. *Ta chérie,* Autumn."

I place the note on top of his easel and notice a red heap in a far corner. As I grab my cloak, a small brass-and-pewter statue with an erect penis falls out and tumbles onto the floor. The thrill of discovery that shivers through me intensifies when I seize it with both hands, press the small statue of the Egyptian god Min between my nude breasts, and hug it tightly like an old friend. How did it get there?

Who cares?

Everything the old artist told me about the statue's power of sexual ecstasy is true. I embraced the statue's black magic and I'm young, beautiful and horny as hell. But I'm scared to death what will happen when this crazy ride is over.

I sold my soul to find Paul Borquet.

I hope to God I won't regret it.

# CHAPTER EIGHT

This dress stinks.

The odor of the previous owner's sweat fills my nostrils, making it impossible for me to ignore the unpleasant smell permeating from the perspiration-stained, brown taffeta dress. Ripped in several places, the dress and petticoat make walking difficult as I lift up my skirts trimmed with white-lace flounces and cross over rue Cortot to rue du Mont, down a quiet alley, around a deserted square leading into more than one look-alike cul-de-sacs, sidestepping the grass growing on the sidewalks, then down a stairway of narrow steps bathed in pale-bronze morning sunlight.

I scratch an itch. Whoever owned the brown-checked dress never washed it. It reeks of body odor, from both sweat *and* sex. It's made so poorly one sleeve came off when I put it on over my head. Worse yet, the top buttons won't close, half exposing my breasts, not that I'm complaining. I've got major cleavage *sans* Wonderbra, though I'm wondering if I should have worn my cloak regardless of the warm, sunny day. But forget the corset. Putting on the red silk corset with lacing up the front and hook fasteners in the

back proved to be mission impossible. I didn't c...
up Paul and ask him for help. He'd want to take the corse...
*off* before he finished lacing me up.

Paul. I feel my pubic muscles tightening just thinking about him. So young and virile. *And* experienced. He knows how to stroke my nipples, then pinch them, not too hard but hard enough to make me flinch with a sudden surge of pleasure and pain. I miss him and I've only been gone an hour or so. I stop, look around. Where am I? I recognize Place du Tertre, a small square packed, in my time, with gawking tourists searching for the cold-water flats of van Gogh and Renoir. Goose bumps inch up and down my bare arms. Who would ever have believed I'd be living in the same neighborhood as these immortal artists?

My stomach growls. Food before art.

Earlier I found a blue-tiled bakery with burnished brass racks stocked with long loaves of fresh bread at least a yard long, tucked a loaf under my arm, then bought smooth yellow cheese in a *charcuterie* displaying tempting *hors d'oeuvres* in the window. Breakfast takeout, thanks to the coins I found scattered among the oil paints and turpentine in Paul's studio. A studio with no hot water or toilet. Luckily the tiny courtyard was empty when I took a piss poised over a hole near a patch of drooping brown weeds.

I continue wandering the streets of Montmartre, heading back to 28 rue Caulaincourt, watching old men in the park playing *bouls,* a kind of lawn bowling, smelling the lovely aroma of roses from the flower stalls, listening to the street cries of the clothes dealer calling out, "*Chiffons à vendre,* rags for sale," drooling over the candy shop selling block chocolate, and reeling in surprise when I see a gilded equine head protruding from the red front of a shop announcing horse meat for sale.

I hold my breath and keep going, only gulping in fresh air when I'm far enough away not to be overwhelmed by the smell. I rub my hands and arms, sticky from the humidity, then wet my lips. My mouth is dry. What I wouldn't give for a cup of coffee, even *café ordinaire,* that mysterious, cheap brew of water and chicory that is so Parisian. I look ahead and push harder, walking faster despite my heavy petticoats, heading down one small street, only to find that one leads into another small street, sucking in warm, moist air until my mouth is so dry my voice is hoarse.

I'm lost. *Damn.*

I keep walking, holding on to the bread and cheese. I *have* to find Paul's studio flat, rising up five stories, the painted-on number visible above the arched doorway, the long louver windows red and battered, the creaking big blue door off one hinge. And the scribbles on the wall that spell Gauguin, Mucha, van Gogh—

—and Paul Borquet.

Broken cobbles crunch under my feet, reminding me how I put my fingers into the grooves on the walls in the court-yard and traced the swirl of the engravings of each name, slowly, as if I were unrolling the pages of history. My hand holding the wrapped package of cheese begins shaking, shaking badly, and a cold tremor chills me with the reality of what I've found. *I'm* part of these times, these artists. I've crossed that threshold to the other side. Is there any going back?

*Do I want to?*

I take a deep breath, and the drizzle of sweat edging down my nose drips onto my cheek. Damn, where is rue Caulaincourt? And the famed quarries of plaster of Paris in Montmartre, used to whitewash the housefronts?

I strain to hear the sound of sand blasting or the heavy arms of the flour-turning windmills, but all I hear is the melancholy music of a man pumping a hand organ. Obviously the mills have outlived their usefulness in a city ready to move into the twentieth century. The only landmark I recognize from my own time—the gleaming, white stone domes of the Basilica of Sacré Coeur—isn't finished yet.

Lifting up my skirts around my ankles, I start up the steep hill, the organ grinder's music fading into the background of clopping horses pulling wagons up the hill with the occasional urging of the crack of the whip.

*Clop-clop.*

I lift my feet in time to the street rhythm. I have to keep going.

*Clop-clop.*

I turn onto rue Lamarck. No matter how tired I am, I'm determined to find my way back to Paul Borquet. Why do I feel compelled to stay with this young man? Because he knows how to make me hot? I'll never forget it: my back against the wall, his hands going behind my butt and pulling it a short way from the peeling paint. Him pressed against me so our stomachs touched. I reached down and grabbed his cock, throbbing, hot and hard, then put it into me. He jerked his hips, thrusting up until he was so deep in me I couldn't breathe. Holding my butt, his chest pressed against my breasts, he moved in me, fast and fierce. When I came, my knees wobbled, my body exhausted, he pulled out, then sapped up more of my fluids in his small clay pot.

His painting of me isn't finished yet. You *know* what that means.

Goody. Goody.

I ignore the circle of perspiration forming below my neck and continue climbing up the hill as the hot sun beats down on my head. An eerie feeling comes over me. Something in the air smells rotten. I get a whiff of the stink of slop tossed out the window of a drab old workshop and onto the gritty cobblestones. I cover my nose with my sleeve. The neighborhood is different. The town houses are rundown and lean against each other for support.

A cold shiver plays tag with my spine at the sight of a crowd of men gawking and making lewd comments in front of the first-floor window of a house. I see a broken tile embedded in the side of a building proclaiming rue Caulaincourt. My heart races, my spirits soar. Somehow I found my way back to the long, curving street. All I have to do is ignore the commotion in front of the window and turn down the street.

All I have to do…but I don't.

Curiosity is a trait that often leads me astray, which can be a good thing when you're moving up the corporate ladder and snooping on the competition is no more dangerous than hiding in a bathroom stall and eavesdropping. Snooping in Montmartre can be lethal, if not unhealthy, for a girl's assets with the emphasis on *ass*.

If only I wasn't so damned curious.

Eager to have a little adventure, I walk toward the crowd. My racing heart begins to pound, then harder as I see a woman in the window, standing in front of a limp curtain stained with red flowers. She holds a flickering oil lamp in one hand while she makes inviting gestures to the men on the street with the other. She's dressed in a printed teagown the color of spotted bananas and her long blond hair hangs down in tight curls to her waist. She's no longer young, but I see a fading beauty struggling to survive in her oval face. Rose-red cheeks. Scarlet lips. Blue eyes that seem neither dead nor alive.

Her gaze meets mine and understanding flashes in her eyes, awakening their blue depths. A moment of sadness for the woman in the window streaks through me. My mouth trembles, my eyes question. The woman sees the look and a tiny tear edges onto her cheek, a word of caution on her lips. In an instant the look in the woman's eyes vanishes when a fat and sweaty workman puts his lips on the window glass and kisses the cleavage between her breasts streaked with brown contour blush. The woman laughs nervously, then beckons him to come inside the town house. The other men join in the game, kissing and smudging the window glass with their mouths and greasy handprints and calling out obscene requests to see *son chat,* her pussy, and *charger,* ride her.

"Here's another one for the window, *messieurs,*" a man calls out, grabbing me by the arm, knocking off my tiny hat and forcing me to drop my cheese and bread onto the pavement.

"*Let me go!*" I cry out, but the man only laughs and drags me back toward the leering men. I scrape my feet on the cobbles, digging in my heels, but the man holds me firmly so I can't get away. *What's happening to me?* Why didn't I go about my business, turn down rue Caulaincourt and back to Paul? How am I going to get out of this nineteenth-century peepshow madness?

"Stop your fidgeting, *mon petit chou,*" insists my captor.

I look him squarely in the eye, summoning up courage I don't know I have.

"You've made a terrible mistake, monsieur. I'm not a prostitute."

"I've made no mistake, *ma belle,* but I've changed my mind about sharing you." The man digs his bony fingers into my arm and drags me away from the crowd. "You're too pretty for any window."

"What are you talking about?" I don't believe what I'm hearing.

"You'll see, mademoiselle." He presses his body against mine, probing his fingers into my shoulders. "I've tasted the pussies of every whore registered in this district. Now it's *your* turn."

I shake my head, not understanding. "Registered? District? What *are* you talking about?" I smell the bitter odor of a strong alcohol on his breath. Absinthe. Doesn't anyone drink anything else?

"*Alors,* mademoiselle, you must be new on the street. Let *vieux* Jacquot be your first—"

"*Take your hands off me!*" I push him away, but he's stronger and grabs my long hair, dragging me toward a freestanding metal alcove.

"Stop fidgeting, mademoiselle. I've got to take a piss."

I blink. *Here on the street?*

Why not? Didn't I take a leak in the garden?

Before I can protest, he pushes me into a circular *pissoir*, its green-painted walls shielding its occupants from scrutiny as they relieve themselves.

"Don't you move, mademoiselle." The man shoves me up against the circular wall, making my head spin, but the stench from the dried-up urine is worse. Overpowering. The smell slams into me and pulls out my insides and shoves them down my throat. Only the chill from the cold metal wall against my back keeps me from losing consciousness.

"This place and you—" I spit out "—make me sick."

"*Alors,* you'll feel better when I pump my cock deep into you and make your pussy throb," he snickers. "First I've got to take care of a mamselle's best friend."

The man holds me tightly by the arm, then with his other hand, fumbles unsuccessfully with the buttons on the front of his trousers. Cursing, he releases me. Rubbing my arm where his fingers dug into my flesh, I think about making a run for it, but it's dark inside the public urinal.

*Which way is the exit?*

I can barely make out where the customers stand with their backs to the outer wall. I have one thing to be grateful for: the relief station is empty. If only I could shrink down to the floor and crawl out on my hands and knees. I have second thoughts about that when I feel the sopping wetness soaking the hem of my skirts. It isn't water saturating my feet.

My heart pounds in my ears, nearly drowning out the sound of the man's feeble spray splattering into the hole in the center of the urinal. *Big talker, small doer.* It won't take him long to finish his business.

Slowly I edge my body along the solid metal wall toward the slender passage opening into the street, feeling my way with my fingertips. Only inches to freedom, my feet sloshing through wet, smelly puddles when—

"Not so fast, mademoiselle." The man grabs me and pushes me out of the *pissoir*. I beat my fists against his chest as he slams me up against a wooden fence, pinning me there.

"Let go of me, asshole!"

"You can't escape Old Jimmy."

*"Leave me alone!"* I cry out, trying to ram my knee into his groin. He blocks my move and laughs in my face.

"*Ah, bien,* keep fighting. I like spirit in my whores." He seizes my wrists and twists them up behind my back. Pain shoots through me. I shriek with agony. He laughs. Then, with saliva running down the side of his chin, he kisses me hard on the lips, trying to force my mouth open with the tip of his tongue.

I squirm and wiggle in his grasp, the odor of decaying food making me sick as he explores my mouth with urgency, his coarse, matted beard pressing into the soft skin on my cheeks. I gasp loudly when he rips open my bodice and rubs his fingers across my nipples, pinching them hard, then begins lapping at my breasts, dragging them into his mouth and sucking on them.

"*Que tu es belle,* you're so beautiful. I'd pay five francs for you."

"She's not worth five francs, monsieur," yells a woman's voice at a fever-high pitch.

The man spins around, his senses alert to danger. Then

he smiles. "*Alors,* Old Jimmy is lucky today—*two* mesde-moiselles want his dick!"

His eyes bulge out on his face and I swear he starts shaking with excitement at the sight of the other woman. Blond, beautiful, and *very* familiar.

It's the blonde from Les Halles. Hands poised on her hips, the young woman called Lillie looks like a character out of a fifties film noir. Her round bosom heaves up and down beneath her tight black jersey, her hard nipples pointing straight out. A faded pink carnation droops on her shoulder, and her long skirt—black with red stripes—ends above her high-buttoned black shoes. Her eyes are big and set wide apart, her long, sooty eyelashes not concealing the anger flashing in her eyes.

"We meet again, mademoiselle," she says.

"I don't know you," I lie. I want nothing to do with this woman, but she won't give up.

"Did Monsieur Borquet throw you out into the street with his come still wet between the cheeks of your ass?" she says, sneering. "*Bon.* I'll be only too happy to warm his bed in your place."

"Not with your cold heart."

"Oh, yeah? I know how to please a man, how to make him crawl on his knees with desire when I lick my hand then close it around his cock and move it up and down on him until he groans with pleasure. Then suck on him until he comes in my mouth—" says the blonde, tasting her lips like she's licking cream off a man's penis.

"Here's an eager customer for you." I point to Old Jimmy, who's gawking at both of us with hunger in his eyes.

"He's all yours, mademoiselle." I sense this woman is dangerous, *very* dangerous, but I can't and *won't* show fear.

"Don't argue, mesdemoiselles, there's plenty of Old Jimmy for both of you whores," the drunk interrupts, a tiny laugh quivering in his voice. He's giddy with anticipation.

Lillie smiles, then, "Get out of my way, *courailleur,* you womanizer."

"*Hélas,* mademoiselle, I have money, lots of money—" the drunk boasts, pulling out folded-up francs from his pants pocket. "And this." He drags out his dick, small but hard.

"And I have *this,* monsieur," Lillie shoots back, drawing from inside her sleeve a clasp knife with a locking blade, something I've seen only in old movies. Old Jimmy knows what it is and takes off down the street, his pants unbuttoned, penis in hand. He never looks back. I sense a new problem, one more deadly than the deflated lust of an old drunk. Lillie approaches me slowly. Up close she's more caricature than woman.

"Why don't you put that knife away, mademoiselle?" I say, not backing down but not feeling as confident as I did a moment ago.

"Frightened, mademoiselle?" Lillie teases, cocking her right eyebrow. "You needn't be. I only intend to take back what's mine."

"*Yours,* mademoiselle?" What kind of game is she playing?

"The artist, mademoiselle. Paul Borquet paid *me* to be his model until you came along."

I laugh. "You're jealous."

Lillie's eyes blaze. Seized by the irrational mood gripping her, she moves closer, never taking her eyes off me.

"You made a fool out of me in Les Halles, mademoiselle," the blonde states coldly, squeezing the words out as if it pains her to say them, yet also playing to the crowd of men beginning to gather around us. "You won't get away with it again."

"I already have, mademoiselle," I say, stalling for time, trying to figure out what to do next. I don't like the idea of having an audience, especially men eager to watch two women fight like alley cats. It's obvious Lillie intends to give them a show.

Lillie says, "I warned you, mademoiselle."

"I've had enough of your games. I'm leaving and I suggest you—"

I turn, then stop. The whistling sound of steel whizzing by my ear cuts my words short. Salty perspiration dribbles over my upper lip when I see the shivering blade of a knife firmly implanted in the wooden fence, only a few inches from my face. I'm not going to find out what Lillie does for an encore.

"I don't frighten easily, mademoiselle," I rush the words, playing for time in a situation that's gone way beyond a curious adventure. "It's a bad habit of mine."

"I have a bad habit, too, mademoiselle—"

I watch in horror as Lillie draws a second knife from inside the sleeve of her jersey, licks the blade with her tongue and takes aim.

"—I hate to miss."

# CHAPTER NINE

Paul lay naked on the silk damask divan in his small studio, in a state deeper than sleep, deeper than a drunken stupor, his body covered with a patina of sweat that glistened and shone like tiny sparks of fire, his heart beating slowly. He was dreaming about *her*. The redhead. Giving herself entirely over to his desires, reveling in her own discoveries.

She was *so* good, grinding her hips when he kissed her in her most intimate place. *Sa huître*, her pussy. Feeling her body tremble against his, she joined him in an explosive climax, his cock bursting with a ceaseless flow of semen. She let out a long moan of pleasure that made even the erotic-loving artist shiver with delight as he scooped up her fluids in the small clay pot.

He'd had many *cavalcades*, love affairs, but nothing like this. *Nothing*. She exhausted him yet filled him with power. She gave of herself with complete abandon, yet she took from him as if she were a goddess seducing him with her extraordinary body as she, in turn, thrilled to his sexual prowess.

As he awakened, his body gathered energy from the memory of loving her, giving him the momentum he needed to finish her portrait. Slowly, making his way through levels of heaven on an orgasmic journey that made him wonder if he'd ever touch down on earth again—did he want to?—he took a deep breath, stretched his muscles and groaned when a pleasurable ache in his knees reminded him of the wanton sounds coming from her beautiful throat as he pumped his masculinity into her, riding her, pulling her back into his cock again and again, grinding his pelvis against the softness of her smooth buttocks.

He must have her again.

He reached down and felt his cock. Erect. With heavy anticipation, he turned over, reaching out for her. He grabbed onto nothing but rumpled silk. He leaned over farther, reached again. Nothing.

She was gone.

He jolted awake, his psyche screaming for sanity to return to his mind. He couldn't believe she wasn't there, disappearing like the smoke from a burned-out match, his dream turning to ashes between his fingers.

No. No. *No*. He refused to believe she was gone, wouldn't, by all the gods in this insufferable world. Putting both hands to his head as if to physically push down that painful and intolerable thought, Paul jumped off the divan, onto his feet. Unsteady and wavering slightly from the effects of not only his furious lovemaking but his intake of absinthe, he reached over to the small table to steady himself. He was afraid of the darkness that began to descend down over him again, pushing his artistic vision into a world without color, without tone, without light. *Without her*. He could never adapt to a world without her. Making love to her, kissing her, being with her, painting her was his *raison d'être.*

His soul.

His spirit.

His immortality.

Although his dream was quickly vanishing from his soul and he felt another raging headache slamming against the back of his skull, he tore through everything in his studio, looking for her, anything that would prove to him she *had* been here. What about the red velvet cloak? No, it belonged to *la comtesse. What,* then? He must prove to himself she wasn't a dream beyond his reach.

Then he saw it. His painting of her.

*Mais oui,* yes, it was there, half-finished, standing against his easel, the paint still wet, her fluids mixed with his oils. His masterpiece. Fresh, beautiful. Enchanting.

But where was Autumn? Where was she?

While his intellectual reasoning struggled to coexist with his artistic madness, he told himself the redhead was *not* an illusion. She had been in his arms, but she was gone. Taken from him because he had allowed his sexual needs to overtake his artistic vision. That fear metamorphosed into anger, the anger into rage.

Now, as his anger pressed upon his resistant brain, Paul descended into his own personal hell, groaning softly, then louder. For years he'd searched for such a woman. Nights when moonlight was his mistress, her belly round and protruding with white light and urging him forward, he went up the stairs to the roof. There, in his haven where he made his magic, where the cold rages brought on by his passion to create erupted inside him, his creative soul flew in a spiritual ecstasy brought on by absinthe, his green enchantress. All the while a pair of green eyes eluded him. *Her* green eyes.

The mewing of a cat startled him out of his thoughts, its loud hiss taunting him. Somehow the animal had gotten in. *Alors,* the big blue door was open. His pulse raced. She could have gone out, up to the roof. Yes, *yes*.

He picked up the tawny yellow creature and cradled it in his arms, realizing too late the paws of his landlady's pet were wet with red paint. He looked down and he could see where the cat had done its business on a brown piece of paper smeared with fresh paint. He didn't remember leaving any paint-smeared paper on the floor and paid no attention to it. He crumpled it up and tossed it into the corner.

Then, putting down the wiggling creature and not bothering to put on his pants, Paul rushed out of his studio, into the hallway, then vaulted up the stairwell, his long legs ascending two, three steps at a time, his naked, muscular body shining with sweat.

"She's gone, Monsieur Borquet," said a woman's voice, then he heard a loud sigh.

Paul turned, aware the woman who had spoken was the concierge. She was of that indeterminate age when the first sign of passing youth produced a sagging bosom, which she hid under a dulled blue shirtwaist dress. Her hair was covered under a gray cap but vanity had prodded her to put two large dabs of carmine on her lips. She licked her lips, gazing longingly at his naked body, then downward to his erect penis. She couldn't take her eyes off it.

"Where did she go, madame?" he urged. "I *must* know."

The woman thought about her answer, then licked her lips again before she said, "I will tell you, monsieur, if you let me touch *votre outil.*"

Her words disturbed him. He said, "Don't embarrass us both, madame. *S'il vous plaît,* please, tell me what I must know."

The old woman sighed deeply, then with a look that said she wouldn't soon forget what she'd seen on this day, she told him what he wanted to know.

I'm certain Lillie hadn't missed her target the first time. I see her grin confidently, revealing small, perfect white teeth. Her words were meant to frighten me with something that penetrates deeper than any blade.

Fear.

I don't back down as a gray shadow rests low over the whites of the girl's eyes and she looks around at the crowd of men watching us, though they keep their distance. I see a few curious residents peeking out from behind half-closed shutters. It's obvious no one wants to interfere with the girl's game. A sideshow for anyone willing to take the time to watch.

Lillie caresses her knife, rubbing some magic onto its fine blade with her fingertips. "When I'm through with your face, mademoiselle, you'll never attract the attention of *any* man, especially Paul Borquet."

"It's not my face he finds so desirable," I shoot back without missing a beat.

Lillie throws back her head and laughs. A deep throaty laugh that shakes her rounded bosom. "*C'est vrai?* Is that true? And who *are* you, mademoiselle? *Un gens du pavé,* a child of the pavements, born under a streetlamp on a po-liceman's outspread cape?"

"I'm not the one they call 'streetwalker,' mademoiselle," I shoot back. "*You* are."

The girl continues her ranting, enjoying the attention from the men whistling their approval. "No, *you* are *une gigolette,* a streetwalker who lures unsuspecting men into an ambush with her seductive smile and promise of forbidden flesh."

"Get away from me. I'm tired of your game!" Brave words, but I'm scared, *really* scared.

Lillie's eyes narrow, her sooty lashes spilling charcoal-gray powder onto her rouged cheeks. "You're young, ma-demoiselle, but soon you'll be old, covering the deepening wrinkles around your eyes and mouth with a smudge of brick dust and haunting the ramparts, spreading your legs and opening your cunt for any soldier with a piece of bread to fill your hunger."

"At least my hair color is natural," I smirk, then point to her crotch. "Top *and* bottom."

"You've insulted me for the last time, mademoiselle," Lillie hisses the words. "You're so pretty…so young," she says, flicking the knife back and forth in her hand. "*Tant pis,* what a pity I must change that."

"Nothing is changing but *your* attitude," I shout back in a voice I don't recognize as my own.

Lillie looks at me for a long moment, questioning, but I hold her gaze, refusing to back down. Finally the blonde glances down at her knife to reassure herself she's still in control. I'm not going to pretend I'm not worried watching her slipping the knife up and down over her sweaty palm, its sharp edges pricking her forefinger. A tiny bubble of blood appears. I flinch when Lillie licks the swelling drop of blood with her tongue, as if she's already tasting *my* blood on her lips.

A fierce pounding throbs through my veins. What the hell's going on here? I never entertained the insane idea I could die in this time. From too much sex, maybe, but not like this. I see the anticipation of the kill in the girl's eyes, the woman's stare tearing through me, cutting my flesh to the bone. I didn't bargain on anything like this happening in my erotic fantasy. I hold my breathing steady, counting the beats of my heart pounding loudly in my ears. I breathe in deeply, summoning up my strength.

*You'll get out of this if you keep your head, kiddo.*

Yeah? I'm running out of options. I have to do something to defend myself. My karate joke isn't going to work on this crazed chick. I pull the knife out of the fence with my left hand and slash it defiantly through the air.

I say, "Looks like we're evenly matched now, bitch."

Lillie pulls back, but only for a moment. Then she regains her control, watching me closely as she continues to flick the knife in her hand. "You've only made the game more interesting, *ma fille*." The French girl grimaces, wrinkling her mouth into an ugly red snarl. I swear I see cat hairs standing up on her back.

With my knife pointed at Lillie in a threatening manner, I crouch down and move from side to side, trying to upset my opponent's concentration. *Damn* these cumbersome skirts, but my opponent is also hampered by similar clothing. As if that evens up the odds. I've no doubt the girl's experience goes beyond giving decent blow jobs. I have to face the truth: this is a fight to the death. I want to turn and run away, but some primeval will to stand up to this girl in this strange environment takes hold of me. I stand my ground.

"*Eeeeiiii…*" Lillie cries, lunging toward me, her knife slicing through the air in a silver blur. For an instant I'm transfixed, watching the scene in slow motion as the girl's body spirals in an arabesque in midair.

Then instinct takes over.

"*No!*" I cry out, sidestepping her attack with a quickness that surprises me. But I'm not fast enough.

Lillie dives into me, slamming her right shoulder into me and pushing me to the ground.

"You're no match for Lillie de Pontier, *ma belle fille*," screams the French prostitute, straddling her legs over me and knocking the knife out of my hand. I hear it rattle onto the cobbles and into the street. A cold darkness passes over my face, blotting out the light promised by the yellow sun overhead as the French girl keeps me pinned down on the ground. I lie helpless, air bursting from my lungs as Lillie grabs my hair and pulls it. Hard. I hold my breath, expecting to feel the sharp pain of a knife pierce my chest. It doesn't come.

I take advantage of the girl's hesitation and bring up my knee into the middle of her back. Lillie yells out in pain and lurches forward, dropping her knife. I push her onto the ground.

"*Quelle catin!* You dirty whore!" Lillie screams, getting up on her knees.

We stare at each other. I grunt in pain. Every muscle in

my body feels like a broken rubber band. Then I see the knife within my reach. Close enough if I'm lucky. I lunge for it, but Lillie grabs the weapon first, a triumphant gleam of sweat glistening on her skin, the taut muscles on her face relaxing. I pray there's some good in the girl, that she stops this insane game, but the jealousy that lives in her soul consumes her. The ugly life of the streets possesses her again.

"You'll be scraps for the dogs," Lillie threatens, then she lunges toward me, the knife pointed at my heart.

"Not if I can help it!" I cry out, flinging out my hands. Somehow I grab the girl's wrist holding the knife with both hands and hold it away from me. I swallow hard. The pointed tip of the blade wavers inches away from piercing my exposed breast. Lillie squeals, pushing down hard. I push back, barely keeping the knife away from cutting me. We struggle wildly, our cries and screams provoking the crowd of onlookers.

"Let the harlot have it!"

"*Alors,* cut out her heart!"

"Kill her…*kill her*…" they chant over and over.

A flood of fatigue overwhelms me but I hold on, even when I hear my dress ripping under my arm and down my back. Sweat plasters my hair to my head. I can't hold on much longer. The French girl has unbelievable strength. I see the triumphant look in Lillie's eyes as she brings the knife down toward my chest, but I refuse to close my eyes in defeat. From somewhere deep inside me, I find the strength to hold on. I *won't* give up.

Then from out of nowhere a piercing whistle screams through the cries of the crowd, drowning out their murderous yells.

*Police.* I recognize the blue uniform of a gendarme grabbing the knife out of Lillie's hand and pulling me to my feet. I relax, a sense of relief flooding my body as I slump down into an exhausted heap. I dare to close my eyes, the heaviness in my lids coming down like the curtain at the end of a bad play. I'm not going to die after all.

"Up on your feet, whore."

"Wait—" I sputter as a pair of large hands grab me roughly under the arms, forcing me to stand up. "I'm not a prostitute—"

A weak smile plays over my lips as I clasp my hand over my torn bodice and gather up my skirts. Who will believe me? I'm dressed like a prostitute. I even smell like one. How can I prove my innocence?

The gendarme holds on to me firmly, twisting my arm behind my back. I wince from the pain but keep silent. I'll have a chance to explain, won't I?

I keep my head up high as the policeman pushes me through the angry mob. The crowd jeers loudly, cursing the men in blue for spoiling their fun. I dodge a rotten tomato thrown at me, but I can't avoid the men grabbing at me with their greasy hands and dirty words. I elbow more than one man, but it doesn't stop them from trying to touch my breasts or smack my ass.

I see Lillie struggling with two policemen. I'm surprised to see fear on the French girl's face. Then her eyes fall on me and that fear turns to anger.

"It's not finished between us," Lillie threatens under her breath as the gendarmes drag her away to the waiting police wagon. "You're already dead, *ma fille.*"

The French girl spits viciously into my face. It's a humiliating gesture. One I won't forget.

I wipe the hot saliva off my cheek. Wipe it clean, but I know the threat is still there.

"*Vien, ma fille,* get along, whore, into the wagon with you!"

Paul spotted the sergeant pushing the redhead toward the *voltaire cellulaire,* the large square-shaped police van. Fast on his feet, he sprang forward, pushing through the crowd of gawking men, looking right and left, shoving his way through without stopping, cursing, until the hard end of a flic's baton stuck into his ribs, forcing him back away from the scene.

"Stay back, monsieur!"

"The redhead is my sister," Paul insisted.

The gendarme laughed. "And the other one is my mother. Get on with you."

Paul continued trying to get through the crowd by turning in the other direction, but something kept him there. Staring. Autumn must have felt the intensity of his look searing through her veneer of despair. She looked up and their eyes met. He drew in his breath. Green eyes with a darkness that seemed to lift when she saw him. The strangest emotion shot through him. A pull that had nothing to do with the heat growing in his groin, the push of his cock against his tight pants. *What,* then? He didn't believe in love. In his world men fell in love only when the woman belonged to another man. It was safer that way. No ties. The redhead was different. He had possessed her body but he wanted something more, yet it was forbidden to him.

"*Vite, vite.* Hurry along," the sergeant ordered, ignoring the mounting protest of the men in the crowd and shoving Autumn into the van, her shock of hair burning a shimmering reddish color even in the deepening shadows surrounding her. "The sooner you get to St. Lazare, *ma belle fille,* the sooner you'll be back on the streets and spreading your legs."

Paul saw the redhead pleading with the sergeant, but he couldn't hear what she was saying over the noisy men in the crowd, cheering. The policeman laughed, then slid his hand up and down her cheek in a familiar manner, then down to her exposed breast, cupping it with his hand. Paul almost lost control then. The sight of the man touching her made him clench his fist, ready to hit him. He hesitated. If he interfered it might go worse for the girl, but it didn't lessen his anger toward a society where young girls were at the mercy of the guardians of the law.

Yelling, hollering, shouting, warning the crowd, the gendarme stayed to his mission, controlling the leering men, while two sweaty horses with sagging bellies waited patiently until the sergeant slammed the door on the van so hard it shook the whole vehicle. Then he jumped on top of the perch, and with a mocking salute in the direction of the crowd, he put the whip to the horses' flanks and the van sped off to the *dépôt* with the day's roundup of prostitutes locked up inside.

Paul ignored the chaos around him, the honking horns, the indignant yells of the men. He stayed in the middle of the street, breathing in the heavily perfumed air of Paris, trying to get the rotten smell of the city out of his lungs. Furious, he beat his fist into his hand, knowing what would happen next to the girl, and his heart was racing. It was no secret she was headed for St. Lazare, a notorious prison for streetwalkers and girls as young as thirteen. Flower girls, seamstresses, shop girls, all looking to earn a few extra sous by the sweat of their body.

To keep them out of prison, Paul gave them money, then sent them on their way without tasting the sweetness of their young pussies. But the day would come when cheap brandy and passionate kisses from other men made them careless and they became fodder for the salad basket, the nickname given to the police van. Then they were hauled off to the *dépôt* and booked as registered prostitutes, their freedom taken away early in their young lives. For those girls, St. Lazare was the last stop.

*She's in for it now. I won't let them have her.*

He knew somehow he must save her from that fate before she was swallowed up like a dot of color blended onto the canvas of a much larger landscape. She was different from the others. Her speech, her mannerisms. She spoke French with a strange accent, even for an American, and she acted so…*what was it?* She was young, *very* young, but intelligent, and seemed out of place in this world, as if she'd been dropped into the city without knowing where she was. She was running away from something, he was certain, but it didn't matter. He would do *anything* to have her back in his arms, kissing her, touching her, pulling up her petticoats, exposing her to him. He imagined her pussy lips opening like a ripening bud, then parting her pink folds and sucking on her...

Think, *think*. If only he'd found her sooner, but he came upon the scene too late, pushing his way through all the gawking men but unable to grab her in time. Damn *flic*, he'd almost had her back in his arms. He wouldn't have found her if he hadn't overheard an old drunk boasting about the beautiful redheaded prostitute fighting with the blonde. Lillie. Although she was clever in the feminine way, changing her moods to fit the moment, he found it puzzling the blonde would engage the redhead in a catfight on the street. Lillie was coquettish, scented and affected a superior accent around men, but it was her body she prized most dearly.

Why would she start a fight and risk scarring her beautiful flesh?

Unless she was so jealous of the redhead she was willing to risk everything to get her out of the way so she could climb back into his bed.

Women. He'd never understand them. *Jamais*. Never.

Propelled by the uneasy feeling the blonde would have used the knife, *couteau à cran d'arrêt,* if she'd had the opportunity, he wondered which one of her *p'tit hommes,* admirers, had given it to her, a knife so sharp he was certain the blade could cut hairs with it.

"Too bad the show's over, eh, monsieur?" said the man next to him, giving a low whistle and making an obscene gesture. "I would have enjoyed seeing the two whores tear the clothes off each other."

"You're speaking out of turn, monsieur," Paul said, gritting his teeth, though the artist barely restrained himself from slugging the man. His jaw muscles tightened and his dark blue eyes turned cold.

"Monsieur?"

"I know the redhead," Paul insisted.

The man laughed. "I'm sure half the men in Paris know those two girls, monsieur," he snickered. "And good they are at swallowing a man's seed."

"Keep your mouth shut, monsieur, or I'll do it for you."

"*C'est vrai?* Oh, yeah? If you lay a hand on me, monsieur, I'll call them *flics* back."

Paul knew the man was bluffing. In this part of Montmartre, the Prefect told their uniformed *agents* of the Brigade Mondaine to look the other way if there was any trouble, except when it came to rounding up prostitutes. Besides, Paul wasn't afraid. When he wasn't behind an easel, he spent time in the *gymnase* located behind the railway yards of the Gare de l'Est. He was rated as a professional boxer, but his painting came first, except when he needed money. Then he'd compete for the hundred-franc purses offered by the more pretentious boxing establishments closer to the center of Paris. He was known for his hard left hooks to the body and wicked right crosses to the jaw that jarred all fighting ambition out of several roughnecks along the railroad yards. Fortunately, he'd never hurt his hands in a fight.

"Don't threaten *me,* monsieur," Paul said, "I have no patience for—"

Without warning the man grabbed him from behind and leaped upon his muscular back, but Paul threw him off easily. The man came at him again, but Paul was ring-wise enough not to telegraph his punches. His right fist moved eight inches and before the man could take his next breath, the hooligan lay on the sidewalk with a cut above his eye that guaranteed he wouldn't be coming back for more.

Unfazed by the attack, sweat pouring out of him, Paul started walking, his long strides taking him somewhere, nowhere. A flash of pain pounded in his skull, as if a door in his mind had been yanked open, forcing him to face the demon who lived behind that door. Before he could catch his breath, calm the unbearable pain of letting his emotions rage, he lost contact with the moment, the present, and the scene changed, jolting his mind into a trancelike state into which he retreated when the old memories dominated his psyche with the pain of his lost youth.

It was always the same. He was in the stucco farmhouse. The moss-green shutters were closed, shutting out the sunshine and the glory of the flowers. Only the bleakness of the gray world inside surrounded him. He saw a huge man in heavy boots. Wearing ankle-buttoned trousers and a white shirt, he stood over him, his straw broad-brimmed hat tossed angrily onto the floor, his fists curled up in balls of fury, ready to strike him with the bamboo stick clutched in his hand. His stepfather yelled at him, trying to make him bend to his will, but swaying on the edge of hysteria himself.

"Put out your hands, boy. *Maintenant*. Now."

Paul refused. As if in a trance, the young man stood in the main room of the farmhouse, eyes fixed ahead, not seeing the charred, blackened remains of his paintings in the fireplace. His veins were on fire, his body convulsing with pain.

His stepfather had destroyed his drawings, paintings, sketches, *everything* he put to paper.

The man was waiting for him when he returned home from the pond, the smoke in the chimney laughing at him as he approached the house. He knew his stepfather wanted him to forget he could see things as no one else did. That he could present images of harmony and beauty that brought pleasure, allowing the eye to see color and line in a new, exciting way. He wanted to run away to Paris, though it pained him to leave his mother, a quiet woman, soft-spoken and gentle. He never knew his father, only that he was an Englishman. After he was born, his father took them to England, but his snobbish family wouldn't accept them and sent them back to France, forcing his mother into a loveless marriage to provide a home for her child. His mother could never have guessed the true extent of the danger into which she had stepped, couldn't have conceived of the horror that would manifest itself as her boy grew into a young man with remarkable talent. A talent that incited both anger and jealousy in the mind of his stepfather.

"You're not talking, eh?" his stepfather said. "Then I'll beat this nonsense of being an artist out of your head."

The blows came. Hard. *Harder.* On his shoulders, his chin, then the side of his head, until blood oozed down the back of his neck and onto his white Cossack shirt. A blow to his neck ripped open the skin, leaving a scar he learned to hide under his long hair. Not even when his stepfather died did the memory soften, grow misty and warm. The man had been evil, unfeeling. Paul shed no tears, nor would he ever. He didn't even know where his stepfather was buried.

But his inner genius continued to see new pictures, new directions that tormented him. When his mother died, her soul gone to heaven, Paul left for Paris. He never looked back. He forgot who he was, put his past behind him and became involved with *la comtesse* and her world of the black arts. A world that brought his youth back to him. A world he embraced with vigor and with renewed sexuality.

*Damn, he wanted it all.* His art. His youth. *And* Autumn. But he could never fall in love with her or he'd lose everything.

Traveling back in his mind to the Normandy countryside where the light was soft, the air sweet, only exacerbated his need to paint, prove himself. Paul leaned back against a brick wall, rubbing his bruised knuckles, and watching the deep cover of night come down over the city. He wasn't surprised by the intensity of the flashback. But the physical pain of what his disbelieving mind had told him was shocking, frightening, and more emotionally gripping than anything else in his life.

He tried to tell himself these sudden bursts of violence were the understandable reaction of a man who lived life on the edge, dabbling in the black arts and paying the price with these illusions. But he knew his sudden outburst was something more than superstition, something darker. The chill edging along his spine became colder. The kiss of a woman could become deadly, penetrate down to his bones. *La comtesse* had warned him she could show him how to achieve the ultimate climax of his passion, but *not* how to love.

He understood that now. *Autumn.* He'd traveled beyond the first blush of desire into a hot, steamy passion; but the wild night of lovemaking that made her body quiver with ecstasy reminded him he hadn't reached her heart. That ache to make her fall in love with him penetrated deeper, deep down into his soul.

He clung fiercely to the idea he could save her from St. Lazare, *must* save her. He wandered up and down the boulevards like a *boulevardier* until twilight cast a purple glow over his face as the gas streetlamps flickered on with their sallow yellow hue. A few electric lights popped on in the city. He couldn't paint. Couldn't sleep. Tonight he'd make his plans, though he knew how quickly a girl could lose her dignity and succumb to the evils of St. Lazare. From orgies celebrating Sappho's favorite pastime with women licking and sucking on each other's cunts, to scorned females taking a knife to a fellow prisoner. Yet he had but one choice, and he agonized over it for hours, until he knew it was his only choice.

In due time Madame Chapet, the notorious madame from the House on rue des Moulins, would be paying a visit to the prison to free Lillie de Pontier. He must convince her Autumn was even more of a prize for her stable of *dégrafées,* unhooked ones, that the girl would fetch a pretty price in her *maison de tolérance,* her licensed brothel, near the Palais Royal.

It was a risk, engaging the help of *la madame,* who constantly badgered him to get her an invitation to a Black Mass. But there was no other way out of St. Lazare. How long would Autumn last *là bas,* down there, the popular phrase used to describe the hell that was St. Lazare? Paul let out his pent-up breath. A day? A week? A month? Not a long time, but it would seem like an eternity to the redhead.

# CHAPTER TEN

*Merde*, Madame Chapet made Paul mad. Flirting with him, plying him with brandy, choking him with her teasing mannerisms. And those two feather dusters in black and white that passed for dogs. Louis and Pompie. Disgusting little animals with cold, black noses and wet pink tongues that licked their mistress's pussy, if rumors were true.

He washed down another warm brandy, cursing himself for not refilling his flask with his green enchantress before he came to the House on rue des Moulins. Saving the beautiful redhead was what he'd come for, not this fleshy mountain of tight blond curls, purple taffeta ruffles and faded carnations sitting across from him with two dogs in her lap. The madam promised many things to any man with gold louis in his pockets and a bulge in his pants.

Paul had neither, despite the array of partially nude beauties lounging in the receiving room of the brothel, nibbling on *tartes aux pignons,* pine nut and creamy almond tartlets. One girl tried to get his attention by sucking the cream off her fingers, rolling her tongue, then licking her moist mauve lips with the promise of what was to come.

Sex wasn't on his mind. Like most Frenchmen who haunted the brothels, he knew all their games, like rubbing their buttocks up against him, their shapely legs encased in black silk stockings, garters adorned with lemon-yellow rosettes circling their thighs. Naked breasts shaking with gold rings through their nipples. The girls would feel his hard cock trapped inside his tight pants, then search inside his trousers with their long fingers, feeling the shape and strength of his erection.

Life was difficult, they'd say. *L'amour* was the answer, *n'est-ce pas?*

To Paul, *art* was more difficult. Life followed a natural cycle from conception to death, but art obsessed a man with its never-ending search for perfection. A constant search that drove him on.

And on.

And on.

Until he could stand it no longer.

And because of his art, he'd committed the unthinkable sin. He'd sold his soul. Nights of black magic under the spell of *la comtesse*, rolling his hard cock between her palms, calling upon the Egyptian god Min to grant him his youth, give him back the years he'd lost, unable to draw, to paint, suffering from the crippling effects of the beatings of his stepfather. And now he must pay the price. He must give up the girl who had stolen his heart.

*She's not like these girls, where lovemaking is a business. They wear the faces of lost dreams and despair. Lifeless eyes. Crude, red mouths. Spoiled youth. Not the redhead.*

*There's a vulnerability in her eyes that touches my soul.*

*Warm, flickering bits of green that seem to flow from a secret she holds deep within her that she wants to share with me, but can't. I won't let her down.*

After much agonizing about his decision, swearing to sell all his paintings and take on every fight offered him to buy her freedom, he'd left Le Café de la Paix before the green hour passed—that quiet recess between five and six in the afternoon when he'd sip his favorite *apéritif* of absinthe and talk to his fellow artists—to save the girl who possessed his soul. Stolen his will. Made him so mad with the desire to work he became frustrated and could concentrate on no other model. No other face but hers.

He nearly went into a rage when he made inquiries at the police *dépôt* and discovered Autumn would be held at Prison St. Lazare indefinitely until the charges against her were decided. A ploy by the magistrate, he knew, to keep the women off the streets and money flowing into his pockets from the local government for a job *bien fait,* well done.

Paul tapped his cane against his shoe in an uneven rhythm, keeping his eyes from meeting those of the clever Madame Chapet. She kept insisting she was recovering from a case of the vapors and could give him only a few minutes of her precious time. *For old times' sake.* Paul frowned. The old fox set her traps skillfully, if not with style. He watched her out of the corner of his eye as she fed the dogs bits of chicken and cream tarts then fondled them in a manner suggestive of the earthly delights going on upstairs.

"Why are you so interested in getting the girl out of St. Lazare, Monsieur Borquet?" Madame Chapet asked.

"I want to paint her, madame."

"Paint her? You can't fool me, monsieur. You're in love with the girl."

"Not I, madame."

It wasn't true. He adored her, but he couldn't love her.

"You say this girl is more beautiful than any girl in my employ?" she asked.

"*Mais oui*, madame, she has a body that defies any earthly creature. She's a goddess with skin so pure it goes beyond perfection and a face that captures a man's soul with her big green eyes swirling madly like whirlpools," Paul said, watching the brothel owner stroke the white dog, then the black. She hugged them in her arms, buried them in her lap, then devoured them with kisses and suggestive caresses. On their floppy ears, their cold, ugly noses. Their tiny, quivering, pink bellies. It disgusted him.

"If the girl is *that* beautiful, Madame Chapet," said a man's voice behind him with a clipped British accent, "you must allow *me* to rescue the damsel in distress."

Paul turned around and scowled when he saw the gentleman, his coat cut away in a curve over his hips and buttoned high over his chest, coming down the stairs with two girls in tow, one on each arm. Something about him piqued his curiosity.

"Ah, Lord Bingham, how kind of you to offer your assistance," said Madame Chapet, her voice light and flirty.

"It's the least I can do, madame, in return for such a lovely afternoon," the Englishman said in bad French, pinching one girl on her rear end and making her giggle. "Your young lady is quite adept at putting her tongue up inside the other girl's cunt while she's crouched over, her lovely arse in the air while I take her from behind. Yes, very nice."

"*C'est mon plaisir,* Lord Bingham. Your generosity facilitates my bringing the girl here for *your* pleasure," Madame Chapet teased, dipping her fat fingers into aërated water. The dogs licked them with their disgusting little tongues.

Paul grimaced. *Where had he seen this Englishman?* To him they were all barbarians in tweed tramping through the streets of Paris with red-covered guidebooks under their arms, speaking the language with savage discord. But this one was uncannily familiar looking.

"Then make the arrangements to bring the girl here," the English lord commanded. "I shall be waiting."

Then it hit him. Les Halles. *Le bâtard anglais.* The English bastard.

"You'll wait in vain, monsieur," Paul said, standing up and swirling his black cape around him. "The girl is mine."

The Englishman narrowed his eyes. "*Yours,* monsieur? By the looks of you, I doubt if you can afford her."

"And by the looks of *you,* monsieur, I doubt if she'd allow you to touch her."

"What insolence! If I weren't in a respectable *maison privée,* I'd call you out—" The Englishman's eyes brightened. "Bloody hell, if it isn't the madman from Les Halles."

"At your service, monsieur," Paul said, bowing with a sweep of his cape, but keeping his eyes on the Englishman. "I'll meet you anywhere, anytime—"

"Why wait, monsieur? I'm ready now to cut you from ear to ear."

"I'll take you down first—"

Madame Chapet interrupted with "*Zut alors,* ah, I can't breathe, messieurs, with all this talk of fighting."

Paul watched in amazement as her eyes rolled back, her lower lip quivered, and she went whiter than the rice powder streaked upon her face. She couldn't speak. He wasn't fooled. *La madame* knew of his skill as a boxer and was taking no chances on losing the bank account of her gilded English lord. The greediness of the woman didn't surprise him. He looked around at the beautifully appointed receiving room, at the rich-looking consoles and silk-covered chairs. Rich, mahogany-brown leather boxes held thin tissue paper, and the hangings and chairbacks were covered with damask embroidery. She was a woman with expensive tastes.

"I don't wish to upset you, Madame Chapet," Lord Bingham said, his eyes never leaving Paul. "But this man insulted me—"

"Monsieur Borquet was just leaving, *n'est-ce pas?*" said *la madame,* feigning a smile.

"*Borquet?*" The Englishman smiled wide, which disturbed Paul more than if he'd taken a punch at him. "The artist?"

"Yes, I am Paul Borquet," the Frenchman said, not liking the Brit's obvious pleasure at discovering his identity. "Does that amuse you?"

"It changes nothing between us. Though I had no idea you were so...*so young.* My information must have been mistaken."

"What information?" Paul asked.

"I, uh, have seen your paintings in London," Lord Bingham

said evasively. "I had no idea you were a madman, like that van Gogh fellow."

"I've had enough of your bullshit, monsieur—" Paul raised up his fists, ready to throw a punch at the English lord.

"*Stop this at once*, Monsieur Borquet," Madame Chapet screamed, ready to faint. "And leave my establishment *now*."

Paul regained control, though anger pumped through his veins. "I'll leave, Madame Chapet, but only after you've agreed to help Mademoiselle Maguire."

Madame Chapet sighed heavily. "As soon as I'm well, I shall attend to it. Now be off with you, Monsieur Borquet, before I change my mind."

Paul slammed the door on the House on rue des Moulins behind him and trotted down the steps briskly. The Chapet woman was inhuman, a monster in curls. *How could she promise the English bastard a night with the redhead?*

As soon as he was through the door, the bargaining began. He could hear the Englishman talking about how he'd come to Paris on family business as well as pleasure, something Madame Chapet was only too happy to provide. Yet something about the foreigner gnawed at his insides, gripping him in a way that made him sweat.

Both angry and frustrated, Paul closed his eyes, trying to understand why the man had such an effect on him. The arteries at his temples throbbed, bursting through his skull. His neck muscles ached, nearly strangling him. But the answer didn't come. Not yet.

He shrugged off the uneasy feeling. Threw his anger to

the night wind. He prayed the fog drifting down from the ramparts would swallow it up and free him from the pain throbbing in his head, squeezing his brain, tightening it, making it fit into a box so small he couldn't think.

He pulled his black felt hat low over his head, matting down his hair wet with perspiration around his neck. With a sweep of his cape he hurried down the boulevard, eager to meet the lights, the clatter, the familiar street noises that would dull his brain. He must get word to Autumn that Madame Chapet would help her.

"I'm *innocent*," I plead, thrusting my bound wrists out in front of me.

Is this really happening?

"A citizen arrested by officers of the law must *establish* her innocence, mademoiselle," recites the magistrate in a tired voice, his eyes scanning the paperwork before him. His attitude says loud and clear he isn't surprised by my declaration of innocence.

"I'm *not* a prostitute," I insist. "You've got to believe me. I'm…I'm—"

What am I going to say? What *can* I say?

I'm a chick from the twenty-first century with a passionate itch in my crotch for a lost Impressionist?

"According to the *Code d'Instruction Criminelle of 1808*," the magistrate continues dryly as if he doesn't hear me, "it's the duty of the authorities to protect the State first, and the State means the people."

He looks up at me. Surprise makes his eyelids flutter. Whatever is on his mind quickly passes. He rubs his beard and nods to the clerk seated nearby, recording every word of the interrogation with his feathered quill. Then he's all business again. "You may proceed with the search, Sergeant Guerlain."

"*Bien, Monsieur le Magistrat.*" The sergeant smirks, licking his lower lip with anticipation, his tongue protruding between thick cracked lips. I can see the saliva dripping from his mouth as he moves toward me. I *hate* the man, remembering how he stroked my cheek, deliberately provoking the crowd. *And* Paul. Somehow the artist found me, but it was too late.

Oh, *why* did I ever leave him? What insane crazy idea made me think I can survive in these times? I'm not a nineteenth-century babe in a corset and button shoes. I'm addicted to downloading cell phone ringtones, I pull into the full-service pump at the gas station so I can check e-mail while I fill up, and I Google everything from market land deals to sale days at Bloomie's. I don't belong here. I'm scared out of my mind.

Who's going to save me?

I'm a fool to believe anything but my own wits can get me out of this mess. I see the sergeant circling me to get a better view. I draw back. The look in the man's eyes sends out a clear signal how much he enjoys his work.

As I steel myself for what's to come, the room begins to spin and the sergeant's face looms up in front of me like a clown in a funhouse mirror. Heavy lids cut his hard stare into half-moons. Dead man's eyes burning into my soul. The effect is chilling.

*I'm not going to let him touch me,* I vow silently, turning away.

"I'm an American citizen, monsieur." I pound on the worn wooden desk with my bound fists. "I demand to speak to someone from the American Embassy."

The magistrate shakes his head. "Your embassy can't help you, mademoiselle. The rules are clear. You were arrested for soliciting on a street where you aren't registered and for engaging in an altercation with a known prostitute. Since you've been unable to prove your innocence—"

"But you haven't give me a fair opportunity, monsieur. I want a lawyer."

"Why can't you accept your fate?" Impatience colors his voice with an ugly, blue tone. He's tired of arguing with me. "I've tried to be patient with you, mademoiselle, taking into consideration the fact women's smaller brains make them more irrational and emotional."

*What did he say?*

I blurt out, "Brain size is *not* determined by sex, monsieur."

"Control your tongue, mademoiselle!" yells the judge, banging his fist on the desk. "Or I'll have the sergeant gag you."

I clamp my mouth shut. That doesn't stop the sergeant from running his dirty finger across my lips, trying to open my mouth. I break out in a cold sweat, trying to figure out what to do. When will this nightmare end? Humiliated and degraded, I can't believe women are treated like hardened criminals without an opportunity to defend themselves with a lawyer present. I'm caught in a system that looks the other way at the oldest profession as long as you obey the rules. But I've broken those rules and the law says I must pay the price. Yet I won't give up trying to prove my innocence.

I say, "You have no proof to support your accusations, monsieur."

"There are witnesses, mademoiselle."

"Witnesses? Where are they?"

Ignoring my question, he continues, grumbling, "You girls get picked up with money stuffed into your bosom and legs spread far enough apart to accommodate the cocks of an entire regiment, and still you proclaim your innocence. I've had enough of your babble." The magistrate nods to the sergeant, raising his reading glass up higher. "Proceed."

To my horror, the sergeant springs forward and grabs hold of the shoulder of my dress, his fingers closing tight around the flimsy taffeta. The material digs into my skin, and before I have a chance to resist, he pushes me up against the railing. Hitting the hard wood knocks me off balance. I struggle to regain control, but he's faster, quicker, more adept at this game. I cry out when the sergeant rips my dress to the waist, forcing open the remaining buttons. My breasts pop out. I can feel his hungry eyes crawling over every inch of my exposed upper torso. Fear creeps up my spine like the fine edge of a silver blade as the man's cold, scaly fingers push aside my ripped bodice and he strokes my breasts. My nipples harden at once under his touch, sickening me. *How can my body betray me like this?* He seems mystified by my lack of a corset, but he doesn't stop.

He's searching for a thrill not a weapon.

Anger replaces my fear. How much longer can I keep from giving him a swift kick where he deserves it?

"You're not like the others," the sergeant says. I flinch when he pinches my nipple, rolling it between his forefinger and thumb. "They've got splotchy skin and are all diseased. Your skin is smooth, unblemished." He strokes my bare shoulder. Satisfied I'm not hiding anything in my bodice, he fumbles with my skirts, reaching inside the leg of my pantaloons. My heart races faster. I sag against the railing as the policeman slimes his repulsive touch over up my leg to my bare thigh. I've got to stop him. *I must.*

"Your filthy hands make me sick," I utter, kicking him in the shin. Not where I wanted to kick him, but good enough.

The sergeant strikes me hard across the face. *"You dirty whore!"*

Pain rips through my jaw from the impact of the blow and my hair swings out wildly over my shoulders.

"When I'm finished with you, mademoiselle, you won't be able to stand up." He laughs, digging his nails deeper into the flesh on my bare breast. "You'll be walking real slow for a long time."

He slides his hands up and down the length of my body, feeling under my skirts with his cold fingers, sliding my pantaloons down to my hips. I close my legs together so tight my thighs hurt. As he tries to push my legs apart, I realize I'm clenching my teeth. I try to relax my jaw. I can't. I'll never forget this.

"I *demand* you tell this man to stop," I blurt out, facing the magistrate. *Damn* if I'm going to let this man go any farther with his dirty hands. "This is an illegal search."

"What?" asks the magistrate, clearly upset.

*Come up with something…c'mon, think. You've watched enough of the History Channel to spin a plausible excuse.*

"According to…uh, the provisions of the Treaty of Versailles," I state with confidence, though I'm making it up as I go along, "it's illegal to search any woman without another woman present."

I watch the magistrate raise his eyebrows. What nonsense is this? he seems to be asking. I hold my chin up defiantly, but inside I'm shaking. The famous peace treaty won't be written for another thirty years and has nothing to do with the French criminal system. Will he fall for my ruse?

The magistrate puts down his reading glass. He's agitated, but thoughtful. "What is this Treaty of Versailles? Another social reform?" Then, not waiting for me to answer, he continues, "Ah, these damned reformers are always butting into police business, urging the protection of women prisoners. Because of these tight-corseted reformers, we had to do away with branding women prisoners. Then they installed female guards in the prisons.

"And now you're telling me, mademoiselle, they've come up with a *new* treaty that prohibits body searches without a woman present? Next they'll be saying women are equal in the eyes of the law. Where will this insanity end?" He takes a drink of wine from the glass sitting next to him and gulps it down. "I ask you, mademoiselle, how could I know about such reforms? I'm only a poor city official who wishes to keep his post." He waves the officer away from me. "That will be enough, Sergeant."

"But, *Monsieur le Magistrat,* I haven't finished—"

"Enough, Sergeant," he orders.

I hold my bound wrists up to my chest. They're numb. "Then I'm free to go?"

The magistrate shakes his head. His breathing becomes heavy. "Treaty or no treaty, mademoiselle, I can't let you go. It's obvious you're a *femme galante*, an outwardly respectable woman who operates in the theaters and dance-halls and spreads disease." He taps his reading glass against his palm. Sweat drips across his hand. "It's my duty as magistrate to keep women like you off the streets."

I can see all too clearly this is how he intends to keep the reformers off his back.

"But I'm telling you the truth—*I'm not a prostitute!*"

"*Alors,* mademoiselle, many innocent women have been sent to Prison St. Lazare on less evidence, especially since the *Préfet de Police* put out a notice that local police have been too lenient on unregistered prostitutes." He puts down his reading glass and wipes his hands with his handkerchief. "I have no choice in the matter. You'll be booked as a prostitute then sent to the prison hospital where you'll be examined by a doctor and held there until your case is decided."

I watch in horror as he signs the record handed to him by his clerk without reading it.

"Don't move, mademoiselle!"

I square my shoulders in front of the camera sitting on the tripod as the photographer puts another plate into the camera and adjusts the lens.

My mug shot. I don't need a mirror to tell me how awful I look. Like a skinned rabbit. Any trace of makeup disappeared long ago, but a flaming streak of red where the sergeant struck my face highlights one cheek. My left eye feels puffy and I taste dried blood on my lower lip. My hair, matted and dirty, is pulled back away from my face, but a few stray wisps hang over my bare shoulders.

Lost in thought, I make a fist in my lap and shiver. The room seems to echo the memory of the sergeant's cold, clammy hands groping me and pinching my nipples as I tried to disentangle myself from his disgusting fingers. A coolness settles over my back, reminding me only a torn piece of taffeta stands between me and full-frontal exposure. What I wouldn't give for a safety pin, but I doubt they've been invented yet. Instead I hold my bodice together by threading some twine I found through the buttonholes.

"*Alors,* mademoiselle, you moved," says the photographer, interrupting my thoughts. "We'll have to start all over again." With a heavy sigh, the photographer removes the large plate from the camera box, tosses it aside, then reloads. *"Don't move!"* he orders.

"*Pardon,* monsieur, but I'm very tired."

I lost track of time hours ago. Or was it days ago? I don't know. From the moment I arrived at the police station, I've been shoved from one room to another, given only water, and that horrible sergeant never stops yelling orders. I wonder what happened to Lillie. Fortunately, we were separated and put into different groups when we arrived.

I look at the gas lamps on the bare gray walls. The light is barely flickering, but a soft yellow haze flows through the nearby open window. It must be dawn. If only I could sit down.

How long does it take to shoot one mug shot?

I look at the photographer huddled under the heavy

draping over his camera. Only his skinny legs show. I hold my breath to keep from smiling. Do I dare remind myself this whole adventure started because I wanted my portrait sketched?

*Do I?*

"Don't tighten up, mademoiselle," he says, exasperated. "That's the quickest way to kill the photo." He comes out from underneath the draping and studies me with interest. Waving his arms about and jerking his head from side to side, he seems to be trying to capture my image in his mind. "If only I had more time, mademoiselle, I could take wonderful images of you for the postcards. *Paris Beauties,* they call them." He smiles at me, then takes the shot. His elusive smile makes me wonder: Does my mug shot end up on a French postcard in the black market?

"*Allons, femme de vie!* Get going, whore!"

I spin around. It's the sergeant.

A momentary fear grips me. Grinning, he prods me in the small of the back with his club and pushes me down the long hallway. Outside several other women shuffle toward a waiting police van.

"Your ladyship's carriage is waiting," the sergeant finishes with sarcasm, leering at me with such intensity I feel his cold hands on me all over again, his eyes betraying hunger and lust. I turn away, biting my lip to keep from blurting out he's a disgusting creep. If I could, I'd give him a swift kick in his balls, then squeeze them hard until he squealed. Loud. Instead I keep silent.

My knees are shaking as I climb the three steps up into the wagon. I know the sergeant is waiting for me to make a mistake so he can grab me and pull down my bodice, leaving my breasts naked except for the ragged remains of my taffeta dress. I stop on the top step, an ominous feeling overtaking me. Whatever brave face I put up for the others, I'm frightened.

Frightened this is a one-way ticket.

"Keep going, *ma petite fille,*" says the sergeant, pushing me into the van. I put my hands out to keep from sprawling on the floor. Keeping my head down, I take a seat in the far corner. No one looks at me. No one speaks. Each woman is alone with her thoughts.

I lay my head back against the boards, trying to think, but it's impossible. A woman begins sobbing, another coughs. The smell of cigarette smoke permeates through the van. I close my eyes but I can't shut out the darkness filling my soul. I have the feeling the worst part of this sinister melodrama is yet to come. The sergeant pokes his head inside and looks around. He counts the women in a deep whisper, hissing the numbers through his teeth, "...five, six, seven..."

Satisfied we're all accounted for, he squints at the prisoners in the dimly lit wagon, wetting his lips and rubbing his fingers together. I feel his eyes on me. "Have a nice trip, mademoiselle. I'll see you soon."

Laughing, he slams the door shut, thrusting the van into complete darkness. I hear him give the driver the order to take off and the van lurches forward with a jolt. I feel myself sliding off the long bench but before I fall onto the floor, someone catches me around the waist. A woman's hands. As they move down to my hips, I hear someone moan with pleasure. A moment later a second woman closes behind me and reaches around me to cup my breasts. A new fear attacks my senses. I can hear my own deep breathing in the dark. Quick, fast breaths. A survival instinct flares inside me. I grab the woman's hands cupping my breasts. Her fingers are cold. "Keep your hands off me!" I yell, then pull the other woman's hands off my hips.

"We're just getting acquainted, *ma fille,*" whispers a husky voice in the darkness.

"Be careful, mademoiselle," warns another voice. "You can get hurt if you don't know the rules."

The sensual undertone in the women's voices is deliberate and inviting. I stiffen. A new danger looms in the prison.

I edge my body into the corner, the wagon wheels beneath me bumping up and down on the cobbles, jolting me about. I hug my knees, burying my head between them. Listening. Feeling. Warm and mysterious is the dark around me. Like a womb it will shield me for a little while. But only for a little while.

Protectively I curl up into a ball and cross my hands over my eyes and prepare myself for the insanity of this place called St. Lazare.

I can think only of escape as I watch the women disappear one by one behind the heavily bolted door in the central waiting station inside the Prison of St. Lazare. I keep my eyes on the long, dark hallway leading to the outside courtyard of the prison, hoping, praying I'll find the courage to try to escape.

Where will I go? Back to Montmartre, back to Paul Borquet? Will he be waiting for me? Or is he like all the other men in my life? Dumped me for a blonde?

*Don't forget, you're young, beautiful, and with a great bod. He'll be there.*

I shake my head. Why isn't that enough for me? Would he love me if I wasn't young? I can't risk it. I might lose him. I can never fall in love with him.

*Damn you, Min!*

I cough. The air is stale and heavy with the smell of the prisoners. It suffocates me. What is taking them so long? I can't stand this waiting much longer.

"Get up, whore," orders a female guard with ugly straw-colored hair. "The good Father is waiting to hear your confession, *ma fille.*"

The female guard leers into my face, licking her thin lips and allowing her eyes to travel down the exposed front of my bodice. Then her hips start moving, rubbing against mine.

"Confession?" I ask, moving away from her. "In prison?"

"So it's your first time in St. Lazare, eh, *ma belle?*" asks the female guard as she unbolts the heavy door.

"What kind of prison is this?" I wonder out loud.

"The original convent was built by St. Vincent de Paul three hundred years ago. Now it's a house of correction for sentenced prisoners...*and* suspects of a crime." She laughs, a wicked laugh. "Like you, mademoiselle."

I don't answer, but I knew by the tone of her voice there's something undesirable about being in that position.

"The prison was fit only for rodents until the Sisters of Charity took over," the guard continues, motioning for me to follow her. "But don't get any ideas, *ma fille.* The only charity you'll find here is the kind that's bought."

"I don't have any money."

"You won't need any, *ma jolie*."

She puts a hand on my shoulder, tugging at the stained taffeta until the worn threads rip, then she moves her hand seductively down my arm. "Eh, your clothes won't bring more than a sou—" she leans up against me, her fingers grabbing my waist, then she moves her hand up my rib cage to my breasts, stroking her broken fingernails across my bare flesh. I wince "—but you'll do all right."

I pull away from her. "I'm warning you, *don't touch me again!*"

Did my voice crack? You bet it did. This is no Catholic school field trip. This woman must weigh 180 pounds. If she ever jumps me, she'll crush me.

"*I* give the orders in here," the guard says, angry at being rebuffed. "Now get on with you."

Breathing down my back like an animal in heat, the heavyset guard prods me up the stairs with the end of her club. I shiver.

It's a cold, unnerving feeling I won't forget.

# CHAPTER ELEVEN

"Come closer, *mon enfant*," urges the priest in a consoling manner. "I won't hurt you."

I step closer, drawn to the quiet but strong voice coming from behind the confessional screen at the far end of the room. The area is dimly lit with a single white candle casting a halolike glow around a dark figure. I squint my eyes. Sitting behind the mesh screen, the priest's face is hidden. His long black habit is spread around his feet like a dark cloud. I try to see his face, but his head is bowed. His dark hair swirls around his high white collar, and his shoulders are surprisingly broad and muscular.

The effect hypnotizes me. The longer I stare at him, the harder I find it to breathe. I grab on to the twine holding my bodice together, twisting it between my fingers. The obvious masculinity of the man in black startles me, tickles my curiosity and makes me yearn for the sensual embrace of my artist lover.

Will I ever see Paul again? I send a look upward, as if my silent prayer might find a faster way to the heavens.

I hear a low mumbling coming from the priest's lips. He's

praying on his rosary, moving his fingers from one smooth black bead to the next. Will he help me if I tell him the truth? He's bound to a code of secrecy, right? I *must* try, though pride and a dutiful convent upbringing prevent me from telling him about my amorous adventures with the handsome Impressionist.

"Leave us, guard," orders the priest without raising his head. "The child will say her confession with the ears of God as her witness."

The guard with the straw-colored hair casts a wary glance at the man in the black habit. Something about the priest makes the woman hesitate, then she changes her mind.

"*Bien, Père*. Very well, Father." She leaves, closing the door behind her.

I look around the room, make certain we're alone. The floor is bare, the wood, old and cracking. A large crucifix hangs on the wall. The wooden kind, all brown and shiny. No furniture except for the mesh screen, a low bench for me to kneel upon, and a high-backed wooden chair reinforced with thin brown rails forming hard ridges against the priest's back.

I look up at the ceiling, trying to find the courage to speak, tell him my story. The only natural light filters through a small window placed high on the outer wall of the building. A colorful mosaic tints the intruding sunlight with muted shades of rose and azure, bathing the atmosphere with a calm serenity. I could be in the parlor of a boarding school. Then I hear the bolt slip into the barred door, and reality taps me on the shoulder. I'm in prison. And there's no getting out.

"Bless you, my child. Now tell me, what have you done

to displease God that you're here in St. Lazare?" asks the priest, shuffling his hands through the pockets of his robe and keeping his head bowed. He seems nervous.

"There's been a terrible mistake, Father. I'm *not* a prostitute. I don't know if you'll believe me, but I'm from—"

"God doesn't care where you came from, mademoiselle," says the priest, raising his voice. Then he does a strange thing. He joins his hands in prayer and covers his face as he shuffles toward the bolted door, puts his ear to the ancient wood and listens. A muscle in my eye twitches. There's something familiar about those broad shoulders and determined walk that stir a pleasurable ache within me. Teasing my mind with thoughts of his muscular body rising above me, his huge cock bobbing up and down, making me come...

...and do I smell absinthe?

"Paul, is that you?" I whisper. Before I can stop myself, a pleasurable sensation shoots down to my pussy, making me vulnerable to my need for him and *that* surprises me more than I want to admit.

"*Mais oui, mon amour.*" He lifts his handsome face and smiles at me, then loses that smile. "There isn't much time. You must listen carefully and do what I tell you or you'll leave St. Lazare lying still and cold beneath the final black veil."

I ask, "How did you get in here without anyone seeing you?"

"A few francs spread over the guard's palm along with a story about my sick sister in St. Lazare who needs money, and *voilà*, I'm here."

"Dressed as a priest?"

He grins. "I borrowed a spare robe from the visiting priest, then lured him away from his post with a phony story about a sick inmate begging for the last rites."

Feeling a sudden need to touch him, make certain he's real, I lay my hand on his arm. My fingers burn, my pubic muscles tighten. "Can you get me out of here?"

Paul shakes his head. "No, *ma chérie*. You've not been tried on the charges brought against you. Only a signed release from the magistrate himself can free you from St. Lazare."

"A release? Can you get one for me?"

"No, but I know someone who can and she's agreed to help you."

"What is her name?"

"Madame Chapet."

"Who is she? The headmistress of a school for wayward girls?" I try to smile, but inside I'm not laughing. Whoever this Madame Chapet is, she's my only way out of this hellhole.

"*La madame* is what you'd call *une architricline*."

"A *what?*" I frown. The meaning of the word eludes me.

Paul doesn't reply, but again checks the bolted door to make certain no one is listening. He seems distraught, an uncertainty about him alarms me, for it implies I'm in more trouble than I realized. And I'm hungry.

"Do you know what time they eat in this place?" I ask, not able to ignore the grumbling in my stomach any longer.

"*Alors*, you have no right to full prison rations, *ma chérie*. Only bread and water, but I brought you some food." He draws bread and cheese from inside his long sleeve and gives it to me. I eat it quickly, not tasting the food.

"What about my clothes?" I pull on the twine keeping my bodice together, forcing my cleavage to swell up over the taffeta. An old trick, but it gets his attention. A sharp longing resonates in his eyes and his breath quickens. As intently as he looks at my breasts, I look at him.

He says, "I like you better nude."

"I'm not surprised. From the sketches I saw in your studio, you have a habit of undressing your models."

"Jealous?"

"Yes. I'm jealous of any woman you've made love to, though for a man so young, you seem so experienced—"

*What made me say that?* It's a thought that's been hanging on the edges of my mind, something I didn't put into words before but it's there, and now I said it. *Why?* Because I feel the need to talk, say something, *anything* to forget I'm behind concrete walls in a world without him.

Abruptly Paul pulls me into his arms and holds me so tightly my breasts flatten up against the rough wool of his black robe. "I'm a man of many arts, *ma chère* Autumn, and someday I'll tell you. But not now. *Alors,* you're so *aimantée,* so desirable, but I must let you go or I won't be able to stop myself from ripping the rags from your body and taking you here on the cold floor, filling you with my cock—"

"Please, Paul, hold me." I lean my head against his broad shoulder, shaking and longing for his touch as he puts his arm around me and strokes my hair. His touch is like a spell on me, drawing me deeper into his world. He understands my innermost sensual desires, even when I don't acknowledge they exist.

"I must warn you, Autumn, St. Lazare is a dangerous place." He's shaking, as if every muscle in his body is taut as he restrains his passion.

"Dangerous?"

"Yes. Never let your head touch the pillow without keeping one eye open. The women in here are thieves, prostitutes and murderers. They have their own society within these walls."

"What does that have to do with me?"

"I saw what happened between you and Lillie. She won't forget how you insulted her. Although she moves in *la haute-bicherie,* the world of high-class prostitutes, she's a girl from the streets and will take back her pride the only way she knows how, with violence."

My mind is scrambling. Is no place safe in Paris? Not even prison?

The door creaks open as someone removes the bar from the other side. I watch the artist, looking for a sign from him. Paul motions for me to return to the kneeling bench. He takes up his position behind the mesh screen, giving no indication he's anything but a devout priest. A guard enters.

"Has the prisoner finished her confession, *Père?*"

I tense up, stiffening my back and making a fist. It's a different guard. Paul reaches around the screen and puts his hand over my clenched fist and shakes his head. This must be the guard he bribed earlier.

"Take her away. *Vite,* quickly!" Paul orders, rattling his

rosary beads for emphasis. "I have no more time for this insolent *fille*."

Playing along, the guard pushes me out of the room and down the stairs. "Get along, mademoiselle."

I keep my eyes straight ahead but I swear I hear a groan filling the high-ceiling room. *Paul.* It's as if a great pain engulfs his soul. The sound shatters the courage I felt only moments before. I try to swallow, but my throat is closed tight. With a sense of time running out, I walk hurriedly to my fate, knowing whatever awaits me, it will change my life forever.

What I believed would be a barely tolerable existence soon takes on the colors of unbearable reality. It starts every morning when the ringing of the convent bell summons the prisoners to chapel in the courtyard. We line up in pairs in our drab blue-and-black-striped uniforms to chant a barely audible hymn to God.

"Please, God," I mumble, joining my battered, bruised hands together in prayer, "give me the strength to survive in this horrible place."

After prayers, I shuffle behind the other prisoners through the square courtyard and into the dormitory for morning ablutions. Seems nature has to wait until *after* we ask for forgiveness of our sins.

Then we make a hasty retreat en masse to the chamber pots. The big, round white porcelain bowls with tiny blue flowers painted around the rim are lined up at the end of the dormitory hall. There's no privacy. We go about our business while indulging in the latest prison gossip: who's sending love notes; who's pregnant; and who's receiving special visitors on Sunday.

After emptying the chamber pot in an open hole in the ground outside, I wash my face in the big, chipped bowl all the women share, the water soapy but dirty. I hum a little tune, trying to drown out the noisy babble in the background. It isn't easy with twenty women sharing a dorm. Cots are lined up on either side of the room, barely inches apart, and we hang our clothes on the low rafters in the cathedrallike ceiling. The only illumination comes from one gas light mounted on the wall.

At night I wait for the popping sound the gas jet makes when it's put out and darkness descends upon the room. All through the humid nights I hear a constant din of wailing and snoring, as well as strange sounds I choose to ignore until—

—one night when I felt someone tugging at the loose chemise covering my body then slipping a hand underneath and up my leg. I shivered. In my dreamlike state, I thought it was Paul. My nipples got hard and pointy in hopeful expectation of what would happen next. My pussy filled with juices and my clit began to throb. A little spark of tension hung over me, waiting to explode. I grabbed on to the sheet, anticipating his touch. I wasn't disappointed. He ran his finger up my thigh in a slow crawl that grated on my nerves, making me clench my teeth so as not to cry out, but I couldn't help myself.

"Yes, yes," I whispered to my fantasy lover, my husky affirmation giving him permission to edge closer to my pussy then draw his finger across my lower lips. He hesitated, teasing me with light caresses on my plump mound, tapping out a signal, waiting me for let him inside. "Please...don't stop" was all I could say, then I moaned when he slipped a single finger inside me, then another. I thrust against him, trying to work his fingers in deeper still, gasping when he touched my throbbing clit. His fingers rubbed back and forth across the hard bud, urging me on. Faster and faster he stroked me, not letting up, my orgasm drawing closer and closer...

I sighed, relishing being so close to the point of losing control, yet desirous of his hands gripping my hips, pulling me back onto him, anticipating the moment of penetration when his thick cock would thrust deep into me. Panting, groaning, I endured long seconds of pain in my stomach as I waited for him to enter me, but he didn't. Why was he denying me release? What maddening game was he playing? I was desperate to come, shivering in spite of the stale warm air, aching to touch myself. I wanted to die of pleasure while embracing the French attitude to indulge in sex without guilt. Frustrated, I dragged my nails down the front of my cotton chemise, ripping the threads. Trembling, I couldn't wait. I let go.

"Ooohhhh..." My sugar walls contracted over and over again in intense pleasure. I closed my eyes tighter, reveling in a shuddering orgasm, though my cunt was empty except for the presence of his fingers moving inside me in a rapid rhythm. Surrendering to the sensations overwhelming me, I didn't want him to stop, but he did. Flushed with the afterglow of orgasm, I turned over and reached out to pull him close to me to embrace him and kiss his lips, when I felt a long finger snake around my butt to find a way inside me, then move to and fro in an intimate manner. I stiffened. Paul teased me, anally speaking, but not like this. His touch educed the promise of intense erotic pleasure, not pain.

I slowed down my breathing, trying to grab on to clues as to what was happening to me. The dreamlike state I'd experienced dissolved into the realization that a creature of flesh and blood held me in their grasp. I let out a strangled gasp as he—no, *she* moaned with extreme pleasure. The mewling of the feminine voice jolted me awake. My first instinct was to let go with a good kick and send my attacker reeling. But another part of me was curious. It was almost as if I could feel the slivers of pleasure creeping up through the woman, who became bolder, flattening herself against me in a long, smooth movement. Her panting body ground hot and sweaty against me, her hard nipples straining against her cotton shift and rubbing across my back evoking sensations in me I didn't expect to be a turn-on. Her erotic movements fired up in me imaginings of the sweetest taboo.

A harking back to my younger days took hold of me, when a flash of bare skin in the girls' gym evoked a curiosity tinged with desire to wonder what was it about a certain girl that made her so appealing to the opposite sex? No one dared admit they entertained participating in what was preached to us as a turpitude of modern society. We were young, our slender firm bodies knowing no shame, hiding no pockets of cellulite, no string-like stretch marks snaking across our bellies proclaiming us as weight loss yoyos and belying our vow of keeping to a vegan diet. Now this. What fervid desire had reawakened in my compliant body?

*Enjoy the ride, kiddo. This is as good as it gets in here.*

That brought up another question. What if I never got out of St. Lazare? I could no longer sustain the pretence of anger I so adroitly feigned a moment ago at the girl's clumsy efforts to stimulate me by forcing her finger into my butt hole. This could be fun. Besides, who else but me would know I tripped the light fantastic with a horny Parisian chick on a lonely night in a stuffy prison dorm? *Sex is sex,* I always say in that flippant "I'm so cool" 'tude while I fight the puritanical urge in me to censor my bohemian self. For years I yearned to play in the sandbox of my id, all the while fearing it was a bottomless pit where my darkest impulses would overwhelm me.

Not tonight. Was the girl's daring presence in my bunk a portent? Or the opportunity to experiment with new ways of finding pleasure?

As if I needed validation my hot bod was attractive to my own sex as well as the male gender, I pulled up my chemise to allow her to run her hands over my slim hips and goddess-smooth skin. An itch in my crotch made me daring, motivating me to travel where I'd never been. A magic place where a feline priestess drew me into her lair with her fragrant scent, offering her fruit to me like Eve before she hooked up with the hunk with the fig leaf.

I proceeded in a slow manner, as if I was sneaking up on my prudish self so as not to forewarn her what was coming. My reward was the sensation of hot breath on my belly then the silky moistness of an eager tongue skipping over my inner thighs in perfect circles. Coming close, so close to my pussy, yet not entering its portal. Oh, God, what the hell was she waiting for? What was I waiting for? I trembled as if I were on the verge of entering a bardo between one existence and another, a place where pleasure existed for the taking. Yet I hesitated. The idea of another woman's softness meshing with mine was a curious affliction hanging on the edge of my mind since my teen foray into watching girls going wild on late night videos. Were they faking it for beer money? I often wondered. Kissing and playing with each other. Or was I missing out on something equally stimulating if not as hard as a guy's dick?

So why not find out with this chick?

If she were a man I would have lifted up my hips and invited him to lick my slickness, but I was holding back and so was she. That surprised me. Who was the dubious mamselle with the eager tongue and good manners? Did I want to know? Or would that spoil the fantasy?

"*Que tu es belle,* mademoiselle," a soft voice whispered, the mellow sounds echoing in my ears, "how beautiful you are."

Her body inched closer to me, her presence enhanced when she raised her armpits and a waft of her personal scent hit my nostrils. I should have been used to the strong aroma, but I wasn't. I turned my face, but not my body. That was her cue to raise up her shift and press her breasts against mine, rub her pussy against my groin. "We are a perfect fit, mademoiselle, *mais non?*"

"Tighter than Cinderella's unholy stepsisters," I quipped. She laughed. The fairy tale obviously had universal appeal to all little girls. It must have been that moment that put me in a dominant mood. I felt powerful and clever and totally in control and not embarrassed as I would have been in my own time. I opened my eyes wider, begging to see her in the dark, but it was as if the bogeyman wanted us all to himself and wouldn't shine any light on her.

Then I would nibble on her.

I kissed her throat. I could taste her sweat, salty but not unpleasant, which surprised me. I dared to grab her breasts, her small nipples brushing against me, hot to my touch. She was petite in the way French girls are, and slender. I slipped my arm around the small of her back and crushed her against me. She groaned, anticipating what I didn't know. This was all new to me, like stepping into a mirror and viewing everything from a different angle. I felt awkward touching her. Between her thighs, then cupping her breasts. Why not her buttocks? I pinched her soft flesh with my eager fingers, making her giggle. Then I slid my tongue between her breasts, no cleavage to bury my face in, but it didn't matter. My whole body was alive with an emerging sensuality, drinking in the spontaneity of my adventure and toasting my daring spirit.

I put my hand down between her legs and was surprised to grab onto a thick triangle of hair much bushier than mine. Darker, too, I imagined for no other reason other than I was certain no blond dye was available in here for touch-ups. Drops of her secretion wet my fingers when I parted her lower lips and entered her. I bit my lip to keep from groaning. Within minutes I was lost in her dark enchantment, marveling in how a tight knot formed in my stomach as I rubbed her little nub, another spiral of an orgasm rising within me as I shared her pleasure. Our bodies rolled back and forth on my cot, like two waves in sync with each other in a compelling rhythm we couldn't stop. My own intense excitement needed release. Again. Whether it was the girl turning me on or me pushing the right buttons, I didn't know. I did know that when the moment came, I wasn't disappointed. I began to twitch and shudder, blood rushing to my face, my fingers aching, but I couldn't stop rubbing her clit back and forth. My other hand found my own hard bean, brushing the ridge of my clitoris and making me moan softly. I switched hands, then back again, my fingers moving in a wild frenzy between her cunt and mine, pressing on my clit while riding with her as she thrust into my hand. Dizzying sensations sent my brain into a meltdown, evoking complete surrender to my newfound freedom to explore my sexuality. Yet something was missing. What was it?

The physical release was there, as well as the peaceful sublime rest afterward and the desire to do it again. I sensed she felt the same way. She dragged her forefinger down the side of my cheek in a slow manner. Tender. Loving. Then with a sweet kiss on my lips, she was gone. Disappearing back into the black void that hid our pleasure as well as invited it.

I lay back, exhausted. Without thinking about what I was doing, I put my fingers up to my nose. A strong aroma tickled my nostrils as I inhaled our scent in one deep breath. Mixed together, it was fragrant, slightly musky. But it wasn't a man's heady pollenesque scent I smelled. Masculine. Strong. Paul. I couldn't deny that I enjoyed the ripples of desire the French girl evoked in me. Her hard nipples. Soft pussy. Tight and wet. But it wasn't like a hard cock penetrating more than my body. My soul. And that's what was missing.

I turned onto my side, huddled into a ball, and fell asleep, my hunger for the artist left unsatisfied. I soon discovered hunger of a different kind was also a problem. Bread and water at every meal. I was surprised to find pieces of dried meat and an orange under my pillow this morning. And yesterday, inside a folded-up note hidden between the towels in the laundry room, was a sou, enough to secure a blanket for my cot. Paul. The artist is watching out for me, but for how long? Where is this Madame Chapet? When will she show up?

An unholy chill comes over me, dragging me back to this morning's service in the courtyard. Someone is watching me. Slowly I raise my head and lock glances with a familiar face. *Lillie.* Her face is washed clean of color and her long blond hair is pulled back into a tight knot on top of her head, but I recognize the feline slant of her eyes and her small white teeth when she hisses at me. The girl's back seems habitually arched, as if poised to strike out at me. I swallow hard, fighting not to show fear in front of her. I haven't forgotten Paul's warning.

"Amen," I whisper in unison with the other prisoners, ending the morning prayers. When I look up, I see Lillie's lips moving silently, a different prayer falling off her tongue.

*I'll get you,* ma fille.

Ignoring her, I fall into line as the prisoners start to move through the courtyard toward the dormitory. Lillie steps out of formation, and I feel the hairs standing up on my neck as the prostitute brushes past me and whispers hotly in my ear.

"Today you die."

* * *

I stand in the doorway of the prison laundry room, the hot, steamy smell of dirty water rolling around me. I take a deep breath and exhale, Lillie's threat echoing in my ears. She won't seek me out here, *will she?* If so, she'll be found quickly. Every moment in the day at St. Lazare is accounted for. Sewing uniforms, embroidering linen, cleaning the convent floors and walls, cooking in the prison kitchen, making artificial flowers. We must think and do exactly what we're told.

Bleary-eyed, with dark circles ringing my eyes, I work in the laundry, folding towels and arranging them in neat stacks. The hot steam devours the air in the closed-off room, making it difficult for me to breathe. How do the others stand it? The women toil under the crude lighting, folding sheets and towels, washing the soiled garments in large tubs, the steam making their faces glow with sweat like shiny, porcelain dolls.

The steam is so thick this morning a prisoner fainted. I'll never forget the woman's face. Pale, then she turned a dirty gray, like the sheets steaming in the giant tubs. I watched warily as two guards dragged the unfortunate woman by her arms back to the dormitory. I closed my eyes and prayed for her. It's well known among the prisoners the poor woman won't escape a beating from the female guards. *Ghouls,* we call them. No wonder. A beating can happen to a woman anywhere, anytime, and for no reason other than wearing her prisoner's cap coquettishly off to one side.

"Back to work, *mes filles,*" yells a guard, twirling her club as she makes her rounds through the laundry room. "Or you'll each take a turn in the yard."

I keep my cap pulled down low over my forehead. Taking a turn in the yard is the euphemism given to the humiliating punishment where a woman's head and hands are imprisoned in wooden stocks. I shiver every time I pass by a prisoner paying the price for stealing food or passing a love note.

I pick up a stack of clean towels already folded, trying to look busy. Stretching on my tiptoes, I place the towels high on the shelf when a piece of paper sticking out between the towels catches my eye. *A note from Paul?* I look over my shoulder. The guard is busy wiping the sweat off her face with a dry towel, and the prisoners closest to me are too occupied dragging the wet sheets and towels out of the huge tub or folding dry ones to pay attention to me. I take the note and open it.

"*Oh!*" I stifle a cry, my hand flying to my mouth. I see the crudely drawn stick figure of a woman with a knife piercing her heart. The figure has hair stained red with dried blood. "Lillie," I whisper, crushing the paper in my hand and stuffing it into my bodice. How did it get between the towels?

I keep looking over my shoulder, folding the towels, doubling them and doubling them again. What I'm doing, I don't know. I have to keep moving. Anything to block out the deadly message of the drawing. My mind scrambles, my mouth quivers, the hot steam drifting around me. I've no doubt Lillie could attack me anytime, anywhere.

"I wonder why Lucie fainted this morning," says the

woman beside me, folding the ends of the sheets into neat squares. Her voice pulls me out of my daydream but the fear stays with me.

"Maybe she's *enceinte,*" says a second woman. A happy murmur breaks out among the prisoners. A woman with a baby is the object of intense and affectionate interest among the female inmates, who are forced to leave their own children on the streets to fend for themselves.

"*Mais non,* Lucie heard the rumor," whispers a prisoner, holding up a wet piece of linen in front of her face so she can't be overheard.

"Rumor? What rumor?" asks another woman.

"*He's* coming today."

I lean in, curious about any man foolhardy enough to tackle this bunch of women. Hair pulling and spitting are commonplace among rivals.

"You mean Monsieur le Docteur Gastonier?" asks a woman with dyed blond hair and a fat stomach.

The woman with the towel nods. "Yes, every month he comes to St. Lazare to examine the prisoners awaiting trial."

A loud moan echoes throughout the steamy laundry.

"Examine the women for what?" I ask. STDs? I wouldn't be surprised, considering the lack of protection available. The others look at me, flickering their eyes with surprise. Snickers and nervous giggles escape from the younger women.

"You'll find out, *ma belle,*" says a prisoner. "Last month a girl committed suicide rather than let *le bon docteur* put his hands on her."

"*Zut alors,* that old bastard nearly tore my insides out

with those cold, sharp pincers of his. His eyes are so poor he practically stuck his whole face up my ass—"

"Quiet down, *mes filles!*" orders the guard in a stern voice. The women fall into an uneasy silence, sending quick, darting glances around the room, signaling each other as the door opens and floating clouds of steam escape into the hallway.

"Here's another prisoner for you," announces a different guard before slamming the door shut behind her. The blonde glares at the prisoners, searching until her eyes find me.

*Lillie.*

I clutch the towels so tightly I feel the soft fibers ripping apart in my hands. I see Lillie glance at the guard, then hiss through her small white teeth. Her coming here is no coincidence. If only the heated room would swallow her up and drown her in this oversize bathtub.

Hands shaking, I crush the note hidden underneath my dress. I feel my heart pounding, my pulse racing out of control.

Lillie is out to get me.

*What the hell am I going to do now?*

# CHAPTER TWELVE

I t isn't that I want to stay and fight Lillie. I just don't have any choice. Even through the dense steam I feel the woman's eyes upon me at every opportunity, never letting go. Never giving up their vigilance. She's taunting me, trying to wear me down and catch me off guard.

*You wanted to be young and beautiful, kiddo. Deal with it.*

I look around at the other prisoners washing, folding, hanging wet linen on wooden poles, unaware of what's going on. The women flit about, nervous energy dissipating the heavy steam into paper-thin water droplets. I hear whispered tittering in every corner. Word spreads quickly, confirming the rumor the doctor is indeed coming today. More than one woman has a story to tell about how the doctor kept her hips on the edge of the cold wooden examination table, forcing her to spread her legs wide as he pawed at her breasts, then drove his pincers deep inside her.

Even the guards seem edgy. They're forced to deal with the skittish females who more often than not test positive for venereal disease. I was right. *Then what?* I asked.

Nothing. No drugs to help them. Just a longer stay in St. Lazare to "cure" them. More often than not, that meant death.

*What's happening to my erotic fairy tale? It's evaporating fast into a graphic novel without a happy ending.*

"Mademoiselle Pierusse," the guard reads names from a list, "Mademoiselle Rolande, Mademoiselle de Fleur..."

A loud, painful moan goes around the room. No one has to announce *le bon docteur* has arrived. The guard rattles off more names, and the women file out the door. Some wet their lips and fiddle with their long hair coming loose on top of their heads. Most wear unhappy expressions. Some are resigned to undergoing the examination, while others are defiant. One young girl has to be dragged out, scratching and screaming at the guard.

I fold and unfold the same towel several times, grateful my name wasn't called. My fingers shake and I can't stop from biting my lower lip. My mind is on Lillie. *What's she doing here?* I was so absorbed in my task I didn't realize the guards had left, leaving the prisoners alone.

"I'm going to kill you, mademoiselle," comes the hot, steamy breath in my ear. *"Now!"*

I shoot around and catch a flash of sharp-edged, copper metal stuck between Lillie's fingers, her raised fist pointed at me through the floating clouds of mist. No one has to tell me the copper fragments can rip my face to shreds with one swipe.

I duck under the heated steam. In seconds I see Lillie's black boots advancing in my direction. I reach out and tackle the prostitute around the ankles, sending the girl crashing to the floor with a thud.

"You'll be sorry you did that," Lillie yells, gasping for breath. She leers at me with hatred so thick it cuts through the spray of vapor rising in my face.

I scramble to my feet and grab a wet towel. Wadding it up into a soggy ball, I pitch it into my attacker's face. Lillie catches it and tosses it aside. Her bosom shakes with laughter.

"Your silly tricks won't stop me, you harlot."

"There's more where that came from," I yell, stalling for time. *When is the guard coming back?* Not until I'm lying unconscious on the floor. Then it'll be too late. Just like the prostitute planned it.

"You'll regret the day you tried to take Paul Borquet away from *me*, mademoiselle." Lillie circles me with careful, precise steps, like a rehearsed dance.

"You never had him, Lillie. Now get out of here and leave me alone."

"I'll leave when I'm finished with you, *mon camelot*, you low-class whore."

The blond prostitute hunches her back in an arc, her shoulders arched up to her ears and her fingers twisted into sharp talons ready to strike out at me, when someone throws a sopping wet sheet over her head.

"*Merde*," comes her muffled yell. "Who did that?"

I don't know whether to laugh or cry at the sight of Lillie grappling with the wet sheet, her struggling form taking on a ghostly shape. I grab on to the wall to steady myself, thanking a prisoner named Yvette. She winks in my direction and I wink back, but the show isn't over yet.

"*Vien-ci,* come on, mamselles, this is our chance to escape the doctor's filthy hands," challenges Yvette, waving another wet towel over her head.

"Or we'll be lying flat on our backs for *le bon docteur* with his pincers up our cunts," yells another, "without a sou to show for it!"

The women begin calling for the guards, squealing and screaming as they slosh water-soaked towels at each other like miscreant schoolgirls at a slumber party. *Are they crazy? Or is taking a turn in the yard more desirable than undergoing the doctor's cold, steel pincers?*

I'm not going to find out. I'm outta here.

I try the door. It opens easily. The guard must have left it unlocked so Lillie could escape. I slip through the door and look up and down the hallway. Empty as a confessional on visitor's day. Escape is mine for the taking, but where can I go? The prison is surrounded by high walls and guards at every gate. A raspy sound jars my senses. *Rats? The two-legged kind?*

"So, mademoiselle, you're still alive?" says a gruff voice behind me. "Lillie must be losing her touch."

I jerk my head around. The female guard with the ugly straw hair towers over me, cracking the whip in her hand against the worn wooden floor. Hard.

"I'm not frightened of you." No, I'm just scared out of my wits, but I'll be damned if I'm going to die in this prison.

"I'll make certain you *never* get out of here alive," the guard threatens, her smile so ugly it oozes vomit. *Crack!* She slices the air with her long whip, dangerously close to the other women filing into the hallway, curious to see what's going on, but her eyes are fixed on me.

Yvette grabs me, her slender hands holding on to me with a fierceness that fuels my courage. "She won't dare touch you, mademoiselle," she whispers. "Only *Mère L'Abbesse,* Mother Superior, can order punishment."

"Are you sure the guard knows that?" I quip. I have to do something. But what? I've just run out of miracles.

I crouch down, absorbing the heat of the moment through the thin fibers of my prison uniform as the guard's whip squeals through the air like a fallen angel's curse, barely missing me. Once, twice, then again the guard slams the worn, leather whip onto the wooden floor with as much force as the devil trying to beat the holy faith out of a believer.

I purse my lips and wipe them dry. I refuse to flinch. Instead, I try to shelter the other women prisoners from the torrent of blubber and fury shrieking and threatening to tear us apart. A surge of anger replaces my fear. Straightening my shoulders, I hold desperately to my mission, watching as the guard cracks her long whip again and again on the hard wooden floor, the woman's extended stomach bulging and heaving when she takes heavy breaths. I cry out as I hold up my exposed arms to protect myself, the juices in my stomach gurgling and chilling me with a panic I can't put into words.

What's clear from the start is the straw-haired ghoul will show me no mercy. Blinking away the dribbles of sweat dripping down my nose, my eyes shoot around the hallway, looking for a weapon. I see no holy stone loosened from its foundation I can grab, but an unholy courage drives me forward when someone distracts the guard with a loud scream. Her confidence shatters. Unwilling to admit she's unable to strike down her quarry, the guard turns and raises up her whip to strike at me again. Creeping up behind the guard, I squint at her, flinching. I'll use my bare hands if necessary, but they're shaking so badly I gather up my skirts and kick the guard in her buttocks instead. Another woman does the same. Then another.

A grunt of surprise stills the whip in the guard's hand as she jerks forward. The muscle in her forearm cramps, forcing her to drop her weapon. I grab the whip and someone screams again. I hear the rustle of a black habit and the hollow sound of large, wooden rosary beads clattering against each other and an older woman's voice giving out a command.

*The mother superior.*

I glance back. The guard stumbles, choking, the breath knocked out of her. Her eyes are droopy and dilated, and in them I see an unyielding hatred, her yellow hair standing straight out from its black roots. I want to run, but my legs won't move. I feel nothing but the heat of the battle warming my blood. I want to stay and fight the straw-haired guard, kick her, knock her down, show her I'm no wimp.

Instead I take a turn in the yard.


My legs are leaden and I'm feeling lightheaded and gasping for breath. It's the impractical position of kneeling with my head and hands imprisoned in wooden stocks. Not just the humiliation, but the damned inconvenience of my situation. I spent the night manacled to the wooden stocks, propelled by terror and the survival instinct, wondering what happened to Lillie, why she hasn't shown up when I'm most vulnerable, knowing she has the advantage. I won a brief reprieve, but for how long? A day? Two?

At least the heat doesn't come down upon me. The gray-cobbled courtyard is steeped in cold shadows. Instead, a slight chill blows through the yard, whipping my skirts against the back of my legs.

My clothes are dry, unlike some of the other prisoners. We're allowed to relieve ourselves in a community chamber pot every two to three hours, depending on the whim of the guard, but many can't hold it. The yard smells of urine, which does nothing to relieve an already unpleasant situation.

I look at the women imprisoned with me. Pale eyes. Drawn mouths. The telling glow of the blue-tinted dawn colors their faces a deathlike gray as if they're stone statues. We spend the time conversing with each other, considering ourselves lucky to be singled out by the mother superior for punishment rather than succumb to *le bon docteur,* though our mood is somber. Some try to sleep, others cry. Is it the power of the wooden stocks that keeps our mood serious?

Exhausted from a sleepless night, I shake my head, squeeze my eyes together tightly, trying to push away my sleepiness as if it were a pesky fly hovering above my nose. It's no use. Fatigue rolls over me like a great ocean wave, dulling my senses and creating a void where my brain was. For hours I watched ghosts dance in the courtyard, flirting with me. I refuse to believe the sheer wisps of fog floating on a breeze *aren't* ghosts. To me they're sneering, leering creatures invading the privacy of my pain with disturbing visions. Teasing my sense of reason with icy-cold reminders that I'm going to spend a long time in here if Madame Chapet doesn't show up.

I shake my head and blink my eyes several times, trying to clear away my fragmented delusions. The dawn is beginning to break but it doesn't change anything.

I'm still in St. Lazare.

I'm defenseless against the prostitute named Lillie.

And it scares the shit out of me.

I close my eyes. I'm tired of watching. Waiting. Any rustle of a breeze can mean the guard is coming by, ready to taunt me with more threats, promising me she'll cut off my hair and make me *sa manguese,* her lover. Make me wait on her at mealtimes and come to her bed whenever she wishes, driving her fingers deep inside me until she makes me cry out with pleasure. Short stubby fingers with broken nails dipping into me and ripping at my bruised flesh, then using my juices to make her dimpled breasts shine with the false blossom of youth.

I shiver, remembering my nighttime encounter with feminine hands stirring raw desire within me. Her richly fragrant pussy tempted me to go beyond my normal world and I don't regret it. I sensed the young woman craved companionship and closeness as much as she did sex. I can't blame her. My loneliness bites deep within me, though it can't be assuaged by the caresses of another female in a wanton mood. What frustrates me more is the need rising up in my belly thinking about Paul, seeing his face, imaging him penetrating the depths of my body, my soul. I yearn to experience the intense pleasure of my cunt humming its favorite tune while opening and closing around his throbbing cock with delightful contractions. Will I ever make love with him again, or will my pussy betray me when the need for release is so close to the surface I can't stop myself from losing control? Sucking in whoever, *whatever*, fills me up?

So what if I'm young and beautiful? It's brought me more trouble than anything else.

Yet I don't want to leave this time. Not until I solve the mystery of Paul Borquet. Okay, and the sex with him is fantastic. Even if I *can't* fall in love with him, I'll always have Paris.

Shutting down my brain, I watch the dawn slowly nudge the spirits awake with a gentle shove of light into the courtyard. I pray the new day will restore my sense of reason, but I'm not betting on it. I shiver as a naughty breeze peeks up my skirt. I wish I could pull it down around my ankles to keep out the draft, but I'm taller than the others and I find it difficult to move anything but my hips. *That* I find amusing. It wasn't that long ago I moved my hips in wave after wave of passion, thrilling to the caresses of my handsome artist.

"*Faites attention, mamselles,* look!" a woman prisoner cries out. "The gate is opening,"

"Who is it?" someone asks.

"No one *you* know, mademoiselle."

The others laugh, but I raise my head, curious. Bouncing irreverently over the rutty road, I see a carriage come through the gate. Squinting, I can make out a woman holding on to the leather strap dangling from the ceiling of the carriage as the team of horses clatters over the cobblestones.

The coach stops and the woman gets out, at the same time shooing a long, black ostrich feather hanging over the enormous brim of her hat away from her carefully made-up face. That doesn't stop her from giving the driver a piece of her mind. She scolds him over his inept driving, frets about her dress catching on the step of the carriage, examines her white enameled face in the tiny mirror she wears about her neck on a gold chain and ignores the guard who wants to see her pass.

Her garish but fashionable appearance announces her station in life. I imagine the woman lying on her back and counting up her fee without missing one beat of her faked orgasm. She must have been pretty once, but years of applying thick white makeup turned the rounded flesh of her cheekbones into a hard mask. Her rotund figure is stuffed into a low-cut gown of rustling yellow-and-pink taffeta with a pinched-in waist so out of proportion with the rest of her it defies all logic. Her gigantic breasts are her best feature, though they sag like water-filled balloons, dragging down her attempt at a youthful figure with them.

No doubt this is one hourglass that's run out of time. And that *hat*. I can't help but smile. It belongs in an old musical. Black feathers protrude from a yellow taffeta frame balanced at an angle on the side of her head. A black satin ribbon is tied in a lustrous bow under her double chins. When she tosses her head, the plumes wave back and forth like wisps of charcoal smoke flirting with the wind.

Everything she does is for effect, from the way she stands in front of the coach, posing, then sashaying across the court-yard with a lightness to her step I never would have imagined. She calls out to the *cocher,* the coachman, to wait for her, then she pulls out a black-and-yellow lace fan from inside her low-cut bodice and fans herself as she scans the shackled women with a quick, experienced eye. Like a housewife sniffing out the gizzards of hanging dead chickens.

*"Who is she?"* I mumble to the woman next to me.

"Madame Chapet," she whispers.

So *this* is the notorious Madame Chapet. God help me. I ask, "What's she doing here?"

"Who knows? Unless she's here with a release for one of her girls *qui vont à la campagne,* doing time at St. Lazare."

"Not her," Yvette says. "She wouldn't lift her little finger or a double chin to help her own mother. Unless there's a profit in it."

"Why do you say that?" I ask.

"She was a clothes dealer and moneylender to the women inside St. Lazare for many years. She knows everyone connected with the prison, including the magistrate."

"The magistrate?" I repeat, interested. *Very* interested.

"Yes. He set her up as an agent for a *maison de tolérance,* a licensed brothel—"

*"A brothel?"* I can't believe it. Paul is sending me to a cathouse. Why should that surprise me? What did I expect from a man who loves pussy?

*You're not outta here yet, kiddo. Don't blow it.*

I hold up my head, trying to see what's happening, as Madame Chapet approaches us, stuffing a piece of candy into her mouth. Her sharp eye takes in every curved cheekbone, every flirty eye, and every set of full, wet lips in the hope of recruiting a new girl.

"Doing a turn in the yard, mamselles?" she mumbles, her mouth filled with sweets. Saliva dribbles down the side of her mouth to her chin. She licks it off with her tongue in a long, slow manner that signals her desire for sweets goes beyond bonbons.

"We're your official greeting committee, madame," one woman says, awkwardly twisting her body and kicking up her skirts. Others do the same, laughing and squealing to get the woman's attention. I'm amazed at the display of flesh put on by these women. Ankles exposed. The flash of bare thighs peeking above tight black garters. One girl kicks up her flimsy skirt so high she shows off her naked pussy. Madame Chapet laughs, then holds her nose in a mock gesture before she saunters over to me.

"And who are *you*, mademoiselle?" She stares at me with eyes so fiercely blue I can't look away. There's no warmth in those eyes, even if her beet red mouth curves upward in a beckoning smile. Greed perhaps, and envy. Her obvious stare makes me uncomfortable. I remember her pointy tongue licking up the sticky sweetness slithering down the side of her mouth. I imagine her putting her mouth between my thighs, her tongue darting in and out of my pussy like a queen bee's stinger. Not a pleasant thought. I feel the sweat oozing down my face in wet streaks. I return the woman's stare with equal intensity and receive only a coquettish fluttering of eyelashes in return.

"Autumn Maguire," I answer.

"Irish?"

"Irish-American."

I see a hesitation slide over her face, then disappear.

Whatever she thinks of the Irish, she isn't going to let it interfere with business.

"*Alors,* Monsieur Borquet told me about you, mademoiselle, about your high breasts, pointy and firm—"

She's grabbing my breasts and rubbing my nipples with
her fat thumbs.

"—and your fair skin shimmering with a golden aura—"

Now she's running the palm of her hand down my cheek
and forcing my mouth open with her finger. I nearly gag.
God knows where it's been. What is it with this woman?

"—and your long red hair that defies the hottest flame
to match its color."

She's running her fingers through my hair. Or is she
looking for head lice? If she goes anywhere else with her
game, I'll kick her in her ass—

"*Mon Dieu,* he's right. You put all my other girls to
shame." Madame Chapet is so flustered she can't reach for
her fan. Instead she makes a breeze by waving the inky black
ostrich feathers hanging down from her hat in front of her
face. She composes herself, a tremendous tide of excitement
and exhilaration sweeping through her. "You'll be perfect
for—"

"I'm *not* a prostitute, Madame Chapet," I retort, believing the woman will help me, but I'm wary of her, reluctant
to believe I'm about to enter the world's oldest profession.

And it's all Paul Borquet's fault.

He's just like all men. Make love, then roll over and fall
asleep until his dick gets hard again. Well, this is one chick
who's not going to let him get away with it.

A bell rings. Morning prayer is about to begin. Nuns,

guards and women prisoners in single file enter the court-yard, jabbering, complaining and pointing to the coach waiting for Madame Chapet. She pays them no attention and studies me a moment or two longer, then glances toward the nuns and prisoners. I notice she's upset by something. Her breathing becomes heavy again. Surrounded by all this new pussy is too much for her, I imagine. I continue protesting my aversion to being referred to as a prostitute, but I have the terrible feeling she's not listening.

"Enough, mademoiselle, I have your release here." She pats her ample bosom with her fan and a light shower of white powder sprays up into the dirty air. "You'll be safely en-sconced in the House on rue des Moulins before nightfall—"

"What about *me,* madame?"

I groan. Lillie stands behind the brothel madame, breathing heavily, hands on her hips.

"Ah, Lillie de Pontier, so *this* is where you've been hiding." Madame Chapet turns and narrows her eyes, her voice sarcastic. "We've missed your charms at the House on rue des Moulins."

"You said *I* was your best girl, madame," Lillie whines, her eyes flashing a warning to me that she isn't giving up her hard-won reputation so easily. "That no one was better than I at cradling a man's balls with my elegant fingers, my tongue and mouth working at his shaft and pleasuring him."

Madame Chapet keeps her eyes riveted on the blonde. "Not anymore, Lillie. I'm going to teach you a lesson."

"Madame?"

"I'm shocked, do you hear? *Shocked.* Getting yourself thrown in here like a common whore. I've lost more gold louis than I care to remember because of you, mademoiselle. Not only have my gentlemen complained about your absence, but Monsieur Gromain has been after my tail when you didn't show up at his studio to pose for the artists."

"It's all *her* fault, madame," Lillie insists, pointing to me. "She attacked me on the street."

"She tried to kill me with a knife, madame."

"Too bad I missed," Lillie says.

"Enough, mamselles! *I* will decide your fates," Madame Chapet insists. The Frenchwoman pulls out a creased, folded piece of paper from her bosom. Not a moment too soon.

"*Faites attention,* watch out!" warns a woman prisoner. "It's Mother Superior."

I see the stern, righteous, and very proper figure of *Mère L'Abbesse* heading toward us, her veils billowing around her like a religious tempest. A storm is brewing under her winged headpiece. A big one.

"Let *me* do the talking, mademoiselle," Madame Chapet says, her words directed at me. *"Say nothing."*

"What about *me,* madame?" Lillie insists.

"If you say one word, mademoiselle, you'll *never* get out of here, I promise you," *la madame* says harshly.

I let my head slump, praying this woman can gain my freedom. I imagine myself selling my soul to this female devil in black plumes, promising her *anything* to get out of St. Lazare. Even lift my hips so she can lap up my juices with those red lips of hers? A horrible revelation hits me. I realize Madame Chapet is having the same thoughts.

"*Bonjour,* Madame Chapet." The mother superior bows her head at a polite angle and folds her hands into her black kimono sleeves. But her body shakes. The Mother Superior is nervous and has lost that inner calm inherent to women who take up the religious life. She's being tested and she doesn't like it. "To what do we owe the pleasure of your company at St. Lazare, Madame Chapet?"

"I'm taking my niece home today," says the madam, fanning herself with the release paper and coming dangerously close to skinning the end of the nun's nose with it.

"Your niece?"

"Mademoiselle Autumn Maguire."

The abbess isn't fooled. "This girl isn't going anywhere, madame, until her case is decided."

"I assure you, *Mère L'Abbesse,* this release has been personally signed by the magistrate," Madame Chapet boasts in a loud voice. Her double chins tremble, the expensive pearls on her choker gleaming a saintly white color.

The Mother Superior's face hardens. "Let me see the release, madame, *s'il vous plaît.*"

Madame Chapet tosses her plumes away from her face, fans the sweat on her brow dry, then adjusts her décolletage before handing over the release paper to the abbess.

I fix my stare on the nun. I know that look—eyes wandering from side to side, upper lip puffed out, the twitching on the side of the mouth. I used to watch the sister walking up and down the aisles when someone talked out of turn, looking at every girl with an accusing stare, daring the guilty one to remain silent, knowing someone would crack and admit the dirty deed and beg for mercy. That same fear revisits me now. A hundred times worse.

"*Bon,* Madame Chapet," says the mother superior. Her

inner calm has returned. The matter is out of her hands now. "Your niece can leave St. Lazare with you. *This time.*" She folds her hands in prayer. "May God have mercy on *both* your souls."

I ignore the warning in the nun's voice. *I'm free.*

Grumbling, the guard with the straw hair unlocks the manacles, releasing me from the wooden stocks. She brushes my breasts with her hand, pinching me like a snake sinking its fangs into my flesh, but I push her away with my shoulder. She groans, but does nothing. I stretch my arms up over my head, but the feeling is gone from my upper body, my shoulders are stiff, and my neck feels cramped. It doesn't matter. The feeling of freedom is inexplicably intense, as if that emotion is my only reason for living at this moment.

I try to walk, but at the halfway point to the gate, I collapse onto my knees, clawing the air and then at the cold, dirty cobbles under me. I continue trying to stand, then crawling, then finally get to my feet toward my freedom. I know that beyond the heavy prison gate, in the bleeding sunshine, the city of Paris waits for me to discover its secrets, to draw me into its myths and mysteries, where no one from my time has ever gone before.

I yank the gate open.

Paul Borquet is also waiting for me.

*Isn't he?*

Madame Chapet pulls at the triple-string pearl choker hiding her double chins, then with two fingers delicately curved, she picks up the last sweet bonbon nestled in the pink velvet-covered box and tosses it to the bundles of fur named Louis and Pompie bouncing around in the carriage. The two dogs immediately fight over the candy.

"*Zut alors, mes petits enfants,* now, now, don't fight. *Maman* will give you more sweets later."

I glance out the side window, disgusted by the two little dogs who won't stop nipping at my ankles. "Where are you taking me, madame?"

"To the House on rue des Moulins…Louis, Pompie, *stop fighting!*" The two little terriers give no indication they heard their mistress and keep snarling at each other.

"I told you, Madame Chapet, I'm *not* a prostitute." I smile thinly, making another attempt to plead my case. "I don't know what Monsieur Borquet told you, but—"

"Monsieur Borquet is a young man infatuated with you *and* a starving artist. You'll be happier without him."

I push down my desire to lose my temper at her audacity, instead asking in a calm voice, "What are you saying, madame?"

"You must forget him. I have plans for you. Big plans. I know several gentlemen, including Lord Bingham, the fifteenth duke of Malmont, who will pay highly to enjoy the taste of *la boîte d'amourette,* the love box, of one so young and beautiful as you."

Young and beautiful. Damn, it's more of a curse than anything else. And an excuse for the old bitch to sell my pussy. I smile. What would la madame say if she knew the truth about me?

"I won't let the duke touch me," I tell her, shivering.

"You *will*, mademoiselle. Or I'll see to it Monsieur Borquet is barred from showing his paintings at any salon in Paris."

"You can't do that."

*Blackmail.* The old witch.

"I can and I will." Madame Chapet fidgets with the plumes on her hat. She wets her lips several times and breathes in and out with difficulty. Then she lights a cigarette to let her threat sink in. I turn my head away. Smoking is a French habit second only to arrogance. I glance around the inside of the coach. Cigarette smoke shrouds the air a dirty gray, adding to the effect of the closed-in conveyance.

We've been riding for several minutes through the streets of Paris, my walk to freedom cut short by *la madame* ordering me into the carriage or back to St. Lazare.

"I've had enough of your insolence, mademoiselle," Madame Chapet says. "I've had nothing but problems with you girls, especially the artists' models. Monsieur Gromain is angry, *very* angry, and desperate for a model. For the last week, he's been spreading gossip that my *maison tolerée,* my brothel, no longer has the best girls in Paris. It's all Lillie's fault. Getting herself locked up in that prison. Cost me quite a bit in lost modeling wages, the little strumpet."

An idea hits me.

"I'll do it, madame."

"Do what?"

"Pose for the artists."

"*You*, mademoiselle? You're beautiful, and from what I see despite that horrible prison uniform, you have a good figure…" Her voice trails off, while her eyes undress me, making me shudder. "But you have no experience—"

"Yes, I have, madame." It's true. I posed for the old artist in Marais, didn't I? A plan is hatching in my brain.

*Use your beauty to get yourself out of this mess.*

"Where did you pose, mademoiselle?" She doesn't believe me. "These artists are very particular and want someone experienced."

"I'll give them something fresh, something new, something they won't find anywhere else in Paris. They won't be able to stay away."

Madame Chapet narrows her eyes. "*Eh, bien,* what?"

"What if I *don't* become one of your girls—"

Madame Chapet shakes her head no.

Think, *think.*

"—at least not right away. You can tell Monsieur Gromain I've just arrived in Paris and *no* man has made love to me."

"*C'est vrai?* Is this true?"

"*Mais oui,* Madame Chapet. Ask your gentlemen callers, ask anyone. No one knows me in Paris. *No one.*"

"Except Monsieur Borquet. Will he talk?"

I take a big breath. "Not if you let me speak to him. *Alone.*"

"*Non.* I'll be there, watching you, making certain he doesn't touch you. From this moment on, mademoiselle, you must let *no* man touch you, you must be as pure as a virgin, not a girl *qui a vu le loup,* who has seen the wolf, *n'est-ce pas?*"

The thought of Paul not touching me is chilling, almost too much to bear, and I realize with a sweet poignancy how tight the bond between us has become in the short time I spent with him.

"…and I'll invite Lord Bingham to the atelier of Monsieur Gromain to see you. *Bien,* you know, mademoiselle," *la madame* is saying, then she bends low, and whispers in my ear, "when you pose for these artists, you must pose nude."

*Pose nude?*

It's too much. I cover my mouth with my hand, but no matter how hard I try not to, no matter how insane this whole situation seems, I start laughing and can't stop.

*Here I go again.*

I'll never complain again about swimming in the corporate mosh pit. Dealing with dirty politics can't compare to doing a turn in the yard. Even when the zipper on David's pants was staring me in the face and I was dreading the sawing sound of metal hitting metal as he pulled it down, I didn't suffer such awful panic.

Now I'm off to a famous Paris brothel to swing the most important deal of my life: saving my butt from getting fucked every which way—off a divan, some taking me standing up, from behind, bent over the banister, and anywhere else the French do it.

But even Nicole Kidman couldn't escape that gentleman devil with the little prick in his pants and the English lisp. Oh, yes, he's in my story, too. The bastard. Don't worry, Paul's got him on his radar.

Oooh, this is so delicious. Two men lusting after me and both of them are filled with:

### Jealousie (Jealousy)

No true love there can be
without its dread penalty—
—jealousy.
—Lord Lytton, English statesman and poet
(1831-1891)

# CHAPTER THIRTEEN

From the moment I see Paul again, I want him. He bursts into the *retiro*, the small receiving room, in the House on rue des Moulins at more of a run than a walk, swirling his long black cape around him like furious storm clouds, as if *la madame* lined up all her girls simply for his pleasure. The whiff of a pampered lifestyle assaults his nostrils as a few girls lounge on divans or silk chairs, while Madame Chapet lies on a *meridienne* with strips of raw veal resting on her cheeks.

He looks only at me, pacing back and forth on the plush white carpeting. He can't stand still, like the dust mote that never settles on the furniture. Back and forth. Back and forth. Watching him, I keep rubbing my fingers on my filmy, silk gauze nightgown the color of crushed pink rose petals—I'm nude underneath—revealing my thigh-high dark stockings, the newest rage among the girls. Backless pink slippers complete my outfit. Madame Chapet refuses to allow me to wear anything else. A ruse so I can't leave the House on rue des Moulins.

I forget about that now. *Paul's here.* I'm relieved to see his handsome face and long dark hair damp with perspiration sticking to his forehead, and his dark blue velvet eyes say, I've missed you, I couldn't wait to get here. I can't wait to touch you.

"*S'il vous plaît, madame,*" Paul says to Madame Chapet, "I must speak to Mademoiselle Maguire." He looks around. "Alone."

"You know the rules, monsieur." The sudden jerking of her mouth muscles makes a sliver of pink-peach-colored meat slide down her cheeks on a veneer of perspiration. "If you don't pay, you must keep to the public rooms."

"If it wasn't for *me,* madame," Paul insists, "Mademoiselle Maguire wouldn't be in your employ."

Madame Chapet chooses to ignore his statement. "I repeat, monsieur, you know the rules. No exception."

"I have money—"

"It's not enough, monsieur."

"Has Lord Bingham enough money, madame?"

Lord Bingham? *La madame* mentioned him earlier, but I've never met him. Madame Chapet keeps me secluded to build up excitement for my appearance at L'Atelier Gromain.

"Go away, Monsieur Borquet. You're wasting my time."

"May I remind you, madame, many of your customers are my artist friends. One word from me and I assure you, they'll seek their pleasure elsewhere."

Madame Chapet considers this a moment. "Five minutes, monsieur. *No longer.*"

Finished with her beauty treatment, she tosses the strips of meat into a crystal bowl sitting on a small table next to her. She waves her hand and *la madame*'s personal maid and seamstress, Delphine, removes the smelly veal. Then she calls her two terriers, Louis and Pompie, to her lap and begins cuddling the dogs, but her eyes never leave me.

Standing off to the side, I look longingly at the handsome artist approaching me. He's no happier with the situation than I am. Nervous. Excited. And yes, a delicious tightening of my pubic muscles jolts my sex energy back into action. A ripple of pleasure sparks low in my belly, a sensation I haven't experienced since we made love in his studio in Montmartre. Not that I can kiss his steamy lips or enjoy his probing tongue. We talk to each other as if we're actors in a play with an audience of one, Madame Chapet watching us with intense scrutiny.

"I want to take you in my arms, Autumn, and kiss you," Paul says, sliding his fingers up and down his cane. Sweat makes it shine. It reminds me of his hard cock slipping into me, my juices making his entry an act of pure pleasure.

"You can't come any closer, *s'il te plaît,* please." I push a tray of Italian figs and sweets between us.

"I can't stay away from you. *I won't.*" He picks up a dark purple fig and breaks it open, revealing layers of rose-pink and deep crimson. The fruit is ringed with seeds. And juicy like my pussy. A delicacy that must be tasted to be enjoyed. He raises his right eyebrow, giving his face a triumphant expression that intrigues me, as if he's savoring that thought. My mouth is dry, imagining his tongue licking and sucking on the sweet fruit. I wet my lips. He's torturing me and he knows I love it.

"Madame Chapet said she'll do something terrible to you if you touch me."

His thumb and forefinger pull back the layers of the fig as if he's holding back the lips of my pussy. He presses his finger inside the fruit, then slides his thumb back and forth as if he's brushing it across my clit. I draw in my breath, still in control, just barely.

He says, "Eh, what can she do to me?"

"Your work, your paintings." My fingers move down to my crotch. *Don't touch your clit. She's watching.* "She'll have you barred from the *salons.*"

"I don't care." He puts the fig into his mouth, runs it around his mouth, to the back of his tongue before swallowing it, juice running down the sides of his mouth. Watching him, I can't help but run my fingers up and down my thigh, ever so lightly, coming closer and closer to my pussy. I clench my pubic muscles as if willing them to behave, but it's not working. A slow burn builds in my belly that I can't ignore. "I can sell my work in the open-air *salons,*" he continues, "hang my pictures on trees, fences, lampposts on the Place Constantin-Pecqueur, *anywhere,* as long as I have you in my arms."

"It's not good enough, Paul." My pussy is wet and swollen, but I can't touch it. *I can't.* I push my thighs closer together, barring entry to my wandering fingers. "You're a genius and your work deserves to be recognized." I rub my fingers on my nightgown, pushing down my sexual urges. A different urge gnaws at me, zapping my physical need, at least for a moment. Years into the future, the name of Paul Borquet will be known to only a few in the art world. *What happened? Am I the reason he gives up his art?* "I won't let you give up your work, Paul."

"I won't give *you* up."

He comes closer, squishing another fruit between his fingers, its juices running down his hand. I imagine him entering me, my pussy as tempting and vulnerable as the succulent fruit. I flinch. *Damn Madame Chapet.* "You must stay away from me...you mustn't kiss me."

"Not kiss you? Are you insane? Just being near you makes me burn with hot desire—"

"Don't, Paul. *La madame* is consumed with the idea of presenting me to the artists at Monsieur Gromain's studio—"

Paul's eyes open wide. "Gromain? That old *sauteur,* womanizer. With you as his model, he'll have half the city of Paris on his doorstep." His artistic jealousy stirs within him, eliciting a surprising response from him. "You'll pose *nude?*"

"Yes."

"I forbid it."

"And who are you, monsieur, to tell me what to do?" My words sting him, as if it never occurred to him I wasn't a slave to his passionate touch. "*You* got me into this mess."

"*I?*" He stares at me in disbelief. "*Merde,* I never dreamed you'd do something crazy like posing nude."

"I posed nude for you."

"That was different."

"Oh?"

"I won't let you pose nude in front of those artists." He moves closer, and I can smell the scent of absinthe and oils on him as he presses his hard muscular thigh to mine. I lay my fingers on his leg and feel his muscle harden. I pretend I'm holding on to his cock instead, making me moan with both pleasure and longing. Madame Chapet clears her throat, but before I remove my hand, Paul grabs my wrist and squeezes it. Oh, how I wish he were rubbing my clit with his fingers instead. Just thinking about it makes the muscles in my belly tighten. "Those lecherous old men think only of titillating a woman's pussy not only with their brushes, but their dicks as well."

"Jealous?" I love it.

"Jealous? *Bien sûr,* I'm crazy with jealousy."

I wet my lips. "Then why did you allow Madame Chapet to secure my release from St. Lazare, knowing she runs a brothel?"

Paul sighs. "It was your only way out of there. I couldn't bear to see you in that miserable hole one more day. I have no doubt you would have died in that place—"

"Lillie."

He nods. "A young girl doesn't stand a chance of keeping her youth and beauty in that prison."

Frowning, I know he's right. How long would have I held out before I succumbed to taking a female lover in St. Lazare? Then what? Drugs, alcohol and who knows what else? That night with the French girl proved to me how vulnerable I am.

"Is that all I mean to you, Paul?" I pull away from him. "Young and pretty?" Except for the pulse beating rapidly at the side of my neck, I sit motionless. In spite of my lively repartee with the artist, I'm hurt at hearing his words.

"I'm a man. I'm human. You tempt me to go where I've never been before. You inflame my artistic vision as no woman has ever done."

*Let him have it.*

"I have a brain, Paul."

"A beautiful one," he says.

*He got me on that one.*

I smile. "You're insufferable. Someday you'll learn to appreciate more than a woman's body."

"Then teach me, *ma belle mademoiselle.*" He tempts me with his dark blue velvet eyes, judging me, mentally stripping off my nightgown so smoothly, so deftly, and with such raw desire, I wiggle my hips and my juices seep between my thighs. He says, "I don't ever want another man looking at you—"

"You mean the way *you* do?" I put my fingers between my legs until they're wet with my fluids, then rub them on his thigh when *la madame* isn't looking. He kisses my hand, sniffing, then waves it under my nose. My musky scent makes us both smile. Does it remind him how he mixed my fluids with his oils? "I revel in your eyes undressing me, burning my flesh down into my soul, making my nipples hard, *ma chatte* wet with desire."

"You're exciting, Autumn. So young, so beautiful, so filled with the blush of a sweet flower not yet blossomed."

I bite on my lower lip. "What if I wasn't young?"

He stares at me, surprised. "But you are. So deliciously young. I never dreamed I'd ever hold a girl like you in my arms, possess you, love you." His fingers gently brush my cheek. "Say you love me?"

"I...I—"

*Don't say it! If you do, you'll turn back into your thirty-four-year-old body, not a pretty sight in a transparent nightgown. Think cottage cheese thighs.*

My heart pounds. What am I going to do? We're so close, our lips nearly touch. For several moments we're silent, submerged in delicious memories of silken bonds, milky white breasts, pink-brown nipples hard and pointy, hips undulating in unison, the hardness of his cock tempting my passion and driving me mad for the want of him. Naked and sweating in the moonglow. When we're but a breath away from a kiss, loud yapping from the two terriers brings an end to our little play when Madame Chapet pushes the black and white balls of fur onto the white carpet.

"Your time is up, Monsieur Borquet," she announces loudly.

Paul asks, "When can I see Mademoiselle Maguire again?"

"When the other artists have that same pleasure, monsieur."

"Madame?"

"Tomorrow. At the *atelier* of Monsieur Gromain," Madame Chapet says, smiling. "*Without* her clothes."

Naked.

Standing on a wooden platform two feet high, with only a thin sheet draped over my nude body, my back facing the curious eyes of the artists, I hear them breathing, feel their eyes staring.

Feel them waiting for me to let go of the sheet.

I hear someone drop a pencil and it rolls noisily along the earthen floor stained with drops of paint. Red, blue. Dirty yellow. Someone else coughs, then sneezes. And is that the sound of a lid being unscrewed on a whiskey flask? The familiar wormwood fragrance of absinthe overpowers the smells of paint and turpentine and unwashed bodies coexisting together in the art studio on rue Fontaine and attacks my nostrils with a strong intensity.

I turn around. Slowly. Cautiously. An early-morning fog frosts the shy sunlight coming through the ceiling skylights with a gray dullness as I look around, my eyes burning with curiosity. I can't see the faces of the artists, especially those seated in the back of the studio, but I know their names: Degas, Cézanne, Pissarro, Monet…and the master of caricature, Toulouse-Lautrec. Each artist waits in front of his easel with pencil, sanguine crayon, chalk or *fusain,* charcoal, in hand, ready to spend the morning drawing a live model.

I study them intently, but I'm too nervous to let my eyes linger on any one face. They're watching me, dammit. It's one thing to pose nude in front of a stranger, as I did in Marais, but these are *the* Impressionists. *Have I gone mad?*

I'm scared out of my wits, yet thrilled and shaking with a strange kind of excitement. I'm the model for the most innovative and creative minds of the Impressionist movement.

All except one.

*Where's Paul?*

"*Le drap,* Mademoiselle Maguire, the sheet…drop it," comes a voice from a dark corner, away from the latticed skylight in the lofty *atelier.* Monsieur Gromain, the owner of the art studio. He's getting impatient. The future of his studio depends on the success of this day. It's common gossip Monsieur Gromain's refusal to change with the times lost him many students to the Académie Suisse, where landscape artists like Monet and Cézanne work to develop a knowledge of anatomy and can sketch a model—stone-faced and haughty women wearing ugly tights—for a small fee. So Monsieur Gromain hired a team of carpenters to refurbish the rundown studio and launched a campaign to attract the artists back. For that he needed a new model. A beautiful one. Untouched. And virginal.

*Virginal?* I smile. I *look* the part, though I don't match up to the desired measurements of 38-18-38 Madame Chapet insists is a perfect body. I'm much trimmer and well-toned. That was enough for Monsieur Gromain. Though I refused to strip for him, my face and legs were enough to redden the fat cheeks of the art studio owner when he left with *sa troisième jambe,* his third leg, stiff and hard.

He's not the only man interested in me. Delphine told me about the mysterious Lord Bingham, Duke of Malmont, who comes calling every day to see me, but Madame Chapet refuses his request. *La madame* insists I can make more money for her by posing at L'Atelier Gromain than going upstairs with a customer. The gossip about the beautiful, virgin model moved quickly through the cafés of Paris and the artists came.

But where is Paul?

My fingers are shaking, my heart beating madly and, God, am I perspiring. Salty beads of sweat roll down the cleavage between my breasts and wiggle down my rib cage. I'm also wet between my legs, both from nerves and arousal. It's disconcerting and compelling at the same time to think I'm about to stand naked before these men. I dare not wipe the sweat away, fearing the sheet will fall to my feet. My white flag of surrender. I'm wearing nothing but my courage underneath and that's about to leave me as well.

I hug the sheet closer to me and shiver. The studio is cold but that's not why I feel a damp, clammy feeling washing over me. Paul hasn't shown up. Why?

I need him to give me the courage to pose nude.

Or is there another reason? A reason that's haunted me since I first explored the silkiness of his dark hair, the strength of his shoulders, the broadness of his chest, then the inescapable joy of having him hard inside me for a long time. No matter how much I pleaded with Madame Chapet, I had no time to be alone with Paul, no time to convince him he's in terrible danger. According to the old artist, he died in 1889. *When?* I'm determined to stop his tragic death from taking place.

Or has it already happened? Is Paul Borquet dead? Gone from my heart forever?

I refuse to believe it.

Standing on the platform before the famous artists, I don't feel so brave, so quick to pose nude. I have the urge to sink down to the floor and curl up in the sheet to ward off the chills sweeping over me in front of all these great men. How am I going to let their eyes and their pencils explore every mole on my body, the dimples on my buttocks, my hard brown nipples, and, God help me, the tuft of hair between my legs? *Le minon,* Paul calls it. My pussy. I can't do it.

"Drop the sheet, mademoiselle," comes the voice of Monsieur Gromain again. *"Now."*

This time he steps out of the shadows, breathing heavily. Wearing a long, flowing tie known as *une cravate flottante* and ill-fitting clothes, Monsieur Gromain senses what's going through my mind. His fuzzy eyebrows wiggle over his angry eyes and his mustache quivers. "Enough of your foolishness, mademoiselle."

He raises his hand and I know what's coming. He intends to rip the sheet off my body. Quickly, dramatically. Like he's skinning a cat. Or pussy in this case.

*No way.* I move quickly out of his reach. A sudden courage overtakes me. Paul isn't here but he's in my heart, giving me strength. I'll give them what they want, show them how a real *woman* can stir their passion with their chalk. If I go through with this pantomime, I have no doubt I'll cause a sensation—my perfect body will see to that—but I'm not going to be plucked naked and served up on a French palette. If I have to go through with this charade, it's going to be *my* way.

Fueled by the wary look on the old master's face and my own determination to reclaim my womanhood, I turn my back to the artists. Then, holding on to the ends of the sheet, I spread my arms wide like an angel testing her wings. My long auburn hair ripples down my back in soft, lazy Marcel waves, the latest hair curling craze. My face is covered with pale Veloutine Powder, my lips painted with *bâtard au raisin,* and my eyelashes turned upward to "look like stars," according to Madame Chapet. But it's the curve of my golden tanned shoulders and the arch of my well-toned back that makes the artists lean forward at their easels. They sense *this* is the moment.

I think of Paul, his dark blue eyes shimmering, his electric caresses, his cock standing up, and I decide that Monsieur Gromain is right. I *am* being foolish.

I take a deep breath, then drop the sheet.

* * *

Between the boulevard des Capucines and the rue Auber, near the Place de l'Opéra, Paul walked so fast even the most hurried pedestrian slowed down and braced themselves, making wordless gestures of dismay as he whirled around the corners of the buildings too sharply.

*Merde.* He was being followed and he didn't like it.

The uneasy feeling was so vivid in his mind he had delayed getting to L'Atelier Gromain. Delayed seeing Autumn and that made him angry. *Very* angry.

*That man wearing the long tweed coat and bowler hat, pretending to read a newspaper every time I stop and gaze into a shop window, who is he? Why is he following me?*

As Paul scurried past the *terrasse* of Le Café de la Paix, his long black cape whipping around his boots, wet from the rain puddles on the streets, billowing out at his sides, he heard someone calling his name.

"Monsieur Borquet, *attendez-vous.* Wait!"

He spun around in surprise at the sound of the man's voice. *He knows my name. How?* He didn't want to stop, not when he had so far to go up the rue de la Chaussée past the rue Blanche and cross over to the rue Fontaine. A coldness rose in the pit of his stomach, freezing his will. The urgency of the voice caught his curiosity, or was it the strange feeling gnawing at him the man had something to do with the Englishman?

Whatever it was, he slowed down, looked past the glass inside the famous café, craning his neck. Flower sellers, a lone accordionist, a waiter bearing a tray with candied plums crowded his view. Where was the man in the bowler hat?

He could see patrons in well-worn topcoats as well as luxurious sable-trimmed capes crowding the entrance. Every table, both inside and outside, was occupied. To warm the customers on the cool rainy day, big open braziers of burning charcoal had taken the place of the dwarf trees on the *terrasse*. With the abundance of top hats and ladies' Reboux hats with their plumes getting in his way, he couldn't see the man who had called out his name.

*Where was he?* he wondered, huffing and puffing, then realizing he'd been running so fast he was out of breath. His heart beat faster, the urge in his groin to see Autumn again making him hard. He had no time for games. She was waiting for him. The pressure for him to create was at its peak, a chaotic storm of hyperactivity. Her lovely, glorious body, stripped of everything but the shimmer of her sweat, was on display at the art studio. He *had* to get there, protect her, *merde*—who was he fooling?—he wanted to drive his cock into her.

He reenergized his creativity from seeing her, touching her, fucking her; yet *she* seemed uneasy with her beauty, as if it were a curse, something he didn't understand. What amazed him even more was her desire he find her intelligent. *That* intrigued him. He'd never questioned that women were either of the fireside or the street. Knowing her made him yearn for the permanency of his own youth. Was such a thing possible? No. According to *la comtesse*, the black magic wouldn't last if he fell in love with the redhead. *What then?* Was passion enough to satisfy the longing in his soul?

Seconds ticked by, the raindrops falling faster, stinging his nose and cheeks with direct hits. He slapped his arms, stomped his feet. If he didn't keep moving, he'd be too wet to go on. Cursing, he went on his way, putting the man in the bowler hat out of his mind. Autumn was waiting for him.

He felt comforted by the falling rain, although a fierce wind was driving swirls of watery drops around him as he pushed forward. He ceased to feel the cold air and the chilly rain beating on his face, his bare hands. He could no longer feel the pavement beneath his feet nor hear the hushed sounds of the *clop-clop* of the horse-drawn conveyances on the streets. He was in the art studio hive consisting of single-story structures looking like tall sheds along an alley.

L'Atelier Gromain was among them.

He turned abruptly on his heel and ran smack into the man in the bowler hat.

"Monsieur Borquet?"

Paul narrowed his eyes. "Why are you following me, monsieur?"

"I have a message for you."

"Message? From whom?"

"His Lordship, the Duke of Malmont," the man said, then before Paul could react, *"Stay away from Mademoiselle Maguire."*

"I'll do no such thing. Out of my way, monsieur, I'm in a hurry."

"You have been warned, monsieur, and since you refuse—"

The man in the bowler hat lurched forward, cursing in English, and swung at him as if to knock his head off his shoulders. Paul ducked under the blow, and without missing a beat, he hit him with a left hook to the stomach. The man reeled backward, caught off balance by the force of the punch.

Paul was ready to hit him again, but a fluid energy was growing in his brain, pressing against the back of his skull, making it difficult for him to see through the gray vapors, the foggy mist. Yet Autumn's face was clear to him in the heat of the moment. An hallucination? He couldn't be sure. He *must* fulfill the destiny torn from him years ago when he'd temporarily lost his sight. No Englishman was going to stop him.

First he must get rid of the pesky man in the bowler hat. With a slow, deliberate hand he pulled his cane apart, exposing the blade attached to the handle. It seemed to float in the air, catching the light in short sparks of energy, taunting their mark.

The man in the bowler hat got uneasily to his feet, saw the blade on the end of his cane, and without hesitation, pulled a small derringer out of his pocket, his finger on the trigger. Paul had no doubt he intended to use the weapon. He wasn't taking any chances on the man being a good shot. With an accurate forward thrust, he slashed a rip across his sleeve, wounding the man. He cried out, dropped the gun, and within seconds, deep red blood oozed through the tear in his tweed overcoat. Paul kicked the gun out of his reach and into an open sewer.

"You bloody French bastard," the man cursed in English.

"You're wrong, monsieur, I'm only half-French. My father was an Englishman," Paul said, his voice hard. "Now you'd best tend to your wound, before you bleed to death."

Ignoring the man tossing off epithets at him, Paul opened the entrance door to L'Atelier Gromain and stepped into the art studio where Autumn waited for him.

# CHAPTER FOURTEEN

P aul wasn't surprised by what he saw. But he wasn't complacent, either. It was the redhead. *Look at her*, flaunting her naked body in front of a room of lecherous men. She was completely shameless, picking up the sheet and twisting it around her body, sliding it down over her moon-white breasts and around her hips to tease the artists like a Pigalle harlot. Nipples turgid, hips slim and smooth, and long, long legs glowing a pleasing golden brown, as if she dared to expose them to the burning, critical eye of the sun. She was tormenting him. Posing nude on the two-foot-high platform, surrounded by the artists at work. Close enough for them to touch her pussy with the tips of their brushes.

He sensed she was enjoying herself. Turning around in a slow circle, facing them, fluffing her hair over one shoulder. He had no idea how long she'd been standing naked on the platform, performing a silent dance with the grace of a bird dipping her wings on a soft, cushiony breeze. A beautiful, pensive smile on her lips dared any man, *every* man, to capture her beauty on canvas. His eyes wandered to her pussy. Curling hairs twisted into a delectable triangular pattern as if she were an edible still life. He wanted to put his cock in her, sliding it in and out, in and out of her cunt until she was liquid and utterly receptive to his every desire.

Paul clenched his fists together with a fierce intensity. How had he survived these past weeks without her?

He took off his jacket and wiped the wetness from around the collar of his white Cossack shirt. He was sweating profusely, in the grip of a feverish urgency. He swore the muses were playing with him, taunting him for all those careless nights and squandered afternoons in the arms of a pretty woman, knowing exactly how to fuck them, the pressure and speed to drive them mad without a thought to what happened afterward.

*Merde,* the pain invaded his head again. Pushing, pulling, tightening his brain. Tearing his heart out. At the same time it was wildly exciting to feel the pulsating erection that made him hard and stiff. He was so tight he felt he would explode. Here, now, if he didn't control himself.

He wanted her. Again and again.

He *would* have her.

He didn't move for several minutes, blink his eyes or loosen the poppy-red scarf around his neck. He was transfixed as the girl turned and faced the artists while rain continued to fall outside. The light and shadow filtering through the thin windowpane glass behind her danced together in riotous excitement over the curves of her body in one perfect line. She shivered as the animated light swirled over her body.

Paul picked up his pencil for the third time, and for the

third time he put it down. His fingers were numb. He couldn't put his chalk to canvas, couldn't get a grip on himself. He put his open flask to his lips and let the absinthe dribble down his parched throat. His heart pumped wildly but he felt his nerves calming. He *had* to get her alone so he could hold her in his arms again. Kiss her, touch her, cover her body with tender pleasures. Having already surrendered to his primal sexual needs, he was surprised to discover it wasn't enough. At the House on rue des Moulins she'd shown him a different side of her, witty, fascinating. He was eager to learn more about her.

Paul closed his eyes and dropped his head into his hands, thinking. He must convince her to leave Paris with him, out of the reach of Madame Chapet. They'd go somewhere, *anywhere,* so they could be together. His old friend, Gauguin, was making plans to go to Tahiti. They could join him on his adventure. Warm sands. Steamy nights. Bare breasts. The thought of it made him hot with an aching desire and frustrated at the same time.

He looked up and saw the wanton, abandoned look in her eyes. She was a wildcat, tawny and bronzed, and he imagined her purring with delight under the reins of a man who could tame her. A man like himself. Roaming his hands over her nude body, marveling at her soft curves, squeezing her small waist, her firm hips, inserting his fingers into her and reveling in the rocking motion of *sa chatte* against his fingers.

It was too much for him to bear.

Heart racing, Paul picked up his cane and walked boldly up to the platform.

* * *

I'm not aware of Paul's presence until he taps his cane on the platform. I look up and see the handsome Impressionist, smiling. Relief floods over me. *He's here.*

He's wearing a black felt hat tipped at an angle and covering part of his face, his long dark hair curling around the collar of his jacket. A bright-red scarf set off with a scarf pin adds a dramatic accent to his otherwise dark-colored clothes. *Wet* clothes.

I want to touch him, make certain he's real, but I hold back. An uneasy silence fills the *atelier* as I continue to stare at him. How long has he been watching me? I wait for the artist to speak, but he continues staring at me, leaning his chin on the cane he holds propped up on the platform.

Fending off my hot desire for his touch, I keep my gaze fixed on him while the others sketch. The rough sounds of pencil and chalk being put to paper in quick, uneven strokes are a strange, eerie accompaniment to the musical sounds of falling raindrops knocking on the windowpanes, trying to get inside.

"I could go on looking at you forever, without eating, without drinking, without sleeping," Paul says finally, smiling and tipping his hat. He's virtually smoldering with ecstasy. I notice his fingers are covered with rough calluses from holding brushes for hours on end. I shiver, thinking about him moving those fingers up my thighs to where my pussy lips open and back down again, torturing me, until I beg him to insert his finger and rub my clit back and forth and bring me to rhythmic orgasm.

"Without making love to me?" I smile back, thinking

about him thrusting into me, my body matching his stroke for stroke. "That wouldn't be any fun, *n'est-ce pas?*"

Paul laughs. "You're not only the most beautiful creature in Paris, but also the most brazen."

"You flatter me, Paul. I'm only an artist's model."

"Ah, but you're *my* model, with a face and body beyond perfection."

Embarrassed, I shrug off the compliment but I can't resist challenging him. "Was it not Delacroix who said the model is merely a point of reference for the artist?"

*Use your brains. Keep him interested.*

"You sound like Monsieur Gromain, mademoiselle. He was a student of Delacroix," Paul comments matter-of-factly. "*Mais oui,* yes, those were the days."

I'm taken aback. What's he talking about? He's young. Not more than his midtwenties.

"I've known Monsieur Gromain since I was a *rapin,* a student," he continues, "carrying my unsold sketches beneath my coatsleeve, sleeping on a stone bench, going without food so I could buy brushes."

I smile weakly. Though I find his conversation intriguing, I can't concentrate on what he's saying. A rumbling in my stomach hits me. Then my head starts to throb and I feel faint. I've been posing, standing, moving, holding my arms up, then down, all morning without a break. I pick up the sheet discarded at my feet, wrap it around me and wipe my face free of the oozing perspiration cooling down my body. I'd give anything for a glass of water. Paul stops talking and stares at me. A look of concern colors his dark eyes a rich blue velvet.

"You look exhausted, *ma chérie*. I'm getting you out of here, now."

"No, Paul," I whisper, "not with everyone looking at us."

I feel the hard stare of Monsieur Gromain watching my every move. With clothes or without, I'm strictly business in his flickering old eyes. He won't let me rest as long as the artists sketch. *Time is money,* I can hear him say. It sounds the same in any language.

Wrapping the sheet tighter around me and trying to take my mind off my sick stomach, I look out the windowpanes. Streaks of silvery rain slide down the glass, but my attention is drawn to a horse and carriage stopping outside the studio. Someone's getting out. A man, then a woman. The woman is wearing a long, blue woolen cape trimmed with feathers, wet and drooping from the rain. Madame Chapet. *But who's the man with her?*

"Drink this, Autumn."

Paul puts a cold, metallic flask to my mouth, and the trickle of a pleasant green liquid kisses my lips with its wetness. Absinthe. I start to push the flask away, but my throat is hot and achy. Dry mouth. Chapped lips. I'm *so* thirsty. Giving in to my need, I take a long sip, then a longer one, surprised at how smoothly it goes down my throat, unlike the first time.

I vaguely remember Paul taking the flask from me and telling me he'll return with more absinthe. I nod, then let the sheet slide down my nude body, exposing my engorged nipples and slim hips as the sound of rain hits harder on the window panes behind me. I pay no attention to it as the alcohol takes ahold of me. I'm in my own universe, sailing, swimming, flying through walls, doors, even time itself.

I turn and see Madame Chapet and the gentleman in the top hat, high celluloid collar and well-cut jacket, chattering, laughing and looking at me. I sense a rapture, a euphoria oozing from the man that goes beyond an interest in art. Then it hits me. This must be the Duke of Malmont.

What is he giving Madame Chapet? Money, I think, and she's putting it into her bosom. Now Monsieur Gromain has his hand out. The gentleman is giving him money, too. How strange.

A man in a bowler hat joins them, though why he has a bandage wrapped around his arm I can only wonder.

Long blissful minutes pass as I continue posing in front of the artists. I've lost any sense of embarrassment. Instead, I flaunt my curves, bumping and grinding my hips and giving them a show they won't forget. I flutter my eyelids several times and by the power of the green enchantress, I feel lighter than air, giddy. I throw my head back, stretch my arms up higher, and sigh deeply. I drift through one seductive pose, then another, my body finding its rhythm in long, graceful movements. I run my hands up over my calves and thighs, then around my hips, then touch myself between the legs, stroking my pussy, then easing two fingers deep inside. Finding myself wet and hot, I circle my clit, moaning when I feel it burn. I hear M. Gromain clear his throat again. With a naughty look in his direction, I remove my fingers but continue to gyrate my hips. I sense the artists are enjoying the show as opposed to sketching a model in pose. I watch my reflection in the shimmering, glimmering windowpanes, my body movements bouncing back and forth in the glass. I forget about Paul, the other artists, Monsieur Gromain, and continue toying with the sheet, twisting and turning it this way and that.

I'm feeling so good, so mellow, I don't give much thought to the Englishman rushing toward me from the back of the room, heading for the platform, his stride long, his intent clearly visible in his eyes. He moves fast, cleanly, and before I know what's happening, he leaps up onto the stage without a word or warning gesture.

"Monsieur, what are you—" I say, blinking.

"*Quiet,* mademoiselle, or I shall have to gag you," he threatens. Before I can close my open mouth he wraps me in the sheet, picks me up in his arms, then slings me over his shoulder. I hear the artists gasp as I thump his back with my fists, my feet kicking wildly, but no one moves. Shocked, confused, flabbergasted, everyone seems frozen, unsure of what is going on.

"*Paul!*" I yell, looking everywhere for him, but he disappeared. Where is he?

"Forget him. I won't allow that artist to have you," the Englishman says, laughing.

"Put her down, monsieur, or I *will* kill you," Paul orders the Englishman, coming from where I don't know, then pulling off the top of his cane to reveal a blade.

"I don't believe you're man enough, Monsieur Borquet," says the gentleman.

Paul says, "We'll see how much a man *you* are, monsieur, after I cut off your cock—"

He starts to rush toward us but the man in a bowler hat

comes up behind the artist and hits him on the back of the head with a lead pipe. He falls to the floor, unconscious. I scream, then scream again, but the Englishman holding me captive pays no attention to my cries. He doesn't wait to see what happens next but runs toward the back door, grunting, with me slung over his shoulder.

"Put me down!" I shout.

"So you can escape? I think not, mademoiselle. I rather enjoy a woman with a reckless nature who engages in such shameless behavior."

"You'll pay for this, monsieur."

"I already have, mademoiselle," he says. "Now be quiet!"

"I will not—*let go of me!*"

"Stop wiggling," he orders.

Damn him. I claw at his jacket, trying to rip it off his back.

"Let go of my jacket."

"You English bastard."

I must get to Paul. He could be badly hurt. Using my strength, I grab the back tail of his jacket and rip open the seam. He curses. Loudly. I sense a deeper brooding, almost evil, lurking behind his gentleman facade.

"You hellion," he yells in English, shocked at my audacity. "If you do that again, I'll dump you in the alley and feed you to the rats." Then he spanks me squarely across my buttocks with a loud smack and tightens his grip on my thighs.

I cry out, hurling every dirty French word I know at him. The blow is so hard it seems to ricochet through my skull. Every muscle in my body tenses in readiness for the next blow. Instead he kicks open the back door of the *atelier* and faces a sheet of driving rain. Big drops splash onto the dirty, slippery cobbles.

"Get ready, my dear," he says. "Your arse is going to get wet."

Dizzy from being slung over his shoulder, I keep beating my fists on his back, calling out Paul's name. It doesn't do any good. The Englishman hurries through the narrow alley, toward the waiting shiny black conveyance half-hidden in a silver-gray fog. He dumps me inside, but not before I glimpse Paul running unsteadily out of the studio toward the carriage speeding off in the rain, horse hooves splashing, wheels sliding, whip cracking. The artist starts after us, his long black cape whipping at his heels, but he can't catch us.

*Paul is alive.* That's all that matters.

Until I look into the cold, luminous eyes of the man holding me captive. In them I see an ungodly desire and a savage hunger to rip the sheet from my body, his fingers tearing at my thighs, then plunging into me, violating me.

My smile disappears.

"You can't kidnap me, monsieur. Madame Chapet will have you arrested."

The gentleman laughs. "I doubt it, mademoiselle. The charming madame has been well rewarded for your services."

"*My* services? Contrary to whatever *la madame* has told you, monsieur, I am *not* a prostitute—"

"Then what are you? An angel from above? A creature from below? For surely with your beauty you have the power to both delight and torment men."

*Damn him.* I'm sick of being treated like a marble statue, a goddess with perfect curves who has no brain, no heart and, least of all, no freedom. My mind races, trying to figure out how to get out of this insane situation. I have no intention of fucking this Englishman. For however long I have this body, I will give myself to *one* man. Paul Borquet.

I can't believe I got myself into such a mess. What if this madman tries to rape me? What then?

In spite of my misgivings, I keep finding excuses to turn around and sneak a peek at him. He's dark and somewhat handsome, although there's a cruelness around his mouth that makes me shiver at the thought of his lips anywhere on my nude body, especially near my soft, juicy pussy, his tongue licking and probing. I tremble, imagining that tongue slithering over the hard ridge of my clit, his saliva mixing with my juices as he proceeds on his journey, darting in and out of me. What if I can't stop him from making me wet? What'll I do then?

I clasp my hand over my chest in a saintly gesture to gather strength and put up an invisible shield between us. Chin up, shoulders back, I try to look defiant but I shiver instead, fighting back a sneeze. What did I expect? A thin sheet isn't much protection from the cold rain. My voice shoots up to a high-pitched tone. "I *insist* you take me back to the art studio."

"No."

"I won't let you touch me."

"I'll tie your hands behind your back."

"I'll kick you."

"I'll tie your legs—spread apart."

He rants on about how he'd enjoy seeing my naked body secured to a metal ring suspended from the ceiling, my arms stretched taut above my head, my breasts sweaty, my nipples hard. I've no doubt his wild fantasy also includes him cracking a thick leather strap over my bare butt.

Fighting to keep my temper, realizing it's useless to argue with him, I turn away, planning my next move. How am I going to escape? The pounding rain on the carriage roof reminds me that I'm trapped inside this vehicle with an insane kidnapper. He won't take his eyes off me, though I wonder what he's looking at. He's already seen me naked.

Embarrassed, I pull the sheet over my exposed thighs, covering them. Nervously I clutch the sheet tighter, ripping it with my nails. I look straight ahead, ignoring the man sitting across from me, staring at nothing, thinking about Paul running after the carriage. He was almost killed trying to help me. *Damn* that Madame Chapet. No doubt this kidnapping scheme is her idea to double her profit.

I pull back the fringed curtain on the carriage window, forgetting the man watching me. Rain pours down in big, heavy drops, gurgling under the coach wheels, the horse hooves sloshing through the puddles. Except for an occasional horse and rider or closed carriage, no one is wandering about on the streets of Paris. No one to hear me if I scream for help. I must convince this Englishman to take me back, even if I have to play damsel in distress.

"If you *are* a gentleman, monsieur," I say with great charm as the carriage slows down to go around a horseless wagon stuck in the middle of the road, "you'll take me back to L'Atelier Gromain so I can get my clothes—"

His eyebrows shoot up at my change in attitude. "I'll buy you new gowns at the House of Worth, mademoiselle. Anything you like."

I sigh, exasperated. "Turn the carriage around...please."

He shakes his head. "You're in no position to request anything, mademoiselle."

I don't answer him. I'll have to try something else.

"I see we understand each other," my kidnapper says. "Good."

"I'll *never* understand men like you," I blurt out, "who believe force is the only way to charm a woman."

He looks surprised at my answer, but he continues with what is on his mind. "I had planned to spend merely an afternoon with you dallying between the sheets and amusing myself by instructing you in the proper manner of pleasing a gentleman, including bending you over and exploring your rear passageway." He rubs his fingers together as if he's stroking my anal hole. I shiver. "That was *before* I saw you naked. Ah, mademoiselle, you were born to massage a man with your beautiful breasts, starting at the navel and working slowly downward until a man's cock quivers with delight and finds itself nestled between your white, rounded orbs."

This time I *do* lose my temper. Making a fist, I stamp my bare feet so hard I feel like I'm walking on hot coals. "Women have come a long way where I come from, monsieur. We bathe without our underwear and we don't act like slaves to men." I stop. I can't reveal any more without arousing his suspicion.

"No need to defend yourself, mademoiselle. I have every

intention of keeping you much longer than an afternoon," he finishes calmly as if I never interrupted him.

"And what does that mean, monsieur?"

He bends closer to me. "I'm offering you my protection."

"Your what?"

"Come, mademoiselle, a woman of your type would gladly give up her position in a *maison privée* to become a gentleman's mistress."

I gulp. "Your *mistress?*"

"Yes. I'm known as a man with an air of distinction. The name of Malmont is highly esteemed in certain London circles."

"Oh? That doesn't change my mind, monsieur. I'm not interested in your proposition," I say, continuing to speak in French, realizing I can't appeal to his sense of chivalry because he obviously doesn't have one, seeing how he treated me like a love slave in need of a good beating. My backside still hurts and is probably glowing red under the sheet.

"You have no choice, mademoiselle. The contract is already done. You are now the mistress of Harry Bingham, Duke of Malmont."

So that's what he gave to Madame Chapet. A contract for my services.

The duke reaches for my hand and brings it up to his lips. I flinch, his touch repulsing me. I pull my hand away, biting my knuckles to stifle the nauseous feeling rising up in my throat.

"Bingham," I repeat, thinking. "You're the gentleman

who's been calling at the House on rue des Moulins every day." It's not a question, but a statement. *Gentleman,* however, is the last word I'd use to describe this raving lunatic.

"Yes. And I've been well rewarded for my patience." He rubs his gloved hand, wet from the rain or sweat, I'm not sure which, over my thigh, pushing away the sheet and exposing my smooth skin. Up and down, in and around, his leather-encased fingers pressing on my flesh and searching for my pussy. What is his game? Does he think I'll get turned on by anticipating his probing touch? No way. I close my legs tighter together to deny him access, though I admit a smoldering white heat settles in my groin, disturbing me. It also gives me an idea.

I'll turn his fantasy into a nightmare. I smile widely, a sign the duke interprets that I'm enjoying myself.

"You'd like it even more if I were to touch you *here,* in your cunt, wouldn't you, mademoiselle?" he whispers, breathing heavier now, putting his finger into my pussy. He bends over me, sniffing and licking his lips as he pushes his finger deeper inside me, searching for my juices. I instinctively flex my butt, drawing in his finger deeper still, though I fight the fiery sensation building in me. "I assure you that you'll scream out with pleasure when I splay the contours of your buttocks with my fingers and fill you with my cock."

*Oh, no, I won't.*

"*You* are the one who will be disappointed, monsieur."

"What?"

"Whatever café gossip you may have heard," I say,

cutting him off. "I am *not* a virgin." I lower my gaze from his surprised face down to the floor of the carriage, waiting to see the effect my words have on him. I sweep my eyes over the rich green velvet fabric lining the coach interior, trying to catch my breath, stalling for time. I can feel the Englishman looking at me, not to mention a chill running through me from a good drenching. I can barely utter a sound, my teeth are chattering so much.

Finally he says, "I should have known better than to believe the fairy tales of a fat, old madam. That bastard Borquet fucked you. Am I right?"

I say nothing. *Don't admit anything.*

"You can't hide it from me, mademoiselle. I see it in your eyes. All dewy and glowing at the mention of the artist's name. I should fuck you now, here in the carriage, and make you cry out for more, *beg* for it." He pulls on my sheet, snarling, ready to tear it off me. Then he relaxes, a different mood settling over him. "However, I need something else from you, mademoiselle, something I can't get if you're lying on your back in ecstasy in what you French call *le petit mort,* the little death."

I look up, surprised. "Monsieur?"

"I want information from you. What do you know about Borquet? Tell me."

He grabs my wrist and holds me tightly. *Too* tightly.

"You're hurting me, monsieur."

He ignores my plea. "Where does he come from? How old is he? Does he have any family?"

"I don't know, monsieur." I bite on my lower lip, trying to keep from crying out.

In disgust, he lets me go. "So, you let him fuck you, but you know nothing about him. Eh, you're just like all the other brothel whores."

"I am *not* a whore," I spit the words out in English, tired of this charade. "I'm an American tourist who happened to find herself in a compromising situation."

His eyes widen. "An American?" He begins laughing. "Well, it doesn't matter. Nobody in this sophisticated world is what they say they are, mademoiselle. Nobody. The pretty clothes, the fancy manners, the coy phrases, they're all a facade." He leans closer and I can smell the fresh rainwater mixing with the woodsy scent lingering on his fine silk jacket. "I thought there was something different about you."

"Does the fact that I'm an American bother you, Lord Bingham?" I ask, hoping to keep him off balance. "Monsieur Borquet finds my colonial humor amusing."

"Forget him. You're mine now."

"I belong to no man."

"You Americans and your bloody independence. It won't help you here. You're bought and paid for with British pound sterling."

"I will *never* let you touch me. Never. I will fight you."

"You'll do as I say or I'll—"

"You'll do what? Whip me with a riding crop until my buttocks are covered with raw red welts? Rape me until I cry out for mercy? I doubt you can even get it up. You're not half the man Paul Borquet is—"

It's the wrong thing to say. I find that out too late when his hand flies through the air and slaps me soundly on the cheek. My face stings as if touched by a searing, red-hot poker from the fire. I put my hand to my cheek, but I don't cry out. Above all I can't let him see I'm frightened. Frightened of being alone with him with nothing more than the flimsy slip of an earthbound ghost between us.

I'm still reeling from his slap when Lord Bingham taps on the ceiling of the carriage and a tiny door opens. Down pops the head of the driver.

"Driver, 64 rue Chalgrin," Lord Bingham says in French, then turns to me. "In spite of your vulgar performance, mademoiselle, I haven't changed my mind. I'm taking you to my apartment on the Right Bank where I can wrap you in fur with only your nude body underneath. Then I will explore your most secret places, while my manservant serves Moët champagne and raw oysters which I will suck off the lips of your cunt—"

"*I will never let you fuck me!*" I yell, jumping up and bumping my head on the padded ceiling. The pain jolts me awake and revs up my courage. I *have* to get out of this carriage. I see the rain coming down in gray, metal sheets and crashing on the cobbles like shattering glass. They promise a better refuge than the padded cell I share with this mad Englishman. No one in their right mind would want to be dumped on a street in Paris wearing no clothes in the middle of a rainstorm. But I haven't been in my right mind since I posed nude in front of the portrait of Paul Borquet.

"I take what I want, mademoiselle," Lord Bingham says, "and I want you."

"*No!*" I cry out, but my voice is stifled as he kisses me, forcing his tongue between my lips and exploring my mouth with a hard driving need fueling his actions with so much energy it startles me. I'm knocked off balance, shaky, repulsed by his kiss. His lips press against mine, forcing my head back, my mouth open, my body jammed against his as I struggle to push him away from me. He keeps trying to expose my breasts, grabbing at my sheet, entangling himself in it, when the padded velvet walls of the coach shake hard, as if the gods of thunder and lightning struck them, rumbling their displeasure. I wiggle, kick, push, flail, *anything* to get him off me. The carriage comes to a sudden stop, tossing us about and pitching the English lord forward onto the other seat, stunned.

"What the bloody hell…" he mumbles.

*This is your moment. Get out of here. Now.*

As I reach for the coach door, the driver, covered from head to toe in a large cape and cap, opens it for me. It's raining so hard I can't see his face under his top hat as he duels with a closed umbrella against a combatant wind, trying to get it open.

"We have a problem, monsieur," the driver says, tilting his hat forward, a well of rainwater spilling from his brim as he continues to struggle with the large, black umbrella.

"What is it, man?" the Englishman asks.

"The wheel is broken, monsieur. We're unable to move on."

I take a deep breath. If I don't make a run for it now, I'll never escape the English lord's cold fingers playing with my wet cunt or him forcing me to suck his cock dry.

Before the Englishman can grab me, clutching my sheet I move toward the door and dash out of the carriage, rain smacking me in the face and the force of the wind pushing me out into the middle of the street. For a moment I wonder if I'm doing the right thing. Half-naked, roaming the streets of Paris, I could catch pneumonia or get lost or worse yet, be picked up by the police again. *What else can I do?* Anyway, I carry with me the feeling some unseen hand is guiding me through this upside-down world and back to Paul.

I see the driver toss his broken umbrella down in disgust, then the Englishman orders him to go after me. The driver tries to explain that's impossible. The duke gets out of the carriage, cracks the whip, cursing without stopping. Yelling at me, calling me names, he starts after me, then with the downpour drenching his clothes, he changes his mind. He gets back inside the coach. He's obviously a pampered Englishman who prefers dry clothes to a naked woman.

I struggle to my feet, but a solid gray wall of bulbous waterdrops blinds my vision, pounding on the cobbles in a steady syncopation and roaring in my ears. Clutching my sheet, pushing my long, wet red hair away from my face, I stumble down a small sidestreet without looking back, down one block, then another through the twisting and turning streets, as far away as I can from the Englishman.

In that moment a man behind me yells out.

"*Faites attention,* mademoiselle. Watch out!"

I turn around in time to see a runaway cart bearing down on me. Speeding, snorting, stopping for no one, the big, brown, ugly workhorses are nearly upon me, so close I can smell the foul odor of their breath mixing with the steamy rain.

I scream but stand as if glued to the spot, my white sheet

slapping around my body in wet bursts of energy. The echo of my own voice is as loud as anything I've ever heard.

"Is she alive?"

"Yes, madame, but she's badly bruised and bleeding."

"I can't bear the sight of blood. I'm going to faint...*going to faint...*" echoes the shrill feminine voice over and over again in my brain.

I moan, moving my head slightly.

"*Ah, mon Dieu,* she's coming to," says the same voice.

"I'll take her back to my studio, madame. There's a doctor nearby."

"No, no, no, she must come with me, monsieur. Put her in my carriage."

"She needs a doctor, Madame Chapet. *Now.*"

"She'll have a doctor, Monsieur Borquet. *Mon cher ami,* Monsieur Lautrec, is on his way to bring his friend, Doctor Bourges, to the House on rue les Moulins."

"I must insist, madame. Your doctor may arrive too late."

"Can *you* pay for a doctor, Monsieur Borquet?"

I hear no reponse, merely a loud sigh.

"Not another word. The girl comes with me."

I feel myself being picked up and carried in a man's strong arms. A warm blanket covers me, and although it's rough against my cheek, it feels good and dry. I snuggle up to the man's muscular chest and grab on to the end of a long scarf, and the familiar manly smell of the artist overpowers my throbbing skull. I must be delirious. I'm in Paul's arms.

The most comforting thing about being in his arms isn't the warmth of them, not the way my head fits into the curve of his shoulder, not the strength and safety his arms give me. Instead, what comforts me most is the perception he cares about me.

"Paul...Paul..." I mouth the words in barely a whisper, but he doesn't hear me. Damn that Englishman for kidnapping me. I'm dazed and disoriented. Drenched to the skin, bruised and nearly killed.

I move. A painful groan escapes from my lips. My face hurts like hell. My throat is raw and raspy. My voice a harsh whisper. Pain inching up my spine. Sharp bursts stabbing, pulling at every nerve in my body. Must be bones broken. But dammit, I'm alive.

I'm going to make it.

I'm a survivor.

# CHAPTER FIFTEEN

Mimosa. I unpin the bunch of wilting flowers from my dressing gown and embrace the simple posies of pink and white blossoms as if they popped through the rich soil and danced on the tree limbs just for me. Most working girls in Paris brothels prefer violets. Big bunches of them, peeking and winking at the gentlemen who take them upstairs and feel them up under their petticoats.

Not me. The light, sweet fragrance of the flower is my favorite scent. Every day for the past two weeks, Paul brings me mimosa, committed to seeing me with or without *la madame*'s permission. He's willing to take any risk to see me, hold me in his arms, his fingers reaching between my legs and moving in me in an intimate manner the second the pompous brothel madam leaves us alone. I could neither resist nor escape his touch. Goody. Goody.

I feel naked this morning without fresh mimosa sitting pretty over my breasts. Paul is late.

Sitting on the divan in the main living room, I close my eyes and hold the delicate flowers up to my nose, savoring the glorious memory that lives on in my mind.

Seeing his handsome face.

Tasting his salty skin with my tongue. Oh, how I love posing for him. Moving my body this way and that. Teasing him. Rolling my tongue over my wet lips. Yesterday he barely touched me, but I was so wet my juices coated his fingers. When he unbuttoned his pants and guided my hand inside his trousers, I felt the huge width of his throbbing cock, making me wish I was in his arms, his bare chest rubbing up against my exposed nipples. Hard and brown, yearning for the bite of his teeth, the caress of his tongue. I, naked as the day I posed in the art studio, and he, wearing only his manly pride, lying side by side, teasing each other with our lips, our fingers. Sighing in ecstasy as his deep kiss inflamed me to want more and more.

My fingers tremble as I pull my dressing gown tighter around me. A different emotion hits me. *Le docteur* is expected any minute for his daily visit. I hate his groping hands and lisping questions as he looks at me suspiciously over his *pince-nez,* tiny glasses. "You have such perfect teeth, mademoiselle, and skin so clear," he says. "I've never seen a young girl with such beautiful breasts. Where do you come from, *ma jolie?*"

His hands and cold fingers linger on my skin, and why is he pinching my nipples? Doctor or not, I'm getting tired of him squeezing my breasts while he pretends to check my heart with his wooden stethoscope.

I smile. Not today. I'm planning a surprise for the doctor to keep his fingers off my flesh.

Doctor Bourges *did* assure me I suffered only bruises. No broken bones. The blow to my head from nearly being trampled by the runaway horses isn't serious. I'll recover in a few weeks, but I need care and rest. That requires money, making *la madame* furious and threatening to throw me out on the street. I made a laughingstock out of her, she insists, acting irresponsibly and running away from the duke.

The Englishman is threatening to ruin *la madame*'s reputation, swearing he won't give her another sou, no matter how much she cajoles him. Worse yet, I can't work as an artist's model *or* a prostitute, which means Madame Chapet receives no commission. Nothing for the time and the money she spent on me.

She showed no remorse about packing me off to *l'hôpital de la charité* until Paul showed up at her doorstep, insisting on paying for my expenses. Not with cash, but with his painting of me. "Let me come every day and finish my painting, Madame Chapet," he insisted, "and you may have it to sell." Only then, smiling and counting up the charges in her head, did she graciously change her mind and let me stay.

And why shouldn't she? Twenty francs each time *le docteur* makes a call. Half a month's salary for the girls in the brothel. Madame Chapet can get a hundred, *two* hundred times that amount for the painting when it's finished. All of Paris is talking about my daring escape from the English duke. The story even appeared in the *Echo of Paris,* a publication which regularly devotes columns to the latest scandals of the *demi-mondaines,* making *la madame* comment: "Ah, *la publicité,* the water that makes my blossoms grow!"

She hired a snooty sick nurse to keep an eye on me, but I threw the woman out on her white starched *derrière* within an hour. I insisted Delphine assist me. I've become fond of the little seamstress and her naughty sense of humor. She's a simple girl, born to poor peasants. She came to work in the House on rue des Moulins because she had nowhere else to go. She's easygoing, quick to laugh but afraid of Madame Chapet, so it hasn't been easy for me to convince her to use her sewing talents to help me.

Humming no particular tune, I sway back and forth, the morning breeze from an open window cooling on my skin before I realize I'm not alone.

"Dreaming of Monsieur Borquet, mademoiselle?"

It's Delphine, her eyes squinting at me and an impish smile turning up the corners of her mouth. She's hiding something behind her back.

"Is it that obvious, Delphine?"

"*Mais oui,* mademoiselle Autumn," Delphine says, then mimicking my accent: "Paul...you are so handsome."

A giggle.

"*Ah, merci,* Paul, you are too kind."

Another giggle.

"What a big cock you have—"

"You were listening yesterday, you little scamp," I tease.

"I was just walking by, and a little breeze whispered the words into my ear, mademoiselle," Delphine says innocently.

"That little breeze didn't happen to tell you where Madame Chapet went this morning, powdered and feathered like a stuffed peacock?"

"*Mais, non,* mademoiselle Autumn, she told no one where she was going, but I heard her say something about a new cabaret in Montmartre."

I frown. New recruits for the brothel, no doubt.

"There's no sign of Monsieur Borquet this morning," I say. "I'm worried, Delphine."

"He'll be here, mademoiselle. I've seen how his eyes glow when he looks at you, then puts his brush to canvas, a look of desire any girl would envy, a deep satisfaction that you belong to him and only him."

"Do I, Delphine? Or do I belong to the strange black magic that brought me here?" I say, knowing the young girl doesn't understand me.

"I feel magic when my Tristan touches me. 'A woman and her petticoats are like the petals of a flower,' he says, 'caressed and adored by her lover as he removes each one.'"

I can't resist asking, "And how many petticoats has your Tristan removed, Delphine?"

"All but the last one, mademoiselle," Delphine says, lowering her eyes. *She's still a virgin.* I'm amused such a thing is possible in the House on rue des Moulins, where the girls are in a constant state of acute arousal and always available to bask in baths of champagne and *monter,* climb the stairs to please a customer.

"I have good news for you, mademoiselle," Delphine announces proudly. Then she looks around to make certain we're alone. "I finished *votre soutien-gorge.* Your bust bodice."

Sticking out her young breasts, Delphine holds up the short breast support she made from two handkerchiefs and satin ribbons. Following my crude sketch, she tied the soft material in the middle to give a clear, natural separation between the breasts and then sewed it to fit over my shoulders, held up by the thin ribbon straps drawn through the hole lacings.

"Oh, it's perfect, Delphine!" I take it from her and hold it up to my breasts.

"*Hélas,* mademoiselle, no Frenchwoman will wear it."

"Why not?"

"It's scandalous. It doesn't cover the midriff."

"A brassière isn't supposed to cover anything but your breasts."

"*Brassière?*" Delphine laughs. "That means 'under the arm' or an undershirt for *un bébé.*"

"Not where I come from," I joke. "Help me into it, Delphine." As she secures the undergarment in back by pulling on the lacings, I see a fancy phaeton pull up in front of the House on rue des Moulins. The doctor's carriage, its black licorice doors shining like polished boots. "We haven't much time." I straighten my shoulders, adjust my straps, and push my breasts upward.

Delphine giggles. "What do you think *le docteur* will say, mademoiselle, when he tries to examine you?"

"I can hardly wait to see his expression."

"Then she is up to receiving gentlemen, Doctor Bourges?"

"Ah, *mais oui,* she is much better, Madame Chapet. She sat up for my morning visit and ate everything I gave her."

I fumble with the wilted flowers, nervously picking off the soft petals and letting them fall to the tips of my backless pink slippers. I suppress my impatience with the doctor— not because I want him to finish the examination, but because I want him out of here quickly before *la madame* realizes I'm well enough to become one of her girls.

"When can she *ouvrir ses jambes,* spread her legs, and go to work for me, monsieur?"

"I can't be sure, madame," the doctor says, holding my wrist and looking into my eyes. I flinch. Finding my pulse and checking my eyes seem to be the extent of his knowledge of neurology. He ignores my questions, pretending he doesn't understand my French, and treating me as if I had nothing more than a fainting spell, then prescribes complete bedrest for two weeks. He enjoys his visits and doesn't want them to end.

"*S'il vous plaît, monsieur le docteur,* I must have an answer." Madame Chapet expresses her opinions boldly, openly, and with little tact, so it should come as no surprise to me when she presses him again with: "When can she fill up *sa jointure,* her money box?"

The doctor clears his throat. "I'll know more after I've examined her, madame." He smiles. I wink at Delphine, grinning. He thinks this is his moment. He takes out his wooden stethoscope and puts it on my chest. The right side. Giving him the opportunity to slide it around, up and over my breasts, then open my dressing gown so he can squeeze my nipples.

"What is this?" his eyes seem to be saying when he feels under my dressing gown. His fingers find only the softness of my bra, blocking his exploration of my flesh.

"Hurry up, *monsieur le docteur,* I have much to do," Madame Chapet urges, fidgeting with her pearl chokers. "I've been invited to the opening of the Moulin Rouge."

"Did you say Moulin Rouge, madame?" I lean forward, sending the doctor reeling backward.

"*Ah, mais oui,* yes, a new dance hall is opening up in Montmartre at the foot of the Butte. It will be the event of the social season. The elite of Paris will be there. *And* the dancers, La Goulue, Nini Pattes-en-l'Air." She leans over and says in a hushed voice, "Monsieur Chéret is working on a poster depicting the *vendeuses d'amour,* priestesses of love, astride donkeys coming to worship at this new shrine of pleasure."

I shake my head in amazement. Hearing about the opening of the Moulin Rouge is like hearing about an old friend.

"...His Lordship, the Duke of Malmont, *insists* I accompany him to the opening," Madame Chapet is saying, removing her tight chokers, one by one, "and that you come along, too, Autumn. I will chaperone you, of course."

Chaperone me? You mean you'll lead me straight to his bedroom so he can manhandle me then fuck me, you old witch.

"But, Madame Chapet, I have nothing to wear," I protest, wondering why Paul hasn't mentioned the cabaret opening to me. A sudden thought makes my throat tighten. Does he disappear *before* the opening night? Oh, God, no.

"Ah, don't worry, *ma jolie,* Delphine will make over something for you."

I look at Delphine. The little seamstress smiles weakly, nodding, telling me she must do whatever *la madame* asks. I understand, but I must talk to Paul. I can't go to the Moulin Rouge with Lord Bingham. I can't.

I look down at the swell of my breasts peeking out from under my new bra. A simple bastion of silk won't stop Lord Bingham from forcing his attentions—and his cock—upon me. I sense a violence in the man boiling below the surface. A violence that frightens me. What am I going to do? *What?*

I raise my eyes and look at Madame Chapet, hating the woman, cursing her. She's fat and greedy and would never open her door to the poor, even if they were dying on her steps. I can expect no help from her. I'm overcome by the terrifying feeling that because of Madame Chapet's lascivious aptitude for money, more and perhaps worse scenarios lie ahead.

I imagine my nude body shaved and oiled, my wrists and ankles tied to a four poster, my skin glowing golden in the soft gaslight. Then what? How many gentlemen will inflict their love of dominance on me in the name of passion, while I lie writhing on a soiled mattress in want of one cock? Paul's.

The doorbell rings and someone announces "the artist" has arrived. For the time being, I fly into my lover's arms and leave my fears behind.


Just inside the receiving salon, seated on a sofa between two mauve silk cushions, I lean back, my body poised toward the intense-looking young man with black, collar-length hair and eyes as dark blue as storm clouds. He clutches a pencil in one hand and charcoal in the other, and although his eyes never seem to leave my face, he moves freely between the two mediums as he puts down his vision on his tall sketch pad.

I can't believe it. Paul Borquet, the lost Impressionist, is in the state of a creative high today *sans* his usual foreplay of caressing my clit with my forefinger, rubbing it back and forth across my hard ridge, the effect of so simple a touch sending pleasurable sensations through both of us. Instead, what he calls his *bouton de rose* throbs for want of release. Untouched. What's a girl to do?

I try to get his attention, moving my hand along my thigh, wetting my lips. No reaction. He hasn't moved for an hour or more, his body rigid, his neck muscles taut like fine steel rods. All he talks about is how he's been waiting so long for this day he won't allow it to slip away. Every second counts. And *please* sit still, he orders me. I long to scratch an itch, but restrain the urge. *That* is somewhat easier to do than trying to ease my discomfort, wishing, praying for him to brush my clit with his lips, then dart his tongue inside me and lap up every ounce of my moisture then do it all over again.

"Is it finished, Paul?" I ask for the third time, wondering why he's sketching me today and not painting me. I was hoping he'd make me come and mix my juices with his oils. Oooh, it's such fun. "My clit is pulsating, clenching and un-clenching, for want of your cock thrusting deep within me—"

"Don't move, Autumn, *please,* I must capture the delicate shadows covering your brow, the rose-peach hue tinting your cheeks, the long curve of your shoulder. You're perfect."

Perfect? Who wants to be perfect?

I want to be normal again. I'd welcome my thirty-four-year-old body with a few extra pounds if it means I can get out of this brothel and away from Madame Chapet and her schemes to sell me to the Englishman. I have one thing to be grateful for this morning. After *le bon docteur* pro-nounced me healthy, with a tormented look in his eyes when Madame Chapet told him his services were no longer needed, the brothel madam went out again, taking Delphine with her, to *Aux Trois Quartiers* department store to buy "the silkiest, shiniest fabric for my new gown," her excitement spilling over about her invitation to the Moulin Rouge. She was so flustered she paid no attention to Paul's arrival, leaving me alone with the artist.

*Très bien,* very well. I wiggle about on the divan, not believing my good luck. The other girls in the House on rue des Moulins come and go at odd hours. This is the first time I've been alone, *completely* alone, with Paul for two weeks and all he wants to do is paint me. I want to touch him. I want *sex,* dammit. What's wrong with the man?

I slip down deeper into the sofa, all the way down, aching to bury my throbbing head in the white astrakhan rugs covering the floor. Soft and furry, the rugs are cut to fit the room, creeping up to the cream-colored walls of the salon. An ache to roll onto the floor wrapped in Paul's arms, his cock pressing against *ma chatte* surges within me, makes me wet my lips. I moan. Loudly. I look over at Paul to see his reaction. Again, *nothing.* His face is sweating, his eyes dilated, his lips parted slightly as if he's experiencing a spiritual high.

Sex isn't on his mind, though he's exciting to watch, his hand moving so quickly through the air, as if an invisible wire guides it through space. All morning he makes sketch after sketch of me, ripping one sheet of paper off the pad then beginning another without pausing for a breath. The curved lines appear quickly, deftly, almost without effort. *Scratch, scratch, scratch.* Pencil on cardboard. Not another sound invades my mind. It hypnotizes me. *Scratch, scratch,*

*scratch*. I don't know how long I sit here, squeezing my pubic muscles together, the sensations burning my cheeks, my dressing gown clutched so tightly in my hand the silk unravels at the ends. I'm totally frustrated. There's no turning on this man.

So, instead, I talk, about how I hate corsets, preferring my bust bodice, which I proudly show to Paul, who insists I take it off so he can sketch my breasts. Well, at least he noticed. I keep talking, he keeps sketching, until finally, he says, "*Je suis fini*. I've finished."

"*Zut alors*, Paul, I thought you'd never say those words." I jump up off the divan and throw my arms around him. I brush his neck, his face with tiny kisses. "Now, my dear sexy artist, it's time for a little artistic expression with your other brush, *n'est-ce pas?*"

Paul seems upset by my request. "There's no time, Autumn. Not now."

"No time to put your cock in me?"

"*Non, ma chérie*—"

"Don't you *ma chérie* me, Paul Borquet. For weeks I've been going through hell, wanting to feel you inside me, filling me—"

"I've got something to ask you, Autumn, but first I want to show you this—"

He lays out his drawings upon the fluffy white rugs. A shiver of anticipation slides down my spine as I lean over to glimpse Paul's sketches of me. A slow pounding beats louder in my chest. The girl in the drawing looks young but sophisticated, in her twenties, *late*-twenties, with green eyes that blaze with the reflection of the hot sun. Seductive, womanly *and* experienced. A lost innocence emanates from those eyes. No hint of youthful wonder or clueless curiosity. Untouchable.

Yet the curve of line, the application of the charcoal, the life he gives to the flat surface are all breathtaking. Frothy chiffon flows up around the young woman's face and her full breasts are like dissipating pink smoke, displaying her exposed flesh, her nipples, and offering the teasing promise of real intimacy to the viewer.

"What do you think, Autumn?"

"Oh, Paul, your work is beautiful, so alive…"

"It's the way I see you, no longer a child, but a woman, the woman I want to hold in my arms…for always."

A shiver settles over me. Isn't this what I want? Yes, but something about the painting disturbs me. Did Paul look into the future? Or am I changing back? *What's happening to me?* I've tried, *really* tried not to fall in love with him. Sex, only sex, but can Min with his perennial hard-on look into my soul? Will I disappear on the capricious whim of a god?

The game is over. I have to tell him who I am, where I come from, before the fates wave their unholy magic and shatter my fantasy like a broken looking glass. I shiver. Why do I suddenly feel cold? Is that the front door opening?

"Paul, I must tell you something—"

"No, first I must ask you to come with me."

"Come with you? Where?"

"To Tahiti."

*"Tahiti?"* My mouth drops open. Is this the answer to the mystery? Paul Borquet doesn't die in a fire, as the old artist

in Marais told me, but goes to Tahiti with *me*. Is it? Did I change the past by coming here?

"My friend Gauguin sold me his ticket on the *Empress of Japan,* the fastest vessel to make a trans-Pacific trip. He'll join us there later. We leave from Cherbourg, then continue around the Cape. I secured your ticket by selling my painting—"

I grab his sleeve. "You sold your masterpiece?"

"Why do I need a painting of you when I'll have the real thing with me always?" The searching look Paul gives me is so penetrating I'm certain he can see into my heart, know my innermost thoughts, and why not? He already has an uncanny knowledge of every freckle on my body.

"But Madame Chapet is expecting you to give *her* the painting."

"*Merde alors,* she can have all the drawings I've done today, more than enough to cover your expenses here."

"So that's why you've been working so hard, why you wouldn't touch me."

"Do you think anything else would stop me, *ma chérie?*" Paul stares at me for a long moment. "Come with me, Autumn, away from Paris, where we can live our lives together—"

"Do you love me, Paul?"

He frowns with the look of a man not used to answering that question. "Love? I...I—"

I barely notice the rustle of a skirt behind me. A man's impatient cough. I want to turn around, but resist the urge to do so.

"You were right, Madame Chapet," says a man's voice. "She is well enough to receive gentlemen."

I pull my hand away from Paul and spin around, my eyes slamming on the tall figure in the dark-gray morning jacket and top hat, his gray-gloved hands clenched into tight fists at his sides. It's the Englishman. Lord Bingham. A sour taste in my mouth makes me grimace. How much did he hear?

"You are intruding, monsieur," Paul says in a grainy tone of voice. The pinched set of wrinkles between his brows clearly says he hasn't forgotten his hatred of the foreigner.

"So I see." Lord Bingham turns to Madame Chapet, tipping his hat and dismissing the artist. He isn't in an argumentative mood. "*A bientôt,* madame. I shall call again when the time is more opportune." Then he leaves.

Madame Chapet runs after him, gasping and choking on her own saliva. "This doesn't change anything, Lord Bingham...the girl is yours...don't forget, the opening of the Moulin Rouge is only a few days away...monsieur... *monsieur!*"

"I should have killed him when I had the chance," Paul mutters harshly under his breath.

"He's not worth it, Paul."

"*Bien sûr,* very well, but I don't trust him. Gauguin told me he's been asking questions about me in the cafés—who my father was, my mother, where I came from, when I came to Paris. *Trou du cul.* Asshole. *Why?* Why is he asking these questions?"

"He's not important, Paul. Not to us," I insist. Squeezing my eyes shut, trying not to think about the horrible Englishman, I reach out to grip his shoulder and wait for him to kiss me.

Sweet, sinfully delicious and oozing with desire, his lips find mine, and the moment is one I'll never forget. The passion is there, yes, and something more. A coupling of our souls catching a ride on a strong tailwind and steering us in a new direction, where we'll be free. *Free to love?* I don't know. I'll tell him the truth about me later.

Paul breaks away first, holding me at arm's length, searching my face for an answer. "You must come to Tahiti with me, Autumn. I won't go without you."

I smile and say simply, "When do we leave?"

# CHAPTER SIXTEEN

I'm in the arms of a man. Naked. His long, dark hair brushes the tips of my nipples, taut with desire as my fingers explore the silkiness of his hair, the strength of his shoulders. His tongue flicks over my breasts, then he bites my nipples and his hands slide down over my hips and move seductively around my waist, squeezing me. His cock is swollen between us, pressing on my groin, begging me to let him in. I smell his desire and sense his urgent need to nuzzle and suck at my throbbing flesh. What more could a girl want? More foreplay, of course.

I part my lips, my head falling backward, and his tongue darts into my mouth, sending warm, delicious sensations through me. He crushes my soft breasts against his powerful chest, pressing his muscular thighs against my firm belly. A piercing hot sensation shoots me, taking my breath away as I surrender to his need. My need. I want to feel him inside me. Hard inside me for a long time until I cry out as he thrusts in and out in a glorious rhythm, faster and faster until—

I sit up with a jolt in the double bed I share with Delphine in the tiny garret in the House on rue des Moulins. My heart hammering. My teeth chattering. I'm dripping with sweat.

I strip off my thin cotton chemise and dab it to my forehead. The room is dark. I'm alone.

Lighting the candle next to my bed, I push the dream out of my mind. I must have been asleep for hours after Paul packed up his paints and brushes and left, promising to come back for me in the early dawn, then going out the back door so as not to run into Madame Chapet. Then *la madame,* smiling and dripping with false concern about my health, insisted I drink a glass of sweet Canary wine.

"Doctor's orders," she cooed.

I pick up the empty glass sitting on the small table next to me and smell it, knowing now why my head throbs. The wine seemed harmless, smelling like cinnamon and cloves. I realize now it contained laudanum, a popular sedative that also includes morphine and opium. No wonder I don't remember climbing upstairs, leaning on Delphine, then falling into a restless sleep.

And dreaming of a realm of secret passions—

"The English duke won't leave you alone, mademoiselle Autumn, until he's plucked *votre gazon,* your pubic hair, with his teeth."

Startled, I look around. I see Delphine. The little seamstress sways back and forth in the old rocking chair in the corner. She's wearing a flannel chemise. Her hands lie still in her lap. What's going through her mind? I wonder as I jump out of bed and sort through the clothes Delphine "borrowed" from the *garderobe* of the girls in the *maison privée.* There has to be something here I can wear.

"Why did you say that about the duke, Delphine?"

"I overheard Lord Bingham tell Madame Chapet he's going to kill Monsieur Borquet because he is a danger to him."

"Paul? A danger to him? That's crazy."

"*Mais oui,* that's what he said and Madame Chapet agreed, but she will say anything if it serves her purpose. Those two are planning something, mademoiselle."

"I don't doubt it. That Englishman frightens me, Delphine."

"*Alors,* mademoiselle, his eyes are angry and swirling with a hatred I don't understand."

"That's why I must leave before Madame Chapet rattles downstairs to have her morning *petit noir,* her black coffee, and pastry."

"I'm afraid for you, mademoiselle Autumn. I don't trust *la madame.*"

I smirk. "You mean the drugged wine she gave me?"

Delphine nods. The girl's brow is moist with perspiration. She becomes quiet and says nothing. She's trying to warn me. I see a dark, brooding look lurking on her face. Finally she says, "Madame Chapet is an evil woman who would just as soon see you dead if she could make a profit from it."

"I *will* be dead if she discovers my plan." I slip into *les dessous,* a linen chemise, along with a pair of knee-length linen pantaloons adorned with white ribbon—slit down the inner thighs and with a convenient back door. And two petticoats—one linen and the other a pale pink silk with a frothy lace ruffle attached to the hem—rolled stockings along with my makeshift bra. I adjust the straps. Despite Delphine's shocked protests, I won't give it up.

She has other ideas about me wearing a corset.

"You *must* wear a corset, mademoiselle Autumn. It's *de rigueur* for a lady," Delphine insists, showing me the whale-boned contraption that begins under the armpits and ends down around the knees with two flat iron springs in the back and two others along the hips, along with a *tirette*, cord, between the legs.

"I'm running away to Tahiti, Delphine, not going for a walk in the woods."

"You don't want to arouse suspicion, mademoiselle. All the ladies of *le gratin* wear corsets, as well as the beautiful *demi-mondaines*."

I smile at her remark. To the young seamstress, being dressed properly, whether born to the manor or on the streets, is what counts in the order of things.

"I'm not a lady, Delphine, I'm…" I bite my tongue. I'm in a dilemma. Delphine will never say it, but I will. I am *une belle,* an artist's mistress. Regardless of any rules I've broken against society, I'm falling in love with Paul Borquet. I keep pushing those thoughts out of my mind, but they keep popping up. Yes, I know what's happening to me. Min's having a laugh at my expense. My waist is bigger, a little tummy is starting to show, and do I see tiny wrinkles around my eyes? How much longer before I change back to my old body?

Smiling at Delphine, who is shocked at my breach in female conduct, I toss the corset aside and finish dressing in a dark blue cloth jacket and skirt worn with a high-necked white surah blouse and blue satin belt. For a final touch, I plop an old hat on my head, taking care to arrange it on my high-piled hair at just the right angle. Its one surviving feather curves down over my cheek, giving me a saucy attitude. Delphine plucks an extra hat pin from her pin cushion and gives it to me: the cabochon of a beautiful butterfly in transparent enamel.

I check my softly rounded silhouette in the mirror, my curves accentuated even without a tight corset. I smile, pleased with what I see. I'm slowly changing back, but I'm still hot.

Though my situation in the House on rue des Moulins has at times been dreadful, I take some solace from the certainty the worst is behind me. I'll soon be with the man I love. I have no place to go but up.

This is Tuesday morning. Early.

Paul stared at the smoky-colored bottle. Stared long and hard. Nothing changed. It was empty. He crushed the crumbly bottle cork between his thumb and forefinger, then put it up to his nose so he could inhale the strong bitters. A redolent aroma seeped up his nostrils but it wasn't enough. He tossed the cork pieces onto the floor and cursed in frustration, as if the green enchantress had deserted him.

*I must appear drunk. Trick the men who are following me.*

He'd been tailed ever since he left his studio in Montmartre, winding his way through the streets of Paris, finally ending up in a brasserie in Montparnasse on the Left Bank. The Englishman had set his bodyguards on him, but another more ominous problem shattered his confidence. His hands were more callused, his face lined, his jaw more angular. His youth, the black magic bestowed upon him by *la comtesse*, was slowly ebbing from his body, a little more each day.

*Why?* He knew the answer. He couldn't stop himself from falling in love with Autumn. *Mais oui,* she stimulated him as no woman ever had, her body eager and hungry to please him, bucking underneath him, grinding her hips and forcing him deep inside her, his cock throbbing as she took him to the point of no return. She drove him mad, making him powerless to love another woman, but he wanted more from her than experiencing her physical delights, her skin as delicate as his most elegant brushstrokes, her nipples as perfect as the tip of his best sable brush, her pussy oozing with desire. She whetted his curiosity to know her as a woman, something he'd shunned away from in the past. He prayed he'd have that opportunity.

Sitting at the table, waiting for his friend Gauguin to arrive, Paul began to sweat. He was at the peak of his genius, and his youth was the price he must pay. But he wouldn't give up Autumn. No, *never.* He loved her deeply.

He moaned, cursed, keeping up his act, demonstrating loudly his need for the strong absinthe. "Like putting on a new skin, it was," he mumbled. Instead he must endure the agony of a symphony of ragged musical notes reverberating in his head, slamming loud noises into the dark recesses of his brain. At least it drowned out the noise of the billiard players cracking the ivory balls against one another. He pushed out the huffing and puffing of the steam organ trying to grind out a tune on worn pipes that had known too many sad and lonely nights. He wouldn't join in the drunken choruses of the revelers spending the late night in the brasserie on the rue de la Gaîeté.

Instead he sat alone, although he was known by the other

artists and poets and writers in the café welcoming in the new day with plenty of drink. He ignored them, wondering who among them was watching him. Instead he focused on the liqueurs in glistening decanters of yellow, orange, white translucence sitting on every table. And green.

"Nothing matters but her," he mumbled loudly, "my green enchantress. Another bottle, madame, *vite, vite!*" He waved his arms about, slapping the air wildly and thumping the fat waitress on the rump with the back of his hand. She turned around, ready to heave a cold, dressed Bresse chicken into his lap, but she let the pullet dangle by its blue feet when she saw who had dared assault her backside.

"Ah, so it's you with the fancy hands, Monsieur Borquet." She shook her bosom and rolled her tongue over her thin lips. "If it was anybody but the likes of you, I'd have their head for grabbing me arse without handing over drink money first." She set the chicken down on a plate and shoved it in front of him, bending over so he was sure to get an eyeful of more than the food. Deep cleavage oozing with sweat and grease grabbed his attention. Then the woman pushed his face into her half-exposed bosom guiding his mouth toward her hard brown nipple. He gritted his teeth to keep his mouth closed, though he was tempted to nip on her breast. "*You* can have what you want, monsieur."

Denying them both that pleasure, Paul slumped down into his seat, pulling his head away from her invitation. He *couldn't* give up his act. Gauguin hadn't shown up yet. Without the identity cards he had promised him, they would only make it as far as Cherbourg.

"Get me another bottle, madame. Another bottle…"

"Eh, you've had enough, monsieur."

Disgust and disapproval changed the tone of her voice, but Paul continued to act too drunk to waste what little consciousness he had left to be charming. He had seen the man in the bowler hat rush off, most likely to inform the duke of his whereabouts, leaving the other man to watch him.

"*Another bottle,* I said."

"I'll be closing soon. Now be off with you, monsieur."

"*No.* I want another bottle!"

"*Merde,* all you artists are alike. Drinking, drinking, drinking. I don't know when you find time to paint."

Paul put his head in his hands, covering his ears. Where was Gauguin? He spread his fingers through his long dark hair, tangled with frustration and worry. Sitting at a dark oak table under copper pots and pans hanging on the walls alongside old weapons and pewter, drinking with other artists and art dealers who often held court here. His brain had been on a strange journey since the night he'd first seen Autumn stripping in his studio, the vision of her, naked, stirring in his soul as well as his groin. Her exquisite body shimmering with beads of perspiration dampening the folds of her *minon* and drizzling down her full breasts like sparkling diamonds melting from the heat of her arousal. Young and beautiful, a sense of magic surrounding her. How long before he would hold her in his arms again? Would she accept him as he was without the vigor of his youth?

"*Hélas,* here's your bottle, monsieur." The waitress held out a bottle of absinthe, pity warming her coarse voice. Paul reached for the dusty bottle, the saliva forming in his mouth, his heartbeat racing.

"First you *pay!*" said the woman.

Startled by her words, Paul held his hand in midair, as if it were made of stone. *Pay?* he seemed to be saying. He couldn't. He had to keep his money for their voyage.

Continuing his act, he fumbled through his paint-splashed jacket, sweat mixing with the scarlets and blues and golds melting into a faded rainbow on the worn fabric. No coin jingled, his eyes told her. Then he looked through his cape. No folded-up franc note rustled.

"Take your money, madame, and leave us alone."

Paul was immediately alert. Who had spoken? The voice barreled out the command with such authority, rich and arrogant. Who was it? Slowly he looked around to see a man shove several franc notes at the woman and grab the bottle from her.

"It's you, Gauguin," he said simply. He smiled, reaching out to hug his old friend.

*"Bonjour, Paul, mon copain,"* Gauguin said, joining him at his table. The imposing artist was a regular at the café, but Paul didn't know the other man sitting down with him. Short, round like a pomegranate, prickly and pock-marked, with a sly glance toward Paul that told him he was used to being stared at but he had gotten over it long ago.

*"Merci,"* Paul answered, drinking a glass of absinthe and keeping his eye on the gentleman. For that's what he must be in his fancy clothes, even if they pulled too tightly around his middle and were wrinkled and ill fitting, as if they weren't made for him.

"Paul, meet Monsieur Morand," Gauguin said good-naturedly, "a junk dealer I've known since my old days as a sailor. He just opened up a shop in the Marais district."

"Antiques, *s'il vous plaît,* Monsieur Gauguin," the man corrected him. Paul noted that his voice, high-pitched and hollow, didn't fit him either.

Gauguin nodded. "Monsieur Morand deals in antiques and art, Paul. *And* items of contraband. I've told him about you."

Paul leaned in, excitement rushing through him and filling him with a different high. *Morand?* Where had he heard that name? "Do you have the identity cards, monsieur?"

Wiggling his nose and jutting chin, the junk dealer removed a brown packet from inside his coat. Monsieur Morand tugged at the tiny pockets on his vest to give himself importance as he said, "Everything you need is in that envelope, Monsieur Borquet."

The man rattled on for several minutes about how difficult it was for him to secure *two* identity cards, and how much it had cost him. Paul nodded. He had given the money earlier to Gauguin; now the junk dealer wanted more. The two men haggled over the price, finally agreeing on an amount. Paul gave him more money; the junk dealer gave him the brown packet. His mind floated in and out of the scene. He was tottering on the edge of his seat when the men finally exchanged goodbyes, Gauguin taking off with the other man.

Standing automatically, then sitting down after they left, Paul finished the bottle of absinthe, singing along with the gentle, puffing notes of the steam organ. He couldn't contain his joy. He hugged the fat, jolly waitress and laughed when she squeezed the bulge between his legs and whispered in his ear how she would open her cunt to receive his cock then move against him, riding his rigid obelisk with abandon. Laughing, he kissed the rounded flesh spilling out of her low-cut bodice, all the while he was making plans. He had more than enough money left for their trip to Tahiti.

Tottering, his bottle in hand, he left the bar. Anxiously he looked around the alley for movement. With the dawn breaking through the fog, he couldn't see if anyone followed him, for the mist swirled around him like ghosts in search of a graveyard. He prayed that, in what appeared to be his drunken state, whoever was following him would be unable to track him on his route to freedom.

I settle back in my chair in front of the window. It'll be 4:00 a.m. if the downstairs chimes stop after the next bong.

*Bong.*

I close my eyes, daring it to chime again. Silence. In an hour it will be 5:00 a.m. and then dawn, and I'll still be here, sitting in front of the open window on the fifth-floor garret in the House on rue des Moulins, waiting for Paul Borquet. Where is he? Is the whole thing a dream, designed to shred the core of my being into a hopeless illusion? But the darkness seems friendly this morning, lifting up its somber black cloak and coating everything with a shimmer of misty fog to hide my secret meeting with my lover.

*If* he ever gets here. Something's wrong. I feel it.

I take a deep breath. The air is cool, inviting. A steady thumping, then clanging, then thumping again disturbs the peace of the night outside, startling me out of my thoughts. A stray cat, a dog, maybe a *chiffonnier,* a ragpicker. I lean my head against the wingback chair and stare down into the street, wondering who the offending culprit is—

I jerk forward, jump up and stare out the window. What if it *is* Paul? Do I dare hope? I see a figure moving quickly through the trash piled up along the pavements, trying to keep out of sight. It's a *chiffonnier,* like the woman I met weeks ago when this whole adventure began. I start to sit down when movement catches my eye and I look toward the street. A man, tall and straight, his black felt hat tipped at an angle, his broad shoulders setting off the classic cut of his long black cape, strides purposely toward the House on rue des Moulins.

*Paul.*

I pull in my emotions, watching him with anticipation and a new fear of the future. I'm not the same young girl I was with the perfect body. I stand up straighter, holding in my stomach. Will Paul still love me?

Cautiously I make my way down the stairs, one floor, then two, three, four, until I find myself on the landing above the grand salon. I take a deep breath, though I'm careful to let it out quietly. Delphine is asleep in the living room, her sewing in her lap. I don't want to wake her.

I inch down the stairway, keeping in the shadows, listening for any sound. Slowly, quietly, I open the door and go outside. I grab the lit lantern *la madame* always leaves on the stoop, shove it aside to set the scene in as little light as possible, then before Paul can say anything, I hug him and utter a word torn straight from my gut.

"Paul."

"Autumn, *ma chérie,* I prayed you'd be waiting for me."

Rich, blue eyes, dark and wary, stare back at me. I gasp loudly, then shake my head, amazed. Paul looks different somehow. Sexier than any male I've ever seen. Athletic and virile with sinewy muscular shoulders, it's as if he's taken on the very interesting aura of a man comfortable with his masculinity, who knows his strength. As for his resilience, well, a slow undulating nudge of my hip to his groin produces a tantalizing tingle that can only be called a tiny orgasm. My pussy starts to contract around what I'd only describe as his phantom cock, finding its own rhythm. In and out...then again and again. *Mmm...*what's happening? Whatever it is, I like it.

"*Allons,* we must go." Paul takes me by the arm. "The train from Gare St.-Lazare to Cherbourg leaves soon."

St.-Lazare? That's a word I hoped never to hear again. Now it means my freedom.

Entering the quiet, fog-shrouded dawn, I contemplate how strange life's twists and turns can be, how only weeks ago I nearly married a man because we had the same tastes, social status, even the same friends. Now I'm running away with a man, *sans* marriage, without money, without a future, without even a place to sleep the next night. Yet I have no regrets.

Whatever happens, I wouldn't change it.

Yet somehow I know I *can't* change anything.

Black magic works that way, doesn't it?

Walking arm in arm with my handsome artist, I realize this is the first time I felt safe since my trip back through time.

*Watch out, kiddo. Tuesday isn't over yet.*

\* \* \*

Through the neighborhood surrounding l'avenue de l'Opéra, past the entrance to the Louvre, then winding through the courtyard to the Jardin du Carrousel, through the maze of the arcade shops along the rue de Rivoli stretching up to the rue Saint-Honoré, we move quickly and silently, our senses alert, trying to shake the men following us.

"We'll *never* lose them, Paul," I say, trying to catch my breath. Sooner or later we're going to turn down the wrong street, find ourselves in the unbelievable situation of having to fight off whoever is following us. Immediately after leaving the house on rue des Moulins, Paul alerted me we were in danger, so instead of heading directly to the Gare St.-Lazare train station, we have to get rid of the men tailing us. Quickly. Or we'll miss our train.

It's Lord Bingham and his men, Paul tells me. The thought chills me. How could I have believed I could run away so easily?

"Stay close to me, Autumn. I know these streets. The duke and his men do not."

He grabs my hand and we shoot across the street in the middle of a chorus of blaring horns as a *cocher* atop a carriage swerves his horses just in time to avoid hitting us. We try to melt into the early-morning crowd of pedestrians with umbrellas under their arms as the fog turns into a graceful mist curling around us.

"Please, Paul, *wait…*"

"We can't stop, Autumn. I can't let them take you from me."

I squeeze his arm. "*No one* can separate us, Paul."

But when I turn my head and spot a man walking fast behind us, then another, I have the terrible feeling our escape is doomed. Why can't we live our lives? What the hell is wrong with this maniacal Englishman who won't leave us alone?

Feeling the tension of Paul's arm on mine, the touch of his body pressed up against me, I don't have to look at him to know what's on his mind. We won't give up.

Paul pulls me inside the passage of the Galerie Véro-Dodat. I feel the magic of a closed silence at work, eager to hide anyone who enters under its invisible cloak of dark, paneled shops. It's only logical Paul will try to lose them here. The passages are familiar to him, the wooden shop fronts intact with their multiple brass-arched window frames and little colonnettes.

The numerous shopping arcades stretch over blocks and blocks, starting near the Louvre and ending at the Grand Boulevard, like a hidden, interior city of skylight-covered passages. Gas lamps, the only light streaming down through the long, pitched skylights, offer a spiritual feeling, reflecting off the diamond-pattern, black-and-white-mosaic tile floor.

I glance behind me down the long passageway. No sign of the duke or his men, yet I sense they're close behind us, like animals tracking the scent of a stray from the pack.

We hurry past a printer's shop, a leather-goods shop, and a tobacco kiosk. Did we escape from the men tailing us? We can't be sure. Running out of time, Paul suggests we split up. He'll take on the duke and his men one by one, he boasts. I say *no*. I don't want to take the chance of losing him again. We've come too far. Reluctantly he agrees.

Then we see the duke, followed by the man in the bowler hat, coming out of a café-brasserie at the west end. Paul turns and, seeing the men in pursuit, we take off through another passageway. The duke and the man in the bowler hat, with another man at his heels, follow us down one long block through a quiet side entrance to the Palais Royal. Then two more blocks. Three.

"Don't let go of my hand, Autumn."

"I'll never let go," I say, my words coming in short breaths as we run through the passage, the seduction of the alcove shadows giving me some comfort. Paul is playing a game with our pursuers, dodging in and out of shops, trying to tire them in their search. With my long dress and petticoats hoisted up around my knees and my boots pinching my feet, I keep going, ignoring the pedestrians, the shopkeepers gawking at us then shrugging their shoulders. *Vivre et laissez vivre*. Live and let live.

"What if the duke and his men catch us, Paul?"

He looks at me, then answers the lingering question in my eyes before I can ask it. "I'll kill them," he says, "rather than let anyone hurt you."

Minutes later, our hands clasped together, our breaths ragged, our hearts pounding, we exit the passage. The canopy of rainy mist has fully arced over the lime trees in the garden near the Palais Royal by the time we cut across the park and reach the entrance to the Galerie Colbert.

Jerking my head around, barely avoiding colliding with a young man rolling a hoop past us, I see the duke and his men not far behind us. Chilling vibrations tingle through me as Paul swirls his cape around us both and we bolt through another passageway. Narrow and crowded with shops, he keeps looking over his shoulder. People crowd behind us and he makes no excuse when he elbows his way through them. He knows this passage well. Here, in these *galeries de bois,* wooden arcades, he tells me, he often picks up prostitutes for his models.

We dash into a *sauna-hamman,* a Turkish bath. Paul holds me close to him. Casually, trying not to bring attention to ourselves, we wander through the bathhouse. The duke and his men won't find us here. They'll be looking for us in the passage, not in a bathhouse where all the patrons are hidden by the hot steam. We duck behind one curtain, then another, naked men eyeing me with interest, their erect cocks curling upward like the curved handle of a gentleman's fancy cane.

"In here, Autumn, quickly," Paul orders, pulling me into a small alcove. A curtain is all that stands between us and a steam room filled with naked men, sweating and muttering among themselves about how they'd like to strip away my modesty along with my clothes, dragging down the frail silk of my blouse to expose my breasts, then ripping away my skirt and holding me down in the steam room while they take turns fucking me in my garters. Their filthy talk disgusts me. And Paul. He holds me closer, protecting me from their stares, if not their thoughts.

I sense someone moving. From a dark corner of the bathhouse, seeped in misty steam spilling out of the heated rooms, the footsteps of more than one man—three? I question—approach us. Loud. Steps that seem at odds with the soothing peace of the quiet, meditative bathhouse, as if they tread with no thought to anything but their mission. Clearly, they have no fear.

"Paul, I hear someone coming."

"Stay behind me, Autumn," Paul orders, drawing the blade from the end of his cane. He swings it forward into the steam, parting the heavy vapor as if it were a flimsy curtain. Before I understand what's happening, someone flashes out of the other side of the curtain behind us and seizes Paul by the throat, cutting off his windpipe with a rope. He tries to yell out, drops his cane, falls to his knees and struggles wildly with his captor. I grab onto the rope but drop it when I feel an arm thrust down around my breasts, holding me fast, but I can still kick my feet and do so, knocking my attacker off balance. The man regains the advantage and holds me tighter.

"Paul, *watch out!*" I yell, warning him as the man holding me raises his foot to kick him in the face. Still gasping for air, the artist blocks the kick and gets to his feet. He reels backward as the man in the bowler hat pulls on the rope, but he lands a solid punch at the other man's face and the man goes down and stays down, dragging me with him.

I hit the floor hard, knocking the breath out of me. I twist my head, my hand reaching out to Paul. He turns toward me and appears to contemplate whether to grab me or punch the man on the ground in the face. Opting to do neither, he surprises the man holding the rope by spinning around so quickly he knocks him off balance and throws a hard punch into his stomach. The man recoils, at the same time pulling the rope tighter around his neck, gagging the artist.

My heart drops like a stone hitting the ground. "Paul! *Paul!*"

Gasping for breath, Paul struggles with the man holding the rope, his fury at what his attacker is trying to do to him makes his hands like steel, wielding an unbelievable strength. It's not enough. He can't loosen the rope cutting off his air. I swear his neck's going to snap.

"Stop, stop, *stop!*" I cry over and over again, my anguish so great, my fear of losing him so absolute, I fail to notice the appearance of the duke from behind the curtain, his dark, somber clothes hiding his intentions as well as his identity.

"Kill him," he orders.

"*No!*" I scream.

Lord Bingham eyes me with a seething lust that even in the heat of his moment of triumph flows to his groin. I've no doubt his dick is hard from the thrill of the chase and catching his quarry more than from the promise of sex. I doubt if the man, repulsive and vulgar as he is, harbors any real feeling for a woman. I imagine he suffers from the grand delusion that money and a title make up for a lack of machismo. I shiver, aware of his eyes slowly crawling over me and lingering on my rear. I'm certain the only affection I can expect from him is the raw kiss of leather on my butt. "And why shouldn't I kill him, mademoiselle? He stole property from me."

"He stole *nothing* from you."

"Oh, no? You're bought and paid for, mademoiselle."

"You're insane!"

"Am I? A contract between the madam of a brothel and her client is as binding as the purchase of any property."

"I don't know what kind of archaic law you're trying to enforce, Lord Bingham, but you can't murder a man for running away with me."

The Englishman laughs, then searches through Paul's pockets, pulling out a brown envelope. He opens it and takes out several pieces of folded papers with official-looking stamps. "What's this? Forged identity cards? Passages to Tahiti? You Americans are so romantic and *so* foolish." He leans over me, baring his teeth. "It's also a matter of convenience for me to be rid of the artist, made-moiselle, though I shall keep my reasons to myself." He walks over to Paul, unable to speak, his throat choked by the rope, the second man now on his feet, restraining Paul's hands behind his back. "And now, Monsieur Borquet, I believe we have a gentleman's score to settle."

With a shudder of horror, I watch as the duke draws a gun from inside his coat and points it directly at Paul's heart. I can't, *won't* let this madman kill him, whatever the cost to myself.

I break away from the man holding me and rush in front of Paul, blocking him, the gun pointing at me. "I won't let you kill him, monsieur."

"Out of my way, mademoiselle."

"Listen to me, *please*."

"Why should I?"

"I'll do what you want, monsieur. I'll go with you to the Moulin Rouge—" I pause "—and I'll cry out with pleasure when you pull up my petticoats then drag down my panta-loons and expose my pussy, then slip your hand between my thighs and—"

"Go on."

I swallow hard, finding my voice and forcing the words. "And moan when you grab me, your fingers working their way inside me and opening my lips to your cock."

Behind me I hear Paul gasping for air, trying to speak, but nothing can stop me from doing what I have to do.

"So the beautiful mademoiselle will give her cunt to me *willingly,* without restraint?"

"Yes, monsieur."

"You will be my slave and serve me in my bed as your master, beg me to crack the devil's tail upon your nude breasts, your arse, making your skin burn and glow before I fuck you?"

"Yes."

"You will caress my balls, lick them, then open your pussy to me *anytime* my cock seeks entry into your trembling cunt?"

"Yes!"

"Allow me to ravish you any way I desire? With one of Madame Chapet's girls sodomizing you with a dildo, another with her tongue lapping at your clit while I watch?" His cruel eyes stare down into mine, savoring my humiliation and distress.

"Yes!"

*What I am saying? What am I thinking? Have I gone mad?*

"You have chosen your destiny, mademoiselle. I accept your proposal." The duke signals to the man in the bowler hat holding the rope restraining Paul. "Loosen the rope but keep his hands tied and escort him to the train station. Both

you men stay with him until he gets on that boat to Tahiti."
He turns to Paul. "I apologize for the inconvenience of your
restraints, Monsieur Borquet, but it is most necessary."
Then he pulls me close to him, running his gloved fingers
up and down my body, cupping and stroking my breasts,
then grabbing my crotch and rubbing his leather fingertips
against my groin, his bold actions claiming me for himself.
I cringe. I've no doubt he'd lift my petticoats and jam his
dirty fingers into me if he could. "I wish you a pleasant sea
journey, monsieur, while I enjoy seducing then fucking the
mademoiselle, so beautiful, so charming…and with so much
courage."

"You *bastard!* You won't get away with this, monsieur,"
Paul gasps, his throat hoarse, his voice cracking. "I *will* kill
you."

"If you try to return to Paris, monsieur, my men have
orders to tie the beautiful mademoiselle naked to four
bedposts and slit her throat." He tips his hat. "*Bon voyage,*
Monsieur Borquet."

Paul turns to me. "I won't let you sacrifice yourself for
me, Autumn."

My eyes fill with tears. "I *must*. I can't let him kill you,
Paul."

My shoulders slump.

My heart sinks into a deep despair.

My body is numb, legs rigid, arms without feeling. Even
my pussy is in a trance, its smooth pink walls still and silent,
no throbbing.

I have no doubt the duke will fulfill all his unholy
demands upon me, and the thought sickens me.

Then I feel nothing at all as the duke grabs me around the waist and leads me out of the bathhouse, out of the passage and into a hellfire from which there is no escape.

Both Nicole Kidman and I agree the duke in Moulin Rouge was not only a schmuck but a wuss. Lucky Nicole. She didn't have to deal with the duke from my story. His sexual appetite is triple X. Men like him think they're doing Madame Chapet's girls a favor if they pay them more to give it to them up their ass.

How did I get myself into this mess? I've lost Paul Borquet and I'm about to go postal—sexually speaking—with a mad Englishman.

But the Egyptian god Min has a surprise for me. Dicks, I mean, things aren't always what they seem. What's real and what's fantasy can exist side by side, the action scrolling from one scene to the next like split-screen TV.

So rev up your mojo and get ready for prime-time entertainment. The good thing is I'm off to meet the voulez-vous coucher chicks from Moulin Rouge. Will I change back to my old body before the big opening night? Will the duke get to fuck me? Or will he discover the truth about me? Stay tuned.

But I'm not the only one with a secret and that leads to:

*Déception (Deception)*

One is easily fooled by that which one loves.
—Jean Baptiste Poquelin Molière
(1622-1673)

# CHAPTER SEVENTEEN

I stand up straighter on the small round platform in the salon of the House of Worth, holding in my breath, trying not to move, though I feel as if I'm being stuck with a thousand little pricks—I mean *pins*. I arrived in a carriage early this morning with Lord Bingham to the couture house on rue de la Paix, met by the famous director himself. Then we were escorted to the salon to watch the parading models present the latest designs.

Turning, raising their arms, bending their heads, stooping, sitting down, the mannequins moved with grace through the salon while *les vendeuses,* the salesgirls, in their plain black skirts and white blouses dotted the room like punctuation marks on an empty page. With their order books in hand, they spoke only when spoken to, ready to suggest a new eccentric color in vogue or assure the client a gown was *le dernier cri*. The duke created a furor, insisting he must have the most expensive gown in the salon for me to wear to the opening of the Moulin Rouge.

He's also driving me crazy. Nudging, touching, cooing dirty words in bad French in my ear—calling my pussy *un mallier,* a spitfire, is too much—squeezing my breasts, licking my thighs with his tongue then nibbling on my labes after he picks his teeth, everything *but* fucking me, although he boasts he has an erect penis just waiting for me.

What he's waiting for, I can only guess, though he constantly drops hints about a night of pleasure where the men wear masks and the women wear nothing but a pretty face and the fucking goes on until dawn. I shiver. A secret ceremony where they worship the devil and deflower a virgin on the scarlet and black altar to atone for their sins. A foul taste from his lips lingers in my mouth from his kiss. Too much about this Englishman disgusts me, makes my body shudder and my stomach clench with dread.

Will I ever see Paul again and feel the strength of his arms around me? His cock arousing me with the need of him? Filling me up? Then coming inside me, the sensation spiraling through me when he explodes like lightning striking us. I remember it was lightning that brought me here. I would crawl to him now if I could, but he's on his way to Tahiti. Without me. He's safe. That's all that matters to me.

I solved the mystery of the disappearance of Paul Borquet, and I wish to hell it hadn't ended like this.

I concentrate on the dress being fitted on me. The décolleté neckline of the silver-rose-blue lamé exposes the upper part of my bosom and arms and shoulders, something the head fitter contends is widely regarded as aristocratic. The bodice is emphasized by added lace, and although I maintain I don't need them, the woman eagerly stuffs pads packed with bleached horsehair in my bra to push my breasts up even more.

"What is *l'amour* without illusion, mademoiselle?" says

the head fitter, trying unsuccessfully to straighten my bra straps, but the silk ribbons won't lie flat. "Men love to be deceived."

*Deceived* is hardly the word. It's my one source of amusement. Lord Bingham believes he's engaging the affections of a young, beautiful girl with a perfect body, but oh what a surprise I have in store for him, what games I intend to play with his mind now that I'm certain Paul is safely out of Paris and on his way to Tahiti.

For surely he wouldn't return to Paris with the duke's hounds after him, would he?

I don't dare dream about escape. The duke is too powerful, has too much money, too many connections to make that possible. All I can do is endure his ridiculous attempts to seduce me, including a night at Maxim's pinching my *derrière* and forcing champagne down my throat, then placing gold coins on the tongues of the waiters and blessing them with the sign of the cross like a bishop. He hinted I could also receive gold coins. Not on my tongue, but between the lips of my pussy, nestled in its moist folds. I finished my champagne instead. I pray when the moment comes when he does more than lean over and amuse himself with a few playful licks, I can close my mind and heart and think only of Paul.

What else can I do? I know exactly what the duke wants and expects. Strictly physical, never emotional. Cold, thrusting movements, flesh against flesh, pleasure for him, numbness for me. Total submission, like a slave girl pleasing her master. He expects me to do exactly as I'm told without hesitation, allow him to dominate me, and make me his, while giving me the excitement he believes I crave and need. Me on all fours, my bare ass raised up to meet the hot sting of his thick leather paddle. I never dreamed I'd end up like this. In Paris. Young and beautiful. And alone. It's an erotic nightmare gone mad.

I breathe out with a loud sigh, ripping apart a temporary seam in my bodice and sending the head fitter into a tizzy. Mumbling, the woman starts pinning up the back of the dress with the small waistline elongated, pointed, and laced up tightly, insisting a young girl's waist should be the same as her age. When I laugh at her comment, I rip open another seam.

"*Alors,* mademoiselle, I must request you remove that…that *thing* you're wearing over your bosom," sputters the head fitter, flitting her hands around her head.

"Why, madame?" I ask. Much to my dismay, I discovered women in this era harness themselves into as much as forty pounds of clothing, what with their arsenal of whalebones, tassels, waistcoats, pearl reins, velvet and belts of satin. And this woman is asking me to remove my little silk bra?

The woman sighs. "It keeps getting in the way when I'm trying to pin up your dress." She waves her hand to a young woman eyeing us with curiosity. "Mademoiselle Sardon, you are a *corsetière,* help us, please. I can do nothing with this dress without the proper garment underneath."

The young woman, dressed simply, though not like the others, crosses the salon and smiles at me. I return the smile.

"Mademoiselle Maguire, *s'il vous plaît,*" says the head fitter. "*Monsieur le duc* will be here presently and if he discovers your dress isn't ready, oh, I can't bear to think what he'll do."

Neither can I. The last thing I want is to give the duke any excuse to put his hands on me and fondle my breasts, flicking his thumbs back and forth across my nipples until they harden under his touch while he leers at me with that vulgar smile of his.

"Very well, madame." I slip the bra off my shoulders, my breasts spilling out over the tight corset. I hand it to the *corsetière,* who runs her fingers over the ribbon straps and studies the bra from every angle.

"Interesting...and practical," says the *corsetière.* "Is this a design from the House of Worth?"

"*Non,* Mademoiselle Sardon."

"I call it a brassière." I smile. Let them figure it out.

"*S'il vous plaît,* madame, I would like to take it to my shop on rue Cambon for further study."

*My bra?* I wonder...

"As you wish, Mademoiselle Sardon, but first we must finish this gown."

Quickly, like marionettes on a string, the two women unpin the gown, slide it to the floor, pick it up and hurry out of the salon, leaving me standing on the platform in a black and pink corset and deep-rose leather lace-up boots with matching stockings. Another girl helps me into a pink wrapper, but I can't stop giggling. Was my bra the inspiration for the first brassière? I shake my head in amusement, laugh so hard tears form in my eyes.

A strange twist to my adventure, I decide, delighted to find something to smile about as I sink down into a silk damask chair and nibble on the pink sorbet and vanilla wafer cookies offered to me. How long have I been standing? Hours, it seems. I'm grateful the duke let me out of his sight. I refuse to think about his fingers in my cunt exploring me, circling the hardening ridge of my clit, skimming his lips over my skin like I'm his personal body slave, every cell in my mind and body refusing to totally submit to him.

Instead I think about the magnificent love I feel for Paul, the way he tried to protect me, his strength, his fearlessness. I had no choice when the duke pointed a gun at Paul. I *had* to go with the Englishman. The irony of the entire situation is I'm giving my gorgeous body to this madman, and in a strange way, in a humorous way, if I allow myself one indulgence, it'll serve him right if I disappear right before he jams his cock into me.

But either way, I'll never see Paul again. I think about it at night as I lie in the darkness in the room next to the duke in his fancy apartment on rue Chalgrin with only a slim wall between us. It's the only thing keeping him from indulging his lust and ripping off my *jeu de corset* with the peacock feather design with a name that makes me laugh: *La Fiancée*.

Well, if I'm going through with this charade, I may as well act the part. I walk round the salon, affecting an elegant, nose-in-the-air attitude. Hips swaying at just the right angle. The proper amount of rouge applied to my cheeks.

"Ah, there you are, *ma chère cousine*," purrs Madame Chapet, her voice a charming trill. I turn around, my ears not believing what I'm hearing, my eyebrows bouncing up to my forehead at being called the woman's cousin.

"Madame Chapet, what are *you* doing in the House of Worth?" I have to ask.

Madame Chapet blinks, then blinks again, staring at me through the lorgnette she wears around her neck on an amethyst chain. "I'm an old customer here."

*Old* is the right word, I dare to think, aloud I ask, "How is business, madame? Picking up? Or are your girls going down for the last time?"

"Watch your pretty mouth, mademoiselle, or I'll use my influence and have you thrown out of here," mutters the madam under her breath.

"I doubt it, Madame Chapet. You're a liar and a cheat and you've humiliated me for the last time. Now if you please, I have to resume my fitting."

I turn away, thoroughly enjoying putting *la madame* in her place.

"Didn't I buy your way out of St. Lazare?" Madame Chapet whispers to me as the older woman fusses in front of a mirror, all plump and pink in silks and feathers. "Give you a chance to model in the best *atelier* in Paris? Put clothes on your back, food in your stomach? You won't find it so easy to get rid of *me,* mademoiselle."

Irritated, I turn to face the woman. My eyes narrow. "What do you mean?"

"In case it slipped your pretty mind, *ma jolie,* the Duke of Malmont engaged me to chaperone you to the opening of the Moulin Rouge tomorrow night. The duke assured me he'll be most happy to include in your purchase a new gown for me."

Before I can utter a word, Madame Chapet snaps her fingers and several girls appear from seemingly out of nowhere, surrounding the madam with ribbons of measuring tapes, throwing bolts of brightly colored silk, fringes and trimmings at her feet, and placing a steaming demitasse of fresh *café noir* with lots of sugar into her open palm. She insists she never places an order without first consuming numerous cups of rich, sweet coffee.

I'm amazed at how the women ooh and aah over the brothel madam, showing her elegant gowns in black-and-white silk, creamy peach satin, faerie-green voile and deep rose-red velvet.

"It makes you look *très* elegant, madame," says *la vendeuse,* clapping her hands. Madame Chapet's chest lifts, and a smile of sheer delight makes her look fifteen years younger, though no less what she is: a fat pigeon in a nest of elegant doves.

"Do you really think so?" Madame Chapet asks, fishing for another compliment.

Trying to look properly bored, I glance up at the ivory and black clock, a Baroque explosion of heavy intricate gold gilding, choking the hours away. Two hours and forty-seven minutes. That's how long I've been standing in the *salon de lumière,* a showroom lit by gas without a sliver of daylight allowed in so the ladies can try on the gowns in the exact same light they'll wear them in the evening. I could care less about the lighting. After standing for so long, I have to go to the bathroom.

"*Pardon,* mademoiselle, where is the *toilette?*" I smile prettily at the salesgirl.

"*En haute,* mademoiselle." She points up the curving staircase. "Up there."

I glance over at Madame Chapet, indulging in a plate of marzipan sweets while she listens to the salesgirl expound on the way the color of the Oriental crépon fabric brings out the gold in her hair. I start for the staircase. Hopefully *la madame* will be gone by the time I return. I wander up and down the hallway until I find what I perceive to be the bathroom with a lovely chamber pot probably used by the Empress Eugénie herself, the first customer of the House of Worth. Afterward, walking along the hallway and in no hurry to return to the salon, I hear women's voices coming from a private fitting room.

One voice in particular sounds familiar, the high-strung notes of the madam of the House on rue des Moulins coming through the door loud and clear. I can't resist putting my ear to the door and listening.

"...it's an unholy ritual where men and women meet in a fancy *hotel privé* and the red Spanish wine casts a spell on all who drink from the silver chalice."

"How can that be, madame?"

"The wine is mixed with both pernicious and mind-changing drugs that produce a sexual magic." I hear high-pitched laughter then, "It's said no woman escapes the night without licking the devil's cock."

"Tell me more, Madame Chapet."

"*Bien,* well, the revelers engage in *le vice anglais,* sexual flagellation, in a secret location. Oh, I feel faint just thinking about it."

"You're going to this Black Mass, Madame Chapet?"

"*Bien sûr*, of course, the Duke of Malmont invited me personally."

"Ooohhh, madame…"

"It is *de rigeur* for a woman in my position to attend these rituals, and since the duke is a member of the Order of the Golden Dawn, well, of course, I couldn't refuse him."

I lean against the door, my body shaking slightly. *Black Mass?* Why does this news about an unholy ritual bother me, set off a burning behind my eyes? The start of a headache. Is this the night of pleasure the duke promised me?

I lean in closer to the door, pressing my whole body against the finely carved oak, gripping the sloped gold-plated door handle. I can't hear anything. It's very quiet. Then—

—is that the sound of a woman sighing? A rustle of silk?

*What are they doing in there?*

Giggling.

"But, of course, Madame Chapet, you have *beautiful* thighs."

More giggling.

"Madame, *please!* Don't close your legs."

"Be quiet, mademoiselle. Your tongue is much better used for something else than talking…"

*Whispering.*

I lean in closer, my head pounding. I must hear more about this Black Mass. I lean forward—a little too far, I realize too late—and lose my balance. I grab the handle for support when suddenly the door gives way—

—and I burst through, landing in a heap on the floor, my hand gripping the door handle.

"I...I was, uh, looking for the powder room," I stutter, attempting to smile.

"Care to join us, mademoiselle?" Madame Chapet asks, running her fingers through the salesgirl's hair, who has her head under *la madame*'s petticoats, her tongue no doubt seeking entry to the woman's pussy through a forest of thick dark hair, her cunt wet, hot, and hungry, and ready to be serviced. The brothel madame laughs so hard, wisps of ostrich feathers scatter like big globs of dust. On the furniture, the carpet, the salesgirl.

And on me. I have the strange feeling the most salacious part of my journey has just begun.

Paul stood outside the door of the House on rue des Moulins, listening to the erotic sounds of a girl squealing with delight, trying not to believe it could be Autumn. He leaned against the bell again, ringing it loudly, cursing the gods, his black felt hat askew on his head, and his long cape flapping in the cold wind. Why didn't anyone answer the door?

*Merde alors,* his feet were wet. Not because of the ghostly traces of rain puddles haunting the boulevards. No, a fierce gale had pitched the paddle-wheel steamer he'd boarded on the pier in Dover to and fro in the green sea all the way back across the English Channel, flooding the ship and his boots with sea water. No one in their right mind would have chanced the bad weather, but he had to get back to Paris. To Autumn. The maritime weather office reported in the papers it was the worst storm of the century. Storms, gales, and God knows what cold-hearted jester from Neptune's court ruled the seas.

Was all of this a dream? No, it was very real, from the grunting of the duke's bodyguards, one with his gun under his jacket and shoved into Paul's ribs during the long train ride from Paris to Cherbourg, and handcuffed to the other man until the ship was ready to sail; then they released him, and the two men took off.

After sailing on the *Empress of Japan* from Cherbourg, he was forced to put into Dover because of rough weather. He held up in the port city on the English coast for several days, wandering up and down the narrow streets and stalking the smoke-ridden buildings with no amusement save the musical imbibing of a few stragglers of British grenadiers. Finally, he was able to book passage back to France on the paddle-wheeler. Paul felt invigorated by the smell of salt water hitting his nostrils with a pleasant sting. He'd discovered feelings he never knew he had during the past few weeks. For the first time in his life he was overwhelmed by a desire that couldn't be satisfied by the pursuit of art *or* sex, but a spiritual need to be close to Autumn. He wanted to love her and her to love him. She was not only beautiful, but intelligent and resourceful. That desire plagued him onboard ship for the entire trip, a sense of urgency forcing him to risk his life by crossing the channel again during a gale.

He had arrived back in Paris less than an hour ago and headed straight for the House on rue des Moulins, intent on taking Autumn with him and never letting her out of his sight again, no matter what he had to do. Yet being able to entertain a wildly romantic image of her in his mind in the aftermath of what had happened didn't help his present situation. He was desperately trying to quell his fear, and more desperately still, struggling to suppress the slow physical changes coming over him.

Unquestionably, he had grown older. A slight graying around the temples. Laugh lines around the eyes, the mouth. Callused hands. Nevertheless, he returned to Paris, ready to kill the duke if necessary. He'd had no problem procuring a pocket pistol from a drunken British grenadier to do the job.

The duke's scornful eyes, seething with hate, haunted him. Why did his eyes seem so familiar? He felt as though some of the darkness in which he'd lived for thirty-eight years was starting to lift and a great secret was about to be revealed to him.

*Not yet. Not until I hold Autumn in my arms and explain to her what's happened to me.*

He hit the bell again. *Where was she?* Were all the girls busy with customers? If so, surely Madame Chapet would answer the door. That same sense of urgency he'd felt on board ship pulled at his mind. This time he was afraid what he felt was more than just missing her. Something was wrong.

When the front door finally opened, Paul was shocked. The little seamstress, Delphine, stood in the archway, struggling to maintain her composure. Her white cap was tilted on her head at an odd angle, her plain blue dress and white starched apron wrinkled and crumpled, her bodice missing several buttons and giving him a peek at her young bosom. And was that her petticoat she was hiding behind her back?

He leaned inside, peeked into the brothel. No one was there.

He looked beyond the genuine onyx staircase and he swore he caught a glimpse of a young man, shirtless, scurrying into another room. He wasn't shocked, rather amused when he realized the young couple had been engaging in *jouer,* making love, when he knocked on the heavy carved door.

"Oh, Monsieur Borquet, it's *you!*" Delphine crossed herself, her eyes filling with tears. "Mademoiselle Autumn will be *so* happy you've returned," she said, surprise filtering through her voice as she automatically opened the door wider for him to enter. Her face was flushed.

"Where's Autumn? Where is she?"

"She isn't here, monsieur. No one is here…except me." She lowered her eyes, though it was obvious she was lying.

"Where did she go, *you must tell me!*"

"She's…she's gone to the Moulin Rouge with Lord Bingham."

"She what?" Paul blurted out in a loud voice.

"Yes, she left with *monsieur le duc* and Madame Chapet a little while ago."

Paul studied the girl intently. She looked frazzled but relieved he was the one to discover her indiscretion. He couldn't blame her. If Madame Chapet found out she was giving away her charms to the lucky young man in an act of love, she'd toss her out into the streets. The vulgar madam held to the axiom that sex not love paid the bills. He looked at the little seamstress's face wet with tears. She was obviously upset, begging him not to say anything to Madame Chapet, but the radiance passing through her eyes at seeing him didn't diminish.

"You must go after her, monsieur. I don't like that Englishman. He is evil."

"He is more than evil, mademoiselle. He's a monster who must be stopped."

Without another word, heart racing, Paul turned and hurried down the rue des Moulins, crossed l'avenue de l'Opéra, heading for Montmartre. Walking, walking, *walking*. He felt a nauseous feeling settle in his stomach. Autumn was with the duke, and he could only imagine what he'd done to her, making her cry out in pain when he laid the whip on her, applying its cruel touch to her nude body with a vigor that was horrifying, her terror exciting him while he shivered with pleasure, his cock swollen with need, nudging its ugly head at her every orifice, thrilling at whatever sadistic act he was doing with her, to her...

He didn't understand why the gods of his black arts tortured him with such debauched thoughts, troubling his soul, but he had a premonition these feelings were only a prelude to a hateful revelation that would take Autumn away from him—

She couldn't leave him. She couldn't.

Unless—

Oh, no, there it was again, that funny feeling she was only an illusion. He shook off that feeling. He was letting his imagination run away with him. Besides, she couldn't simply vanish from his world, go back to where she came from. Like human dust dissolved into a memory.

*Could she?*

He wanted so badly to believe she wasn't hurt, her soul pure. Even if her body was touched by another man, it wasn't of her own desire. All that mattered to him was *her,* the woman. Yes, yes, yes, she was a woman, though with the body of a young girl, firm high breasts with nipples so nut brown and perfect he ached to twist them, creamy buttocks that tempted him to ride her with abandon, a tight, moist cunt that sizzled at his touch. He was certain some magical force had brought her to him. The question was whether the black art that opened a doorway to him was from *this* world or a heaven beyond the world he knew.

Would he live to see that world? With her?

He kept walking. He prayed he would.

# CHAPTER EIGHTEEN

"Higher, mademoiselle. Kick higher!"

"Show us your bloomers, *nana*, dearie."

Shading my eyes from the blinding light, coughing from the hot and smoky air, taking in the giddy atmosphere festooned with paintings covering the wall spaces, even the mirrors, I watch the dancers in fascination. La Goulue with her topknot and arrogant *grandeur*. Grille-d'Egout, precise and dignified. La Sauterelle. And Cri-Cri. Screaming. Doing cartwheels. Kicking their legs up high. Flinging back their petticoats to reveal their buttocks. Rivaling each other with competitive acrobatic steps. Raucous, bawdy cries. Ear-splitting whistling.

Having arrived only minutes ago, racing over the tiled floor from one story of the cabaret to another, I'm already gasping for breath, my heart beating faster. And now this. The cancan. *Le chahut*. The word means din, rambunctious. The quadrille is a world of feminine enchantment that thrives on its guttural instincts, its crude displays of flesh and its naughty behavior that shocked and titillated an entire world.

Women scream and men lean forward when La Goulue

pulls up her skirt and salutes with her behind, revealing lacy drawers with a heart embroidered on it. I watch in amazement as the other dancers reveal their naked skin between their garters and petticoats when they lift their legs. Garish costumes. Windmills, cats and rats decorate their dresses. The only thing pure about them is their white petticoats and long pantaloons with fluffy, creamy ruffles nipped in tight around the knees. A pleasant heat grows in the pit of my belly, making me think about their clits pressed against and restrained by their pantaloons. Do they feel a tiny orgasm spark in their pussies each time they kick theirs legs up high? I tap my feet in time to the music, pretending I'm one of them and in step with their little secret.

Meanwhile, the crowd surrounding me presses up against each other, punching out their demands in an orgasmic frenzy as I sway to the combustive racket of the orchestra, tapping my feet and clapping my hands. A delicious sweat covers my face and my quivering bosom with a shining polish that glows amber under the flaring gas jets and sparkles under a single row of electric footlights. Fiercely, and with a passion that makes me tremble all over. I love it.

It's maddening.

Exhilarating.

Vulgar.

Sublime and sordid.

It *is* the Moulin Rouge.

A dance hall, a bordello, offering all manner of entertainment, sex, drugs and alcohol, all flowing in abundance. A wild world of red velvet all around me, lush yet brassy. Pagan. Primitive.

Standing on the large, wooden dance floor surrounded with galleries where the customers can sit and drink or watch the dancing from raised platforms, I can see everything going on. Oh, the fierce excitement that races through my veins. A red heat tempts my nipples to harden then shoots down to my pussy, setting me on fire.

For the most part I can control the heat, but then I can't, rising up from my crotch, scorching my skin, sparking my cheeks with a cherry blush rouge when the alloxan oxide in my makeup heats up. It makes my cheeks glow, then melts on my lips when it makes contact with a dab of cold cream *la madame* insisted I put behind my lower lip to keep me from biting it.

*Who cares?*

I yell. I scream.

I tap my feet, sway my shoulders.

"Oh, the joy, the thrill of this night will live with me forever," shrills Madame Chapet. "I adore all the excitement, but it's making me want to pee." She pauses, puffing on a cigarette. "Perhaps you'd accompany me to *la toilette, ma jolie,* and we can indulge in a few moments of pleasure, my tongue probing your mouth with a deep kiss before you return the favor with your pretty pink-rose lips giving me *un cachet de l'amour* on my pussy—"

"Satisfying your Sapphic urges isn't part of the deal, madame," I say bluntly, still seeing *la madame* at the salon with her skirts pulled up around her waist and the salesgirl with her head between her legs sucking on her with as much enthusiasm as her two insipid little dogs.

"Pity. However, I *am* pleased with your success tonight."

"*My* success?"

"Look for yourself, mademoiselle. Everyone is watching you."

I look around. It's true. *Demi-mondaines* drop curious glances my way and working girls openly ooh and aah over my gown, my hair, my entire ensemble. Small curls are dressed over my forehead and piled up high in front to give a rounded effect to the top of my flaming red hair. A fan, long gloves and simple pearl earrings complete my look.

I should look good. The gown cost the duke more than the affections of ten of Madame Chapet's *nymphes,* her prostitutes.

Fanning myself, I look around and see snooty, elegantly dressed ladies of *le gratin* pushing their lovers over in my direction to find out who I am. Something *la madame* is only too quick to take the credit for achieving.

She says, "*Bien sûr,* of course, you owe your success to me."

"*You,* madame? If it hadn't been for your meddling, informing the duke of my every movement, I'd be with Paul now, under the hot sun, bare-breasted, and wearing nothing but pineapple leaves around my hips."

"You girls are so ungrateful," *la madame* complains. "However, I shall overlook it, mademoiselle, considering the fact I intend to ask the duke for an additional stipend for your services tonight—"

I groan. "Haven't you caused me enough pain?"

"Pain? It is pleasure I will bring you, mademoiselle, when the duke fucks you, *n'est-ce pas?*"

I stick my tongue out at her from behind my fan, then

ignore the rest of her comments as I yell as loudly as the rest of them, from royal wastrels to starving artists to students. The diversity of the clientele of the Moulin Rouge includes aristocrats, entrepreneurs and artists. Bohemian Paris. My dream. Here life is lived passionately and frankly.

Who cares? It means nothing to me without Paul.

I'm like a beautiful rose in the full bloom of her red passion, soft, silky, existing in a lush and vibrant garden, reaching for the sun, reaching, reaching, but dying at the root.

A hand presses against the back of my waist. It's Lord Bingham, dressed in an elegant black evening coat with tails, white satin vest, cravat of white embroidered quilting. Shiny top hat. As is the custom in the Moulin Rouge, and to keep away the hat bandits, he keeps his hat on. I pray he also keeps his dick in his pants.

"Enjoying yourself, mademoiselle?" he whispers, a hot puff of air chilling the back of my neck.

"I was," I say coldly, "until you arrived."

He laughs. "You will enjoy much pleasure, mademoiselle, very soon. The evening doesn't end until the feathered cock mates with the velvet blackbird of night."

I pull away from him. What's he talking about? Does it have something to do with the Black Mass Madame Chapet mentioned? God, I hope not.

I pretend to be confused. "*Pardon*, monsieur?"

"You'll find out soon enough, *ma belle*." He grabs a bouquet of Maréchal Niel roses from a passing waiter and presents them to me. I give him a narrow look, then toss the flowers onto a small table, defiant. He laughs again. What's going on in his dark, staring eyes? A dazzle of rich, black oil seem to pump through them, graying the whites of his eyes, giving his face a haunting, sadistic look. It hypnotizes me and frightens me at the same time.

I look away and fan myself by swishing my skirts, showing my pink petticoat under my long, slim silver-rose-blue lamé gown. The air is suffocating, but there's a seductive eroticism that waffles through the air, dabbing the spectators with a magical, heavy perfume, a lusty fragrance that induces an almost savage response in men and women alike. A response that isn't lost on the Englishman.

I feel a wandering hand pinching my hip. The duke. He tracks his fingers over my breasts, caressing the swell of my bosom, then slides his hand down my rib cage. I'm powerless to stop him in the crowd of people crushing me against him. To make matters worse, Madame Chapet keeps thrusting her corpulent body into my hip in time to the music, allowing Lord Bingham to position his body so it presses against mine. He massages my shoulders with his hands, then his touch becomes more intimate, his hand reaching down toward my inner thigh, massaging my pussy through the silk. The sudden touch of his hand, rubbing my crotch, pressing through the thin fabric to my pussy lips as if his fingers can't wait to dive into me, makes me flinch and gasp with surprise. I pull his hand away. He narrows his eyes with a look of well-bred annoyance. I don't like what he's doing but I can't stop him without making a scene.

Trying to avoid him, I edge my way along the perimeter of the dance floor, the electric footlights creating a pattern of light that falls down and across my face. Damn him, damn *la madame,* damn *everything.* How can I go on, let him touch me, running his fingers everywhere, parting my lower lips and allowing his tongue to invade my wet folds, licking and sniffing, when my heart is skipping in an uneven rhythm, my body tense and hot, my emotions ready to explode.

*No!*

*Where are you, Paul?* Aboard ship, looking out to sea, riding the crests of the waves, taking you farther and farther away from me? Is your heart lonely like mine?

I yearn for his touch, the intense pleasure he gave to my bare flesh with his tongue, his cock, thrusting, tender, sending a sexy chill through me, then the afterglow that resonated whispers and moans, sighs and words of desire. No man ever made me feel so loved, so adored, so *alive.* And he's gone. *Damn, damn, damn.* Until this moment I wouldn't allow this melancholy to overwhelm me. Now I can't stop it from pressing down on me. Once, I'd been so sure who I was, where I was going, with never a doubt. But Paul changed all that. He taught me how to love like a goddess, and for a little while, I reveled in that role. Then my world crashed, my erotic fantasy turned upside down, into a debauched nightmare.

I grip my fan tightly, opening it, closing it, then breaking it in two. To save the man I love, I must become a whore. I recall again the duke's threat: "I will take you as I want you. Fuck you. Sodomize you."

His words are branded on my soul. Oh, God, help me.

The raucous music of the cancan fills my body, from my taut nipples to my swaying hips to my pantaloons wet with my juices. I grit my teeth, break out in a sweat, and with the sweat comes passion heightened by a need to soothe my soul even as my sexual urges grow. I imagine I'm nude, crouched on my hands and knees, moving my hips back and forth over Paul's busy tongue, my body wired as what to expect as he brings me closer and closer to the edge, knowing I'm about to explode. I struggle to compose myself, take a breath, but I'm consumed by my fantasy. I can't come, not here, but the passionate urge won't go away. Attempting to quell the rising fire within me, I sway my hips, roll my shoulders, tap my feet, another idea forming in my mind...urging me forward. I smile. *Can I do something crazy, wild?*

Then, without thinking about the consequences of my actions, I step out of myself and join the dancers on the floor, ready to deal with the excitement that overtakes me. My body seems to be melting, leaving only the raw essence of desire to be part of this night. A hidden sexuality that began when I stripped off my clothes erupts within me and a loud sigh escapes from my lips. I won't rein myself in. I can't help but lose myself to the pleasure of the moment, the music, the excitement, the dancing. The wooden floor shakes underneath me, my feet stamping out a few simple steps, turning, clicking my heels. The brassy sound of the orchestra seems to be blasting out its raucous notes just for me, every beat matching my own thumping, pounding heartbeat. I dare to leap into that world, ready to face it head-on.

Amid the swirl of white petticoats and whiter pantaloons, I pick up my legs, my pink petticoat crackling through the air with the sharpness of a whip, demanding to be noticed. The audience surges forward, unhampered by the lack of a barrier, eager to glimpse the naked flesh naughtily exposed by the teasing dancers. Will they catch a peek of a thatch of pussy hair—red, blonde, or brunette, does it matter?—curling around plump outer lips? Not one of the girls will disappoint.

Not me.

Not for a second.

Nobody is going to stop me from becoming a part of history. *Nobody*. I don't care if I'm ripping through a page in time and shredding it to pieces. So what if there's no record of a redheaded dancer in pink pantaloons dancing the cancan at the Moulin Rouge? More than half the spectators are in a drunken stupor. By morning they will have forgotten me.

Standing on the toes of one foot, I grab my other foot as high as I can with my hand, then I bounce around in a circle, wobbling, pitching forward, then tipping backward and barely keeping my balance. My voice rings out with the others, screaming like a wild banshee. I can smell the melee of earthy, fragrant, unwashed scents of the spectators, the wine on their breaths. They move in so close to me I can hear them whisper naughty words in my ear. Especially the duke.

"Tonight, mademoiselle, I tip the velvet of your cunt with my lips," he says, "then I'll spread the cheeks of your arse and anoint your tight dark hole with the most fragrant of oils before I plant my cock firmly in you, inching into you slowly until you take *all* of me."

*No, no, no.* I can't do it, *won't* do it, dammit. I want to bolt out of here, race down the *butte sacre*, celebrated butte of sin, and into the Paris underworld of prostitutes, pimps, white-slavers, thieves, escaped criminals, deserters and libertines. Anything is better than the duke. But how long could I last in that world? *Do I care?*

The tempo of the music goes faster and faster, and I dance faster and faster, kicking higher and higher, sweat bubbling down my breasts swelling out over my corset cinching my body and nipping my flesh, but making me aware of my wild twists and turns. My nipples press against my silk bodice, hard and pointy, and aching to be rubbed. I spin round and round, a high sense of expectation sparking again in my belly. It chills me, sends me to a place I've never been before. I can do *anything*.

Something dark and wild in me is set free when the music reaches the rousing, primitive crescendo. As the dancers leap into the air, one by one, and crash down to the floor doing the splits, I run forward when it's my turn. I embrace the chaos of the evening with open arms. Petticoats in hand, breasts heaving, my eyes light up just before my dress flies up over my head, creating that magic connection between me and the audience as I soar into the air and hang suspended for a split second before slamming to the floor in a pandemonium of female screams and yells.

Stretched out horizontally, my legs go numb, the wooden floor cold and hard beneath my soft flesh. Splinters of wood prick my skin. My heart is pumping so fast I swear it'll burst through my corset. God, my face burns. I gasp for breath, not moving. I don't dare.

My pantaloons are ripped wide open.

My wet pussy oozes my love juices all over the wooden floor, my pubic muscles contracting with one, then two orgasms as spasm after spasm of ecstasy overtakes me. I close my eyes.

*Yes, yes, yes!*

A cool draft slipped through the front entrance of the dance hall and all the way to the back of the establishment. Long, wavering feathers on ladies' hats and loose wisps of their hair fluttered on the night breeze as a man came in. Tall, imposing, he swirled his long, black cape around him, his eyes searching the flushed faces of the wasp-waisted women. Red, black, pink, green silks and velvets. A rainbow of feminine treats. He was searching for a particular sweet, yearning in his soul to drink deeply from her well of desire.

Paul smiled. Overwhelmed by the past days and nights he lay in his bunk in a fever of frustrated desire, his cock hard and straight, pushing up the thin sheet like the pole of a tent. He could see her in his mind, her beautiful face, her luscious body, and him behind her, reaching around her to open the lips of her pussy to explore the pink moistness within while he breathed in her scent. He had never known such torment, such despairing emotions tearing at the very core of his being. How he missed Autumn. And now he was back in Paris, close to her. She was somewhere in this mass of humanity, sweating and drinking and—

*There she was,* squeezed in between the woman in the peacock-blue gown he recognized as Madame Chapet and that damn Englishman. A silver lamé cape hid her figure from him but he remembered how her breasts curved full, her waist in, her hips slim. She was waving her arms about, talking without stopping. She was excited about something. Smiling. Laughing. Her face flushed. Her hair hung down to her shoulders, glimmering a soft red under the gas jets. God, she was beautiful.

The trio was leaving the establishment, heading for the exit. Paul eased through the crowd of unshorn men with greasy collars and black nails in the company of resplendent girls, manicured, coiffed, often bizarrely dressed. He pushed past gentlemen wearing an air of aristocratic boredom as if they were suffering this experience for the sake of later in the evening, and ladies peeking at the perverse goings-on. He ignored the clatter of conversation and laughter filling his ears, hearing only her voice.

"Why do we have to leave, Lord Bingham?" Autumn was saying, pouting. He smirked. He knew that pout well. But did she have to look so damned seductive when she did it in front of that Englishman?

"Lord Bingham has been a patient man, mademoiselle," said Madame Chapet, shivering with excitement, "your moment to deliver *votre bonbonnière,* your pussy, is now."

"I won't go with either of you." She turned on her heel, but the Englishman grabbed her by the elbow.

Lord Bingham shook his head adamantly. "You're coming with me *now.* I've waited a long time for this night."

"But my pantaloons are ripped—" Autumn argued.

"It will save me the trouble of sliding them down your lovely thighs, mademoiselle. Let's go."

The bastard. *He'll be dead before that happens.*

Paul could see her flinch. She said, "I'm not leaving until you tell me where we're going."

The duke smiled. "To a place where the night never ends and the Prince of Darkness rules."

Paul saw a frightened look etch itself on Autumn's face, and then they were gone. Disappearing into the crowd like ghostly apparitions taking leave of the earth. He tried to follow them but he lost them in the swelling crowd. Damn, he didn't like the look on the duke's face. Evil, calculating.

Prince of Darkness?

Of all the amusements and gaieties that captured the fascination of aristocrats, Paul knew, the most debauched and the most disturbing was the Black Mass. Human sacrifice. Sexual perversities. The Prince of Darkness held court in an arena that catered to such perverted tastes.

But *where?*

The location was always secret, and though he was familiar with many hôtels privés in the Marais district where such revels were held, it could be any one of them.

*Which one?*

He asked two artist friends of his, each with a husky, sweaty dancer on one arm and an iced bottle of champagne precariously balanced between them.

"Haven't you heard, Paul? There will be a Black Mass celebrated tonight at the *hôtel privé* of the Marquis de la Pergne."

Paul froze. The marquis was a reincarnation of the devil himself. Known for his elaborate orgies, his notoriety whispered on the lips of every sexually perverted gentleman in Marais, the nobleman engaged in blasphemous goings-on that defiled the most sacred beliefs, using bondage, drugs and ancient demonic rituals that demanded the complete subjugation of the sacrificial virgin to reinstate the masculine vigor of the gentleman chosen to be the guest host for that night.

The duke.

He *must* save her.


My blindfold is too tight.

I raise my hand to loosen the black satin band covering my eyes, but gloved fingers grab my wrist, followed by a hot, warning breath whispered in my ear.

"*Attend,* mademoiselle. Wait. You'll see soon enough where you're going."

It's Lord Bingham's voice. Icing my neck with a cool spray of fear that reaches down to the unseemly tear in my drawers. Open. Wet. And inviting. My pussy dripping with juices, waiting for his caress of my cunt and clit, probing, exploring me with his finger and thumb, doing anything he can to bring me to the very edge of orgasm, knowing I can't stop him. What have I gotten myself into? Games? Masquerades? I can only guess. According to Madame Chapet, who hasn't stopped chattering since the duke ushered us into a carriage with a princely coat of arms emblazoned on the side, we're going to a party. What kind of party is it where the guests can't see where they're going? *La madame* thought the idea of blindfolds was exciting. I don't. The darkness hides too many secrets.

Instinctively I close my legs tightly together, but the duke's fingers seem to trace my fear with their touch. He slides his other hand under my cape and up and down my body as if

I were a living *poupée,* puppet, and his traveling fingers are the strings that will make me do his bidding.

*Spread your legs,* mademoiselle, I imagine him saying. *Touch yourself. Yes, there, now deeper, open your pussy lips a little bit more please, oh, what lovely moist pink flesh, ah, there it is, your, how do you say,* petit bouton? *Your clit? Now, I must insert my fingers in you so I can breathe in the warm scent of your sensuality—*

I push his hand away, disgusted. I've never felt more naked, more exposed. And it can only get worse. We're going to a Black Mass. No doubt in my mind. The ramblings of the brothel madam were not merely spicy gossip but a trap. And I fell into it, eyes—and pantaloons—wide open.

I push myself as far back into the velvet padded seat as possible. I'm not in the mood for a party. I want to go back to the apartment on rue Chalgrin and sink into a tub of lukewarm water—hot water is out of the question without indoor plumbing—and let my dancing bones remember what it's like to be back in their sockets again. That seems unlikely now.

"*Zut alors,* my heart is beating so fast, Lord Bingham," Madame Chapet says. She can't see where she's going but that doesn't prevent her from talking incessantly. "I can't believe tonight I will worship at the altar of Luxor, drink the wine of the priests, partake of the sacrifice—"

"Hold your tongue, madame," the duke says harshly. "Or you will find it missing before the evening is over."

I bite my lip to keep from smiling. A bitter taste makes me grimace. Damn, I forgot about the cold cream, but it was worth it to imagine Madame Chapet's jaw hanging open, her heavy bosom heaving up and down. I hear the older woman clear her throat nervously, then silence.

The ride in the coach is smooth. No jostling about or rough bumps in the road. We can't be headed to the poor section of Paris with its heavily cobbled streets. I sniff the air. Cinnamon, cloves, sandalwood and others I can't name drift up from the direction where Lord Bingham sits. I draw in my breath. Did he open up a vial of scents? Is he trying to drug us?

Finally the coach stops.

"We're here," Lord Bingham announces.

A skittish dread shoots through me. I don't resist when the duke takes my hand and helps me out of the coach. I have no choice. The night wind blows a welcome kiss on each cheek before I'm led into a house, then up a flight of steps to what is called *la premiere étage,* the first floor, then another floor. A sweet, spicy odor tickles my nostrils. Incense. I can hear the heavy pounding of Madame Chapet's tight-fitting satin evening pumps in front of me, although not a peep comes from the capon in a corset.

Lord Bingham stops on the stairway.

Madame Chapet stops.

I stop.

Still wearing my blindfold, I listen to the unnatural silence. It's as if everything in Paris has evaporated into darkness and I'm suspended between this time and my own.

What a strange thought to strike me at this moment. I had the same feeling before, yes, when I went down that dark alley, then turned a corner and found myself in old Les Halles. I was in the Marais district. Am I again in that marvelous and fascinating quarter of beautiful houses where every street, every alley has a personality and a life of its own? Am I?

Is that feeling creeping just at the edge of my mind trying to tell me I can find a way back to my own time?

Only a little while ago, when I was in an orgasmic frenzy dancing the can-can at the Moulin Rouge, I might not have dared to dream there's a way out of this nightmare, though my heart pains me terribly to think about leaving this time without Paul. Yet the idea of flight is overwhelming. I shiver from head to toe, and pricks of perspiration escape from underneath the black satin covering my eyes and trickle down my face.

"You may take off your blindfold, *ma belle.*"

My instinct is to rip it off so I can see, run, run, *run,* but I overcome the urge and remain motionless. Voices whisper in my ear. I can hear sensuous laughter trickling through the darkness as if someone suddenly turns up the volume. A low chanting. Monotone masculine voices. Then a soft hiss. I continue to stand motionless. I hesitate to remove my blindfold. Something isn't right. Only in the deep blackness behind the satin mask can I keep my fear locked up, resist whatever is in this room. Make plans to escape.

I step backward and strong arms enfold me in a tight embrace, cupping my breasts as if calculating their firmness, then twisting my nipples but not too hard. I have the feeling he can ill afford to damage the goods. I squirm in his grasp, holding my breath then forcing it out in a big push to free myself, but all to no avail.

"Don't be afraid, mademoiselle," says a smooth voice I

don't recognize. "The Prince of Darkness awaits you at the Altar of Luxor."

*Prince of Darkness.* The duke mentioned such a creature earlier. Who is vile enough to assign himself that role? What does he want with me?

The male chanting becomes louder, surrounding me. Before I can react, the arms release me and someone rips the blindfold from my eyes. I remain still as my eyes adjust to the soft pinkish aura floating around me. My breathing eases, my pulse beats slower. Struggling fiercely to regain my composure, I let the power of the images overtake me. Men in searing red robes with animal heads—fox, goat, dog— encircle me, the crunch of their brown leather sandals stepping in sync with their chanting, their robes flapping open against their legs.

They carry censers with intoxicating fumes invisible to my eye but not to my senses, giving me a heady feeling and sending my brain spinning. I gasp when I realize they're naked underneath their robes. The rogues. And their cocks! Some long. Some short. Some thick. Some slim. Some with their owners' hands urging them upward into erection. Others already hard and stiff and bouncing up and down like elephants waving their trunks about in a circus. *All* of them in search of a vessel to receive the ultimate moment of their ecstasy. A willing pussy. Pink, wet and tight.

The men in red robes step aside so another man can come forward, cloaked in a billowing black-hooded domino covering his face with two horns of black velvet attached to his head and a live green-silver-scaled snake slithering down his arm. A hissing sound, warm and seductive, crawls down the length of my spine. It's a sight I never thought to see.

Standing before me is the Devil himself.

"Strip her to the waist."

It's the duke.

Before I can turn, think, run, do *anything,* a man in a red robe wearing a goat mask moves forward and rips my bodice open, pushing down the silky smooth lamé, and tearing the sheer silk of my chemise into shreds of frayed threads, exposing my breasts and my very hard, very brown nipples. I try to cover myself but he pushes my hands away and traces the soft curve of my breasts, pulling on my nipples and commenting on their plum brown color and erect peaks. I refuse to cry out, give him *any* satisfaction.

The man in the black-hooded domino—I'm *sure* it's the duke—stares at my naked breasts bobbing up and down to the uneven rhythm of my ragged breathing. My muscles tense and my head falls backward as the man grabs me roughly and anoints my breasts with champagne flowing from a silver chalice, then sucks on my nipples. One, then the other, then back again. His actions surprise me, his teeth biting on my nipples and sending spark after spark through me of what I can only describe as shooting pain.

"This is how the ritual of the Black Mass begins, mademoiselle," he says in a low, husky voice. "With the blessing."

I spit on him. "You and your Black Mass disgust me."

He slaps me hard on the cheek. I feel the sting from his hand, but I refuse to back down. "As the night progresses, mademoiselle, you will change your mind. You'll beg for my cock, the mere thought of it inside you will have you so excited you'll do *anything* I ask of you or you'll meet the same fate as the goose."

"Goose?" I ask. "What goose?"

Before I can protest, the man in the black-hooded domino pulls me over to a table covered with rich gold velvet. A cackling white goose waddles back and forth, shoving its beak into my face. The man grabs my hand and points my finger at it. The goose sticks its long neck out and nearly bites off my finger. Instinctively I pull my hand back, holding it to my cheek. He throws his head back and laughs.

"You see what I mean, mademoiselle. Danger lurks everywhere."

"I don't frighten that easily, monsieur," I say.

"Are you sure, mademoiselle? I haven't finished yet."

"Monsieur?"

"On the night of a Black Mass before the dawn breaks, the black bird of death cries out, heralding the killing of the sacrifice."

Before I can blink, the man in the black-hooded domino cuts off the head of the goose, laying it on one end of the table and the body of the bird on the other. I cover my breasts with my hands, wanting to turn my head away but refusing to show this fiend any sign of weakness. I squint. If he cut off the head of the goose, where is the blood? The lighting is dim, pinkish, but I see no stains of red on the gold velvet.

Turning away from the table, frowning, puzzled, I look around for a way out. Somehow, someway, I've got to make a run for it. By the high, high ceiling in the salon, I'm certain I'm on the top floor in a grand house. But where is the stairway?

"I tricked the black cock tonight, *ma jolie,*" whispers the duke harshly, grabbing me, twisting my head around and forcing me to watch him wave his hand over the goose as it gets up on its feet and up pops its head. The trained goose fooled me by tucking its head under its wing. A carved wooden head and neck sit on the other side of the table. "*Voilà,* the goose has her head again."

Unimpressed, I say, "I don't intend to lose my head *or* my dignity."

"It's not your dignity I intend to fuck, mademoiselle," says the man in the black-hooded robe. He throws back his head and laughs.

A rushing energy kicks through me, heating up my insides as an overwhelming fear creeps back in at the inner workings of my mind. I won't let him touch me. He's an aristocrat, debauched, yes, and not entirely rational, but unfortunately, from what I've seen on this night, he's lost none of his passion or desire for me. What I see the problem to be is that the voice of reason goes unheard when a gentleman's cock *and* his imagination—if he has one and from what I've seen the duke has a doozie—is aroused. It's one thing when he stares at my groin as if he's trying to discern the shape of my mound through the silk. It's quite another when he insists on a backdoor delivery with his eager cock. I've no doubt that's his plan. He has a habit of sliding his hand down to my waist then lower still until his little finger rests in the crease of my buttocks. I have no intention of allowing him to indulge his anal whims.

Standing here, looking at the deformed shadows deepening on his hooded face, the demonic stance of his body, I'm too frightened to move. I *will* escape this madman, this purveyor of the Black Mass, even if I have to kill Satan himself.

\* \* \*

Paul stared at the fox mask and the voluminous red robe he held in his hands, letting the rich red velvet lined with soft red satin slip through his fingers, every sense in his body alert. Naked women. Heaving breasts, buttocks jiggling. Gold rings through their nipples. Filmy wisps of silk strung around their hips. Their pussies, moist and yielding to his touch. Ecstatic sighs. Dancing. Flirting.

Where would he find Autumn in this orgy obsessed with fulfilling a man's every carnal desire?

Upstairs in the second-floor bedroom of an elaborately furnished *hôtel privé,* Paul was among several well-bred gentlemen exchanging their evening clothes for red robes and animal masks. He took off his white Cossack shirt, revealing his muscular chest, but it didn't loosen the tightness in his throat. He declined the silver bowl of dark liquid the manservant offered him. Even though he no longer had the unbelievable endurance he had enjoyed with his youthful body, he refused to rub the juice of *belladonna,* a powerful narcotic, over his cock to stimulate himself. Every muscle in his body coiled in revulsion—yet he *must* take part in this debauched ritual; it was the only way to save Autumn from this godless coven of devils. Slaves to the flesh and the power of the black arts. Why had he never before questioned the vileness of this naked display? *Why?*

*Am I not also a slave to the black magic that gave me back my youth? Am I not as debauched, as godless as the men who feast their eyes upon the shimmering, wet flesh of nude women?*

Paul was suddenly aware he *had* changed, that he no

longer coveted the mask of youth, no longer needed anything but the love of the redhead, this beautiful woman, to assure him of his manhood. He had conviction in himself, in his art, and in his ability to love and be loved. Whatever danger there was to his own life, he was in more of a panic about Autumn.

He imagined her surrounded by naked men…the chant of a devil's prayer…numerous hands holding her down, she wiggles and squirms to avoid their probing touch in her pussy, her anal hole, dizzy from body smells and redolent spices overwhelming her…a man forces her legs open… rams his cock into her…

That horrible scene shook him so badly he dared not dwell on it. He wouldn't allow it to happen, no matter what he had to do. Although he'd taken part in the upside down ritual known as the Black Mass, never had he been present when it was celebrated by members of London's notorious Order of the Golden Dawn; but he'd heard the gruesome stories about the secret caves, the rapes, the sacrificial mutilation of women's bodies, the drinking of the blood of a virgin.

What if she were already defiled, already dead—

*Don't think about that. Keep your eyes open, ready to grab her and run.* He was burning with hot desire, a fury making him hard like he'd never known, a furious challenge stimulating him to find her. Only then would he find peace.

"Messieurs, gentlemen, make haste!" a voice called out. "Abbé Bescanon and his most honored guest, the Prince of Darkness, await your presence."

Paul donned his robe and fox mask, noting the garment

contained an inside pocket for a gentleman to carry his snuff. He grinned. It was also big enough to hold his pocket pistol: a .31 caliber, six-shot multi-barreled weapon. Wrapped in his folded-up pants, he slipped the walnut-handled pistol inside his robe, then followed the other red-robed gentlemen up a secret stairway to a padded door opened by unseen hands. He stepped through the door, noting the image of Medusa carved into the wood, and into a chapel glowing pink and red from the blush-colored sanctuary lamps hanging from bronze chandeliers.

The scene before him was macabre but spellbinding. Men in red robes, all wearing animal masks, anointed themselves with champagne, then imbibed from golden goblets as they fondled and caressed naked women, licking their breasts and nipping at their cunts. In the middle of the chapel he could see an altar covered with black velvet cloth and six tall black candles. Incense burned. He recognized the fragrances of myrtle, sandalwood and the powerful narcotic, thorn apple.

"*Regarde,* monsieur, look," said the man beside him, "at the female sacrifice for this evening. What lovely breasts she has."

Paul stiffened. "Sacrifice?"

He riveted his eyes on the naked back of a beautiful young woman in a lamé gown stripped to the waist, her red hair hanging long and full over her shoulders. She turned toward him, her breasts white and perfect. Her nipples hard. When she looked up, her eyes were questioning pools, praying for redemption.

Meeting her stare—she couldn't know it was he who

looked at her through the eyeholes of his fox mask—he felt his cock harden, then pulsate with desire. His passion for her told him to find an empty and convenient room, alcove, any place where he could relieve the tremendous need she had aroused in him. His rational self said otherwise, though that had no effect on his erection. He was harder than he'd ever been. He no longer had any doubt he'd rather burn in hell than lose her again.

# CHAPTER
# NINETEEN

The world as I know it appears to be dissolving at the end of my fingertips, as if everything I touch isn't real.

Red-robed men disappear in screens of smoke, then reappear behind me. Trumpets play by themselves. Ghostly images appear in columns of smoke. A door swings open mysteriously and no one is there. Young women wearing only wisps of silvery threads giggle and tease men hiding their identities behind fox, goat, dog and sheep masks. Statues seem to speak to me, soliciting lewd comments about tempting my darkest desires with the sting of a leather-covered rod between my pussy lips. An immediate surge burns between my legs. I ignore it.

I'm tempted to make a run for it and take my chances. Even if I escape, I won't get far. Something more sinister than cheap magic tricks is going on here.

Anyway, who would help me?

Madame Chapet gleefully abandoned me for the company of two nymphets wearing only strings of pearls and pink posies in their hair, pinching their taut nipples and slapping their bare buttocks with the back of her fan, branding them with fresh red welts. And the duke? Gone as mysteriously as he appeared, though I have no doubt he'll make his demonic presence known when he's ready to torment me. I haven't forgotten his sadistic, perverted threats, making me equally fear and despise him.

I close my eyes, trying to block out the disturbing sights, but the exotic smells, pleasing and mindbending, catch up to me, making me feel light-headed. I fight against the power of the drugs, refusing to join the revelers in their dreamy, playful spirit and be rendered into a state of submissiveness. I refuse to give myself completely to the will of another, surrender to whatever slave training the duke has in mind.

I look around and see couples involved in intense sex with an edge, including three-ways, four-ways, and bi-curious girls wearing strap-ons, even a double-dong. I can't look away when I see a large blonde spread her legs then bend over and pull apart her buttocks to reveal both her cunt and the tight puckering of her anus. She moans in a loud voice when a monk slips his finger into her anal hole then waves an incense burner over her nude body while he chants in Latin. I keep my head high, my shoulders straight back. I can't let them see I'm frightened. *I won't.*

I open my eyes and resist violently when a half-naked priest grabs me and tries to tie my hands in front of me. I twist and turn my body, falling to my knees, biting his hand, kicking him, though my long skirt and petticoats hamper my efforts. I look around, screaming for someone to come to my aid, to stop this debacle, but all I hear are snickers, crude jokes, even applause for what some deem my "theatrics." I squeeze my eyes tight, shutting out the humiliating sight of the priest tying my hands together with red silken cords. *They've won.*

"*Bon.* You have accepted your fate. Come with me, mademoiselle," says the priest, wearing only a crimson chasuble, a sleeveless outer robe, embroidered with a triangle on the back depicting a black goat with silver horns. I flinch when I spot a pentagram tattooed at the corner of his left eye. The sign of evil. I grit my teeth, resisting when he pulls on my silken bonds. He jerks me forward and I get a good glimpse of his nude side view. His short cock lies flaccid between his legs.

*I'd like to twist it off with my hands.*

As he walks in front of me, I see black crosses painted on the soles of his bare feet. As if he curses the very symbol he walks on. I pull back. What clandestine order of renegade priests haunts this aristocratic refuge steeped in sexual fantasies and hidden from the outside world?

"Where are you taking me?" I dare to ask.

"To the altar of worship, mademoiselle, where—"

"I will take her, monsieur."

I turn and see a man wearing a red robe and a fox mask. *Where did he come from?*

The priest asks, "On whose orders?"

"Abbé Bescanon."

"As you wish, monsieur."

The priest nods and, with regret, hands the silken cords to the stranger. The man in the fox mask grabs me before anyone else can challenge him. I edge back, out of the way, studying him. He's tall, broad-shouldered, his eyes boring into mine, taking in my bare breasts with a groan, though his manner isn't threatening. As he pulls on the cords, his red robe billows open, revealing his naked torso. My bewilderment gives way to a tremulous sense of the unbelievable. I look again at him. *Those deep blue velvet eyes behind the fox mask. Those shoulders.* That *cock.* Long and hard. I'm aware of a wonderful feeling that instills in me a new courage. Before I can express my emotion, I must keep these emotions tantalizingly just beyond my fingertips, though I ache to touch him. *He's here. How?*

"Paul," I whisper low. "It *is* you, *n'est-ce pas?*" A warming sensation thrills me, along with a chilling fear.

"*Mais oui, ma chérie,* no one can keep me away from you."

Before I can say, think, do anything, he pulls on my bonds, leading me through the *grand salon,* past men and women sighing, giggling, lying about on divans in various stages of copulation: naked breasts, legs spread, pussies pink and juicy, cocks hard, bodies squeezed in between two portly *génies* sitting astride horns of plenty. I wet my lips when I see a red-robed man wearing a dog mask inserting one, two, three, then—yes, four fingers into a girl's cunt, then laying the palm of his other hand flat on her tummy to squeeze in time with his rubbing gyrations and her grinding hips. She begins to squirm wildly, spreading her legs as far apart as she can. Her eyes bulge, her mouth falls open and I sigh along with her when she reaches the pinnacle of her climax.

Fearing my panting sounds will give us away, Paul pulls me underneath an overhang of heavy-winged eagles with two straining Atlases on either side, hiding us from curious eyes. The chanting of the priests muffles our voices. No one is likely to overhear our conversation here.

I'm safe.

With Paul. For the moment.

My mind is so filled with frightening speculations related to the events of this night, I fall into his arms. He unties my bonds, then lifts my hair off my neck, his mouth pressing against my skin, sending a wave of heat throughout my body. His teeth nibble at my ear, and a pleasing chill spirals down my spine, making me shudder. He reaches down and slips his hand over my bare breast, finding my hard nipple. Rolling it between his thumb and forefinger, he plays with my nipple, cupping my breast while running his hand down my ribcage, moving slowly toward my pussy. Goody. Goody.

"I don't know how you found me, Paul, but we *can't*, not here," I say, but the breathless sound of my voice betrays me. This is insane, teasing me like this. I have to admit I don't want him to stop. I push him away when what I really want is to feel the tightening in my belly and legs, the sensation of him entering me from behind, lifting me, pushing into me faster and faster, harder and harder, parting my pussy lips with his fingers and rubbing my clit, low raw sighs coming from my throat—

I hear a sound.

A groan. He seems to be holding back, trying to speak, but the words pain him.

"I have to touch you, *mon amour*, make certain you're real," he whispers. "I have the strangest feeling you're slowly dissolving from my world."

"Paul, I...I—" I can't speak. How can I tell him I also feel the mysticism of the black magic here in this house, stronger than ever, pulling and twisting at my sanity, as if warning me that I can't control my destiny. My instinct is also reacting to a deeper need for him. One I pushed aside when I entered this unholy place. His touch is so hot, reaching not only my body, but my soul.

"Don't try to explain," he says. I hear the frustration in his voice. "Whatever it is, I will fight this—this dark force trying to tear us apart. I will never let you go."

"Hold me tight, Paul. Please."

He pulls me close to him, crushing me against his hard chest, my face buried in the curve of his shoulder. Neither of us utters a word, but our bodies speak to each other. A white heat ignites a tantalizing need in my groin and matches the hardening of his cock as his hands reach down and grip my hips, pulling me closer toward him. Stifling a moan, I arch my back, bending like a taut bow ready to spring forward for want of an arrow. Lifting up my skirt, then my petticoats, his fingers squeeze my thighs but he doesn't enter me. I know what he wants, what I want.

*Who will notice if you slide your cock into me?* my eyes ask him. I tease him by showing him the slit in my torn pantaloons. Curling red hairs from my pussy protrude through the tear, tempting him.

He shakes his head. *I'm not a fool,* he tells me. Filling me up with his cock, a move I so desperately need and cannot have, would make us both vulnerable. Instead he seeks out the curve of my buttocks, massaging my flesh before he reaches between my legs and inserts his fingertips through the torn cotton and inside me. I move against him, feeling my body open to his touch. He brushes my clit with his thumb, pressing on its delicate hood and urging me to find my rhythm. I smile. Why not? Playing with my pussy allows me to relax and him to keep an eye out for trouble. The swiftness of his action is a welcome counterpoint to the wild fear I experienced moments ago in this house of the devil with its blue satin walls and corniced ceiling filled with satyrs hotfooting through reeds after bare-bottomed nymphs. I should call it madness, run from him, but I don't. It's that madness and my need for him that keep me close to him.

Back and forth I sway my hips, slipping my hand down over my belly, inching closer to my pussy, crying out in a strangled gasp when his fingers press down on my clit, teasing me, working hard to make me come. Here, now? Yes! Wet and hot with excitement, I throw reason to the ill wind that brought me to this house, close my eyes, and enjoy it. Oh, it feels so good I don't want him to stop. I struggle to make my body obey my desire and let go, my pleasure building until I can stand it no longer and it takes my breath away. I gasp and begin to moan, overcome by all the sensations swirling through me, half of me fearful we'll be discovered, the other half afraid he might stop.

Just when I think I'll go mad if my body doesn't find release, a wave of intense pleasure overcomes me. I cry out with relief and joy, thrusting my hips to capture every sensation rolling over me. My breathing is heavy and ragged, my pulse pounding, but I can't stop. When Paul feels me peak, he rides the wave with me, his fingers pressing hard, but not too hard on my engorged bud. Then he slows down, keeping his rhythm in sync with mine until I slump against him, exhausted.

Twisting my hair through his fingers, he murmurs words of endearment in my ear, comforting me, though I sense the tension in his body building. I want to satisfy him, but I fear what will happen to us if we're discovered indulging in a passionate cock-to-pussy embrace.

Opening my eyes, determined not to cry, I'm at last forced to come face-to-face with the reason why the warm stirrings in my belly remain unsatisfied. I came, yes, but I want more. The hardness of the man pressed against me is maddening, his muscular body pushed into my breasts, my hips. Shivering, I try to hold my breath, to keep the exotic incense from entering my brain and flying me to a place where I have no intention of landing. I can't stop the heat from him touching me, tempting me. I want him inside me, need him, but I have to resist. Keep my senses.

I put my hand up to his face. He doesn't stop me when I push his mask upward, revealing his face. I pull back surprised, though pleasantly intrigued by what I see. He's lost his youthful aspect, and a more noble masculinity has taken its place. Even his hair is slightly gray at the temples and the planes of his face are pulled toward a more mature appearance, making him even more handsome. The effect on me is immediate. Here is a man with a raw sex appeal that sends my senses reeling. A question, however, lingers on the tip of my brain, though I don't dare ask it. Not yet.

I shudder, confusion swirling around me. Who is this man who sends my pussy into overdrive? From the thrills I've experienced in his arms, I fancy he belongs to a new breed of Parisian libertine who shuts their door on the outside world and celebrates the art of love, the dream of seduction, and the promise of satisfying sex. I long to linger in his world and partake of this bohemian attitude with my lover. He's in the full éclat of his masculinity and artistic genius. His longish black hair sweeps untamed over the top of his mask in a swirling tempest, his eyes are the color of a moonless night, his mouth set in a determined line to keep me close to him.

Knowing he's satisfied my immediate need, he responds to the smell of my sweet honey drizzling down between my thighs and staining my white pantaloons, inhaling my scent into his lungs. His hands move over my body, touching and probing me everywhere, much to my delight. I return the favor, reaching under his red robe and grabbing his erect cock, then lightly running my fingers up and down his shaft. My eyes never leave his face. I can't stop looking at him, as if I'm seeing him for the first time. I feel like an artist trying to capture the movement of the clouds. There's a uniqueness about him that defies understanding.

"Paul, you're as handsome as a god—"

"We must escape," he says, dismissing my remarks. "The duke is planning some macabre ritual to increase his virility by worshiping at the altar of the demons. To do so, he must create a night in hell with intoxicating smells, sounds, and colors. An alchemy of the senses to stimulate his cock, which means a virgin sacrifice."

I nod. "And *I'm* the virgin."

"Yes. He'll consummate his virility as the Prince of Darkness by having sexual intercourse with—"

I cut him off. "But why this Black Mass?"

"The ceremony is a parody of the Catholic ritual with prayers recited backward and an upside-down cross. But as celebrated by members of the Order of the Golden Dawn, it's simply a convenience to satisfy their lusty, sexual appetites for orgies rather than worship. Dominance. Violence, cruelty."

"Who is this Abbé you mentioned?"

"Abbé Bescanon is a defrocked priest who believes God should be worshipped naked, as Adam did, and the Devil rewards his followers with pleasure and power."

I draw a deep breath. "What are they planning to do with me, Paul?"

"After the duke fucks you, he'll take a sheet soiled with his semen and offer it at the altar for the sacrifice—"

"*Listen!*" I grab his arm. "Someone's coming."

Paul moves in front of me. Above the loud chanting of the men in red robes comes the chatter of someone running past us, then stopping.

"Stay back," Paul orders.

We hear a giggle. "You can't hide your pretty pussy from me, mademoiselle," a female voice murmurs. "I've found you—"

Poking her head between the two towering statues, Madame Chapet squeals with laughter, pressing her half-exposed breasts out in front of her, sticking out her tongue, wiggling it in anticipation, until she sees us, embracing.

"*Merde alors,* it's Monsieur Borquet!" she cries out, then before she can utter another word, Paul grabs the woman, encircling his arm around her corpulent waist and lifting her up off her feet and, although she sputters and curses, he succeeds in keeping his hand over her mouth.

"*Run,* Autumn—through the salon. The great Medusa-masked door leads to the secret stairway. Now, *go!*"

I hear Madame Chapet gasping for air, struggling, as Paul pushes her big, sagging breasts out of his face and ties her hands together with a red silk cord. I rush through the upstairs *grand salon,* my boots tapping on the polished wooden floor.

Don't look back.

*Don't look back.*

Running, running. The scene chills me. The chapel is glowing with an eerie golden-pink fluttering of shadows, like an old silent movie. *Where's the door with the Medusa mask?* I keep running until I hear the soothing notes of voices chanting monosyllabic sounds. I stop, peek around the corner and see rows of men in red robes and animal masks lined up in front of the altar. Some are masturbating, others offering their erections swaying in front of them like candy treats.

Naked women anoint the rosebud tips of their breasts and their pubic hair with unholy red wine then genuflect in front of an upside-down crucifix. Six tall black candles burn on top of a black-draped altar, and the smoke of the incense permeates throughout the chapel from swinging censers suspended from the hands of two celebrants. A flash of nausea hits me in the stomach, my tongue swells in my mouth, my teeth clench together. *What insane beast has been unleashed in this house?* Tears sting my eyes. I've been thrown into a snake pit of devil worshipers.

"Grab her!" someone calls out.

I spin around, feeling the heat of their gaze. *They've found me.* I try to run, but two men in red robes grab my arms, nearly pulling them out of their sockets.

"Let me go!" I yell. "You're all insane."

A man in a red robe says, "We've got her, Lord Bingham."

The creature in black appears in front of me from out of the smoky haze drifting around me. I scream when he yanks my head back by my hair. *Hard.* A hissing snake slithers down his arm, edging so close to my face I can hear the flicking of its tongue. The duke positions his arm in such a manner that the snake is so close to my nipple if I so much as breathe, the serpent will bite it. I keep still. I don't dare move when the Englishman laughs, then leans down and looks into my eyes. I refuse to show fear, but his voice chills me as he announces in a loud, bold voice:

"Let the sacrifice begin!"

Paul raged inside, spittle drizzling down the side of his mouth as he carried the heavyset woman over his shoulder, so incensed was his anger toward her. She beat on his back, but he grabbed her flabby toes and squeezed them hard.

"Be quiet, madame!" he ordered. He was grateful no one had seen them.

"*Salaud,* bastard," she sputtered, kicking her feet. Madame Chapet snarled at him as he opened the door to a tiny, round room slightly bigger than a priest hole and pushed her inside. Women's petticoats, corsets and dresses hung neatly on racks, along with several pots of rouge, black kohl and lip salve arranged on a tray. Pink-yellow candleglow reflected off red glass hanging pendants and flickered over the erotic mural on the wall highlighting slim, naked women draped over high back vespers chairs, spreading their legs and playing with their cunts. The air smelled of cinnamon-scented wax.

He dumped her onto the floor, knocking over the tray of cosmetics and sending the little pots cascading to the padded floor without a sound. Unloosening her silken bonds, the woman rocked back and forth, one hand on her hip. She couldn't resist asking him, "Why did you return to Paris, monsieur?"

"That's none of your business, madame." He looked around for something, anything to stuff into her mouth.

"What kind of game are you playing with me, monsieur?" She dropped some of her anger and hoisted up her sagging breasts. She licked her lips and looked at him with desire in her eyes. "Unless you have a different game in mind."

Paul shook his head. "You're to stay here until Autumn and I are safely out of this place. Do you understand?"

She pursed her lips, then wet them with her tongue. "I want twenty gold louis for my trouble."

Paul smiled. "I don't have any money."

"Then I'm not staying, monsieur," she said firmly, trying to get to her feet. She took a deep breath. "Although from what I see revealed underneath your robe, you possess *un coursier*, a cock any woman would gladly open her legs to receive. I regret not having had the opportunity to know you on more *intimate* terms."

She bolted for the door, but she wasn't fast enough. Paul

grabbed her around the neck, pulling off her pearl choker. "I should strangle you with these pearls, madame—"

"Monsieur...*you wouldn't!* I'm just a poor soul in need of a helping hand," she pleaded, gasping for breath. "Please!"

Paul changed his mind and slipped the pearl choker into the pocket in the folds of his robe under his pistol. He'd returned it to her after he and Autumn were safely out of Paris. "You're a liar and a cheat, madame, but you're not going to stop us from escaping."

Still holding her by the neck, he grabbed a corset and tied her hands together with the long lacings. Then before she could kick him, her eyes riveted on his thick cock, still erect though in need of the attention of a pair of pretty pink lips. Ignoring her gaze, he dumped her onto the padded floor and tied her feet together with a ruffle he tore off a hanging petticoat.

"It won't do any good to restrain me, monsieur. The duke will find you," she spewed, "and when he does, he'll kill you, and as for that girl, he will—"

"Enough of your vile talk, madame," Paul said, stuffing a black stocking into her mouth then tying a second stocking over her eyes. "I bid you and your greedy disposition *adieu.*"

Ignoring her muffled cries, knowing it was only a matter of minutes until someone heard her kicking her feet against the wall, he closed the rounded door, sealing her inside.

He walked back toward the *grand salon,* his senses alert. Someone had left open a long, six-paned window on the top floor, letting in a cool breeze scented with the acrid smells of the city. And was that thunder he heard? A storm was imminent. Wiping the sweat from his brow, he looked out the window down to the ground below, planning his escape route. In the night creeping closer to the edge of dawn, a black cock cried out.

*Autumn was in danger.*

He ran back to the *grand salon* to find her.

Again the feeling that he'd lost her came back to visit him.

Lying nude from the waist up on a hard mattress on an altar covered with black velvet with a pillow beneath my head, tilting my face upward, I feel as if I'm floating in deep space. My ripped pantaloons and petticoats are pulled up around my waist, exposing me. My legs dangle down over the end, and my arms are spread out. In my hands I hold two black candles. I'm not tied down, but a heavy leaden sensation in my limbs keeps me pinned to the altar.

I roll my head, slowly, in denial, as if I'm caught in a spell. *Where is Paul?* Was he only an illusion, brought on by the strange, weird thoughts floating around in my head? Sensations of something pulling me and—do I dare say it?— urging me back to my own time? A crippling loneliness takes hold of me and suffocates me, making me take deep, heavy breaths. I long for the safety of his arms, but all I feel is a rising nausea creeping up through me like a squirming mass of snakes.

I groan softly and open my eyes. Fuzzy, hazy images blur in front of me. Kneeling before the altar, I hear the duke, in his black-hooded domino, invoking Satan, reading prayers from a missal with red, black and white pages and bound in wolfskin. Around me the worshipers chant hymns, draping their naked bodies over prayer desks and chairs covered in crimson velvet and gold. I see a man reach over the back of a chair and grab a woman's bare breast while another man laps at her pussy, sucking on her. Then a slender dark-haired priestess leans over and runs her devil red lips up and down the man's engorged shaft, licking all around the sensitive head and sending him into a deistic ecstasy.

*"Sanguis euis super nos et filios nostros,"* they chant, lost in their pursuit of pleasure, their eyes hungrily drinking in the nude and debauched delights on display in the name of devil worship. "His blood be upon us and upon our children."

Pulling my head up, I see the celebrants forming a semi-circle around the altar, writhing, screaming hysterically, howling like animals, grunting, then prostrating themselves on the ground, eager to grab a ready cock or a wet pussy, a pert nipple or a fleshy buttock, whatever was closest to satisfy their depraved need to quench their red-hot lust.

I watch in disgust as the duke pulls out small, round *oblata,* hosts, from a chalice and holds one over my head. *Holy Eucharists?* No, they're not the flour and water wafers, but slices of turnip, stained bloodred. I watch in disgust as he chews on the make-believe sacramental wafer, then washes it down with wine from a silver chalice studded with rubies and diamonds.

Next, the duke places the chalice between my breasts, then dips his fingers into the cup and sprinkles the drugged wine on my body, taking care to let it drip over my nipples then lick it off with his pointy tongue. Next, he drizzles it over my belly and down lower to the soft mat of damp curls between my legs. I flex my pubic muscles in protest when his tongue eases my labia apart, tormenting me as he bites on my delicate flesh. I will my senses to go numb, but the aromatic haze of drugs dangles under my nose, shooting up my nostrils. I hold my breath, but the incense is so thick it seeps into the pores of my skin as he removes his tongue and licks his lips. Then with a look toward the men watching him as if to say the exploratory part of the ritual has ended, he sets fire to a paste in a copper tray, burning the strong-smelling herbs under my nose. A paste of myrrh, incense, camphor and cloves.

I struggle fiercely, but I can't free myself. I'm exhausted. Sweaty, dripping with perspiration. My hips and thighs, as well as my pussy are exposed, my nipples hard. My nearly naked body glows a hot pink under the gleaming red-lit pendants of glass. I watch in horror as the duke lays out a sword, a knife with an ebony handle and a wand on the altar alongside me. As if in denial, the old house shakes, rumbles. Or is that thunder?

A flash of anger rips through my terror. *"Release me!"* I spit at him. "I want nothing to do with your godless magic."

"How *dare* you speak, whore!" He slaps my face soundly on both cheeks. "You have no will. You must obey your master."

I feel the sting of his hand, but it doesn't dull my spirit. I twist my head from side to side as the duke holds my chin and forces a strong, pungent-smelling wine down my throat, choking me. The taste burns my tongue, making me sweat as I swallow it, then makes me turn cold. Its effect is immediate, rendering me confused, terrified. The fear of certain death rushes through my veins and I've never been more powerless to stop it.

Next, the duke waves a slender crystal wand with a pointy end over my body from head to toe, sweeping it down over my shoulder and rubbing it back and forth across my taut nipples and sending sparks down to my belly. The constant friction makes the sensitive peaks on my nipples raw, but he's not finished with me. He follows his unholy trail down to my mound and pokes the hard object into my cunt, sliding it inside me, then slipping it in and out until it's dripping with my juices. I buck my body hard, trying to expel the object, but he pushes it in deeper, making me scream. I can't stop screaming. Whether my cries unnerve him or he's tiring of the ritual, I don't know, but he removes the crystal and shakes a human skull in front of my eyes. I cry out again, but this time my voice cracks from the terror pumping inside me. I draw back, but I can't escape the tiny, black maggots peeking out at me from the deep, sightless eye sockets in the skull. Nausea wiggles through my guts. I struggle to keep from throwing up and choking on my own vomit. Reluctantly I force myself to stare back at the duke, daring him to face me. I'm not prepared for the dead stare of the man's eyes. Penetrating, hard. His fingers seem to twitch with a supernatural energy as he holds the knife poised over me.

The voice of the duke comes again, cold and inhuman, chanting the words backward, then forward: "You will die, whore of the master, then be reborn with the seed of the Prince of Darkness in you."

I hold my breath, my heart pumping wildly as the long

blade of the knife comes down toward my nude breasts like a silver-blue flame burning brightly against the backdrop of deep blackness. The howling frenzy of the celebrants around me, urging the duke to fuck me then finish the deed, fills my ears. I hear a loud scream of shock, horror, pain.

*It's my own voice.*

Then someone throws a black veil over my face and darkness overcomes me.

# CHAPTER TWENTY

Paul pushed the barrel of his pistol into the back of the duke's skull. He cocked the trigger, then pulled it back, slow and easy, his finger just a breath away from squeezing it. Then for some reason—call it a deep sense of humanity—the steel fiber of his being telling him not to kill this man, he stopped, unable to pull the trigger and murder him in cold blood.

*Why can't I pull the trigger, why can't I shoot him? What is it about this Englishman that makes me fearful yet draws me to him?*

The duke had no idea what conflicting, tortured thoughts were running through Paul's mind. Wary of the feel of cold metal pressing up against his brain, Lord Bingham stiffened, his body rigid, his senses alert to danger from the man in the fox mask. The surprise of the action made him curse, but he held fast to the knife in his hand.

"Drop the knife, monsieur," Paul ordered. *"Now."*

"What stupid game are you playing, monsieur?" demanded the duke. "The girl is ready to receive my seed, her cunt moist and wet." He waved the crystal wand wet with her juices in Paul's direction. The sweet scent of her fragrance drifted to his nostrils, making him both angry and erect. "You and the others will have your chance to fuck her when I'm finished with her—"

"You will never touch her, monsieur," Paul said. "Never!"

His anger fueled by the duke's words, but unwilling to admit he should have killed him when he had the chance, Paul pushed the duke aside with such force the Englishman dropped both the knife and the crystal and stumbled backward, collapsing on top of several female celebrants. The man in the black-hooded domino scrambled out from underneath the naked women and got to his feet.

"What do you want, monsieur?" the duke yelled, angry that his sexual games had been disrupted by this intruder. *"Who are you?"*

Paul ripped off his fox mask. And grinned. "Paul Borquet, at your service, monsieur."

*"Borquet!* Where the bloody hell did you come from?" Then the duke did a strange thing, something that unsettled Paul, made him thrust the pistol in front of him, keeping the Englishman in his sights. The duke stared at him, long and hard, as if trying to make up his mind about something, then he said, "You look different, *older,* much older…old enough to be—"

"I'm warning you, monsieur, no tricks."

"—my brother!"

His *brother?*

Paul snapped his head around, shocked by the unbelievable words, the completely maddening statement that this

Englishman was his brother. He'd thought he knew what he had to do, rough him up, *kill* him if he had to. But for the first time since he crossed paths with this crazed aristocrat, Paul studied the man's face. Startlingly blue eyes, angular jawline, dark hair, chiseled face. Yes, the resemblance was there. He just hadn't wanted to see it before, but he'd *felt* it, known *somehow* this mad Englishman shared a bloodline not impossible to believe. His mother was French, but his father had been an Englishman. There was a special license, a quick marriage and a child, before his father's family had sent her packing from England.

So many years ago.

So far away.

*Why?*

The duke said, "I see in your eyes you believe me, Monsieur Borquet."

Paul nodded. "I do."

"I assure you, it's true," the duke spat. "You are my older half brother, erased from the official family records until my father's death several months ago. A copy of the marriage license and your birth certificate with your mother's name on it were discovered among his papers." He paused. "I traced you to Paris through your artwork which had made its way to London. When I first discovered who you were, I didn't believe it. You were much younger than the age on your birth certificate, yet now—"

"If I am your *older* half brother, monsieur," Paul said, cutting him off, not wanting to explain his dabbling in black magic, as well as the unpredictability of the black arts that had unexpectedly returned him to his mature appearance, "—I am also heir to the title you covet so dearly."

"Exactly, my *dear* brother," said the duke, staring at him, his face creased and puckered up like dried leather, "which is why I regret you didn't heed my warning. Now I have no choice but to kill you."

Paul was so close he could see the unspeakable hatred in that gaze. The Englishman gave no quarter, stood fast, even his breathing seemed to have stopped.

"You won't get away with it, Lord Bingham."

"Won't I? My men are stationed at all the exits. I have nothing to fear."

"I believe *I'm* the one with the pistol."

"You won't even get to the stairway," the duke threatened, indicating the group of men in red robes and masks, rallying around him, mumbling at Paul.

"You will be cursed, monsieur, your rebellious spirit broken."

"The Devil himself will strike you down."

"The woman has bewitched you with her hot cunt, monsieur. You will pay dearly."

Paul shook his head, tossing off the insults and lewd comments thrown at him. "I doubt if *any* of you will try to stop me. I have six bullets. Enough for all of you." The men backed down. They were gentlemen with a perverted taste for pussy, he surmised, but little gumption. The duke's bodyguards, however, could be a problem.

He looked down at Autumn, lying prone on the altar, her naked breasts shiny with sweat, her chest rising and falling with heavy breaths. He pulled off the black veil covering her beautiful face. Her eyes were closed, her eyelids dark and smudged with purple shadows. He was about to pull her to him when—

"I should have killed you when I had the opportunity, monsieur." The duke reached for the knife on the floor.

Paul caught the movement out of the corner of his eye, swung away from Autumn, and fired twice. The pistol roared, and fire flashed from its barrels. Both shots ripped into the duke's long black domino, jolting him, hitting him in the shoulder, the heart, Paul wasn't sure where, before he fell backward into the long, six-paned window behind him. His head struck the glass, and several of the panes cracked. He dropped to the floor and was as still as the dawn creeping inside. He lay silent, motionless, his hood covering his face.

"He's dead, monsieur!" a woman cried out.

*I don't trust him. It could be a trick,* thought Paul.

With the duke's bold confession still echoing in his head, Paul was torn between doing what his conscience told him to do—check the condition of the man claiming to be his half brother—and the fear edging along the perimeters of his mind that if he didn't leave quickly, he'd lose Autumn forever. He hadn't aimed to kill—would he have tried to kill him if he hadn't told him he was his half brother?—but he dared not get any closer to the body, knowing if he *were* alive, the duke wouldn't hesitate to end *his* life.

Pushing aside the smoky inhalants invading his brain, Paul kept his pistol aimed at the duke and, holding Autumn around the waist, he lifted her up off the altar.

"Autumn...*Autumn,* wake up!" he cried out. Her cold,

unconscious body pressed against him sent a momentary fear through him that she was dead, but he could feel the beating of her heart against his chest.

She shook her head slowly, then opened her eyes. "*Ooohhh*...my head. What happened?"

"They drugged you. Quickly, we're leaving this unholy place."

She looked up, then grabbed on to his robe with immense relief when she saw him. "Paul! How did you—"

"No time now." Did she have to look at him like that, eyes all dewy and wanting? This was no time for him to feel the heat of her desire, the pink moistness of her cunt against him, making him so hard his cock jutted out in front of him. "Can you walk?"

"Yes, I think so." She put her hand to her mouth. "Paul, what happened..." She gasped when she saw the duke's prone body lying on the floor, several women leaning over him, crying, moaning. "Is he dead?"

"I don't know and we can't stay to find out. *Allons*. Let's go."

"Paul, did you—"

"Yes, I shot him. He forced my hand. I don't know why, but I'm sorry I did. The bastard was my brother."

"*What?*" Her voice was incredulous.

"No time to explain. *Allons*. We must move quickly."

"Even if he *was* your brother, Paul, he would have killed you," she said softly, laying her hand on his arm, and for a brief moment that comforted him. Crazed, half-insane by the churning emotions pulling him in several directions,

Paul held her in his arms. *I can feel her heart beating quick. I won't let anything happen to her.*

"Hurry, Autumn!" he urged.

"Help me down, Paul."

She gathered up her skirt and petticoats, and with a little difficulty he helped her ease her body down from the altar, one leg, then the other. He cursed when her long skirt caught on the edge of the altar and, as she tugged on it, she knocked over a tall, lighted black candle.

"Autumn, watch out!" he yelled, but it was too late. Instantly, the altar cloth caught on fire and golden orange flames licked the candles like giant tongues, melting the black wax into big, ugly puddles on the floor.

"My God, I'm on fire!" she cried, gathering up her skirts around her and trying to smother the growing flames with her hands.

"Don't move—don't move!" Paul yelled, refusing to panic. He peered into the flickering brightness growing around her, stomping out the yellow flames with his sandaled feet, the crackling sound echoing in his ears. He blocked out the cries and panicked voices of the naked women and nearly nude men scrambling to put out the fire springing up around them. The smell of singed hair and burnt flesh assaulted his senses with a pungent stench that choked him and made him gag. The fire was out of control, devouring the altar, the window hangings, the tapestries on the walls, the flames jumping onto chairs, turning red velvet to charred black. The sight of the screaming naked women and cursing gentlemen repulsed him, dragged him down into a subliminal world he never wanted to see again.

He was fearless of the danger to his bare skin. Nothing mattered but her. He ripped off her flimsy gown and crushed the burning material with his hands, feeling no pain, nothing, though the smell of his singed flesh reached his nostrils. And the smoke. Mixing with the incense, the spices, and creating a wildly intoxicating and deadly vapor that choked him. Choked Autumn. She was coughing, sputtering, sweating, her nude breasts glistening with sweat. He pulled down a hanging red velvet drape and threw it around her shoulders. She thanked him with her eyes and held it tightly around her. The bottom of her petticoats were singed, but she was unharmed.

He cursed his own stubbornness for allowing her to be subjected to this horror. If he hadn't taken leave of his senses, intent on satisfying his need to settle his account with the duke, they wouldn't be suffocating and gasping for breath in this third-floor deathtrap. All he could think about was getting out.

Getting *her* out. Fast.

"Head for the secret stairway," he yelled. "Stay with me. Don't stop."

In the minutes that followed, the atmosphere was chaotic, the mood of the celebrants both angry and fearful at having their fun spoiled. Paul kept to his mission, grabbing Autumn's hand then pulling her through the *grand salon*. With his arm around her waist and her arm encircling him, he kept his pistol drawn, his eyes straight ahead, pushing with the others toward the exit. In the middle of the smoke, with burning rafters falling around them, furniture turning to cinders, the fire consuming everything in its path, he saw two girls wrapped in curtain hangings dragging Madame Chapet down the hallway, looking for a way out. Where was the secret stairway? The Medusa mask door?

Where was it?

By now the flames from the fire were coming close, windows exploding everywhere around them. Paul ducked into a small alcove, pulling Autumn along with him. Lightning zapped through the broken windows, followed by thunder. But the rain didn't come. He pulled out the rolled-up pants hidden in his robe and put them on quickly to protect his body from the fire. Coughing, choking, he could see little through the smoke. He turned and saw a small door etched into the painted mural of a garden scene behind them, a door so small he would have to bend over to go through it. Or was it simply a *trompe-l'oeil*, a deception to the eye, like so many of the wall paintings? He had to try something, *anything* to get them out of here. He kicked open the small door with his foot, and darkness greeted them, cool and welcoming though without light, unlike the stairway he had entered through earlier in the evening.

"Is it a way out of here?" Autumn asked.

"I don't know. Stay back, I'll find out," Paul said, stepping to the side, and in a macabre way, the flames of yellow behind them threw enough light into the stairwell for him to see a small, winding stairway going down at least one, maybe two floors. He couldn't see any farther. "Take my hand, quickly, before the stairwell fills up with smoke."

Taking a breath, not looking back, he was about to pull Autumn with him into the small stairwell when—

"*Borquet!* Help me, *please!*"

Paul spun around, his pistol thrust out in front of him, his finger on the trigger, his heart beating fast, his mind spinning in so many directions at once. The duke staggered toward them, holding his chest—or was it his shoulder?—his other hand outstretched, blood running down his fingers. In his eyes he saw a tremulous fear, his features twisted into an expression that grated on his nerves. The Englishman knew he was going to burn to death. He collapsed on the floor.

*The man was his brother.*

Paul knew what he had to do.

First, get Autumn out of here. Make her go, don't stop, *don't!*

"Run, Autumn, down the stairway, *now!* I'll follow you."

She turned and a wrenching cry came from her throat. "No, Paul, I can't. I *won't.* I have the most horrible feeling if I do, I'll never see you again."

"I can't let my brother burn alive, Autumn. Go, quickly."

She hesitated, only a second, then said, "I understand."

Paul could see the rising fear in her eyes, but she didn't question him. She bent down, holding up her petticoats around her, and went through the tiny doorway. She started down the stairwell. He could hear her footsteps, tiny tapping sounds that seemed to echo, then disappear, as if she had disappeared. But he couldn't dwell on such thoughts; the fire was at his back, hot, crackling, dancing yellow flames with silver edges.

Where was the rain?

He raced over to the duke, replacing his pistol in his pocket, knowing now he wouldn't need it, then picked up his brother's slack body and slung him over his shoulder. He wasn't dead; he could hear him breathing, choking for air. With one hand shielding his face, the other holding on to the man on his back, Paul looked behind him for the small stairwell. *Merde,* the entire alcove was now consumed in red flames, the doorway gone, the entire wall of *trompe l'oeil* gardens and colonnades burning quickly, only charred fragments of paper remaining. Where had he sent Autumn? Where? To her death?

*No, I won't believe it.*

For the next few minutes he wandered around in circles, avoiding falling beams, pools of flames, his face sweating profusely, his brother slung over his shoulder.

"Over here, monsieur!" he heard a voice calling out to him from the other direction.

Where? *Where?*

He followed the sound of the voice, and the smoke seemed to dissipate a little. He must be in an area of the house the fire hadn't yet consumed. Leaning forward, squinting, with the duke's limp body slung over his shoulder, he saw two men also wearing red robes running toward an open doorway with the Medusa mask door. *Yes,* that was it. He grunted, gathered his strength and moved quickly, taking both himself and the unconscious duke down the lighted stairway. One, two, then several steps at a time, nearly falling at times from the weight of the man on his shoulder.

All the time his mind racing. Where had he sent Autumn?

Did she make it?

Did she?

Finally he neared the end of the stairwell. He was afraid the door might be locked, that he was destined to die saving his brother but losing Autumn. Without hesitation he kicked open the door and almost shouted with relief as he rushed into the fresh, dewy dawn of light raindrops. Filling his lungs with clean, cool air, he laid the duke on the ground. Out of breath, his pulse beating wildly, he put his ear to the man's chest. He was breathing and, from what he could see, his wounds were not serious. The duke was immediately surrounded by his bodyguards, who gave the artist a strange look, then turned their attention to the unconscious man in the black-hooded domino.

"Take care of my brother, *messieurs,*" was all he said.

Paul walked through the crowd gathered outside of the *hôtel privé,* an assortment of women crying, men cursing, most trying to cover their nakedness with singed pieces of clothing. Bare breasts flamed red from the fire, buttocks painted with strokes of fine black soot, pubic hair tinted charcoal from the cinders. A melee of quivering flesh that moments ago resembled sophisticated creatures with lust as their common denominator. Now they cried and shrieked like frightened animals. He looked right, then left for the redhead.

*She's not here. She's not here.*

That meant that she—

*No!*

Paul groaned. Loudly. Before his eyes, in only a few minutes, the *hôtel privé* burned—flames leaping out of the third story windows, seething, roaring. The light rain wasn't enough to put out the fire. He looked on in silence, unable to speak. The sky was aflame with mustard-orange streaks swirling through imperious white clouds and black smoke. The elegantly carved wooden door, smooth Roman sculptures, furniture, even the courtyard were being consumed in the belly of the advancing fire.

*Where was Autumn? Where was she?*

He continued walking up and down, grabbing everyone, asking them if they had seen the redhead. Several celebrants, shivering, crying, cursing, shook their head. A woman stifled a scream as the wooden archways framing the first floor went up next in spiraling red flames. Singeing embers flew through the air in a strange pattern against the black smoke.

Paul swept his eyes over the hot, roaring fire, but it was cold fear that rolled through his body. He shielded his face with his hand from the red glow of the fire. Husky emotion boiled over in his voice and he cried out, moaning with pain. Ugly, raw sounds filled the air around him. Was that *his* voice? Then an unfamiliar echo sounded again and again in the hidden depths of his mind. The pounding of his heartbeat?

He had to do something, *anything*. Autumn was still in the *hôtel privé* somewhere, overcome by smoke, and God help him, burning alive.

Moving, not thinking, he rushed back toward the *hôtel privé*, intent on going after Autumn. Into the fire. He would find her. He couldn't fail. He had to save her—

He stopped. A deafening roar of fire jumped into his path, burning balls of fire falling from the first-floor balcony, blocking him, its wavering human form licking his face with its hot, steamy breath and daring him to come closer. The air turned heavy and dark, choking him. Lightning crackled overhead. Thunder rumbled. Churning black smoke closed in around him, snatching the hope of seeing her again from the workings of his mind. The suffocating darkness held him tightly in its grasp and reminded him of the look in her eyes just moments ago and the words she'd said to him: *I have the most horrible feeling if I do, I'll never see you again.*

Her words hurled him into a cold well of fear that wouldn't let go. He couldn't stop shivering. His teeth chattered. His lips trembled.

He ran back toward the house.

"You can't go back in there, monsieur!" someone yelled after him. "The whole house is burning!"

"I *must,*" Paul yelled back, not heeding the warning. "I must save the woman I love."

A moment before I head down the stairwell, just after I leave Paul, I hear a tremendous roar. *Thunder.* Then I feel a chill so intense I shudder, as if someone presses a knife against my flesh, its silver blade sliding up and down my bare back, teasing, pricking my skin until tiny bumps appear.

What's happening to me?

I tremble as if I'm being dragged down, *down,* farther into…into *what?* I don't know, don't have time to think, just run.

My high-button boots pound hard on the steps of the narrow stairway, my loud footsteps drowning out the sounds of doubt in my mind. I descend the stairs two and three at a time, my mind racing, my heart pounding, mixing with the hot sweat seeping over my brow. My moment of desperation comes when I least expect it. Cold stings my face. An electricity zaps through me, hot, burning my skin. My boots feel damp and moist, and the velvet material covering my shoulders sticks to the bare skin on my back. A wave of dizziness makes me lose my step. I'm afraid.

Afraid of never coming back.

Of never seeing Paul again.

I trip over my own feet, stumbling, my knees buckling underneath me. Before I can steady myself, a daring thought edges into my mind. *The same bone-chilling cold and electricity came to visit me before when—*

My heart drops to my stomach. Everything comes back to me in a rush. The studio in Marais, the feeling of darkness, the sound of electricity zapping and buzzing around me. *Am I going back to my own time? Oh, God, am I?*

Somehow, some way, I've come full circle, lost in a darkness so black it can only exist in that indescribable hole suspended between the present and the future. I'm trapped in a burning house, but I'm going back to a house burning in my own time.

Filled with despair, hope drained from me, I continue down the stairs. I can't think. My heart is exploding. I'm going to die in a fire.

I scream.

Just as Paul rushed through the front entrance of the *hôtel privé,* back into the house, shaking, sweating, he heard a woman scream. Autumn was alive. Had to be. Where was she? Where? As if defying him, a wall of flames rose up before him, daring him to find her.

*No, no, no!* He couldn't let anything stop him. Clenching his fists, steeling himself against the fire, he picked up a chair, held it out in front of him, then lurched forward and rushed up the main staircase, his pulse racing madly, his breath coming fast. He didn't get very far—the fire was blocking his path, forcing him to go back.

Cursing, he threw the chair into the flames, then yelled out her name, "Autumn, *Autumn!*" He ran back and forth on the bottom floor, shielding his face from the fire roaring down the grand staircase, praying he'd hear her scream again. He heard nothing. Sweat trickled down his forehead, oozed down the front and back of his red robe. He had to do something, anything.

Crouching down low, Paul crept between piles of burning, charred debris, looking for another stairway. He saw what was left of a garden *trompe l'oeil* wall scene with hanging vines, painted on flowers, statuary, and a small door. The scene was similar to the one on the top floor. Did it also hide a secret stairwell?

Feeling the heat of the fire advancing in his direction, choking on smoke, he felt around the edge of the wall, looking for an opening, something—all these old houses in the Marais district had secret stairways added during the Revolution—but he found nothing.

The fire was at his back, so close he swore it singed the hairs on the back of his neck, but he wouldn't stop looking for an opening. It had to be here, *had to be.* Covering his mouth with part of his long robe, he started banging with his fists and pushing on the small door on the wall. He blinked sweat out of his eyes, coughed, choked on the smoke, when—

—suddenly the door gave way and a burst of cold air hit him in the face. Anticipation, excitement, even relief rushed through him as if an unseen force reached out to him and pulled him inside. Holding his robe close around him, he bent down low, and in a crouching position, he slipped through the door and into the small stairwell. He paused to peer up the stairs, through the deep shadows, half expecting to see fire. As far as he could see, only darkness. Then a loud noise behind him shook his nerves. Thunder. A strong wind blew by his face, stinging his cheeks with cold, and the door closed behind him. He cursed, but he wasn't going back without Autumn.

He put his hands out in front of his face, at least where he *thought* his face was, but he could see nothing. He must be in the dark, secret stairwell, and no matter what happened, he wouldn't stop, wouldn't give up looking for her.

He pulled the collar of his red robe up around his neck but it didn't keep out the clamminess crawling all over his body like a cloak of maggots already claiming him for the grave. He shivered. *Merde,* it was cold in here. And black. Midnight black. As if the ends of the earth all came together in this one spot and dissolved into a heavy fog of nothingness so thick that the present coexisted with the future.

He kept moving up the stairs, walking, if it be called that, for he felt as if he was floating. An unearthly tremor went through him as though some unseen, irresistible force pushed him from behind. He was certain he would find Autumn. He had to believe it. Had to. He'd go mad if he didn't.

To keep up his spirits, he recalled the pleasure of shining green eyes, *her* green eyes, captivating him with their desire. He thought about the touch of her, the feel of her body pressed up against his, her pussy boiling with the heat of her desire, her cunt lips swelling, her clit hardening into a pink pearl, her juices covering his fingers—

He stopped. Wait. There was something strange about this area, something he couldn't put into words. By the feel of the steps beneath his feet, the balustrade under his fingers, he sensed this was the secret stairway where he'd find Autumn.

I shiver as cold fingers press possessively around my shoulders, urging me forward. Blind hands, seeking, groping. Whispers, soft yet demanding, push into my ears, telling me my deed in the past is done, complete, and I mustn't resist. Not resist? I can't go back to my own time. Won't, dammit. Leave Paul? For what reason? To live without him? The only man I ever loved? No, I can't, I *won't*.

As if the fates can read my thoughts, an unknown force pulls harder on me, jerking my head back awkwardly and nearly bringing me to my knees. A clammy, moist cold seems to encircle my body a little at a time, like the moldy wrappings of an ancient mummy freshly unearthed from its tomb.

It's the Egyptian god Min. His black magic is pulling me back. I sold my soul to him when I wished to be young and beautiful. I broke the spell when I fell in love with Paul Borquet and now it's time to pay.

Then it's true. Paul *did* die in a fire trying to save the woman he loved, as the old artist told me. A heavy sadness drags me down. Did I also die? Or is there another ending?

I'll never give up.

I pull the soft material covering my shoulders closer around me. I feel something pressing up against me, its breath cold and frosty, blowing on my neck. I begin shaking. I can't stop shaking. Though wet with dampness, the velvet material offers some protection against...*against what?* I can't see anything. Not a glimmer pierces the heavy blackness. A strangeness hits me. It isn't something I can feel, smell or taste, but a deepening of my own consciousness. As if I'm reaching down into myself, into the core of my soul.

Oh, this is insane. I pull my arms to my breasts, trying to keep warm. It's a cold, damp stairway, that's all, dammit. Not some supernatural passageway between life and... what? Death?

*"Autumn...Autumn!"*

I stop, listen hard. It *has* to be Paul. His voice sounds garbled, as if it's filtered through a mechanical device. Then his voice fades, winding down, slower, slower. Until he sounds like an old vinyl record losing speed.

Before I take another step, my feet start sliding from underneath me, as if I'm tumbling, riding in the center of a rolling barrel in an amusement park, the kind that goes round and round and round. My hair blows wildly around my face as though I'm in a wind tunnel. The force of the wind is so strong it pulls the velvet drape off my shoulders and sends it flying down through the stairwell. Instinctively I cover my bare breasts with my hands as my petticoats billow up around me. Even my teeth ache, and I can't catch my breath.

Struggling to keep my balance, I try to turn around, but a ghostly hand tightens around my throat and a great rush of wind pushes me down the stairway. Down...*down,* I fall, tumbling over and over, black spots pushing in front of my eyes, driving out hope as I slide awkwardly, recklessly, back down the stairway into a timeless vacuum.

Paul couldn't see anything. A cold fear gripped him, but he couldn't stop. No matter how exhausted, how much his body ached, he had to go on. Find her.

He stumbled over the rolling floor beneath him, managing to regain his equilibrium, forcing one foot in front of the other, aware the stairway was changing, flattening out though he couldn't see it, making it harder for him to climb up. A flurry of softness—it felt like velvet—blew past him, brushing his face. He reached out to grab it, but it flew over his fingertips and he couldn't hold on to it.

With the demon wind whipping him in the face, he made his way up the steep stairs, though he faltered a few times, losing his balance again and again. He was determined to push his way through the great wind attacking him from all sides as if he were fighting against a living creature of the night. He didn't think about himself. Only

Autumn. He never cared for another human being as deeply as he did for the redhead.

As he pushed forward, he realized a great whooshing sound was headed toward him, would smack directly into him and push him farther back into the blackness if he didn't hold on to the balustrade.

He held on to the thin railing that shook wildly, rattling his body, his brain. He thought he'd lost his mind when he heard the screams of a woman coming straight toward him.

I tumble down the rolling stairway, my body jerking through the air awkwardly, my petticoats wrapping around my legs. I'm out of control, trying to grab on to something, anything, when my body slams to a stop as I run into something or someone.

*Someone?* my mind questions, disbelieving. *Who?*

The rush of the wind pulling at me can't drown out the deepness of the voice shouting my name or tear away the feel of his hands pressing me close to him as strong arms wrap around my waist, then covering my bare breasts with his burned hands, caressing me, comforting me. I lay my hands over his, trying to soothe his pain. I can't speak, but a loud moan escapes from deep within me. Even in the deadness of this dark place I feel alive again, my soul reborn with a new, enduring spirit.

Somehow, some way, Paul found me.

"*Autumn...*" I hear him yell, fighting against the power of the great rolling wind driving us downward.

"Don't let go of me...don't let go!" I call out, holding on to him and trying to keep my long hair blowing wildly about me from hitting him in the face. I can't see him, but I sense his features are twisted by fear.

"What's happening?" he yells into my ear.

"Someone…something is pulling us forward to my time," I yell back.

"*Your* time?"

"Yes, over a hundred years into the future."

Paul says nothing. I can imagine what he must be thinking, feeling. For several long minutes he battles his way slowly down the stairway, with me holding on to his waist. My tender nipples press hard against his muscular back, the incessant rubbing making me mewl and gasp in surprise at finding pleasure while fear courses through my veins. Fighting the whirlpool trying to swallow us up, forcing our way through the inner guts of the beast of darkness trying to keep us prisoner, our faces burned by wind, our limbs aching from the struggle, we keep going, our efforts sagging only when the forceful wind makes us stumble. The cosmic forces can't beat us. I know it as surely as I know that I love Paul more than anything else in the world, past or present.

"There's less wind here," I hear him say in a normal-sounding voice.

"We must be getting close to the end of the stairwell," I answer back, noting my voice sounds sharp and clear.

Moving slowly. Carefully. Our arms reaching out to touch something solid, *anything* that indicates a door is within our reach. I can't believe it when my fingertips brush up against something solid.

"I've found it, Paul," I call out, running my fingers over the outline of a small panel door. I can't see him but I feel

Paul's body brush up against mine, the touch of his skin electrifying every hair on my body, including the curling strands on my mound. His touch is also reassuring as he leans his shoulder into the door. I'm surprised when the rolling floor beneath us stops, the wind merely a restless breeze making a nuisance of itself around our feet. The sudden change in the stairwell seems as strange as the initial appearance of the fierce wind striking out at us. Do I dare hope we've beaten the dark force?

"The door won't open," Paul says. "Stand back."

I hear him grunt loudly, then push his shoulder against the door, but it won't budge. As he does so, I feel the moldiness again creeping into my bones. I cry out when the space beneath me shifts, pulling me downward, away from Paul. *My God,* the dark force is trying to claim me. Panic rattles in my bones.

*"Paul!"* I yell.

"I've got you." He reaches back and pulls me to him, wrapping his arm around my waist and pressing my bare breasts against his nude chest, our warm embrace completing the erotic arc we began that first night in his studio. Then, before I can take a breath, Paul kicks open the door. We both gasp loudly, dumbstruck, as a glorious, white light hits our eyes, blinding us so we can't see. I smell burning wood, charred fragments, gray smoke swirling upward in lazy curls, but the fire is out. A light rainy mist mixes with the wetness on my cheeks. And is that moistness I feel seeping between my legs? A slow fire is building in my pulsing pussy, and though I strive to hide my expression, I've no doubt my eyes sparkle with suppressed pleasure at the

I'm not worried about Nicole Kidman's Satine in Moulin Rouge. Movie star heroines never die, they just play over and over again on DVD, swinging through the same hot musical number ad infinitum. She's happy, looking gorgeous, and singing her way through one orgasm then another on a plasma TV somewhere in the universe.

And me? I won the hero lottery. Big-time. I got Paul. A hunk in any era.

Oh, but what about me changing back to my old body, you ask? Will Paul love a twenty-first century chick with wrinkles and a few extra pounds? Hey, I lost five pounds just traveling through time—now to keep it off. Or will he view our relationship as an affair played out on the whim of an ancient Egyptian god? I'm confident in my love for Paul. You see, I've got some black magic of my own. And it's not the candy box between my legs.

The fantasy may have ended, but there's still:

### La Joie de l'Amour (Joy of Love)

She fills my life like air, laden with the
smell of honeysuckle. And my insatiable soul
she fills with longing for eternity.
—Charles Baudelaire
(1821-1867)

# CHAPTER TWENTY ONE

*Paris Today*

The heavy blue door of his art studio creaked as Paul opened it. *What will I find?* he wondered. *Something, anything that says Paul Borquet lived here over a hundred years ago?*

The strong smell of turpentine and oil paint clinging to the walls told him the rooms had been rented out over the years to other artists; in addition, there was a lingering odor of mildew and dry rot. Autumn followed him as he ventured inside the second floor studio where the hard wooden floor cracked underfoot and where the reek of many nights of passion was as thick in the air as that first night he made love to her, bound by silken cords to the divan.

Even now, he couldn't stop a slow heat from growing in his groin remembering his lips sliding down her body, kissing her everywhere, his thumb and forefinger opening her cunt, then sucking every pink fold, the standing ridges, her helpless clit, all into his mouth at once. Then he lifted her onto his hard cock, her slim, elegant body positioned on top of him, her sighs of wonder and delight, her passion matching his as her cunt bore down on his hard cock, competing for contractions and throbbing at each other as his come seeped down her thighs. Her joy of making love to him was total, her acceptance of him as a man unchanging even as he changed, her beauty of face and figure living perfection. He held his breath, then let out a moan as he struggled to hold on to the memory. So long ago, and now he was back here. He didn't know what he'd expected, only that he *had* to come as soon as he was able to face his past.

They didn't speak as they looked around, pushing aside several rush-bottomed chairs, boxes of junk, bits of clothing, broken palette knives, and an open paint box filled with tubes of crusted paint, crowded together and not closed. He bent down and grabbed the hardened tube of paint, realizing he was also hard. He smiled. As soon as he could, he'd make love to Autumn every way, him on top, then turn her over and fuck her from behind, then on the edge of the bed, inserting his cock in very rapid strokes, until her clit hovered on the brink of orgasm and her body gave in and exploded, convulsing with pleasure as she opened up to him, her body arching to draw him deeper in her. He delighted in the idea of mixing her juices with his oils in this new century to create new works of art. He'd always told his artist friends the future of art was in a woman's face. He just hadn't known then he'd have that opportunity in the future. He didn't intend to waste it.

He looked around. The only other furniture left in the

studio was a broken-down divan, its stuffing long gutted from its frame, pushed next to the wall, as if the last occupant spent a lot of time staring out the window. Silently Paul sat down on the divan. Autumn sat next to him. It had been several weeks since the terrible fire and she'd never left his side. He was grateful for her presence, her understanding, her *everything* in this new world that fascinated him, at times frustrated him, and always amazed him. She was his greatest joy. *Sa joie de l'amour.* And why not? He had been pleasantly surprised when they'd entered her world and he found this luscious creature in his arms. She was no longer a girl, but a *woman,* curvy and sensuous—a paradise of delights where a man could bury his fears and, with her help, discover his true meaning in life. He could ask for no more.

When they ran from the *hôtel privé* in Marais, *les pompiers* of the Paris Brigade were firefighters with a sense of duty, but they weren't prepared for the man and woman who ran from the smoldering house, their clothes practically burned off their bodies. No way could they have explained to the firemen *who* they were, *where* they had come from, *what* they were doing in the grand house. Though shocked and dazed, Paul wasn't totally disbelieving that somehow, some way, Autumn had pulled him along with her when the black magic sparked her reentry back to her own time.

Everything happened so fast after that: he was whisked off to a modern hospital, hooked up to strange machines, Autumn convincing him to take the medicines that took away his pain, doctors checking him. Then a stay in a special hospital, where he spent weeks recuperating from the burns on his hands. Each day, slowly, he began sketching, praying he hadn't lost his art, knowing he would have to face coming back here to his studio in Montmartre to make peace with his past before he could secure his future.

He sat for a long time in purple-gray shadows with Autumn at his side, holding on to her hand, he, trying to draw in the creative energy he felt in this place, she, speaking only once to ask him if he was "okay," a strange-sounding word to his ears, only one of many he had learned since his entry into her world.

He shut his eyes and drew in a deep breath, drinking in the familiar smells of the past. Strong, pungent smells. The scents didn't overcome him, for the studio was the pulse of his life, its churning memories gurgling in his ears. It was also the place where he could rid himself of the effects of the black magic, cleanse his mind and purify his soul. Only then, could he go forward and meet his destiny.

For more than a hundred years, his acceptance into the art world had been slumbering in a suspended sleep, as if under a spell. During that time, the destruction of the art world as he had known it occurred, gone mad with its abstract shapes, maniacal disorder. A new natural order had progressed almost as slowly as a drip of paint dribbling down the side of a canvas, but he suspected that at last *his* moment had arrived.

A bare lightbulb hung down over their heads from the low ceiling, where a row of mirrors had once looked down upon them during their passionate lovemaking, when they were oblivious to everything but the intense sensations engulfing them and sending them on a compelling ride to total release.

The mirrors were gone now, only bits of broken glass stuck on the ceiling, but the memory remained. Her tight wet pussy sucking him in, his groin slapping her buttocks noisily in a fast rhythm, then exploding in her. His fingers stirring her fire until it burned bright again and she cried out, calling his name and writhing in ecstasy. Only she had the power to make him forget the long periods of loneliness and darkness in his life.

In his time, he had pursued women in a forbidden garden, reveling in the joy of illicit sex and sensual desires. Red wet lips, heaving breasts, and throbbing pussies tempted him. Vibrant youth, reckless passion, wild emotions. It had all been his for a while, and although he regretted nothing, there was a quality of excitement and awe about who he was now, in *this* world. Whatever connections he had to the past, he had to let them go.

Switching on the bare lightbulb with his callused fingers, intending to prove to himself this wasn't a dream, that *she* wasn't a dream, he reached out with his other hand into the light. And touched her face.

"*Alors,* Autumn, you're so beautiful. And I'm a lucky man to have you."

"No regrets?" she asked.

"Never. Whatever happens, you'll always be the woman I love." He brushed his lips on her neck, tasting the sweetness of perfume on her skin, loving the glint of sunlight reflecting off the long windowpanes and onto her red hair. Oh, how he loved her, and yet he hesitated to ask, but did so anyway, "And you?"

She shook her head. "I love you more than anything,

Paul." She moaned in delight as he kissed her neck, her face. Then, on a more playful note, she added, "Although I wish I could have kept my great body."

"What do you mean? I *adore* your body. Your full breasts—" he cupped them in his hands, then pinched her nipples "—your waist, your hips, *ta chatte.*"

"*Silence, mon amour,*" she teased, putting her fingers to his lips, "who knows what ghosts might be listening?"

Playfully he put the tips of her fingers to his mouth and kissed them, making her laugh.

"If you don't stop teasing me," he said, "I won't be able to control myself and I'll make love to you even more passionately than I did more than a hundred years ago." His mouth slid down her neck, licking, biting, teasing the soft spot he knew would send her blood surging through her veins. "I could tease you with my cock, poke it between your legs or enter you a little bit before pulling away."

"You wouldn't torture me like that—"

He smiled. "Or I can make you come with my fingers with the tip of my penis against your clit, then make you come more with my cock deep inside you."

"Mmm...I like that idea better."

"*Bien,* well, it will be my...or should I say, *your* pleasure, mademoiselle."

"Oh, Paul, I wish we could stay here always," Autumn said, leaning her head on his shoulder. He got a whiff of her luscious red hair, smelling like mimosa. He put his arm around her. She felt good.

"Why don't we fix up this old place, make it our home?" he said. "From the roof, we have the best view in the city—

gleaming stone curbs and blue-tiled rooftops at dawn, a horse-chestnut tree blowing in the evening breeze, and in the distance, the moonlit swell of the River Seine."

"And you could paint all day, all night, without stopping."

"Except to make love to you," he whispered, nuzzling his face in her hair. "Whispering to you my insatiable desire to fuck you, then fill you completely, your body moving in tandem with mine as wave after wave of pleasure surges through us, all the while knowing my hunger for you can never be satisfied."

"That can be arranged," she teased. Then she became silent before saying something to him he sensed had been on her mind for a long time. "Will you miss your old life, Paul?"

He took a deep breath. "Love is a great healer. Looking into your eyes, I can forget my past…"

His voice trailed off, a sadness masking his face as he gazed into her eyes. He wanted to say more, but he fell into a heavy silence, breathing in the musty air, inhaling the view of both the past and the future, pulling memories out of his psyche occasionally, unexpectedly. His old friends, Gauguin, Monet, Degas…all dead. Everyone he knew was dead. Even his brother, the duke. Strange, he should think of him now. Autumn had done what she called an Internet search, and she discovered the Duke of Malmont had recovered from his wounds, then gone back to England and lived to old age. He never returned to Paris.

Paul took in a deep breath. His thoughts *must* escape the

past. The future was theirs, if they had the courage to grab it. With Autumn at his side, his art was their future.

It had taken time but his burns had healed, and he worked hard, *very* hard, the creative sparks flying from his fingers, to animate the poetic dimension of what he saw all around him in this new era. He was ready to challenge the art world.

"Are you ready to go, Paul?"

"Yes. I'm ready."

He picked up the bundle of his artwork, sketches he had made during his recovery, along with some paintings, and held on to them tightly. With Autumn at his side, he walked out of his studio, out of the past. The morning fog had cleared while they'd been inside the building, and the sun popped out and shone high in the sky, as bright as his future, the shadows of the past behind them.

"Your ancestor Paul Borquet was quite a handsome devil, monsieur," says the old artist, sucking on the butt of his Gauloise cigarette. With a nod, he indicates the life-size self-portrait behind him as he spread Paul's paintings on his easel, studying them intently. I have the strangest feeling he knows about Paul. Or am I just imagining it?

"And quite the lover, monsieur, from what I've heard," Paul comments, winking at me.

I roll my eyes, then open my mouth to speak, but decide to keep my comment to myself. *He is handsome, and a genius, and only I will ever know what a brave man he is. I owe my life to him.*

I shift my weight from one foot to the other, trying to appear businesslike in my new role as curator for Paul's work, resisting the urge to tell the old artist about my adventure into the past. It isn't easy for me to keep quiet. For the past few weeks I've been telling the same story over and over again, how I was dazed by the electric jolt and wandered outside into the *hôtel privé* down the street, now divided into apartments. How Paul saved me from the burning building struck by lightning, although my mother doesn't believe a word of it.

Although I wasn't gone for more than an afternoon, my mother is convinced I'm having an affair with this handsome artist and didn't want to tell her about it. I don't try to change her mind, though she made me promise to call her on her cell if I needed her, then took off for her bra fitting at the Cadolle lingerie boutique.

"Did you know bras were invented in Paris over a hundred years ago?" she asked me, peeking at Paul out of the corner of her approving eye.

*Oh, boy, do I, Mother.*

My heart is pounding, my sanity fraying at the seams. Bras. Brothels. And my bad-boy artist.

Did it all really happen?

I'm back at the same art studio, standing in front of the life-size portrait of Paul Borquet. Each time I look at the handsome Impressionist in the painting and then at the man standing next to me, I see the same man, dark hair curling around his white collar, dark blue velvet eyes, broad muscular shoulders, trim hips.

And, oh yes, that squeezable butt.

But this time I'm not a jilted bride. I'm a bride-to-be. As soon as we come up with the official paperwork, using the money Paul received from selling Madame Chapet's pearl choker he stuffed into his pocket, we're going to be married.

Finally, after several long minutes, the old artist speaks.

"You're a very talented painter, Monsieur Borquet, but with a very modern approach to art," the old artist says, lighting up another Gauloise. His third in the last half hour. He seems nervous, and excited.

"*Merci,* monsieur. My ancestor was also a man who kept trying to experiment, to innovate. If he had lived, I'm certain he would have moved to a Modernist style."

The old artist agrees. "Your free and vivid use of color is similar to his, so simple, so pure." He studies Paul, then his self-portrait. I hold my breath. Will he challenge him?

"You have inherited his gift, monsieur, although your application of paint is looser, more free, your colors more intense. I've never seen anyone with a more penetrating and powerful pictorial vision."

"Then you'll show Paul's work?" I ask.

"*Zut alors,* but of course, mademoiselle." He turns to Paul. "I assure you, monsieur, the art world will soon be at your feet." He gathers up the paintings, the sketches, then grabs his jacket. "And now, I must make arrangements for a showing of your work, Monsieur Borquet. Wait here."

He closes up shop, then he's off, carrying the bundle of paintings and drawings, smoking and mumbling to himself about discovering a lost genius.

Paul tries to contain his excitement, can't, grabs me, picks me up and spins me around. "*A showing!* Autumn, do you know what this means?" he says enthusiastically.

"The art world won't be able to get enough of you," I say smugly, then add, "And neither can I."

"Don't tempt me, Autumn. You know I can't say no to you."

"Then say yes."

He holds me closer, inhaling my scent. "You seductress. You haven't changed. This is how you looked the first night I saw you, heaving breasts, sparkling green eyes, your hair glowing in the dark. My redhead." Paul puts me down and points to his self-portrait. "Of course, I can't blame you. *Alors,* I was young and handsome, wasn't I?"

"I like you better now."

"Oh?"

"Yes, you're even sexier." As if to prove my point, I run my fingers over his thighs, his hips, his butt, then even slower over the bulge between his legs, a slow, white heat growing in my belly. I growl. I want this man. A buzzing current in my pussy makes me moan as I work my fingers under the waistband of his loose pants and down to his cock. I clench my hand around him, squeezing it, then stroke my fingers up the shaft, rubbing ever so gently with my fingernails before releasing him.

Barely able to catch his breath, he says in a husky voice, "You vixen. You're more beautiful than ever."

*I love hearing you say that, my darling, that you want me as I am now.*

I begin humming, swaying my hips. "I wonder what it would be like to strip off my clothes in front of the *live* man in the portrait?" Already I can feel a series of tiny orgasms building inside me, heating me up, making me warm. Oh, it feels delicious. As if I'm about to lose control, lose myself in moments of pure sensation. I ache to feel my hips grinding against his, riding up and down on him, my body pulling him in deeper, my pink walls contracting around him, my pleasure building. I rub my crotch, pressing down on my magic spot. I'm not surprised to feel dampness wetting my dress. Tears and a kind of weariness sting my eyes as instant fire erupts between my legs. The skin on my breasts and belly crawls with desire. I can't stand him not being in me.

"Here? *Now?*" Paul takes a deep breath, his juices also flowing. I watch his face and see his expression change, his eyes half closing. His cock bulge just got bigger.

"Why not? We're alone." I reach around behind my back and find the zipper of my dress.

*Zip.* I pull it down, letting the front of the silky garment fall away from my nude breasts. A shimmering sheen of sweat makes them shine, inviting him to nibble on my nipples, taut and flushed with my desire. I may have invented the first bra, but I'm not wearing one.

Paul's eyes open wide at the sight of my breasts as I take his hand and guide him, so his fingers touch naked flesh. "And then what, *ma chérie?*" He's breathing fast and hard. His thumb and forefinger rolling my nipple, not stopping. His desire for me is fierce. The look in his eye tells me I'm playing with fire.

"I'll show you, Paul."

I grab him and pull him behind the black-lacquered screen. I let out a cry of surprise when I see a small Egyptian statue with an erect penis standing in the corner. How did *he* get here? Or maybe he never left. After all, it *is* black magic.

"Look, Paul, it's the statue of the god Min." I hold it between my nude breasts. "What should we do with him?"

"Put him back in his corner," Paul says, burying his face in my hair, then kissing my neck, sending his own brand of electricity down my spine and shooting up the heat a few notches between my legs. "I don't need his black magic. I've got you."

I smile, putting my arms around my handsome artist, feeling protected, feeling loved. But something else is on my mind. "Paul, he *is* the god of fertility. We can't disappoint him."

"*Zut alors,* are you suggesting I fuck you here?"

I nod. "Mmm-hmm…if you would be so accommodating."

Paul holds me close, his hands moving slowly up and down my body, making me purr with delight, then he slides my panties down over my hips. "It will be my pleasure, mademoiselle."

Standing, with my butt pressed up against the wall, the sweet, sensual scent of my pussy fills the air as his fingers part my swollen lips, his thumb rubbing the tiny bud that glows deep within me until I cry out in pure pleasure. Then before I can take a breath he pushes his cock into me. I lift my hips to meet him stroke for stroke, linking our bodies with an intense dual feeling of satisfaction.

I sigh and savor the sensation, my breath quickening as he pushes deeper in me, his throbbing cock hitting my G-spot with his rhythmic thrusts, making me tremble then cry out as my orgasm starts and goes on for a long, *long* time. Each pulse of pleasure is followed by another and another, our bodies slick with sweat and the heady perfume of the past and present mixing together. I sense a certain wildness in the air as I did that night when I danced the cancan at the Moulin Rouge, when enchantment and reality came together in a thrilling experience.

My orgasm now is just as real as Paul holding me, just as real as our future together.

*And Min?* Who needs an Egyptian god with a perennial hard-on to make me feel young? Not when I've got Paul. *His* hard-on never stops. And it's *soooo* big.

Goody. Goody.

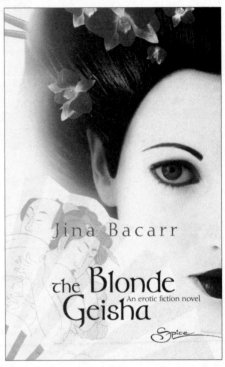

# the Blonde Geisha

An erotic fiction novel from
## Jina Bacarr

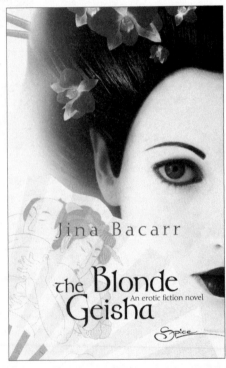

On sale August 2006.

When Kathlene Mallory's father makes an enemey of the prince of Japan, he leaves his daughter in the world of geisha. Kathlene becomes an apprentice geisha, until age eighteen, when she becomes one of the most sought-after geisha in the land.

Visit your
local bookseller.

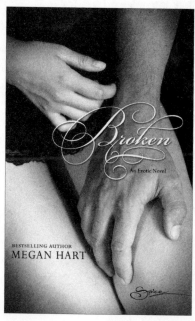

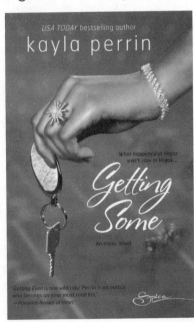

# A One-Year Anniversary has never been this hot...

Celebrate the first anniversary of SPICE by indulging in the sexiest, most scintillating stories destined to ignite your senses!

# Jina Bacarr

In addition to being the author of the award-winning book *The Japanese Art of Sex*, Jina Bacarr has also worked as the Japanese consultant on KCBS-TV, MSNBC, Tech TV's *Wired for Sex* and British Sky Broadcasting's *Saucy TV*. Enamored with all facets of Japanese culture, Jina is able to speak the language, which helped her find jobs acting in Japanese television commercials. Jina is also a successful playwright and has written over forty scripts for daytime television (including thirty animation scripts). This is her first novel.

Jina can be reached at her Web site, www.JinaBacarr.com, or by e-mail at jinabacarr@jinabacarr.com.

Spice